THE No.1 LAWYER

A list of titles by James Patterson
appears at the back of this book

JAMES PATTERSON
& NANCY ALLEN

THE No.1 LAWYER

C
CENTURY

1 3 5 7 9 10 8 6 4 2

Century
20 Vauxhall Bridge Road
London SW1V 2SA

Century is part of the Penguin Random House group of companies
whose addresses can be found at global.penguinrandomhouse.com.

Penguin
Random House
UK

First published in the UK by Century in 2024

www.penguin.co.uk

A CIP catalogue record for this book is available from the British Library.

ISBN 9781529136395
ISBN 9781529136401 (trade paperback)

Printed and bound in Great Britain by Clays Ltd, Elcograf S.p.A.

The authorised representative in the EEA is Penguin Random House Ireland,
Morrison Chambers, 32 Nassau Street, Dublin D02 YH68

www.greenpenguin.co.uk

To Sarah, Yancey, Matthew, Meredith, Elizabeth, and Mallory

PART I

CHAPTER 1

IT WAS a Monday morning in Biloxi.

I had on my best suit, fresh out of the dry-cleaning bag. I wore my lucky tie, the one my wife, Carrie Ann, had given me two Christmases ago. I'd bought a new pair of cap-toe oxfords for the occasion because my old ones were worn down at the heel.

I didn't want to look shabby next to my client on this big day.

The capital murder trial *State of Mississippi v. Daniel Caro* was set to begin.

I took a deep breath to center myself, gave a final glance at the note card in my right hand, made eye contact with my audience.

"I'm Stafford Lee Penney, attorney for the defendant, Dr. Daniel Caro. Ladies and gentlemen of the jury, this is what the evidence will show."

I'm a second-generation Mississippi attorney. My father, Charles Jackson Penney, is also a trial lawyer in Biloxi, Mississippi. He has been known to proclaim—so often over the years that I've lost count—that a lawyer wins or loses his case in the opening statement.

The old man is half right. After fifteen years of practicing law, I know you can lose a jury with a weak opening. But the opening is too early to win the case. Witnesses will take the stand and evidence will pour in; there are too many unknowns, too many battles to be fought.

Particularly in the Daniel Caro murder trial.

"We all heard the district attorney, Henry Gordon-James, outline the evidence he plans to bring before you," I said. "He went on and on about exhibits and experts, didn't he? Made all kinds of promises. But you need to think about what Mr. Gordon-James failed to mention. What word did he *not* say?"

I took a step forward. I wanted to move closer to the jury to ensure they'd listen to my key point.

"Ladies and gentlemen, that word is **circumstantial**. All the evidence in this case is purely circumstantial. The prosecution will not produce a single witness or a shred of evidence that directly ties my client to the crime he's been accused of committing."

I was warming to the speech. I could feel it. My blood was pumping; the words flowed easily.

"The criminal defendant in this case, Daniel Caro, is highly regarded in this community. He grew up in Biloxi, received his medical degree from Duke. His ob-gyn practice is a blessing to this town. For over a decade, he has delivered our babies and cared for our mothers and wives and daughters. Dr. Caro is an asset to this region. I've known him all my life. We played Little League baseball together. He's my client and my friend."

That last line contained a gross exaggeration. Caro and I weren't friends. In fact, I'd never particularly liked him. He wasn't my kind of cat. But the opening statement was my opportunity to humanize him before the evidence demonized him.

After I wrapped up my client's glowing bio, I took two steps to the right to signify a change of direction.

"The events that you'll hear about in this trial are tragic, undeniably horrific. They never should have happened anywhere, certainly not in Biloxi."

Careful, I thought. It was time to mention the murder victim, to speak her name. It was imperative that I proceed delicately.

"Aurora Gates's untimely death was a terrible loss. She was an exceptional woman: Valedictorian of her class at Biloxi High School. A promising law student at Ole Miss. Her future was bright. Someone took a gun and stole that future from her, cut her life short."

Time to switch it up and alter the tone.

"But the person who committed that vile act was not my client, the man who sits in the courtroom today."

I teased a few items after that, hinting at important evidentiary points I intended to score at trial without directly revealing the strategy. My father has another saying about the start of a jury trial: A defense attorney who shows his hand in the opening is a damn fool.

The old man's not wrong. We see eye to eye on that one.

CHAPTER 2

I GLANCED at the clock just before I wrapped it up. Good — not too short, not too long. I said thank you and smiled warmly but without flashing any teeth so the jury could see that I was not flamboyant or showy, that I respected the gravity of the situation.

I stood there waiting. When I didn't get a reaction, I said: "Well? What do you think?"

Mason grimaced. "Meh. Not your best effort, Stafford Lee."

I tossed the crumpled note card onto the conference-room table. I'd been gripping it too hard. "Really? That bad?"

The guttural noise Mason made in reply could have been interpreted as neutral, but he followed it up with "Pretty bad."

"No!" Jenny, seated next to Mason, leaned over and swatted the back of his head. "Are you trying to jinx him? It was great, Stafford Lee. Really good."

"I've heard better," Mason said under his breath.

"Mason, quit being so negative," Jenny snapped. "You always do that."

Jenny was right. Over the past fifteen years, we'd done the ritual of the trial run scores of times, and Mason did always do that.

I performed these run-throughs at my law office for an audience of two: Mason Burnett, a trial attorney with his own law office, and

Jenny Glaser, a licensed private investigator. They were my closest friends and both were excellent sounding boards. Helpful, even when it hurt.

Predictably, Mason skewered my weak spots, especially what he called my lackluster delivery. Without Jenny's supportive yin to balance Mason's criticizing yang, on the first day of any jury trial, I might have walked right past the courthouse, kept going until I reached the waters of the Gulf, and dived in, fully clothed.

Mason said, "All right, it wasn't a total flop. Remember the first time you did your opening for me, right after we graduated from Ole Miss? You essentially admitted your client's guilt in the first two minutes."

Jenny snickered. I didn't blame her; that misstep could have destroyed my legal career before it began. But on that long-ago occasion, Mason had pointed out my gaffe, and we fixed it. To the surprise of everyone in the courthouse, I went on to win the case even though it was a loser, almost as tough as the case I was handling now.

Since that first jury trial fifteen years ago, I had managed to win them all. Whether that was due to good luck or good tactics, I'd be hesitant to opine. Criminal defense lawyers are supposed to lose, so mine was a pretty unusual record.

If it ain't broke . . .

Leaning on a chairback, I asked, "Was there too much bio? Or not enough?"

Across the table, Jenny said, "The background on Daniel Caro was effective, the part about delivering babies and caring for mothers and daughters. People will respond to that."

"They'll like him until they hear the evidence." Mason put his feet up on the conference table.

He was pushing my buttons, but I kept going. "Did it sound genuine, the stuff I said about Caro being a great guy?" I worried that the jury might detect a note of insincerity.

"Yeah, that was all right," Mason conceded. "They'll buy it. Unless they know him very well. Or know you at all."

We were all Biloxi kids with a shared history going clear back to grade school. Mason's mom had been my Cub Scout leader. She'd been like a second mom to me after my own mother passed away from non-Hodgkin's lymphoma in her thirties. Jenny and I had had a brief romance in fifth grade—we went steady for almost forty-eight hours.

Jenny reached into a bright red attaché case and pulled out a stapled sheaf of papers. As she slid it across the varnished table, she said, "I did the background you wanted, ran more information down on the jurors and the alternate. No big surprises which ones might be defense-team-oriented and which lean toward the prosecution."

Even from a cursory glance, I could see it was stellar work. "Jenny, you're worth every damn cent I pay you."

Mason chuckled. "Paste that quote on a billboard for your PI business, Jenny, right smack next to a picture of Stafford Lee. His fan club will love it."

Jenny rolled her eyes. "Have you always been jealous of Stafford Lee, Mason? Even back when we were kids?"

"I'm not jealous of him." Mason made a show of peering down at my feet. "But I'm seriously impressed by those shoes."

I ignored the comment about my footwear and checked the clock again. I met Mason's eyes and said, "Any final suggestions?"

Mason the irreverent comic disappeared. He was shooting straight and serious when he said, "The jurors are going to need a tangible reason to root for the defendant, so give them something to sink their teeth into. Go ahead and call the murder victim a floozy."

I must have recoiled.

"Do it." He raised his voice. "Call her a home-wrecker. Give her a black eye at the outset. They love that shit in Biloxi."

Not my style, trashing the victim of a violent crime. But in this situation, it might give me a boost. God knew I was going to need one when the evidence started rolling in.

Jenny weighed in, playing her part in the ritual. "Mason, you can't try the case in opening. And attacking that young woman is a dangerous gambit. If Stafford Lee offends jurors on day one, he'll have trouble winning them back."

We could have gone more rounds, but the chiming from my phone ended the fight. I turned off the alarm and slid my phone into my pocket.

My parting question: "What are the odds of winning this one?"

"Of getting a not-guilty verdict?" Jenny asked. "I'd say fifty-fifty."

I swallowed down a groan. "Your odds, Mason?"

"Sixty-forty."

Better.

"Sixty percent that your client will go down," Mason added. "Just to be clear."

I'd preferred the fuzzy odds.

I picked up my briefcase and shot a wry grin at my two closest friends. "Thanks for the vote of confidence."

CHAPTER 3

THE HEAVINESS of my briefcase as I walked to the courthouse provided a physical reminder of the weight of the Caro case. My briefcase wasn't a slim nylon bag designed to carry a laptop and nothing else. Constructed of black leather and secured with nickel locks, it was more like a mobile filing cabinet. Mason thought I was crazy to haul the massive briefcase the blocks from my law office to the Biloxi Circuit Court.

Taking this solitary walk on the first day of trial was another of my long-standing rituals. Even when hurricanes threatened, I stubbornly adhered to it. Today, the September sun reflected off my sunglasses; the Gulf breeze blew balmy.

Big casinos lined the water's edge. People pointed to them and said, "We're the New South now, not the old fishing town famous only for shrimp and oysters and Jefferson Davis. It's twenty-first-century progress, these hotels rising up twenty-five stories, hotels that dominate local revenue. Biloxi has changed."

That's what people say, anyway. But we're still a small city with one public high school that serves a population hovering around fifty thousand.

The first couple of blocks cleared my head, and I girded myself for battle. I was acutely aware that I was in for the fight of my life against my opponent, Henry Gordon-James, the district attorney for Harrison County. Harrison County has two county seats, Biloxi and Gulfport, and Gordon-James served in both communities. He was personally handling the trial, and he was a powerhouse in the courtroom.

A whole lot was riding on the outcome of this trial. First and foremost, my client's life was at stake. It was a death-penalty case.

Tensions around town were running high, and when the jury returned its verdict, Biloxi would likely be in an uproar. Whichever way the case went, there were many issues that would leave people fired up.

Issues like race.

The murder victim, Aurora Gates, was a person of color. The population of Biloxi was about 21 percent Black, but the defendants charged in local criminal cases were about 75 percent Black. This defendant, my client, was a white man. And the particulars of the accusations against him were extremely inflammatory.

For several blocks, I had the sidewalks to myself. I turned the corner, and the courthouse came into view. The Second Judicial District Courthouse is a flat-topped, two-story structure built in 1968 for function rather than architectural style or grace.

Even from a distance, I could see the gathered crowd of onlookers and the news vans circling the building. I switched the briefcase from my right hand to my left and picked up the pace.

A woman coming off the graveyard shift at one of the casinos, still dressed in her poker dealer's uniform, called out, "It's Stafford Lee Penney! Hey there, Stafford Lee!"

I paused to return her greeting. "Good morning to you, ma'am."

As the woman shouted, "Good luck," the crowd surged toward me. A guy from my high-school class pushed through to clap me on the shoulder excitedly, like he'd come to watch the state football championship. I smiled, said hello, and continued on my way.

Standing near the courthouse entrance was a former client of mine, a young woman I had represented on a minor traffic charge. I had gotten her a good deal on a plea bargain and charged a reasonable fee. I hoped she was there to support me.

I stepped up to her, extending my right hand. "Hey, it's Arnette, isn't that right? It's been a while. How are you doing?"

She stared at my outstretched hand without moving. Finally, she met my eye. "I went to school with Aurora Gates," she said.

I dropped my hand. Clearly, trying to get the man who was charged with her schoolmate's death acquitted made me a villain.

But it bothered me that my former client might misunderstand my motivation for taking on the Caro defense. Whether we like our clients or not, criminal defense lawyers sincerely believe in the Fifth Amendment right to due process for everyone. A person's entitled to a defense, and I was in the business of providing one — for a price.

Still, I wanted to show Arnette that I was not a heartless guy, not just another white good ol' boy.

"I'm sorry for your loss, Arnette. Ms. Gates was an exceptional young woman. What happened to her is a tragedy."

Her face was stony, her expression unforgiving. "Right. If you're so sorry, why are you trying to let her killer walk?"

She turned and left. I wanted to reach across the abyss, but this was not the time. I headed for the courthouse door.

Just before I entered the building, one of the locals who had come to witness the ruckus shouted, "You'll get him off, Stafford Lee!"

When the door shut behind me, his voice rang in my ears.

Two women, clerks from the recorder's office, grabbed me before I reached security. One of them, Liz Craig, was remarkably pretty. Mason had asked her out more times than any sensible man would have, but she invariably rebuffed him.

Breathless, Liz said, "You're famous, Stafford Lee. Did you see the cameras following you to the door? Do you think you're going to be on TV?"

"I don't know, Liz. I guess we'll have to tune in and see."

"I love watching you in court. When we take our break, Renee and I are going to come and sit in for a minute just to see you do your thing."

Her eyes were shining with admiration. A man would have had to be blind, senile, or both to miss it.

"That's a real boost for me, knowing I have your support." I gave the women a friendly smile. "Thank you, ladies, both of you. Now, I better get on upstairs."

Before I stepped through security, Liz tugged on my sleeve and whispered, "Good luck, Stafford Lee."

Walking up the stairs to the second floor, I was glad that Mason had not witnessed the exchange. He frequently claimed that I had a flock of lawyer groupies. Unfortunately, he'd been known to joke about that in the presence of my wife. Carrie Ann didn't think it was funny.

In fact, it was one of the reasons she'd kicked me out of the house five weeks ago.

CHAPTER 4

I PEERED through the glass panel into the courtroom. It was too early for the press or the public to be admitted, but my client was already inside, seated on the front bench of the spectator section, his wife next to him.

I called out a greeting and hurried down the center aisle to the defense table. I set down the briefcase, shook out my left hand to get the blood flowing, and reached out to Caro with my right. "Daniel, join me at the counsel table as soon as you're ready." I smiled warmly at his wife. "Iris, how are you holding up? I know this is a difficult day for you."

I liked Iris. Caro's wife and I had gone on a couple of dates in college, when she was the reigning belle of Ole Miss. I'd stepped aside when Mason fell for her; he'd even escorted her to a sorority formal. All of this predated her romance with Caro and my marriage to Carrie Ann by many years. Ancient history, but I'd always had a soft spot for Iris.

Iris began to say something, but her husband cut her off. "Where the hell have you been? I've been waiting here for twenty minutes. Do you know how much I'm paying you?"

I certainly did know, down to the penny. Like a lot of defense attorneys, I charged my clients on a sliding scale, based in part on their ability to pay. Daniel Caro's lucrative medical practice netted him almost half a million a year, and that annual income put him in the top 1 percent in the state of Mississippi.

Caro's income was one of the few things I liked about him—it enabled him to pay his attorney fees in advance and in full—but the money wouldn't necessarily endear him to everyone. I made a mental note to check Jenny's background information on the jurors' household incomes. One in five people in my community lived in poverty.

Iris Caro eyed her husband warily as she scooted down the bench, creating distance between them. Obviously, she didn't like to be too close when his temper flared. Daniel got up and came over to the counsel table.

Caro's father claimed the family had roots in Sicily, and my angry client did resemble Michael Corleone. His hair, longish and slicked back, added to the *Godfather* aura. We had to work on that. In front of a jury, it wouldn't be a good look. "Daniel, you need to calm down."

"Calm down? Really?"

Two people took their seats in the back row, and Caro dropped his voice to a whisper. "There are people here today who are out for my blood." The newcomers were too far away to hear him, but the deputy standing near the judge's bench wasn't. She was serving as bailiff, and she was listening.

I could not deny that Caro was right, so I didn't try. Nonetheless, I had to reassure him. "Daniel, thanks to trained personnel from the sheriff's department, the courtroom is the safest place a person can be." I turned to the deputy. "Isn't that right, Charlene?"

She nodded. "We are on top of it, Stafford Lee."

Caro grabbed my sleeve. "That little girl is supposed to protect me? That's the best you've got?"

I looked down at the hand clutching my suit jacket. When he released it, I said, "Charlene is extremely competent. And she won't be alone. They're doubling up on officers for the trial. You've got nothing to worry about."

His eyelid twitched. "Nothing to worry about? I stand to lose everything. It's preposterous that you ever let this matter reach the trial stage. I didn't do anything wrong."

That wasn't entirely accurate, but I wasn't going to argue about it, not in front of his wife.

He continued. "You should know that I heard threats when we arrived. Actual threats from people milling around out there."

I was running out of patience—and time. I was due in chambers to meet the judge and the DA, so I made a statement certain to shut him up: "If you really feel unsafe, you should talk to your father. Maybe he'll provide a security detail for your protection."

Caro blanched. He re-joined his wife on the bench and said something into her ear; her face crumpled, and she raked her fingers through her carefully styled ash-blond hair.

It was no surprise that Caro backed off when I mentioned his Mob-connected father. I picked up my briefcase, recalling my client's embarrassment that his medical education at Duke had been paid for with money from Hiram Caro's casinos. Daniel distanced himself from his roots. If he could have, he'd have rewritten history. But that's hard to do in Biloxi, where roots are deep and memories are long. Everyone knew that the seed money for old man Caro's casino complex had come from underground gambling in the 1970s and 1980s. Before casinos were legal in Mississippi, Caro ran slots and card games in the back room of the Black Orchid, his seamy striptease joint. The rest of the Dixie Mafia was taken down in 1985, but my father kept Caro's father out of prison.

And here we were, the next generation, with a Penney again defending a Caro in court.

Things never really change in Biloxi.

CHAPTER 5

SPEAK OF the devil and he shall appear.

On my way to chambers, I ran smack into my old man. He was at the top of the courthouse stairs, leaning on the railing for balance.

"Hey, Dad. How you doing?" Without waiting for a reply, I veered to the left, giving him a wide berth. But he followed me.

"Hold up, Stafford Lee. I've come all the way up here to wish you good luck."

I didn't believe that, not for a minute. He had come to offer me unsolicited and unwanted advice. And the truth was, I didn't have time to fool with him. Over my shoulder, I said, "Dad, Judge Walker is waiting on me. And you always told me never to keep a judge waiting."

"Horseshit. I never said that. And Tyrone Walker isn't a stickler for timeliness, never was." Running a hand through his mane of white hair, he tried to keep up with me. He wore that bulldog look he got when he was determined to say his piece.

I paused at the door to the clerk's office. "Later, Dad. Thanks for checking in."

Something must have made him change his mind. He waved a hand, releasing me. "Go on, then."

I did go, speeding past the judge's clerk, Megan Dunn. The young woman glanced up at me with the serene expression she always wore, regardless of the circumstances. "Judge is waiting on you, Stafford Lee."

"Thanks, Megan."

When I stepped into chambers, Judge Tyrone Walker was perched behind his desk. Across from him sat the district attorney of Harrison County, Henry Gordon-James, somberly dressed in charcoal gray. Though the DA was about my age, his grave demeanor made him seem older. We weren't close, but I respected his talent and his experience. He was the first Black man to serve as the district attorney of Harrison County.

As soon as the door shut behind me, I picked up the uneasy vibe; the tension in the room was so thick, the air seemed to vibrate with it.

I nodded at them. "Morning, Judge, Henry."

The judge pointed to a seat. "Join us, Stafford Lee. Henry has been wondering whether you'd be here. But I assured him you wouldn't bail on us."

Gordon-James's eyes briefly met mine. "I don't believe I suggested that Penney would be a no-show. I did, however, mention that he had failed to appear on time."

I was late by three or four minutes. But my old man was right; Walker's nose wasn't out of joint about that. The DA, however, was less forgiving.

The judge announced, almost gleefully, "We are going to have the battle of the gladiators in the Second Judicial Circuit today. Did you see the crowd out there? TV cameras, the whole nine yards. Good thing that jury is sequestered."

I nodded in acknowledgment. Henry Gordon-James did not react.

The judge didn't seem to notice the DA's lack of enthusiasm. "In this trial, we've got the hottest district attorney in Mississippi duking it out with the best defense attorney in the state. Henry, you're still undefeated, right? No acquittals on your personal trial record?"

"That's correct."

The judge chuckled, shaking his head. "Somebody's record is going to take a hit this time. Stafford Lee has never lost a case before a jury either. I expect y'all both got a copy of the *Bar Association Journal*."

The judge held up the publication. My photograph was on the cover above the words *The #1 Lawyer for Southern Mississippi*.

He tossed the magazine onto his desk. "I wouldn't be surprised if people all over this town were laying bets on the outcome."

I caught the distaste that flashed across the prosecutor's features. "Surely people aren't making wagers on a case involving a young woman's grisly death," he said. "People wouldn't do that, not even in Biloxi."

A timer dinged, and the judge pulled a tea bag from a steaming cup. He squeezed the bag, discarded it, pulled out a penknife, and, using his desk as a cutting board, sliced a lemon. I could smell the citrus as it sprayed into the air.

Walker sipped his tea, his eyes crinkling at me over the mug he held. "Stafford Lee, is your daddy retiring soon?"

I was surprised by the change of topic. "He's slowing down these days. I'd say he's semiretired."

The judge snorted. "Well, that explains why the ERs and funeral parlors haven't seen much of Charlie." To the DA, Judge Walker said, "In his day, Charlie Penney had a deal with all the undertakers in town. He handed out business cards at every funeral. And he was notorious for jawboning injured people being carried into the hospital on stretchers." He gave us a sly wink. "You know what they called him."

Gordon-James avoided my eye and said shortly, "An ambulance chaser."

The judge nodded, chuckling.

What Walker had said about my dad was true. But there's a thing called family loyalty, and it chafed me to hear my father belittled, even if he deserved it. I had to exercise profound control to keep my fists from clenching and my jaw shut. This was no day to pick a fight with Judge Walker. Judges wield tremendous power over the outcome of a case. A trial lawyer is absolutely obligated to remain silent in these situations. The judge holds all the cards.

Maybe my discomfort showed. The judge took a swallow of the tea and set the mug on a coaster on his desk. "Stafford Lee, don't get your hackles up. I'm not putting you in the same class with Charlie, no, sir. You've got star quality. Charisma. You don't need to chase down widows and orphans." With a nod to the prosecutor, he added, "Henry's got it too—the magic. I say with total honesty that Henry here is the best DA in Mississippi."

"A lot of people in Harrison County were shocked when I was elected to this office," the DA said, his voice cool. "Others called it progress. But you know what they say: Progress in Mississippi is one step forward, one step back."

The judge leaned forward, interested. "Who said that? Faulkner?"

The DA's face looked chiseled from granite. "I'm not talking about literature; I'm talking about the Caro case." His gaze slid to me. "I'm determined to see justice done in this trial."

I said, my voice ringing with all the sincerity I could pump into it, "We are all interested in justice here."

"I'm getting justice for the victim, for Aurora Gates," the prosecutor said, his voice sharp as a razor. "It's personal for me. This shit keeps happening, and I'm sick of it. My people are dying."

After a moment of silence, he repeated, "It's personal."

CHAPTER 6

AFTER THE jurors took their seats in the box and listened to the judge's instructions, both sides hit the ground running, moving straight to opening statements.

The jurors need to like the defense attorney and think he's a good guy; it's a way to build trust and score allies. God knows the jurors are not usually impressed with the defendant.

At the defense table, I placed Caro in the seat directly next to the jurors. The physical proximity could provide an advantage as long as the client behaved himself. I hoped I wouldn't regret the decision.

Since our table was so close to the jury box, Henry Gordon-James stepped within a couple of yards of us during his opening. I listened closely, appraising him with a careful eye. He was good, passionate but controlled. I had my work cut out for me.

When my turn came, I was ready. I recited the speech I had rehearsed an hour prior in front of Mason and Jenny. I was better in court than I had been in the office, and early on in my opening, I hit my groove. The jurors were listening; eye contact was good. When I talked about Caro delivering babies, one of the women nodded—a lawyer's fondest hope. I finished and sat down, pretty sure I'd hit the mark.

Judge Walker turned to the DA. "You may call your first witness."

Gordon-James stood. Speaking with deep solemnity, he said, "The State calls Harley Oates to the witness stand."

Caro whispered to me, "He's the fisherman?"

"Right," I said, keeping my eyes on the jury. They watched Oates make his way down the center aisle of the courtroom and up to the bench.

After Oates was sworn in, Gordon-James commenced direct examination. "Please state your name."

"Harley Oates."

"Where do you live?"

"Biloxi, Mississippi."

"Occupation?"

"Plumber. Well, I was a plumber, had my own business here in town. I retired two years ago."

He wore his retirement well. His face was ruddy with sunburn; his frame looked lean, and he sat up straight in the witness chair.

"Let me direct your attention to June fourteenth of last year. What were you doing on that date?"

"I was out in my fishing boat. I've been doing a lot of fishing since I retired."

"Whereabouts were you fishing that day?"

"Just the other side of Popp's Ferry Bridge. They have some pretty nice big reds there."

The witness had not violated his oath with that statement. When Mason and I were growing up, his dad often took us fishing for red drum by the bridge. We'd caught some big bull redfish there back in the day.

"While you were fishing by the bridge, what, if anything, did you observe?"

The witness paused as he remembered, shaking his head in disbelief. "A body was floating in the water over by the old pylons."

Gordon-James's voice was tight: "What did you do?"

"I steered my fishing boat over there. Shoot, I thought maybe I was just seeing things, a trick of the light on the water. But there it was, kind of bobbing up and down."

"What did you do then?"

"I pulled it into the boat. Her, I mean. I've got a twenty-one-foot aluminum semi-V. It took some doing, but I managed to pull her in over the starboard side."

His face expressionless, Gordon-James said, "Describe the body, sir."

The witness cleared his throat. "It was a woman, like I said. She was bloated, looked like maybe the seabirds had got to her. But she was female, I could tell that for certain, because she didn't have a stitch of clothes on. It was a young woman. A young Black woman."

"After you pulled the body into the boat, what did you do?"

Oates puffed his cheeks out and exhaled. "I picked up my phone and dialed 911. My hands were shaking so hard, I almost dropped the phone overboard."

The DA walked over to the counsel table and tapped the keyboard of his laptop. On a large overhead screen adjacent to the witness stand, an image appeared.

Gasps and groans sounded in the courtroom.

I fixed my eyes on the screen and was careful not to wince or grimace at the sight of the corpse of Aurora Gates.

Her skin, wrinkled by exposure to water, was discolored and marbled, the soft tissue bloated. Her hands were clenched into fists. Abrasions bloomed across her body. Portions of her face had been eaten away, presumably by fish, crab, and shrimp in addition to seabirds. One eye socket was empty. Her nose was mostly gone.

A long hush fell.

Gordon-James began to speak, then broke off and stopped to breathe. When he started again, his voice cracked. He turned away from the screen, placing his back to the jury.

I looked at his hands. They were shaking. He made fists and shoved them into his pants pockets.

This was not a neophyte lawyer's nerves. When Gordon-James had said in chambers that the case was personal, it wasn't an overstatement or a figure of speech.

The case *was* personal. Aurora Gates, whose body had been found floating in the water near Popp's Ferry Bridge, was the district attorney's niece.

CHAPTER 7

I THOUGHT about the relationship between the DA and the crime victim as I watched Gordon-James.

When he'd revealed it, early on, I'd raised an objection. The judge said he didn't think there was a direct ethical prohibition, but he required the DA to make a showing that would affirmatively establish that the relationship didn't create a conflict of interest. After Gordon-James filed a sworn statement, the judge said he wouldn't require him to hand the case off to another attorney.

I thought they were both nuts, but it was an adverse ruling I could keep in my pocket and use in the event that my client was convicted and I needed grounds for appeal. I hoped, of course, that it wouldn't come to that. I intended to win the case.

I kept an eye on my opponent. My position at the defense table afforded me a unique view of Gordon-James's face. Furtively, I watched as he regained his composure: he straightened his shoulders, tightened his jaw, and hardened his expression. Watching the transformation, I believed that I could read his mind—he wanted vengeance and would marshal all his strength to take my client down.

Moving with athletic grace, he turned to face the jury and the bench. "I apologize for the interruption," the DA said, sounding entirely poised. "Mr. Oates, directing your attention to the photo on the screen, State's exhibit number one, do you recognize it?"

"Yes, sir."

"What does it depict, Mr. Oates?"

"It's a picture of the body. The woman I found by the Popp's Ferry Bridge and pulled into my boat."

"Is State's exhibit number one a fair and accurate depiction of the body of Aurora Gates when you discovered her that day?"

Harley Oates shivered, and I suspected the reaction was genuine, not the product of witness coaching. "Yes, sir. It sure is."

"Your Honor, I request that State's exhibit number one be admitted into evidence."

Judge Walker glanced at me. "Objection?"

I stood. "May we approach the bench?"

He nodded, and I hurried up to the bench. The DA joined me. Speaking softly so the jury wouldn't hear, I said, "Your Honor, I object to the exhibit on the grounds that it is inflammatory and prejudicial, outweighing its probative value."

Gordon-James's response was terse. "It's essential evidence."

The judge glanced at the screen, wincing. Shaking his head, he said, "It's gruesome, no denying that. But the jury needs to see the condition of the body to understand the testimony of the witnesses, including the medical examiner. Overruled."

The ruling wasn't a surprise; we'd duked it out over the photo prior to trial. But I had to make a record of my objection to preserve the issue for appeal.

I had barely gotten back to my seat when the DA announced: "No further questions of this witness."

Judge Walker said, "Mr. Penney, you may inquire."

I rose from my chair. "No questions, Your Honor."

Caro turned to me, lifting an eyebrow. I shook my head. There was no point in questioning Oates; we weren't disputing the information he'd provided, that a dead woman had been found at Popp's Ferry Bridge. The faster we could get through the evidence regarding the discovery of the corpse, the sooner that picture would be off the screen.

During the lunch break, the DA and I wrangled in chambers over the admissibility of other photographs Gordon-James intended to use. The judge listened patiently as he ate a sandwich at his desk and washed it down with a can of Coke. I lost the battle; Walker ruled against me. The photos would be admitted into evidence.

The next witness to testify was the patrolman who'd responded to the 911 call and overseen the transfer of the body to the coroner. I let him go without cross-examination too.

Judge Walker called a brief recess. After the jury left the courtroom, Caro said in an indignant whisper, "Are you going to try this case or not?"

I didn't get ruffled or take offense. The choice to forgo unnecessary questioning was tactical on my part. Some defense attorneys believed they should go after every witness who took the stand. My father was a member of that particular school of thought, but it was not my way. I continued sorting through the autopsy report, surveying my notes. I said, "We've been over this, Daniel. We aren't contesting anything those folks offered on the stand. There was no need to subject them to cross."

"So cross-examination isn't important to you."

"Sure it is. When the circumstances call for it."

The underlying friction at the defense table threatened to become a full-blown conflict. With a mighty effort, I ignored it—until he spoke again.

"I would think that a murder trial constitutes compelling circumstances."

At that, I shut the autopsy folder and shoved it to the side of the glass-topped table. "We need to reach an understanding. You don't tell me how to practice law, and I won't tell you how to practice medicine."

He looked like he intended to prolong the dispute, but the door to the jury box opened and the jurors filed back into court, so I no longer had to defend my tactics.

Gordon-James called his next witness: Miles Ellis, the Harrison County medical examiner. My adrenaline started flowing again. I knew what was coming.

The DA asked him to recite his qualifications. I kept a poker face. I knew Ellis; before he moved to Gulfport, we'd been neighbors for a while. But we were never friendly. The guy was a prig, the kind of neighbor who picked up the phone to complain if the music was loud on New Year's Eve. More than once, I'd caught him peeking in our recycling bin at the curb. Looking for what, I don't know. Maybe he was counting the beer cans.

"Dr. Ellis, during the autopsy you performed on Aurora Gates, did you do an external examination of the victim?"

"Yes, I did."

"What injuries, if any, did you notice on the exterior of the body?"

"Aside from postmortem injuries that occurred when the body was submerged in water, I observed a gunshot wound on her chest and marked fingertip bruises on and around her neck."

"Is it possible to tell if the gunshot wound was an entrance wound or an exit wound?"

"It is. The entrance wound was in the center of her chest."

"Doctor, I'd like you to explain to the jury the significance of the fingertip bruises."

"They are consistent with strangulation, someone using their hands to forcibly choke the victim."

"Dr. Ellis, regarding the gunshot wound—please describe the path of the bullet through her body."

Ellis walked the jury through it. As a witness, he was wooden, but he got the point across. And there were more photos—the entrance wound, the exit wound, the bruises circling the neck. One close-up of the neck displayed the bruises so vividly that the killer's grip was apparent even to the untrained eye.

"Did you observe other injuries during the external exam?"

"I observed genital injury—abrasions and bruises in the genitals and a laceration in the vagina. Upon discovering the injuries, I took forensic samples and preserved them."

"Doctor, tell the jury what this forensic medical examination is commonly called."

"It's called a rape kit."

The jury understood the significance of that response. A female juror in her forties closed her eyes and bowed her head. The stuffy medical examiner was a star witness in this trial. And Gordon-James wasn't done with him, not by a long shot.

"Doctor, did you perform an internal examination of the body of Aurora Gates?"

"I did."

"What were the findings of the internal examination?"

Ellis didn't answer immediately. From the stand, he looked past Gordon-James and stared at the defense table, first focusing on Daniel Caro and then shifting his gaze to me. Then he swiveled his chair slightly toward the jury and addressed them directly.

"At the time of her death, Aurora Gates was pregnant."

CHAPTER 8

IF THE prosecution had concluded questioning at that point, I could have jumped into the fray and used the cross to redirect the jurors' thoughts. But the direct exam went on.

The medical examiner said, "I found the fetus during the internal examination when I performed an internal pelvic dissection. I removed the pelvic organs and inspected them."

Gordon-James nodded. "Describe the fetus, Dr. Ellis."

"It was fully formed, about two and one-half inches in length. It weighed half an ounce. I estimate that it was at approximately twelve weeks gestation."

As the testimony continued, my eyes slid to the jury box. The jurors were hanging on his every word; several of them were literally sitting on the edge of their seats. I glanced surreptitiously at my client. I wished that Caro would display some compassion or concern, but he just sat there, unemotional and aloof, looking unaffected by the revelations coming from the witness stand.

Gordon-James said, "Based on your experience and training, do you have an opinion to a degree of medical certainty as to the cause of death of Aurora Gates?"

"I do."

"What is that opinion?"

"Aurora Gates died of the gunshot wound to the chest. It injured one lung and the aorta and also the superior vena cava, the large vein that carries blood from the head and upper body to the heart."

"Doctor, you have testified that you also observed bruises around the victim's neck. Can you describe those further?"

"They were patterned abrasions and contusions of the skin of the anterior neck."

Gordon-James tapped his laptop's keyboard. The photo of the victim's neck reappeared on the big screen. The DA circled parts of the image with a virtual pen. "What are these marks, Doctor?"

"They are superficially incised curvilinear abrasions. In other words, fingernail marks."

"Whose fingernails made those marks?"

"Aurora Gates's. In my opinion, she made the marks when struggling to pry the attacker's hands off her neck."

The testimony from the medical examiner was a kick in the gut. In a way, it was more powerful than the gunshot evidence, even though the bullet to the chest was the cause of Aurora Gates's death. But the photo of the bruises and fingernail marks conjured up mental images of the attack—a man's hands around her throat, cutting off her air as she struggled and scratched into her own flesh in a fruitless attempt to break his hold.

Anyone would be affected by such evidence.

Not my client, though. He sat like a stone.

Gordon-James displayed another photo from the autopsy. But it wasn't an image of Aurora Gates; it was a picture of the twelve-week fetus.

I watched the jury after the image of the lifeless fetus appeared. Heads were shaking. My favorite juror, the one who had given me a nod during my opening statement, crossed her arms over her chest. So much for the hope that she would side with the defense. The fetus pushed her to the other side.

"Doctor, did you see any evidence of injury to the fetus?"

"Specific signs of injury? No. But the fetus was dead. It died in utero because the mother died."

At that, Gordon-James enlarged the image of the fetus on the screen, perhaps to illustrate its increased significance in the case.

Because the two-and-a-half-inch fetus was not merely a footnote in the autopsy report.

It was a homicide victim in its own right.

The Mississippi statutory code states that killing an unborn child is murder. And that includes an unborn child at every stage of gestation, from conception to birth.

Gordon-James said, "Doctor, are you telling the court that two separate bodies were the subject of your autopsy?"

Dr. Ellis's forehead puckered as he thought this over. "Yes, that is correct."

Gordon-James made a three-quarter turn and stared coldly at Daniel Caro. He didn't bother to frame his next words as a question.

"This is a double murder case."

CHAPTER 9

I LEAPED out of my chair.

"Objection, Your Honor! The district attorney isn't asking questions—he's making statements. And he's not under oath, not sitting on the witness stand."

Gordon-James pierced me with a stare. "If Mr. Penney wishes, I can rephrase and put it in the form of a question."

I stepped away from the counsel table, itching to confront the DA head-on. Gordon-James had gone too far, and he knew it.

"I request that the court order the district attorney's words stricken from the record."

Wearing a baffled expression, the DA looked from me to the judge and back again. "I'll concede the point, agree to strike. But I fail to understand Mr. Penney's vehemence. The defendant is charged with two counts of murder. That's not a matter in dispute. It's why we're here in this courtroom."

From the bench, Judge Walker nodded in agreement. Things were going from bad to worse, and I needed to steer the conversation away from the jury box.

I said, "May we approach the bench?"

With a weary gesture, Judge Walker waved us forward. When I reached the bench, I had trouble keeping my voice down.

"Judge, the district attorney is out of line, and I ask that you instruct him to refrain from inappropriate commentary in the presence of the jury. He knows full well it's prohibited, and he's intentionally disregarding proper conduct of trial."

The judge rubbed his brow with a liver-spotted hand. "Stafford Lee, not sure why you're picking this particular battle. What Henry said is true. Your man is on trial for two counts, and everybody here knows it."

I couldn't back down. If the judge didn't restrain my opponent on the first day, the DA would continue the same tactic throughout trial, popping off in front of the jury whenever he took the notion. That was not correct procedure. Lawyers were supposed to ask the questions, not give the answers. And we couldn't comment on the answers either.

So I stuck to my guns. "Judge, we need to shut this down, right here and now."

Walker sighed. As he adjusted his glasses, I noticed his hand had a slight tremor. "It's close to four o'clock. Henry, how much longer are you going to spend on direct with Ellis?"

"I'm done, Your Honor." Glancing my way, the DA added, "For now."

His announcement gave me a surge of energy. It was my turn, time for my cross-examination. I was ready for my shot.

But Walker pushed his chair back from the bench.

"Enough for one day. My cardiologist has put me on beta-blockers and blood thinners, and when they're not kicking my tail, they're sucking the sap out of me. You young guys are lucky. Enjoy your health while it lasts."

For the defense, it was a bad stopping place. The jurors would sit in a hotel room overnight, reflecting on the uncontested testimony of the State's witnesses.

But Judge Walker was already instructing the jury not to discuss the case or listen to news reports about it. I stood in place near the bench as the jurors rose from their seats and filed out. Not one would meet my eye.

Court was adjourned. When the door behind the jury box closed, I stepped back to the counsel table, prepared to consult with Caro. But he was already on his feet; he signaled to his wife with a jerk of his head.

"Daniel, you want to talk? We should review today's testimony, and I can outline what we expect to see tomorrow."

He shoved his chair under the table and from an inside coat pocket pulled out a monogrammed linen handkerchief that he used to wipe his hands. Maybe they were sweaty. Could be the medical examiner's photos had had more impact on Caro than he'd let on.

"I'm out of here. Iris!" He raised his voice. "We're going to the car."

If Caro didn't want to do recon, I couldn't force him. To his retreating back, I said, "We can talk in my office if that suits you better."

Caro didn't respond. I shrugged it off, gathered up the papers from the counsel table, and organized them in my briefcase.

Mason sauntered up. "How'd it go today?"

I answered with a rueful look.

He chuckled, shaking his head. "My car's in the lot. You want a ride so you don't have to haul that monster briefcase away on foot?"

I was grateful for the offer. The briefcase was always a heavier burden at the end of the first day.

As we walked down the courthouse stairs, he said, "How about making a stop at the Salty Dog?"

It was our favorite watering hole. We'd been going there since we were a couple of college kids with fake IDs.

Mason didn't have to talk me into it.

I was ready for a drink.

CHAPTER 10

THEY WERE doing a brisk business at the Salty Dog. Crowds of early-bird diners were eating platters of fried shrimp and oysters, and Mason and I were lucky to snag a corner table.

The barmaid dropped off the first round: a bottle of Stella for me, an Absolut martini for Mason.

"Keep them coming, Scarlett," Mason said. "We're thirsty. Me and Stafford Lee, we've been working hard today."

Scarlett said, "I bet that's half right." She winked at me and walked off. As soon as she was out of earshot, I asked, "How much of the trial did you catch today?"

"Stuck my head in for a minute this morning, then came back twice in the afternoon, waiting for my turn in chancery court."

"How do you think it's going?"

Mason stirred his martini with the plastic toothpick. He ate both green olives before he answered.

Oh, shit, I thought. *Better brace myself.*

"You're getting your ass kicked, Stafford Lee."

I picked up my bottle and chugged half of it down as he continued the critique.

"Every time I walked in there, the DA was scoring all the points while you just sat in your chair. Pretty poor showing for the dude who's supposedly the number one lawyer around here. You're running behind, Stafford Lee. Way behind."

Mason's bald assertion put me on the defensive. "Damn, Mason, it's only the first day. The prosecution has the burden of proof. They call their witnesses first."

Mason belched softly and repeated, "Way behind."

He knew how to get my back up. I shook my head in disgust. "What were my options? Dispute that the woman was dead? Claim she hadn't been pregnant? Explain away that fetus?"

I was starting to get worked up, so it was a relief to see Liz Craig and another young woman shoulder through the bar crowd. When she approached the table, I rose from my seat.

"Oh, Stafford Lee, sit down—you're too polite! We just wanted to come by and say hi."

"Ladies, join us," Mason said.

Liz took an empty chair, but her friend hung back, looking bashful. Liz ignored Mason and directed her considerable sparkle at me.

"Stafford Lee, everybody at the courthouse was talking today about what a great job you're doing."

"Is that right?" I asked, glancing at Mason.

Mason rolled his eyes, but Liz wasn't paying attention to him. "We were on break, and the lobby was so full, we couldn't even sit down. And people wanted to know if you'd ever lost, and I told them, 'No, Stafford Lee has never lost a trial. Because he's the best.'" She paused for breath, smiling her megawatt smile again.

I'd be a liar if I said I wasn't flattered.

Mason checked out her friend, who'd remained standing. "Like to join us?"

She glanced at Liz, then looked down at her phone. "I'd like to, really, but we're supposed to meet our ride outside. Come on, Liz, or he'll be mad."

Liz heaved a sigh. "Gotta go." As they moved away, she called over her shoulder, "See you tomorrow, Stafford Lee!"

Mason drained the last of his martini. "Scarlett!" he called, raising the empty glass until the barmaid acknowledged the signal. He set the glass down and scowled at me. "Why do you get all the positive attention? The women scamper to you like ants to a birthday cake."

I laughed. "Mason, you're imagining things."

"I'm stating a fact. Is it because you played football? Or do you put out some pheromone? Because I'm better-looking than you, obviously. But you always get the best lawyer groupies. Women must believe that 'number one lawyer' bullshit."

I took the last swallow from my bottle and shook my head. "No groupies for me. I am a happily married man."

"Damn it, Stafford Lee!"

The voice came from behind me and almost made me jump out of my skin. She was at my elbow before I had a chance to turn around. Her face was pink with anger.

"Drinking again, of course. Where else would you be but in a bar?"

CHAPTER 11

I HADN'T seen my wife in five weeks. Her choice, not mine.

I was out of my chair in a wink. "Hey, honey. Good to see you. Mason and I were just talking about you."

Carrie Ann was wound up, her eyes flashing. I considered giving her a peck on the cheek but thought better of it.

Mason said, "Stafford Lee just said he's a happily married man."

"Well, that's a big fat lie," she said. She dropped into the seat Liz had recently abandoned and focused pointedly on my beer bottle.

Her accusation wounded me; I hadn't intended to lie. Admittedly, it was an exaggeration. "Carrie Ann, can I get you something from the bar? Or Scarlett can bring you a sandwich or a shrimp basket." I took a step, intending to flag the waitress.

"Sit down, Stafford Lee."

I sat.

Mason tried to calm the waters. "How's everything over at the high school, Carrie Ann? Stafford Lee tells me they've put you in charge over there."

"That's another fib. I'm the assistant principal, not the principal. Jim Boyd is still in charge."

After a moment of uncomfortable silence, Mason scooted his

chair away from the table. "I'm going to see a man about a dog. Nice to see you, Carrie Ann. You're looking good."

As Mason walked off, I studied her. Her face had lost some of its softness; her cheekbones were prominent. Could she have lost a noticeable amount of weight in five weeks? Or had I not been paying attention for the past few months?

"Are they working you to death over there?" I asked, genuinely concerned.

She narrowed her eyes. "What's that supposed to mean?"

I was treading on perilous ground, walking through a minefield, but I couldn't shut up. "You look kind of tired, that's all."

She tilted her head to the side and eyed me with disbelief. "Really? I'm the one who's putting in too many hours? I've sat alone in that house for seven years while you stayed night after night in your office."

It was an old argument. I had been almost thirty-five when Carrie Ann moved to Biloxi. As soon as I met the pretty new middle-school teacher, I fell hard for her. We married in a fever, just like that old song goes. But Carrie Ann was younger, and I was set in my ways. It was tough for us to adapt. "Carrie Ann, you know what trial practice is like. It's not a nine-to-five job."

She talked over me. "Here's what's funny. Now that we're separated, you're free to work as late as you like. But you're not at your office in the evenings. You think I don't hear the talk, Stafford Lee? You're in the bars every night. They have to kick you out at closing time."

It wasn't strictly accurate, but there was a kernel of truth to the gossip.

She lowered her voice and said, "You're turning into a damned drunk. That's a deal-breaker for me, Stafford Lee."

I started to deny it, but she cut me off again. "I didn't get married to be your nursemaid and designated driver. I refuse to be an enabler. I'm not my mother."

Her nose reddened as she teared up. She shook her head, plucked a paper napkin from the metal dispenser, and dabbed at her eyes.

Carrie Ann wasn't a crier. She hated to let anyone see her break down, even me. I wished we were alone. We could fight it out, hopefully end up in bed together. I had to settle for reaching out and clasping her hand.

When she didn't pull away, I said, "I have been spending more time here at the Salty Dog and some other places. Goddamn, Carrie Ann, sitting around in that hotel room makes me crazy. I miss you."

A tear ran down her cheek. She turned her head away.

"Carrie Ann, I want to come home. I'm not like your father. I'll cut back on my office hours. Tell me what you want, I'll do it."

She breathed out a ragged sigh. When she spoke, she wouldn't meet my eyes. "I don't know what I want anymore."

After seven years of marriage, my spouse should be an open book. But when she chose to, Carrie Ann had the capacity to lock me out.

"Tell me about the new job. I know you were afraid you'd miss the classroom, but you are a natural for the assistant-principal spot."

She shrugged. "I don't know about being a natural."

I still held her hand. I squeezed it. "Well, you are good at kicking kids' butts and keeping them in line. You got a lot of practice on me."

She laughed at that. Just a chuckle, but it was progress. I wanted to seize the moment. I leaned in close to her and said quietly, so no one else could hear, "You know, Carrie Ann, maybe something's missing. We can talk about that. Give it another try." She looked at me warily, but I couldn't stop. "You'd be an incredible mom. It's not too late."

She jerked her hand away and jumped out of the chair. Her face contorted with pain as if I had struck her. "Don't. Just stop it. Never bring that up again, never."

I didn't have a chance to undo the damage. Jenny Glaser walked up, a beer in each hand. She set one bottle in front of me and said, "Hey, Carrie Ann! Good to see you."

Carrie Ann wiped her nose with the soggy napkin she still held. Her voice was frosty when she said, "Jenny. Hi."

Jenny held the other beer out to her. "You want this? It's untouched. I'll tell Scarlett to bring me another one."

When Carrie Ann didn't take the bottle, Jenny pulled it back and turned to me. "I thought I'd find you here. How's the trial going? I saw some of it, but I want to hear all the deets." Jenny took a sip from the bottle. Glancing at Mason's empty seat, she said, "Okay if I join y'all?"

Carrie Ann backed away from the table. "Yeah, this is perfect, absolutely perfect. You always appear right on cue." Carrie Ann tore off, making a beeline for the exit. I watched her go. She didn't look back.

I could have chased after her. Maybe I should have. But I didn't.

Jenny still stood by the table. She grimaced, looking chagrined. "I should go."

Deliberately, I picked up the beer she'd delivered and took a swallow. Nodding at Mason's deserted spot, I said, "No, stay. Tell me—was I as bad as Mason said?"

She sat, set her beer on the scarred table, and said, her voice reassuring, "You were fine."

I searched her face, looking for the truth. "You wouldn't lie to me, now."

"No!" she insisted. "Not that bad. Really."

CHAPTER 12

IT WAS Tuesday morning, a brand-new day. I had the medical examiner, Dr. Ellis, on the stand for cross-examination. And it was time to do some catching up.

"Dr. Ellis, you stated during direct examination that you performed a rape screen on the body of Aurora Gates, is that correct?"

"It is."

"And you took those steps because you observed injuries to the genitalia that were consistent with forcible sexual assault, correct?"

"Correct."

"How many swabs did you obtain during the forensic exam?"

"Four. That's standard."

"Those four swabs — where, from what areas of the victim's body, were those swabs obtained?"

"Two swabs were from the vaginal pooled fluid. The other two swabs were obtained from the cervical area. The cervical os."

"Cervical os? What does that mean?"

"The cervical os is the opening in the center of the cervix."

I turned to face the jury; the follow-up question was for them. "So, to be clear, you swabbed the vagina twice. And you also placed two swabs in the opening of the cervix."

"Yes. That's the standard protocol."

Four of the jurors showed visible signs of confusion—they were squinting, their foreheads furrowed. That was okay. They were paying attention. The seed I'd planted would be harvested later on.

"Dr. Ellis, when you gave the jury your qualifications yesterday afternoon, you stated that you're vice president of the Coast Counties Medical Society, isn't that correct?"

"Yes."

"Congratulations, Dr. Ellis. It's quite an honor to be awarded that post, is it not?"

His face froze. In an unfriendly voice, he said, "It is." He knew what was coming next.

"Who is the immediate past president of that medical society?"

His eyes darted to the defense table. "Dr. Caro."

I stepped back so he could have an unobstructed view of my client. "Are you referring to Dr. Daniel Caro, who sits in this courtroom today?"

"Yes."

"Dr. Ellis, how long have you been acquainted with Dr. Caro?"

He paused to think. "Ten years. Closer to eleven, maybe."

"Did you know him in a personal or professional capacity?"

"Both, I guess."

Henry Gordon-James had tensed up at the counsel table. I saw him drop his pen and press both hands against the table's edge, ready to rise.

"And in those ten—eleven?—years, isn't it true that you have known Dr. Caro to be a peaceable, nonviolent man?"

Ellis started to agree, but his response was drowned out by Gordon-James.

"Objection! This is improper cross-examination, a flagrant violation of the rules of evidence."

I stayed cool. "Your Honor, Mississippi Rules of Evidence four-oh-four permits the defense to offer evidence of character."

The DA pointed an accusatory finger at me. "This is not your witness! You're outside the scope of direct examination."

Judge Walker took off his glasses and rubbed the bridge of his nose. "Sustained. But the defense may call the doctor during their case and inquire, if they wish. Defense counsel is correct about rule four-oh-four. The time isn't right, that's all."

It was okay. I'd made my point. And Gordon-James knew it. He looked disgruntled as he sat down.

When cross-examination was over and I joined Caro at the defense table, my client and I exchanged a glance. For the first time since the trial began, he gave me a nod of approval.

CHAPTER 13

I WOULD have appreciated Caro's nod more if I'd known it would be the high point of my day.

Things went downhill fast. The DA called witnesses to piece together the last time the victim was seen alive, a story that was pretty damning from a defense point of view.

A waitress from the high-end steak house at Lucky Sevens, Hiram Caro's casino, testified she'd served dinner to my client and the victim on the night she went missing. After the server cleared the salad course, she saw Daniel Caro and Aurora Gates arguing, flinging angry whispers across the table. The fight grew so heated that the waitress was hesitant to interrupt. Their fish entrées grew cold while she waited for the spat to die down.

I'd glanced at the front row of the courtroom and seen Iris Caro step out prior to the waitress's testimony. I couldn't fault her for that. It would have been tough for Iris to listen to the waitress describing the lovers' spat between her husband and the victim.

The next witness was a young guy who worked in valet parking at the casino. He'd brought Aurora's 2017 black Volkswagen Jetta to her. Caro's car was much more distinctive; everyone knew he drove a silver Bentley coupe. He tooled around town in it like he was a member of the British royal family.

The valet was young, but his testimony was unshakable. He'd held the door open for Aurora Gates as she got behind the wheel. He said she looked like she'd been crying. And when he was asked to identify the man sitting next to Aurora as she drove off that night, he pointed his finger straight at Caro.

It looked bad.

And then the DNA expert from the crime lab took the stand. As the DA questioned the witness, I sat at the counsel table trying my damnedest to look relaxed. It was a challenge.

Gordon-James said: "Mr. McNabb, what experience and training do you have in regard to forensic DNA analysis?"

He had plenty, and he didn't omit any of his education, training, and certifications. We wouldn't have grounds to attack his expertise. I tapped my pen on the legal pad, waiting for the bomb.

Gordon-James asked, "What is DNA?"

I blinked. Gordon-James had just made his first mistake.

When the expert replied, he sounded like a human science textbook. "DNA is deoxyribonucleic acid, a complex molecule that contains each person's unique genetic code. It is composed of two polynucleotide chains that coil into a double helix carrying genetic instructions for development, growth, and reproduction. It contains all the information necessary to build and maintain an organism."

The expert was glowing with excitement. The dude waxed eloquent on the science of DNA. He left out no technical detail.

Wise lawyers say that, for expert testimony, give the jurors a KISS: Keep It Short and Simple.

I swiveled in my seat and sneaked a look at the jurors. He'd lost nine or ten of them already. They sat with glazed expressions, like kids forced to watch a boring video in biology class. Some of them seemed about to nod off.

The witness finally wrapped up the lecture, beaming. And the DA said, "Mr. McNabb, how do you develop a DNA profile?"

And the expert was off again, describing a world that very few people in the courtroom understood. I inspected my client a couple of times. Caro was following the thread. He looked interested.

No one else did.

That changed, though.

The overhead screen flashed to an image of State's exhibit number ten, one of the swabs that the medical examiner had taken from the deceased as part of the rape kit.

"Did you perform a DNA analysis on State's exhibit number ten, Mr. McNabb?"

"I did."

"How does that profile compare to the DNA sample taken from the defendant, Daniel Caro?"

"There are no differences in the DNA sample from exhibit ten, taken from the deceased's cervical os, and the known DNA sample we took from the defendant."

I swallowed, resisting the urge to look at my client.

"What are the odds that someone else would have the same DNA profile as the defendant, Daniel Caro?"

"Negligible. One in four hundred quadrillion people would have the same profile. But there are only seven billion people on the planet."

I checked out the jury again. They weren't sleepy any longer. Some were watching the expert witness. Others were staring at my client.

So. They got it, despite the expert's loquacious overkill.

The rape kit picked up semen. It had been found on the swab taken from the victim's cervix. And the DNA from that swab matched Dr. Caro's DNA.

It might not be his, of course. There was a one in four hundred quadrillion chance it was someone else's.

CHAPTER 14

AT MIDAFTERNOON, the DNA expert was still on the stand, and I was doing my cross.

I'd been trying to build to a big breakthrough, but I wasn't anywhere close. Finally, Judge Walker cut me off. "We're adjourning for the day, folks."

I checked my watch. *Really?* Walker was shaving off even more time from the courtroom proceedings today than he had yesterday. I suspected the old guy was suffering from burnout. He waved us up to the bench.

He whispered to Gordon-James and me, "Juror number seven says she's got a migraine. She told the bailiff it's getting so bad, she can't concentrate. She needs to take her medicine, but it'll knock her out."

So that was it.

After the judge and jury left the courtroom, I didn't linger. My client wasn't disposed to talk to me. It was an appropriate reaction on his part; it had been a bad day for the defense.

Gordon-James was huddled up with the family of the deceased. As I walked past them, Aurora's father looked over at me, but I avoided meeting his eyes.

Inside my car, I checked my cell phone. Jenny wanted to schedule a meeting with a defense expert on Saturday. Mason had invited me to meet him for a drink at Mary Mahoney's. Carrie Ann had texted too. Her message was terse: the house payment was due.

She'd finally gotten in touch with me, and it was a reminder to pay a damn bill. I hadn't missed a house payment in the seven years we'd been married. I deleted the text without answering and drove to my office.

I had my evening mapped out. There would be no detour to Mary Mahoney's. I'd be spending it at my office, alone.

That was my intention, anyway. Until I got to the office lot and saw a familiar vehicle, a shiny black Cadillac Escalade with a personalized license plate — LUCKY 7S — parked in my usual spot.

I pulled up to the passenger side of the Escalade. A hand holding a cigarette extended from the open window. My client's father, Hiram Caro, had apparently decided to pay me a visit.

I stepped out of my car, and Caro said, "You got a minute?"

"Sure, Mr. Caro. Come on in."

I hauled the big briefcase up the front steps and unlocked the office door. Caro followed me inside, and right behind him was his driver and bodyguard, Joey Roman. I led them past my office and flipped on the light in the conference room; I thought I'd feel more comfortable if I kept some distance between us.

I took the chair at the end of the long table, nodded in their direction, said, "Have a seat."

Caro pulled out the chair opposite mine at the other end of the table. The bodyguard dragged over a chair and set it next to Caro's so they sat shoulder to shoulder, facing me.

There was an uneasy silence. I broke it. "What can I do for you, Mr. Caro?"

"We need to talk, Stafford Lee. I'm not happy with the job you're doing in court."

I wasn't especially happy with it either. But I tried to keep my game face on. "Can you elaborate on the problem, sir?"

He lifted his eyebrows in disbelief. "You can't guess? You're not winning the case. My boy hired you with certain expectations about your legal ability."

"Mr. Caro, it's the second day of evidence. The trial has barely begun."

Caro pulled a pack of Marlboro Reds from his jacket pocket. He shook out a cigarette, held it between his thumb and forefinger, and waited for his bodyguard to flick a lighter.

When Caro exhaled his first cloud of smoke, I spoke up, trying to cover my irritation with joviality. "I don't run this office on casino regulations, sir. This is a nonsmoking business space. No free drinks and no ashtrays."

Caro took another hit and blew it out. The gray ash of the cigarette grew longer.

"Mr. Caro, you'll have to smoke outside."

Caro's bodyguard cupped his hand. After Caro flicked the ash into his palm, Joey Roman rubbed the fabric covering his thigh. It left a gray stripe on the black denim.

Caro puffed on the cigarette again. "My son could have hired anyone, here in Mississippi or out of state. He chose you. Because everyone said you were the best. But you're letting that Black DA from Gulfport beat you." He inclined his head to Roman. "What do you think, Joey?"

"I think he's phoning it in."

Shaking his head with regret, Caro ashed the cigarette again, this time directly onto my hardwood floor. "What's it gonna take to motivate you, Stafford Lee?"

It was a clear threat. Everyone in Biloxi knew what getting on the wrong side of Hiram Caro brought. And Joey Roman was the current guy in charge of inflicting the penalty.

I was framing my reply when I heard the front door open. A voice called out, "Stafford Lee! You in here?"

Jesus. Not the old man.

CHAPTER 15

JENNY WAS determined to find Stafford Lee. She had an important insight to share with him before trial resumed. When he didn't respond to her message or show up at the Salty Dog, she shot off a text to Mason, who was waiting for Stafford Lee at Mary Mahoney's.

She took a roundabout route to the bar on Magnolia Street that passed Stafford Lee's office. Everybody in Biloxi knew where Stafford Lee parked. The blue Prius was a sign that he was open for business.

In the lot, Jenny saw three cars side by side: Stafford Lee's Prius flanked by Hiram Caro's LUCKY 7S Cadillac and Charles Penney's Buick sedan. Undeterred by the visitors, Jenny pushed the door open, followed the voices to the conference room, and announced herself by knocking on the wood-trimmed doorway.

"Hi, Stafford Lee." Wrinkling her nose, she said, "Is something burning?"

Stafford Lee rose from his seat at the far end of the table and said, "Jenny, I wasn't expecting you."

"I've got something for you." With a swift glance at Caro, Roman, and Charles Penney, she said, "I'll wait out in reception until y'all are done here."

Stafford Lee said, "No need to wait. Come back in about an hour—I'll be free then."

"Join us, Jenny." Charles Penney acted like he hadn't noticed the tension in the atmosphere. Offering the chair beside his to Jenny, he asked, "Do you know Hiram and Joey? Joey Roman's about your age. He played ball at Clemson, years back."

Jenny, perched on the edge of the seat, had no intention of feeding Joey Roman's ego. She said, "I don't follow Clemson."

Charles continued as if hosting a cocktail party. "Jenny is a private investigator," he told Hiram and Joey. "She looks too pretty for that line of work, wouldn't you say? But my boy has a lot of confidence in her. She gives him some real good help."

"He needs it," Joey said.

Jenny saw Hiram Caro tug back his sleeve and check his watch. Mississippi had legalized gambling, and Caro supposedly operated on the right side of the law now, but his dangerous vibe had a lot of people convinced that he paid no attention to the line between legal gaming and organized crime.

Jenny silently urged, *Go, please. Get out of here.*

When Caro stood up, pocketing a pack of cigarettes, Roman also rose, pushing his chair back with his shoe. The movement caught Jenny's eye and she observed a crushed cigarette butt on the floor.

What a jerk.

"No need to show us out," Caro said.

The moment the front door closed behind them, Jenny asked, "What was that all about?"

Stafford Lee shook his head. "Caro just stopped by to complain. Nothing to worry about."

"The hell you say." Charles Penney spoke sharply. The jolly host had disappeared. "Stafford Lee, you've got a problem. Why do you think Hiram Caro paid you a visit tonight?"

Jenny found a disposable glove in her bag and picked up the cigarette butt. It had left a scorch mark on the floor. "I'm going to toss this," she said.

While she flushed the cigarette in the restroom, she heard the elder Penney railing at Stafford Lee. "That was a message of disrespect."

Even in the hall, Jenny could hear every word. She returned to the conference room, hoping that her presence would provide moral support for Stafford Lee.

Charles Penney continued upbraiding his son. "I heard you didn't make headway with a single witness today—and not just the forensic scientist. The DA bested you with a waitress and a kid who parks cars for a living. A valet!"

"Are you done?" Stafford Lee asked. "Because I need to get to work."

Penney shook his head in disgust. "Mr. Nice Guy. That's not your job." He pushed away from the table. "I'm leaving." On his way out, he patted Jenny's shoulder. "Try to set him straight, Jenny. He never listens to me."

"Night, Mr. Penney," she said. "Good to see you."

When the old man slammed the door shut, Stafford Lee slumped in his chair with a comical grimace. Jenny laughed, grateful to feel the atmosphere lighten.

He said, "Please tell me you haven't come here to kick my ass, Jenny."

"Nope. Not today," she said.

"Thank God. I think I've reached my limit."

Jenny crossed her arms and said, "When I was waiting at the bar this afternoon, I saw the witness who identified the car. The woman with pink highlights in her hair."

Stafford Lee checked the witness list. "Brandy Mitchell?"

"Yeah, that's the one. She was at the Salty Dog holding court, telling everyone she's testifying tomorrow."

"That sounds right."

"The way she was acting, Stafford Lee, gave me a feeling. She wants to be a hero."

Stafford Lee listened, nodding. "Right. I know the type." He reached into the big briefcase and unearthed a file.

When he flipped it open, Jenny picked up her bag. "I'll let you get to work. Are we good for Saturday? Can I confirm the meeting with the witness?"

"Yeah, thanks."

She'd almost reached the door when Stafford Lee called, "Hey, Jenny? The next time I ask you to leave and come back later, I'd really appreciate it if you'd do that. It's for your own safety."

Jenny swung the door open. Stafford Lee sometimes forgot that she was her own boss; he needed a reminder. "Go to hell," she said.

CHAPTER 16

AS I headed to the courthouse on Wednesday morning, I should have been weak and bleary-eyed from getting only three hours of sleep, but I was in fighting form. Whether it was Caro Sr. or Jenny or my old man who'd gotten my wheels spinning was tough to say, but I appreciated the push.

The first person I spotted in the lobby was the victim's father, Benjamin Gates. I glanced away quickly, but not before seeing how the tragedy had grayed his hair and carved deep creases into his brow. He sat in one of the upholstered seats, flanked by a preacher on one side and a woman who I guessed must be Aurora's stepmother on the other. Her mother, the DA's older sister, had passed away years ago. Cancer, I seemed to recall.

Both days of testimony, I'd glimpsed Benjamin Gates in the courtroom gallery several rows behind Gordon-James's counsel table. I'd dodged his gaze there and in the hall during recess.

Now he saw me walk across the lobby; he handed off his coffee cup and rose from his seat. I looked away, heading straight for the security station. There was nothing to be gained by a public encounter with Benjamin Gates.

He was following me. I whispered to the security guard, a deputy who'd been in Carrie Ann's English class a few years back, "Yancey, can you let me pass? I'm in a hurry."

He paused for a split second, then nodded and stepped aside. I walked around the metal detector, grateful for the favor, and strode to the stairway.

Gates trotted up to the security post, calling, "Stafford Lee Penney! I've got something to say to you!"

I took the stairs two at a time, distancing myself from security, where the young deputy ordered Gates to empty his pockets and step through the metal detector. It sounded like they were having words.

When the courtroom door closed behind me, I put the minor commotion out of my head and focused on the job I had to do. It was time to turn the screws on the DNA expert, McNabb.

Twenty minutes later, I commenced my cross-examination. "Mr. McNabb, did you have occasion to review the autopsy report in connection with your role in this case?"

"I did, as part of my preparation."

"So you're familiar with it."

"I am. Generally."

"And you're aware that the deceased, Aurora Gates, sustained multiple injuries, including injuries consistent with forcible sexual intercourse."

"I am."

I was feeling so sure of myself, I asked an open-ended question: "What DNA evidence can you provide that proves my client, Daniel Caro, inflicted those injuries?"

McNabb blinked his eyes repeatedly. Kind of reminded me of an owl. "I testified that the swab from the victim's cervix—"

I cut him off. "No, Mr. McNabb, we all know about the DNA in the cervix. I'm talking about the other injuries. The gunshot wound, the strangulation, the abrasions on the genitalia. Is there DNA evidence from those injuries that matches Daniel Caro's?"

The expert cleared his throat. "There is not. No DNA evidence obtained from the injuries you described matched the defendant's DNA."

I stepped closer to the witness stand. "Then it's possible, isn't it, that those injuries could have been inflicted by someone else? Someone other than the defendant?"

He nodded. "It's possible."

"Mr. McNabb, let's focus on the injuries to the genitalia. You're telling us that those injuries are not tied by DNA evidence to Daniel Caro, correct?"

"Correct."

"And isn't it true that the semen taken from her cervix could have been there for days?"

"It could have."

"Because spermatozoa can be found in the cervix for up to two weeks after intercourse, isn't that true?"

"Yes."

I wanted to check out the jury, see if they were surprised to hear that sperm could last for two weeks. But I was on a roll. "Mr. McNabb, to your knowledge, was the deceased tested for condom lubricants?"

"No."

"So no one performed condom trace analysis?"

"Not to my knowledge."

That's when I glanced at the jury. *Well, shit.* Three of them were confused. Time to quit dancing around and get to the point. "Mr. McNabb, if the man who strangled, raped, and killed Aurora Gates was wearing a condom when he assaulted her, you would not have evidence of his DNA in the cervix, isn't that true?"

Gordon-James stood up, looking disgruntled. "Objection. Speculation."

I raised my hands, palms up: *Not hiding anything, not me.* "I'm just asking if it's scientifically possible, Judge. The prosecution says this witness is an expert."

"Overruled."

I swung back to face McNabb. "Isn't that possible? If the assailant wore a rubber, you wouldn't have his DNA in the cervix."

He gave a stiff nod. "True."

"So it's possible, isn't it, that Daniel Caro had unprotected sex with the victim, and then days, or even weeks, afterward, she could have been raped and killed by an unknown person who wore a condom during the sexual assault. And because of the condom, you wouldn't find the killer's DNA when you did the rape-kit swabs. Correct?"

Gordon-James pounded the counsel table with his fist. "This is improper cross-examination, Your Honor, without a doubt. Calls for speculation!"

"I'm asking a hypothetical!" I protested.

It was a close call.

Judge Walker's cheeks puffed out before he released a thoughtful breath. "I'll allow it. You may answer, Mr. McNabb."

Walker was doing me a favor, and I knew it. The expert might have known it too. But he made us wait. Finally, grudgingly, he answered my question. "It's possible."

CHAPTER 17

AFTER THE DNA expert was excused, Gordon-James said, "The State calls Brandy Mitchell to the witness stand."

Mitchell stepped forward, dressed in faded jeans and a GOLDEN NUGGET BILOXI T-shirt, unruly hair streaked with hot-pink highlights. The young woman didn't cut an impressive figure, but her testimony was crucial for the prosecution. She'd claimed that during her shift as an Uber driver, she saw Aurora Gates's car parked near Popp's Ferry Bridge the night before her body was found floating in the water.

Keeping in mind Jenny's hunch from yesterday when she'd seen Mitchell at the bar, I watched her intently. Testifying from the witness chair, Mitchell conveyed a sense of self-importance, showing a marked willingness to play amateur sleuth. When she identified Aurora Gates's car from a photo the DA provided, she volunteered that the car was distinctive because it had a crumpled bumper.

Mitchell went on, "There was only one person in the car that I could see. It was a man. He was sitting in the driver's seat."

"Can you describe him for the jury?" Gordon-James said.

"A white male around forty years old. He wore dark clothes, had dark hair that was combed back."

Six jurors glanced at our counsel table. The description wasn't specific, but it arguably matched Caro. He wore his medium-length hair slicked back, like a vain imitation of Brad Pitt.

But the worst was yet to come. I tensed up, waiting for it.

"Is the man you saw in Aurora Gates's car at Popp's Ferry Bridge in the courtroom today?"

To her credit, she hesitated—briefly—before she pointed her finger. "He's right there, in the gray suit with the blue tie."

Daniel Caro's left eyelid twitched. Other than that, he didn't react.

The DA asked that the record reflect that the witness had identified the defendant. He gave Mitchell a nod of approval and said, "No further questions."

Gordon-James hadn't settled in his seat before I was up and swinging.

"Ma'am, you testified that it was just before midnight when you saw the car. Is that correct?"

"It was eleven fifty-four. I'm certain, because I keep a log of my pickups."

"And it was dark, right? We all know that spot you're talking about by the bridge. It's poorly lit. No streetlights nearby, isn't that true?"

"Yeah, that's right. But—"

I didn't wait for her to qualify the answer. "The interior of the car you saw—it wasn't illuminated in any way, was it? No overhead light was on?"

With a dogged look, she said, "No. But my headlights were on, obviously. And they lit up the car."

"So you're telling us that your headlights were the only light source by which you could see the interior of the car parked near the bridge. Okay. Now, you just stated under oath that you saw the car as you drove by, correct?"

"Yeah."

"You didn't stop, did you?"

"No."

"So you were driving down the road around midnight and saw the parked car. How long would you say you looked at it? For what amount of time?"

"Can't say exactly." The chatty sleuth had disappeared, replaced by the recalcitrant witness.

"Tell us generally, then. Because you've said you were operating a motor vehicle at the time. Did you turn your head and look out the driver's window to see it?" To illustrate, I gave my head an exaggerated turn and peered into the jury box.

"I could see it through the windshield. I didn't have to look through the driver's window."

"So you didn't take your eyes off the road."

"No. Well, yeah, just long enough to look at the car."

"How fast were you driving?"

"I don't recall."

"Well, you're a driver by profession, right? On your way to pick up a customer in downtown Biloxi? Let's have some parameters. Were you driving a hundred miles per hour or ten? Or driving the speed limit?"

"I was driving the speed limit," she snapped. "I'm a good driver."

This was going better than I'd dared hope. "I'm sure you are, ma'am. So, isn't it true—because you were driving in the dark at forty-five miles per hour en route to downtown—that you just gave that car a glance before you passed it by? For a second or two?"

"I guess."

"You didn't stare at it through your driver's window as you passed. You kept your eyes on the road, gave it a glance. Because you're a good driver."

Still defiant, she said, "I saw a man."

"Wearing dark clothing, you said. How do you know for sure that the man you supposedly saw was wearing dark clothing?"

"Because I saw him."

"Was he wearing a dark jacket? A dark shirt? Dark pants?"

She hesitated again, probably suspecting a trap. "A dark top. I think."

"Was he wearing glasses?"

That's when she gave herself away. Her eyes darted to the defense table.

I stepped in front of my client. "No, ma'am! Ms. Mitchell, don't try to bolster your testimony. You just looked to see whether the defendant was wearing glasses, didn't you?"

She wore the guilty expression of a kid caught cheating in class.

The jurors saw it. They knew she had tried to see if Caro wore glasses. And he did, rimless glasses with rectangular lenses.

Still blocking Caro from her view, I said, "Isn't it true that when you gave your statement to the police, you didn't say anything about clothing or hair or glasses? That you didn't provide a description at all?"

"I told the police I saw a man."

She was faltering. I stepped closer to the stand. "And you never identified anyone to the police, did you?"

"Not to the police, no."

I turned to the jury to convey my incredulity. "So how could your recollection magically grow sharper over time? Come on! You're not really certain that the person you glimpsed in a dark car is sitting in the courtroom today, are you?"

The witness didn't answer. She looked like she was torn between fight and flight.

I pushed her. "Are you certain? Remember, ma'am, that you're under oath."

She didn't want to back off, I could tell. So she hedged. Her voice held an aggrieved note when she stabbed Gordon-James in the back: "The DA said I'd need to identify him in court. He told me I had to. So I did."

Booyah!

CHAPTER 18

I MADE my case right where I stood, by the witness stand. "Your Honor, the defense moves to strike from the record this witness's in-court identification of the defendant."

Gordon-James was on his feet. "Objection, Your Honor."

I didn't give him an opportunity to argue. "She just stated under oath that her identification testimony was coerced by the prosecution!"

"Gentlemen, please approach," the judge said.

When I joined the DA at the bench, Gordon-James said in a low voice, "Request to discuss this matter in chambers, Your Honor."

He wanted the conversation outside the hearing of the jury. But I sure didn't. My words rang out. "Your Honor, we need to resolve this issue right here. We just heard Ms. Mitchell state that her in-court identification of the individual she allegedly saw in the victim's car resulted from the DA's insistence rather than her own recollection of the events."

Judge Walker toyed with his gavel, rubbing the end of the wooden handle under his chin. "I don't think she went quite that far." The judge turned to study her as if that might help him decide how to rule on my motion. Brandy Mitchell met his eye, appearing

65

unperturbed by the uproar. She lifted her shoulders in an unrepentant shrug.

When Walker grimaced and shook his head, I sensed that he would, like King Solomon, try to split the baby and give each side a partial victory. "No need to go into chambers. You can't unring that bell, Mr. Gordon-James. But I'm overruling the defense motion to strike."

I edged closer to the bench. "Your Honor—"

"Mr. Penney, the witness's testimony speaks for itself. The jury heard what she said. It will go to the weight of the evidence." He set the gavel down. "You may continue with your cross-examination."

I was done with Brandy Mitchell. I didn't intend to give her a chance to back down from her statement. Gordon-James wanted her gone too. When the judge asked the DA whether he wished to ask questions on redirect examination, he declined.

When the courtroom door shut behind Mitchell, the DA announced, "The State calls Detective Stokes to the witness stand."

Stokes was a career cop who had worked his way from traffic patrol to the detective division. I didn't expect to gain any ground with him. My only hope was that his stint in the witness chair would be short, because I knew what he was going to contribute.

Gordon-James said, "Detective, I'm handing you what's been marked as exhibit number thirty-nine. Can you tell me what it is?"

"It's screenshots of a series of text messages taken from the cell phone found in Aurora Gates's vehicle on the day her body was discovered."

"With whom was Aurora Gates having this text conversation?"

"With the defendant, Daniel Caro."

"And how do you know that?"

"Dr. Caro's phone number was in the contact list in Aurora Gates's cell phone."

"Who took the screenshots of the text messages contained in exhibit thirty-nine?"

Detective Stokes directed his response to the jury. From long experience, he was comfortable on the stand. He conveyed the right note of gravity as he said, "I did, in the course of my investigation into her death."

"And is a screenshot a reliable method of capturing what is on the screen of a cell phone?"

"It is."

"Your Honor, I offer State's exhibit number thirty-nine into evidence."

Gordon-James was too eager. He was in such a hurry to get those texts up on the overhead screen, he hadn't jumped through all the required hoops.

"Objection, Your Honor," I said as I rose from my seat. "The exhibit hasn't been properly authenticated, and the detective hasn't provided evidence that it came from my client."

Looking thoughtful, Walker scratched the back of his neck. "Mr. Gordon-James, you haven't sufficiently linked the defendant to those texts. Objection sustained."

Gordon-James backtracked. "Detective, were you present when the defendant was booked?"

"I was."

"On that occasion, did you ask him for his phone number?"

"I did, as part of the standard booking procedure."

"And what number did he provide to you?"

Stokes glanced at the defense table. "He gave a personal cell phone number that is identical to the number in Aurora Gates's contacts and displayed on the texts in the exhibit."

In fact, my client had handed the number to Stokes.

Caro thought he was being smart on the day he was booked when he invoked his *Miranda* rights and told Stokes that he wouldn't submit to any police interrogation. My client had deleted from his phone all romantic texts, and he assumed his extramarital girlfriend had done the same. Big mistake. For a man whose professional life was devoted exclusively to the female gender, he didn't know women very well.

Again, the DA said, "The State offers exhibit thirty-nine into evidence."

Exhibit thirty-nine wasn't particularly inflammatory, but more exhibits were coming. "Your Honor, there's been no showing that my client was in control of the phone at the time the texts were sent."

"Overruled. The exhibit will be admitted."

Bam! Gordon-James hit a button on his laptop, and on the wall by the jury box the texts appeared, enlarged and easy to read.

The jurors swiveled in their seats, hungry to see the messages the DA and I had argued over, successfully building up the suspense.

The first text exchange had happened seven months before Aurora's death, on the day of a chance meeting between my client and Aurora, who at the time was an intern working in the office of the DA, Henry Gordon-James. Her uncle.

> Really good meeting you at the courthouse today, Dr. Caro! 😊

You too. Good luck with law school.

> I was thinking you'd be a GREAT resource for my project in Trial Practice class! Any chance we could talk over coffee? Or lunch? I know you're super-busy!!!

Let me check my calendar. 😉

Exhibit thirty-nine was light, friendly. With the possible exception of the winky-face emoji from Caro, nothing pointed to the beginnings of an intimate relationship. Still, a person might conclude that my client was trying to send a subtle message.

Fast-forward about six weeks to the next authenticated screenshot.

> Good morning, Doc! I had a sexy dream last night... Guess who was in it? Hint: U.

I hope you rested well. 😜

> Someone at the courthouse tried to flirt with me today. He asked me out... RU jealous???

I'll have to tell you in person. Tonight?

The prosecution threw up another series of messages from February. As the jurors read the exhibit, I saw one young woman look at Iris with an uneasy expression. Presumably, at 6:53 p.m. on a Thursday, Caro would have been at home with his wife.

Iris Caro was seated behind us in the courtroom, her eyes averted from the projector screen.

> Bored right now. Thinking naughty thoughts about U. Want to hear?

Sure.

> 🌶️🐱

69

Lol! U know wut? I'm going to shut the door and
take off my panties & pretend ur here with me.
What does that do to you?

And we were only through exhibit forty-one. *Jesus.*

CHAPTER 19

GORDON-JAMES REQUESTED that Detective Stokes read the texts aloud. He read them soberly, without inflection.

I glanced over at my client. If he could sit like a statue at the sight of his lover's corpse, he should have had the strength to withstand the sight of an eggplant emoji. But hearing those texts read on the witness stand finally made him crack. He shifted in his chair, fumbled in his pocket, pulled out a monogrammed handkerchief, and wiped sweat from his forehead and upper lip.

Caro's discomfort was obvious to some of the jurors. The young woman who had checked out Caro's wife now gave our defense table the side-eye. And a middle-aged man frowned at Caro, seemingly in judgment.

While Caro sweated, Gordon-James was going for maximum impact. The date on the screenshot flipped to March. "For the benefit of the jury, Detective Stokes, what is the eggplant emoji generally believed to represent?"

I was halfway out of my seat, primed to object on the grounds of speculation, when a cry from the spectators' section stopped me.

"That's enough!" Benjamin Gates was on his feet, struggling to make his way to the center aisle. He shook his finger at the DA. "Henry, no! I told you—you can't do that to her!" His anguish was plain as he pointed to the screen on the wall. "Take it down now. Now!"

Gordon-James stepped away from his laptop and said, "Please, Benjamin. Go back to your seat." He turned to the judge. "I request a recess, Your Honor."

Walker rapped the gavel, but it didn't stop Gates. The courtroom had no barrier to keep spectators back, and he continued down the aisle, now focusing on Daniel Caro.

I jumped out of my chair, but the bailiffs were already moving. Two uniformed deputies, Charlene and a stout, gray-haired man, restrained Gates by the arms while the judge addressed the jury.

"Ladies and gentlemen, we apologize for this interruption. We'll have a brief recess."

Gates spoke over the judge, calling out to the jury as he struggled with the bailiffs, "Why's the judge apologizing about *me*? Caro's a monster, a damned monster! My baby was an angel until he corrupted her and sucked her into adultery."

Judge Walker beat his gavel on the bench. "Order! Bailiffs, escort the gentleman out."

"What if it were your daughter?" Gates shouted to the jury as the deputies hauled him to the door. Charlene kept a tight grip on him, but the older bailiff must have loosened his hold, because before they reached the exit, Gates broke free so unexpectedly that Charlene stumbled to her knees.

Gates roared as he charged back down the aisle. "He soiled her, then he killed her! And now y'all think you can smear her name and her memory?"

He was coming for Caro. At the defense table, I got into position and put my hands up. When Gates tried to shove me out of the way, I planted my foot and pivoted my torso counterclockwise. My body block didn't budge, so he swung at me and hit me squarely in the left eye.

Charlene tackled Gates. It was a dogpile, and I was on the bottom of it.

She cuffed Gates and jerked him to his feet. The judge tried to speak to the jury as Gates broke down. Sobbing, he said, "She was my baby girl. I had one daughter, and he took her from me. Don't let him get away with it."

As the bailiffs hustled him down the aisle, I picked myself up off the floor. I adjusted my jacket, straightened my tie, and sat back down beside my client. My eye ached from Gates's blow, and my ankle smarted, but my pain was nothing compared to the raw agony in the voice that now echoed in the hall outside the courtroom.

"Did you see what he did to my little girl? I can't stand it! My little girl!"

CHAPTER 20

AFTER THE jurors filed out of the courtroom, Judge Walker pointed his gavel at Gordon-James. "I need to see counsel in chambers."

Before I could rise, Daniel Caro leaned toward me and whispered, "I want a new trial."

Pushing back from the table, I said, "I'll see what I can do."

He followed me and seized my arm. "I'm serious. Do you understand? I demand a new trial."

We were in complete accord on that point, but it was the second time in three days he'd grabbed me. I shook him off. "I heard you. Why don't you go talk to your wife? She looks pretty upset."

Iris Caro was sitting on the front bench. Her head was bowed and her sideswept blond hair shielded her face, so I couldn't read her expression, but her posture conveyed her shame and misery. I decided that if Caro was too thickheaded to console Iris, I'd give him a shove, but he went over to her.

When I entered chambers, I found Gordon-James seated across from Judge Walker's desk, arms folded, listening to the judge's tirade.

"Damn it, Henry, you get your man under control." The judge jerked off his robe. "Hear me?"

"I will, Your Honor."

Walker tossed the robe onto a coatrack. "You better. Because if he pulls that crazy act in my courtroom again, I'll hold him in contempt. I don't give a good goddamn if he's the victim's father. He can't go off in front of the jury, you understand?"

I shut the door behind me and leaned against it. "This jury is finished, Judge."

Walker shifted his ire from the DA to me. "What the hell does that mean?"

When I squinted in response to his inane question, my left eye throbbed. "Come on, Judge Walker. We all saw what Mr. Gates did. The jury's been tainted by his outburst."

Walker eased into his chair. "Have a seat, Stafford Lee. Let's work this out."

I couldn't refuse the judge's invitation. I took the seat beside Gordon-James, and the judge reached for the landline on his desk. "Let's cool off. Who needs a cold drink? Stafford Lee, what can I tell Megan to get for you?"

"Nothing." He couldn't buy my cooperation with a can of Coke.

He took his hand from the receiver. "When we reconvene, we'll patch this up. My first instruction to the jury will be to disregard the incident with the victim's father." Looking to the DA, he said, "What's his name?"

"Benjamin Gates," Gordon-James said.

"Right. And in front of the jury, I'll threaten with contempt anyone who disrupts my courtroom. Any outburst will land them in jail. Okay, gentlemen? Henry? Stafford Lee?"

I didn't respond. But Gordon-James said, "All right."

Walker leaned forward and placed his elbows on the desk. "How about that, Stafford Lee? I'll throw a scare into them."

I made both men wait a moment for my response to that shabby, insufficient remedy. "I request a mistrial, Your Honor."

"Oh, come on, Stafford Lee," he said in a wheedling tone.

He was trying my patience. "My client has been prejudiced by Benjamin Gates's breakdown in front of the jury."

Gordon-James said to me, "Penney, be reasonable. You've got to take into account that this is a double murder trial."

I was about to argue when Judge Walker snapped at him. "Are you the judge? Is this your call?" When the DA backed off, Walker said, "Come on, Stafford Lee. This kind of case, it's natural for emotions to run high. I can tell you from my years on the bench, it'll blow over. No need to start from scratch."

Gordon-James was quick to agree. "The judge is absolutely right. The jury will follow the court's direction. They've all sworn an oath to base their verdict solely on the evidence."

I wasn't fooled by the DA's pitch. From his perspective, the trial was going great. And the scene with Gates would create more sympathy for the prosecution. I couldn't let it happen. "There's no point in continuing. It's a waste of everybody's time."

Walker's brow furrowed. "You've got that backward, Stafford Lee. Between jury selection and three days' worth of evidence, we've already invested a big mess of time. And you know how tough it is to squeeze a two-week trial into my busy docket."

Gordon-James chimed in again: "The judge is right."

The judge was dead wrong. I was beginning to suspect that he was beyond convincing, but I had to try. "Judge, if this case ends with a conviction, you'll be overturned on appeal."

Stubbornly, Walker repeated his offer. "I'll instruct the jury to disregard. Your man will still get a fair trial."

It was a bald-faced lie. "How can they possibly disregard that scene?" I asked, my anger rising. "The victim's father was shouting, crying, making accusations against my client. And he physically attacked me. I got punched and ended up on the floor just feet away from the jury box. You think the jury will forget that?"

The judge looked mulish. "They'll do what I tell them. That's how it works."

The discussion was so absurd, I couldn't remain seated. I jumped up and said, "Going forward with this trial amounts to a denial of due process. I want my motion for a mistrial on the record, Judge. The court's insistence that we proceed is blatant trial error. It's insane."

I'd gone too far. He was glaring at me. "You can make your motion. Then I'll bring the jury back and give them my instructions. After that, we'll adjourn until morning."

It was crucial that I demonstrate effective assistance of counsel and make a strong showing on the issue. I cut a cool look in the DA's direction. "I want to brief it. I'll submit a written motion with suggestions."

Gordon-James sighed, the sound of a man who bears a heavy burden.

The judge said, "You can spend your night buried in books if you want, Stafford Lee. But I don't think you'll write an argument that will make me see this differently." The judge picked up the phone and hit a button. "Megan, tell Charlene we're ready to bring the jury back. I need to give them a talk."

As Judge Walker zipped himself back into his robe, he glowered at Gordon-James. "If you're smart, you'll keep that crazy father out of the courtroom until we put this case to bed."

The DA said, "I can't keep him from observing the trial. His daughter was raped and murdered."

"Bullshit. He's your kin, isn't he? You tell him that if he does it again, he'll be in a jail cell while the defendant's out walking the streets on bond. See if that makes an impact on him."

While they argued, I carefully ran my fingers along my aching eye socket. Judge Walker caught me at it. He stepped up close and inspected me.

With a rueful grin, he said, "Damn, Stafford Lee. Looks like this trial is gonna give you a black eye."

The statement was the literal truth. But as I followed him out of chambers, I wondered whether he also intended it as a metaphor.

CHAPTER 21

MY HOTEL room didn't have a desk, but it did have an ice machine directly across the hall.

When I'd checked into room 221 of the Beachside Inn, I hadn't given the furnishings much consideration. I'd never anticipated that my overnight lodgings after an ugly blowup with Carrie Ann would stretch into a five-week stay.

Now, propped up against the bed's headboard, I balanced my laptop on my legs while I consulted legal authorities on my iPad; it was an unwieldy setup. Eventually, the pain in my eye interfered with my concentration, and I took a break from drafting legal suggestions in support of my motion for a mistrial, walked to the bathroom sink, and, from a plastic bucket of melting ice, packed a handful of cubes into a thin hotel washcloth and gingerly pressed it against my eye.

Back on the bed with the ice pack, I gave a careful read to a Mississippi Supreme Court case. While the defendant was on the witness stand, the murder victim's mother stood up and shouted, "He cold-blooded killed my child!"

What the Mississippi Supreme Court held in that case would be an excellent authority—for the DA. The court said that the harm from the mother's outburst was removed by the judge's instruction to the jury to disregard the incident, that it must be presumed that the jurors put the event out of their minds.

A stream of icy water from the sodden washrag ran down my face and dripped onto the keyboard. I returned to the bathroom and tossed the rag into the sink.

I inspected my eye in the bathroom mirror. Benjamin Gates's punch had left its mark. From my eyelid to my cheekbone, an irregular circle of tissue and skin was swollen and discolored. In the coming days, the bruising would turn from purple to black and then fade to green.

I'd expected that. But the blow had also given me a bright red eyeball. When I noticed that the white of my eye looked bloody, I googled it. According to a medical website, a subconjunctival hemorrhage, which was apparently what I had, would take a couple of weeks to heal.

So every time the jury looked at me, they would get a colorful reminder of the scene between me and Aurora Gates's father in the form of my red and purple eye.

The ice in the bucket had nearly melted. I dumped the few remaining cubes into the sink and headed for a refill. When I flipped the lock and jerked open the door to my room, I found Carrie Ann standing in the hall. She looked startled.

After an awkward moment, she said, "I was just about to knock. I didn't know if you'd be here."

A barbed response came to mind, but I suppressed it.

She focused on my bruised eye, then lifted her hand as if to touch my face, only to slide it into the pocket of her shorts. "Looks like they weren't exaggerating. That's going to be a bad one, Stafford Lee."

I leaned against the doorjamb. "You're probably right. How'd you hear about it?"

"Marla, in the attendance office. Her brother's the in-house investigator for the Biloxi DA."

"Yeah, well. That's a pretty good source."

She backed up a step. "Were you heading out someplace?"

"No." I lifted the ice bucket. "Just an ice run. For the eye."

The hum of the ice machine was audible. Carrie Ann took the bucket from me and walked across the hall to the room marked VENDING.

She returned with the refilled bucket, and I took it. "Appreciate that, thanks."

She dismissed my thanks with a wave of her hand. "Just checking on you. The way people talk in Biloxi, you never know what to think."

Condensation from the icy bucket dripped onto the carpet. "I need to set this down. You want to come in?"

She peeked around me, looking into the room. What she thought she'd find, I couldn't guess. "You're probably busy working. I don't want to bother you."

"I'm drafting a brief, but I don't mind taking a break. Come on in."

When she crossed the threshold, I let the door swing shut. "Take a seat," I said. I stepped over to the particleboard dresser and set the ice bucket next to the coffeemaker. An arm's length from the rumpled bed, an upholstered chair—the room's only seat—was positioned under the window.

Carrie Ann sat down, looking ready to bolt.

"Nice of you to come up here just to see if I'm okay."

Her face flushed. She toyed with her wedding band, twisting it on her finger. "I was heading in this direction anyway. There's a scrimmage tonight at the high school. Varsity against JV."

"What?" I couldn't keep a note of skepticism out of my voice. "You want to sit in the bleachers in September? Football wears you out even after the temperatures drop. Who tricked you into coming out for a practice game?"

She glanced out the window, looking irate. "I'm an administrator now. My responsibilities are different than they used to be."

My phone hummed. Carrie Ann said, "You gonna answer that?"

It lay on the bedspread by my iPad. The screen displayed Jenny's name. I was in trial, so I couldn't ignore a call from my investigator. I picked it up. "Hey, Jenny. Can I call you back in a minute?"

"No problem," she said.

I hadn't even ended the call before Carrie Ann was out of the chair and digging in her purse for her keys.

"Hey! No need to go. Sit back down. We have to talk, Carrie Ann."

"You're busy. It's obvious." She spoke in a clipped tone, the one she used when I did something that hurt her feelings.

"I'm not too busy for you. Damn, Carrie Ann, we need to have a conversation. It's way overdue." I reached out. "Come on, sit back down."

She jerked her arm away so I couldn't touch her. "Oh, please, don't play me. I'm not stupid."

I knew what had set her off. We'd gone around on this before. But she was dead wrong. "Carrie Ann, there's nothing going on between me and Jenny. I've told you that."

I had told her repeatedly, every time Jenny worked on a case for me.

I'd been a bachelor for many years before Carrie Ann and I met, and in the early days of our relationship, I'd found Carrie Ann's jealous tendencies flattering. After we married, the appeal quickly wore off. In my contacts with women—clients, courthouse staff, waitresses, old friends—I'd never given my wife any reason to doubt me. It must have been insecurity that made her continuously suspicious.

She clutched the keys. "All my life, Stafford Lee, men have been coming on to me. But I can handle it—I nip it in the bud. You encourage it." She stalked to the door, turned, and looked me in the eye. "Stafford Lee, I've been watching you for years. I've heard your closing arguments, heard you tell juries to cut people loose when they're guilty as sin. You're the best liar in Biloxi."

As she walked out, she said over her shoulder, "I can't believe a goddamn word you say."

CHAPTER 22

AN HOUR later, a second woman appeared in my hotel room. Before this, during my five-week stay at the Beachside Inn, the only females who'd been inside room 221 were the housekeepers, so two women was a record.

Jenny walked in bearing a cardboard beverage tray with two steaming cups and a paper bag stuffed into the space between the hot drinks. "I brought coffee and burgers because I figured you'd forgotten to eat." After she set the tray on the dresser, she took a look at my face. Wincing, she said, "Damn."

"Yeah, I know. Hey, thanks for the coffee." The cup was still hot enough to burn my hand, but I lifted the lid and took a sip.

Jenny pulled one of the burgers from the bag, and the odor of hamburger grease and onion kicked my appetite into gear. While I wolfed it down, she studied an open file folder that lay on the rumpled bedspread.

"Are these the text messages that came into evidence today?" she asked.

"No. The DA only made it through the early ones, during the happy phase of the tryst. Those are the ones they'll show tomorrow." I went to the bathroom to wash the burger grease off my hands. When I returned, she was still scanning the file.

"Yikes. I'd forgotten how ugly it got between them. She threatened to tell his wife. Are you sure Gordon-James will let the jury see that text? She sounds a little crazed."

In the DA's position, I'd opt to show it. It provided a motive for the offense and an unsympathetic reminder that the defendant was breaking his wedding vows.

"He'll introduce it. The threat leads right up to the next screenshot, where he agreed to meet her at the restaurant."

"Oh, that's right. The dinner at the casino steak house."

"Yeah." I caught her eye. "The last supper."

"That's not funny, Stafford Lee."

"I wasn't trying to be funny. Just stating a fact."

She put the pages back in the folder. "Were you working on this when I called? Is that what I interrupted?"

"No, it wasn't that." I hesitated, not sure if I should mention Carrie Ann's visit, but she was my wife, for God's sake. "Carrie Ann stopped by for a minute."

Jenny took the other burger from the paper bag and sat in the chair that Carrie Ann had recently vacated. As she peeled the paper from the burger, she said, "That's great. I hope y'all are patching things up."

"I don't know. She only dropped in because she was on her way to a school thing."

She took a bite, swallowed. "What kind of school thing?"

I had to stop and think. Carrie Ann claimed I didn't listen to her closely enough, and maybe she had a point. "A scrimmage? Yeah, that was it. Varsity versus junior varsity."

Jenny's face was expressionless as she said, "Huh."

The reaction irritated me. "What?"

"Nothing."

"Bullshit. 'Huh'? What's that supposed to mean?"

"Quit being so defensive. Stafford Lee, I hope you work it out—I really do," she said, sounding earnest. "My marriage was a total disaster. I had to get out. But a breakup leaves scars." As Jenny's attorney in the divorce against her shithead husband, I was entirely familiar with her story. "I don't want you to suffer like I did."

"You're right. I know that." I backed off, but the conversation about Jenny's marriage and my own was making me uncomfortable. I wanted to put space between us, but the room was too small, so I sat on the very edge of the mattress and changed the topic. "Did you meet with our character witnesses today? Are they lined up?"

She nodded. "Some of them. That's why I called earlier. Some of the staff from Caro's medical practice had contact with Aurora Gates when she was his patient. Do you want to scratch them?"

Jenny had raised a touchy point. Aurora became Caro's patient as well as his lover, which was a breach of professional ethics. Gordon-James would jump on it in cross-examination. The jury wouldn't like it. I knew that, because I didn't like it.

"I need you to feel them out. At the top of each witness summary, make a note. If the potential witness encountered the victim in the office, I don't want to call them. I don't care how loyal they are."

She nodded with a sober expression. She'd hardly touched her burger and now she picked up the coffee but set it down on the dresser again without taking a drink. "Okay, but how should I break it to them? Maybe I could just tell them we'll put them on call? Or I could—"

My in-room air conditioner kicked on with an earsplitting squeal. Jenny jerked back, almost knocking the coffee off the dresser, and clapped her hands over her ears. When the noise dwindled to a rumble, she said, "Good God, Stafford Lee! How can you work in here?"

"You'd be surprised at the conditions a guy can adjust to." The AC sputtered as if to prove my point.

Jenny glared at the window unit, then looked at me. "We're old friends. You're welcome to the spare bedroom in my house." With her forehead wrinkled, she said, "That doesn't sound weird, does it?"

My eye had started throbbing with a vengeance. I reached across the bed and picked up the soggy ice pack I'd dropped on the bedside table when Jenny knocked on the door. As I pressed it to my face, I said, "Thanks for the offer, but your spare room doesn't have a commercial ice machine right across the hall."

It was a reasonable explanation. I didn't add that if I took up residence with a woman other than my wife, all hell would break loose.

CHAPTER 23

BEFORE COURT the next morning, I stopped by my office. I was in the back of the building, watching pages shoot out of the printer, when I heard pounding on the front door.

When I opened it, Jenny charged into the reception area, looking fired up. "What's going on?" I asked.

Without answering, she walked into my office.

I went to get the hard copies of my motion and suggestions, which were still in the printer tray, and when I returned to my office, I found her seated and rubbing her forehead—her tell that she was thinking through a problem.

I sat across from her, behind the desk, and spread the printed pages across the surface. "I'm about to proofread my suggestions. Something we need to talk about first?"

Her hand dropped to her lap. "Yeah. I'm pretty freaked out."

That got my attention. She wasn't disposed to overreacting. "What happened?"

"I had an early meeting at Daniel Caro's office, remember? To talk to one of the nurses. Her name's Darinda Johnson. Have you met her?"

When I shook my head, she continued, "She's been on staff for eight years. She's sharp, well-spoken. Loyal."

I picked up a pen and started to read through the document. "Sounds like she'll be a Caro-stan. Say he's a peaceable and non-violent guy, right?"

"Stafford Lee." Her voice was strained. I looked up. "There was another incident. Another victim. Did you know a patient of Caro's was murdered a couple of years ago?"

"No, I don't think I'd heard that." I looked down, spotted a typo, and marked it.

She said, "It was another Black woman. Young. Pretty."

I turned to the computer and corrected the error. "Yeah, well. The man's got a lot of patients."

"Are you hearing me?" she asked, her voice rising. "The MO is similar. They found the body in Gulfport."

I scanned the document on the monitor, looking for more errors. When I glanced down at the clock in the corner of the screen, I saw that it was 8:36 a.m. Court convened at nine o'clock. "I really don't have time for this right now."

She stood and leaned over the desk. "Stafford Lee, listen to me. Another murder. Also Caro's patient, same MO. It's still unsolved, a cold case. What if he did it?"

I saved the document and hit Print. I needed to e-file the motion before court, but Jenny refused to let this go.

"What if he did it?" she repeated.

My hands were on the keyboard while I kept an eye on the time. "Don't even go there, Jenny."

"What the hell is that supposed to mean, 'Don't even go there'? Is that all you've got to say?"

"Yeah." Once the e-filing was complete, I pushed my chair away from the desk; I had to take the corrected hard copies to court. She followed as I made my way back to the printer, righteous anger radiating from her. I sorted and stapled the papers.

"You can't ignore this, Stafford Lee."

"Sure I can." I unearthed a box of file folders, pulled one out, and slid in the documents.

"So what am I supposed to do with this information?" she said.

"Nothing. Put it out of your mind." When she started to protest, I cut her off. "Jenny, I'm Caro's advocate. You understand? I'm trying to get him acquitted."

"The MO—"

"Damn it, Jenny, I don't care. It doesn't matter to me. I'm not the judge or the jury. I'm his defense lawyer."

"But what if it's true?" Her voice cracked, a sure sign of distress. "What if I'm onto something?"

I checked my watch. I needed to be sitting at the counsel table when the jury filed in. "You're speculating." While I packed up my briefcase, I said, "Don't pretend you don't know the law on this. If Caro told me he committed murder, I'd have an obligation. But he denies it, as I'm sure you recall."

"Yeah, but these new facts—"

I didn't want to hear her reasoning. "Just because you harbor a suspicion doesn't change my professional duty. Or yours, for that matter."

She pulled out her phone. "I recorded the interview, so I can make a transcript. When you read it, you'll understand where I'm coming from. Can we meet here during the lunch break?"

I snapped. "Goddamn it, Jenny, listen. You're working for me on Caro's case, and that means you're cloaked by the same attorney-client rules. We fight *for* our client, not against him. You better remember whose side you're on."

She followed me to the door. After looking pointedly at my wristwatch, I held it open for her. She shot me a stubborn glare.

"Since you won't hear me out, I'm going to talk to Mason," she said.

"Don't you dare," I said.

She walked down the steps, then turned around to face me. "The family of the woman—the victim in the cold case—I think I really need to contact them."

"Jenny!" I said as she started walking away. "Absolutely not! You can't do that!"

When she didn't look back, I shouted, "Are you trying to get me disbarred?"

That didn't slow her down either.

CHAPTER 24

I TOOK the stairs to the second floor of the courthouse at a dead run and managed to reach the counsel table just before nine o'clock. When Charlene saw me slide into my chair, she touched her eyelid, mouthed *Ouch,* then phoned the judge to report all parties present.

Judge Walker emerged from chambers.

I stood and said, "Your Honor, in light of the events that took place in open court yesterday, I've prepared a written motion requesting a mistrial along with suggestions in support. I'd like to urge the court to give serious consideration—"

"And you e-filed it this morning. My clerk alerted me."

I stepped forward, holding out a hard copy of the motion. "I'd like the opportunity to present my argument on this matter, Your Honor."

Walker sighed wearily. "I assume the motion speaks for itself." He tossed it, unread, to the side of the bench. "Overruled."

As the judge had warned, my hours of overnight work proved a poor investment. The jurors filed in and took their places in the jury box, and I returned to the counsel table.

Caro leaned toward me and said, his head inches away from mine, "You didn't even make an argument for stopping the trial?"

"I didn't have the opportunity." I had an overwhelming urge to physically distance myself from him, to pick up my chair and move it away.

The DA called back to the stand Detective Stokes, who continued reading the text messages aloud.

I was acutely aware of my client's presence beside me. With a cool demeanor, he listened to the evidence without showing any reaction. Though I was determined to suppress Jenny's speculations, the detachment he displayed made me wonder: What if my client, a doctor who was responsible for protecting the health of his patients, had intentionally killed two of them?

The text messages kept on coming. They told an old story.

> Why didn't U call? Did U get my message?

> U can't just drop me like this. Y R U being so mean 2 me?

> U R breaking my heart, U know that? 💔

> U know what??? UR AN ASSHOLE!!! 😡

> I'm not some dirty whore U can pick up & throw away. Maybe UR wife should know what U do when she's not around.

> U think I'm kidding??? Wait till U see me at UR house.

> I'm gonna tell her about it, I'll be doing her a favor.

The final text exchange occurred on June 12, the day before her death.

You're right, we need to talk.

I KNOW, RIGHT???????

Can't meet at my office. I'll get a table tomorrow at the steak house at Lucky Sevens, 7:00.

Pick U up by UR office?

Sure.

There were no more texts. Stokes left the stand.

Gordon-James said, "The State calls Dr. Matthew Clark to the witness stand."

At the announcement, I sat up straight, bracing myself for the testimony. Beside me, my client picked up a pen and coughed. Maybe the cough was a tell.

Clark raised his hand and swore to tell the truth. Once he sat in the chair, Gordon-James walked him through a recitation of his education, training, and qualifications.

"In regard to DNA testing, have you previously testified as an expert witness in the courts of Mississippi?"

"I have."

"Approximately how many times?"

"A ballpark figure, I'd say twenty."

From the bench, Judge Walker spoke up. "The court finds that the witness is qualified to render an expert opinion."

The court had supplied materials for jurors to take notes, and one of the older male jurors retrieved his pen and notebook. He looked ready for a detailed lecture on the structure and function of DNA. That's not what he got.

"In your expert capacity, what kind of DNA analysis do you conduct?"

"I conduct genetic testing, DNA tests to determine paternity."

My client placed his pen by the legal pad on the counsel table. No need for Caro to take notes; he knew what was coming.

The witness said, "I compared the DNA samples of three subjects: Aurora Gates, the fetus taken from her body, and the defendant."

"Based on those tests and on your education, training, and experience, did you form an opinion within a reasonable degree of scientific certainty as to the paternity of the fetus taken from the body of Aurora Gates?"

"I did. In my opinion, the probability that the defendant, Daniel Caro, is the father of Aurora Gates's fetus is greater than ninety-nine point nine-eight percent."

I'd figured that the jurors had all been following the thread of the direct examination and they'd anticipate Clark's conclusion. I was wrong. A woman in the jury box gasped with shock. She fumbled in her pocket and pulled out a packet of tissues. Shaking her head, she wiped her eyes and blew her nose.

The remainder of the jurors didn't register surprise, but their reactions were easy to read. I saw three of them fold their arms across their chests.

When I took my eyes from the jury box, I gave Caro a passing glance. He hadn't flinched during the DNA testimony. And his face wore an expression that could only be interpreted as indifference.

Which struck me as perverse. Maybe it was due to the years Carrie Ann and I had tried unsuccessfully to have a child or the knowledge that Iris and Daniel Caro were also childless. Or maybe it was the seed that Jenny had planted in my head that morning.

And despite what I'd told Jenny, I was uneasy about the murder of Caro's other patient a couple of years prior and her allegations that he'd been involved in the crime.

After all, a man who'd kill his own child was capable of anything.

CHAPTER 25

WET BOOTS slapped against tile.

"I know I stink," the young man said to Jenny.

It wasn't an apology. The man was a deckhand on a shrimp boat. He had worked through the night, dropping the nets at sunset and pulling them up in the wee hours, then dumping the catch on the deck and pinching the heads off the shrimp.

In Mason's office, Jenny greeted their visitor and made introductions. "Mason, this is Germain Whitman. He came straight from work because he wants to talk to you."

The man sat down and gripped the arms of the chair. He bowed his head for a moment before he raised his eyes to Mason's.

"My wife, Desiree, was killed two years back. It's closer to two and a half years now. Her body was found in Gulfport, just outside the Biloxi city limits. Maybe you remember hearing about it on the news."

Looking appropriately solemn, Mason folded his hands on the desk. "I don't recall the details. Can you help me out, refresh my memory?"

Whitman's shoulders twitched. "She was shot right in the middle of her forehead. The police called it an 'execution-style' murder."

The man released one arm of the chair and ran his hand across his face. "Me and Desiree, we had two kids, little boys. One was just a baby when she got killed, but Lyle—he's the older one—he still cries for his mama. For a long time, he kept waiting for her to come home."

When he shuddered, Jenny reached over and placed a hand on his arm. His shirt was damp and reeked of shrimp, but Jenny wasn't bothered by the smell. Briefly, she worried about Stafford Lee's reaction to the step she'd taken. He wouldn't like it, that was guaranteed. But she'd come this far. She edged forward to see how Mason responded to the man's grief.

Mason cleared his throat. "I'm very sorry for your loss, sir. And it's a tragedy that those boys lost their mama."

His eyes on the floor, Whitman nodded. And then he raised his head and gave Mason a guarded look. "Both our boys were delivered by Dr. Caro. He was Desiree's doctor when she got pregnant." Whitman's hands began to tremble. He clasped them together and thrust them in his lap as he shook his head in bewilderment. "How could he kill a woman after he helped bring her babies into the world? He delivered the boys himself. I was standing right there beside him."

Jenny watched Mason, knowing he'd been caught off guard. She hadn't told him that Whitman believed Caro was responsible for his wife's death. She'd thought the young man should relay that to him in his own words.

She was disappointed when Mason turned the interview away from the accusation against Caro. "How was your wife's body discovered?"

"She was a cocktail waitress. Her shift ended at midnight, but she never made it home. Her body washed up on the beach two days later."

Mason's voice was uncharacteristically gentle. "Were there any injuries other than the gunshot to the head?"

That's when Whitman broke down; sobs wrenched his chest. "He raped her. He raped my wife."

The room echoed with the man's grief. When the tears subsided, Mason said, "Can you tell me about the condition of your wife's body?"

The man touched his throat. "There were bruises around her neck." He went on, his voice breaking again. "I could see the marks from the guy's fingers. It was like I could see the dude choking her. I still can't get that picture out of my head."

Mason raised his eyebrows. "Strange that Harrison County let a homicide go unresolved. What did the police tell you? Why was no one prosecuted?"

Whitman said, "I kept calling them and asking that same question. They got to where they wouldn't take my calls, wouldn't return my messages. So I went over in person and asked the detective. He just told me to go home."

Mason frowned. "Seriously? He really said that?"

Jenny wasn't surprised. The detectives wouldn't hesitate to give a poor Black shrimp-header the brush-off. Things hadn't changed that much in Gulfport or Biloxi.

"Yeah, he told me it wasn't going anywhere. They didn't have leads. And I asked, didn't they do that rape kit? But he said someone messed it up."

Mason said, "What happened to the evidence?"

Jenny answered for Whitman. "Germain told me the sexual assault kit wasn't properly stored, so the DNA sample was lost."

"But that was two years ago," Whitman said. "Now they know about Caro, what kind of man he is."

Mason shook his head. He picked up a pen and tapped it on a legal pad while he regarded the man. At length, he said, "Mr. Whitman, I have to ask you: What do you want? What have you come here for today?"

Whitman shifted in the seat, looking uncomfortable. "I don't understand."

"When you hire an attorney, it's because you want a remedy.

Usually it's money—damages. But I don't think you can win a judgment against the Gulfport or Biloxi PD on these facts."

"You think I want money?" Whitman's eyes glinted with tears. He didn't bother to wipe them away. "I want the police to open up that investigation and get some justice." His voice rose. "How do I get them to do that? I hear all about Aurora Gates, it's the same goddamn thing that got done to Desiree. I want Caro to go to trial for killing my wife. How can I make it happen?"

As Jenny waited for Mason to answer, she felt her stomach sink. Watching his expression, she knew what he would say. Still, she winced when he spoke the words.

"You can't."

CHAPTER 26

BETWEEN THE jabbering on the twenty-four-hour news channel and the rattle of the air compressor in my window unit, I almost missed the knock on the door of my hotel room.

I checked the time. It was past eleven o'clock, pretty late for a casual visit. The door to the room didn't have a peephole, so I cracked it open.

Joey Roman shoved the door wide, came in, and kicked it shut with his booted foot. His voice was entirely cold when he said, "I'm here to give you a message."

He delivered an uppercut straight to my gut. I dropped to the floor, unable to breathe. Roman stood over me, watching me writhe on the carpet. Then he took a half step back and kicked me in the nuts. "Mr. Caro gave strict orders that I couldn't hit you in the face because he wants you to look presentable in court tomorrow. You need a full set of teeth."

I rolled onto my side and curled up in a fetal position. In my agony, I heard high, keening noises. On some level, I was cognizant that the sounds were coming from my own throat.

Roman gazed down at me with professional interest. Then he walked to the bedside table, picked up the TV remote, and turned up the volume. He sat in the chair, propped his feet on the bed, and flipped through the channels while I convulsed on the floor.

When I'd recovered sufficiently to quit wailing, Roman muted the TV. "Penney, it looks to Hiram Caro like you picked the wrong line of work. You're not tough enough for the law."

I took a shallow breath and said, "Tell him I'm doing all I possibly can to show the jury his son's not guilty. I swear to God."

Roman leaned over me and said, "Jesus, Penney. You still don't get it. Dr. Caro needs to walk out of that courtroom a free man whether he's guilty or not."

I stared up at him, praying that he wouldn't choose to inflict another blow because I was physically incapable of fending it off. He frowned at me. "Do you understand, Penney?"

In a hoarse whisper, I said, "Yeah. You've made yourself absolutely clear."

"That's good. I'm relieved to hear it." He opened one side of his jacket and displayed a handgun in a holster he wore on his belt. It seemed entirely possible that Hiram Caro had decided that the best way to guarantee a new trial was to kill the defense attorney.

He dropped the jacket, stepped over me, and made his way to the door. I followed him with my eyes. If he was done, I was a lucky man.

But then he delivered his parting words.

"Hey, Penney. I know where your wife lives. That's a nice house you've got on St. Charles Street."

A knot of dread formed in my gut, right where he'd struck his first blow. We had a security system on St. Charles. But it wouldn't keep Roman out.

In an offhand voice, he said, "I almost forgot. We've got our eye on your friends too. The lawyer, Burnett. And the woman, the PI."

I wanted to shout at him, tell him to leave my wife and friends alone. Counter his digs with threats of my own.

But he wouldn't have heard me. He was already gone.

CHAPTER 27

THE PROSECUTION rested its case on Monday. It was finally our turn, time to present the evidence for the defense. It looked like Caro was going down, and I had serious doubts about my ability to turn it around.

I kept my expression neutral. We were in trouble, and I needed to be sharp, to fully immerse my brain in the strategy of the trial. But my focus was seriously distracted.

Directly behind me, next to my client's wife, sat Hiram Caro. And he was accompanied by Joey Roman.

Under my shirt, right at my waist, I had an ugly souvenir of my recent visit from Roman. Every time I moved, my belt rubbed against the bruise and reminded me of the threats he'd tossed at me before he left.

When the judge invited me to call the first witness, I tried to push Roman out of my head. We kicked off the defense with our own DNA expert, hired from an independent lab in Jackson. He did a credible job on the stand, as he damn well should have. The guy's testimony didn't come cheap.

Our witness was just as qualified as the witnesses from the state lab Gordon-James had put on the stand. And our man was a lot better dressed and gave a smoother presentation. I walked him through a short and sweet explanation in which he made it clear that none of Aurora Gates's injuries could be tied to Daniel Caro by any trace evidence collected in the investigation. He also helped along the seed I'd planted when I cross-examined the DA's experts: he reiterated that the DNA match with Caro was taken from the victim's cervical os and he explicitly stated that sperm can survive for as long as two weeks after intercourse.

I checked out the jury while my witness testified. They were attentive. They got it. But they weren't necessarily convinced.

Gordon-James did a perfunctory cross-examination just to flex some muscle. He didn't hurt my guy. When he was done, I wasted no time getting my next witness on the stand. She was bringing an exhibit to court that would shake things up, no doubt about that.

I called the records custodian from Dr. Caro's office. I had issued a subpoena duces tecum, which required her to bring documents to court. My direct examination wasn't flashy or dramatic. We walked through the foundation. When she authenticated the exhibit, I offered Aurora Gates's medical records into evidence.

Our character witnesses took the stand next, a string of upright citizens from Biloxi and Gulfport who swore that my client was a peaceful man with no reputation for violence. It was hard to judge their impact on the jury. But the character evidence was the classic lead-in for my next step.

"The defense calls Daniel Caro to the witness stand."

His hand didn't shake when he raised it to take the oath. In a criminal trial, that was generally a good thing. But seated on the stand, he looked stiff, wooden.

"State your name, sir."

"Daniel Caro, MD."

I blinked, trying to keep my irritation from showing. I'd specifically told him not to do that. His professional occupation was not his goddamn name; I'd explained that to him when we rehearsed over the weekend. The jury knew he was a doctor, our evidence would show he was a doctor, and I intended to call him "Doctor." He didn't have to insert the information himself. In the current circumstance, it sounded pompous, and we didn't want that.

"Where do you live?"

"In Biloxi, Mississippi."

"And what is your occupation?"

To his credit, he looked abashed. "I'm a physician, a medical doctor. I guess I already said that."

"You did." Though I smiled at him, it was intended as a message.

"Sorry about that. I guess I'm a little nervous. I have a clinic here in Biloxi. I'm an ob-gyn."

"And what do you do in your clinical practice?"

He sat back and lifted his eyebrows. "I'd guess that half the people in this room know firsthand what an ob-gyn does."

Someone in the jury box snickered. I was glad to hear it. Caro was going off script, but this time I didn't mind. It might loosen him up. Giving him an encouraging nod, I said, "For the record, please, Doctor."

He turned and addressed the jury. "My specialty is female reproductive health. My patients are women from the community and surrounding areas. I care for them during and after pregnancy and deliver their babies, and I treat patients for a wide range of conditions involving the female reproductive system from adolescence through menopause and beyond."

"How many years have you been in practice, Dr. Caro?"

He returned his focus to me. "I've had the privilege of serving the women of Biloxi for eleven years."

That was a line I'd given him. He carried it off.

Caro had won several awards, done some community service and philanthropy. We covered that, continuing to build his profile as a guy who wouldn't murder his pregnant girlfriend.

"And, Dr. Caro, did you have occasion to be honored by the Harrison County Chamber of Commerce?"

"Yes. They named me Man of the Year in the under-forty category four years ago." He sounded appropriately humble.

I checked my notes. "Did you say four years ago, Doctor?"

He paused, squinted at the ceiling. "Sorry, Stafford Lee—it was five years back, actually." Looking sheepish, he grinned. "I should have remembered that. I don't qualify in the under-forty category anymore. Not since my birthday. Plus I'm getting too much gray hair."

A couple of jurors seemed to be warming to him. The oldest lady on the panel cracked a smile at the gray-hair reference.

"Directing your attention to the last calendar year, did you have occasion to meet Aurora Gates?"

He sobered immediately. "I did. We met in November, approximately seven months before she died."

"How did you meet?"

"I was at the courthouse testifying as an expert in a civil lawsuit. And we met in the lobby. She came up and introduced herself."

"Did you have occasion to meet with her after that?"

"She texted me and said she wanted to use me as a resource for a class project. We met for coffee two days later."

I walked to the wooden lectern and rested my elbow on it. "And did you discuss a class project on that occasion?"

"No. It was a pretext. Aurora told me she was suffering pain and bleeding and asked whether she needed medical care. She'd recently had an abortion."

I let that sink in while I waited for Gordon-James to fly out of his chair.

CHAPTER 28

THE DA'S voice bounced off the walls of the courtroom. "Objection, Your Honor! Request to approach the bench!"

He was so angry, his hands were shaking. From his reaction, you'd think he'd been blindsided.

But Gordon-James already knew. Under the Mississippi Rules of Criminal Procedure, prior to trial, the prosecution must disclose all of its evidence to the defense, so I was aware that during the course of the investigation, the police had obtained from Caro the victim's medical records. And because I'd served Caro's records custodian with a subpoena duces tecum, the copy of the subpoena was in the court's file. He surely couldn't claim surprise.

But damned if he didn't act surprised. Also indignant. "This is wholly irrelevant, Your Honor. It's an unjustified attack on the character of the murder victim, an attempt to sway the jury against her. The outcome of her prior pregnancy is not relevant to any issue of this case."

"Judge, it's not character assassination, it's a statement of fact. The pregnancy that she terminated and the symptoms she suffered afterward are why she wanted to meet with my client. It's entirely relevant."

"The objection is overruled. You may continue, Mr. Penney," Judge Walker said.

After we turned away from the bench, the DA muttered a message meant for my ears alone. "You son of a bitch. When you attacked my niece's reputation, Aurora was assaulted yet again. I won't forget this, Penney."

I let it bounce off me. Of course the DA wouldn't want the jury to know she'd had an abortion. Their sympathy for Aurora Gates would take a hit when we displayed the medical records that confirmed the truth of Caro's testimony.

A woman's decision to terminate a pregnancy wouldn't have created a ripple in a lot of other places, but this was Mississippi, where antiabortion sentiment ran high. After the U.S. Supreme Court overturned *Roe v. Wade,* Mississippi passed a law banning abortion in most cases. Abortion was also illegal in the adjoining states of Alabama and Louisiana. Aurora Gates had had to travel to Illinois to have the procedure performed.

Though we hadn't polled the jury on the issue, many of the jurors sitting in that box were bound to sympathize with the pro-life movement. And people in that camp viewed abortion as murder.

I resumed my spot at the lectern. "Pardon the interruption, Doctor. What did Aurora Gates confide to you?"

"She'd searched for the closest place that performs abortions. With the help of a friend, a student at Northwestern, she'd secured an appointment at a clinic in Chicago. Aside from telling the friend who accompanied her, Aurora said she'd kept the pregnancy and the subsequent abortion a secret — to the extent of remaining silent about her post-procedure complications."

"Did she explain why it had to remain a secret?"

"She did. Aurora told me she'd been involved in an abusive relationship and —"

The DA's voice rang out: "Objection! Stop right there." Gordon-James was out of his chair and heading for the bench. "Request to approach, Your Honor."

I joined him at the bench. The judge whispered to the DA, "What are the grounds for the objection?"

"Hearsay. I didn't raise a hearsay objection earlier, Judge, when the defense was establishing background. But the testimony the defendant just offered is clearly inadmissible hearsay, and I want the jury to be instructed to disregard."

I sounded cool when I responded. "Judge, this is res gestae. I'm not offering it for the truth of the statement; I'm simply showing the jury what Ms. Gates said and did at the time of the events in question."

Gordon-James lowered his voice to a growl. "The defense is most certainly trying to persuade the jury—"

The judge cut him off. "Objection overruled. Res gestae is an exception to the hearsay rule. Defendant is entitled to inquire." He pushed back his chair and nodded at me.

I'd lucked out on that ruling. I wanted to keep the testimony rolling. I turned back to Daniel Caro and said, "Dr. Caro, what was it that Ms. Gates told you about the relationship?"

Caro said, "She said he was abusive, and she wanted out. If her boyfriend had discovered she was pregnant, she thought she'd never get away from him. And if he knew she'd aborted his baby, she was afraid he'd kill her."

So now we'd done it. We had introduced the specter of the shadowy "other guy," the bad dude who might have killed her in a jealous rage. But we'd have to flesh it out to create reasonable doubt.

"So after she confided these personal matters to you, what did you do?"

"I examined her in my office that week." With an expression of gravity, he added, "I saw marks on her, healing contusions consis-

108

tent with abuse. The injuries were on areas covered by clothing—not an unusual circumstance for victims of domestic violence. When I asked, she refused to reveal the man's identity. She said even her own family didn't know about him, and she intended to keep it that way."

"What else occurred on that occasion?"

"I advised her about the bleeding and cramps and we discussed birth control options. I wrote a prescription for her. I asked whether she was in danger from the abusive situation, but she informed me that she'd left him and she never intended to see him again. She was adamant about it."

"Did you make any written record after the examination?"

"I did."

Luckily, he had the notes in his office's electronic records, which had been provided to us today by his staffer. As the office notes were displayed for the jury on the overhead screen, I glanced at the DA, wondering whether Gordon-James had misread them earlier or failed to decipher Caro's abbreviations and codes.

And then I refocused on my client. Caro's direct examination was coming along better than I'd expected, and I didn't want to break the rhythm. "What, if anything, occurred after that initial office visit?"

"I called to check on her, to see whether the bleeding and cramping had subsided."

"And thereafter, did you communicate with Ms. Gates again?"

"I did. We did." He rubbed his forehead as if he were in pain. "I stayed in touch with Aurora because I was worried about her. I wanted to help her. She had a special quality, the kind of charisma and enthusiasm I admire—probably because I lack those traits. She was a young woman who could achieve great things. But she had a vulnerable side."

His voice wavered. Caro paused to pull out one of his monogrammed handkerchiefs. This part wasn't scripted. As he dabbed at his eyes, I wondered how many of these handkerchiefs he owned. He seemed to have an inexhaustible supply.

After a moment, I said, "Over time, did you develop a relationship with Aurora Gates?"

"I did. I admit that. It started as professional concern for her welfare, but that changed. We developed a personal relationship." He balled up the handkerchief in his fist. "I never intended that, but it just took off. I swear it."

I manufactured a look meant to convey sympathy for his dilemma. "What is your marital status, Doctor?"

"I've been married to Iris for eighteen years. Iris and I met in college. We married the summer before I started medical school. She's a supportive partner, a loving wife, and we've always been faithful to each other. The situation with Aurora—that's no pattern, not in my life. Our friendship went too far, became physical."

When Caro referenced Iris, the eyes of the jurors darted in her direction. I almost turned to check on her but stopped myself in time.

I sounded chilly when I followed up. "And whose fault is that?"

"Mine. I take full responsibility for the improper relationship. It was improper for any number of reasons. I was older; she was in her twenties. I was married; she wasn't. But also, it was an unforgivable breach of professional ethics. When I accepted her as a patient, I owed her a duty as a medical doctor. I violated that duty when our relationship became sexual."

"How long did the sexual relationship between you and Aurora Gates continue?"

He gave a shaky sigh. "It's complicated. There was a point, two months before her death, when I came to my senses. I tried to end it. She refused to let go, said she was in love with me."

"What happened after that?"

"I tried more than once to cut off all contact with her. But she'd demand to see me, insist on talking about the decision. We'd get together, and I was so stupid. Stupid and weak."

"What happened on those occasions?"

His shame was apparent as he slouched in the witness chair. "We'd end up having sex."

"Where?"

"In a hotel room, usually. Occasionally in my office, after hours. Sometimes in my car." He shook his head. "It was crazy. And of course she was confused about my intentions, because my actions weren't consistent with my words. She'd send more texts, making demands, professing love. Threatening to reveal the affair."

"When did the affair actually end?"

"The last time we had sex was about two weeks prior to her death. I was so ashamed of myself. After that, I finally said, 'That's it, we're done.' I blocked her number on my phone."

"What happened then?"

"When she couldn't reach me, she came to the office. I walked into the examining room, and there she sat. She insisted that I unblock her on my phone. She made threats, said she'd expose the affair, tell my wife."

"What else happened on that occasion?"

"She told me she was pregnant. Her periods had been irregular and scant, so she'd done a home pregnancy test and it was positive."

"What did you do?"

"I had a nurse test her. She was pregnant. It's in her file. I went back to the examining room and told her that the pregnancy didn't change my decision to end the affair. It was over."

"What did she say?"

"She said we still had to talk, to discuss the pregnancy, what I intended to do about it. I knew that a conversation was inevitable. But we couldn't have it in the middle of the workday, with my patients and staff nearby. I said I'd be in touch, that I'd meet her at a later date. I texted her the next day. We agreed to meet the following night, June thirteenth."

"Tell the jury about your last encounter with her, the last time you saw Aurora Gates."

He turned to address the jury. "We agreed that she'd pick me up at the office and we'd drive to a restaurant. A restaurant at my father's casino. Most of the patrons are hotel guests from out of town."

"Why did Aurora drive?"

He turned back to me. "I told my wife I was working late. I wanted my car parked by the office in case someone we knew drove by. It was part of the pattern of deception I'd used during my relationship with Aurora."

"What happened?"

"I tried to talk to her at the restaurant, but she was unreasonable. She wanted me to get a divorce and marry her. She was living in a fantasy. I'd never led her to believe that was a possibility. I love my wife." Speaking to the jury, he repeated, "I love my wife."

I heard an audible sob from directly behind me—where Iris sat. I didn't pause. "And what next?"

"There was a scene at the restaurant. She was angry—she accused me of taking advantage of her. She said I had broken her heart, ruined her life. I got angry too, said things I shouldn't have. I told her that she was the one at fault, that she'd created her own problems because she was reckless and immature. That she shouldn't have gotten involved with a married man. And I blamed her for having two unwanted pregnancies in a year. It was terrible. I was insensitive and cruel."

"And then?"

"And then we got in the car. She drove from the waterfront casino directly back through downtown Biloxi. She pulled into a parking lot near my office. I got out there, and she drove off while I walked to my car."

"What time was that?"

He responded immediately. "About eight fifteen."

"What did you do then?"

"I walked to my office, got in my car, and drove home. I got there at eight thirty."

"Did you ever see Aurora Gates again?"

"No."

"Did you have sex with Aurora Gates that night?"

"No."

"Did you sexually assault her in any way?"

"No."

"Did you wrap your hands around her throat and choke her?"

"No!"

"Did you kill her?"

"I did not. I did not."

"Describe Aurora Gates's condition the last time you saw her."

"She was upset, angry. She'd been crying. But she was alive. I swear it." Caro turned to the jury. His eyes were red; his face was marked with the strain of the testimony. "She was alive, I swear to God."

He sounded sincere. It didn't look like his anguish was manufactured. But I wasn't a mind reader.

CHAPTER 29

DESPITE A grueling cross-examination by Gordon-James, Caro didn't back down. When the DA was done, Caro joined me at the counsel table.

We had only one witness left. It was time to establish my client's alibi.

Judge Walker chose that moment to push his chair back from the bench. "We'll take a brief recess. Court will reconvene in ten minutes."

The interruption came at an awkward point. I'd hoped that we could rest the defense case on a high note, and that Iris Caro would provide it. Both Jenny and I had worked with her; she was the only person who could establish an alibi for Caro at the time of Aurora Gates's death. Iris was prepared.

As the courtroom emptied, my client said, "Where's Iris?"

I turned around and scanned the room. "She's probably out in the hall. I'll find her. You stay here."

Members of Aurora Gates's family stood in a cluster just outside the courtroom door, Benjamin Gates at the center. It was his first day back since he'd created a scene and punched me. The black eye he'd given me had changed color, but it hadn't faded.

I saw Iris emerge from the women's restroom. When the door swung shut behind her, Gates broke away from his supporters and ran to her. I wasn't fast enough to prevent him from reaching out and clasping her arm.

He said, "You don't have to get up there."

When I pulled her away from Gates, her eyes were wide with apprehension. I said, "Come on, Iris." I put an arm around her shoulders and escorted her to the courtroom door. Gates followed right behind us. His voice was low, but I heard him clearly: "You know what he is, what he's done. You don't owe that man a lick of loyalty. He hasn't done right by you."

I shuttled her into the courtroom and down the aisle. When she slid into her seat, I moved to the prosecution table and bent over the DA's chair.

"You said you'd keep Gates under control. He just accosted my client's wife on her way out of the damned restroom."

Gordon-James glanced over his shoulder at Iris. "She looks fine."

The problem was, she didn't look fine. The incident had shaken her. And she hadn't been rock solid to begin with.

I left the DA's side, determined to calm Iris down before she was called to the stand. But the door to chambers opened, and Judge Walker returned to the bench. As soon as the jury settled back into the box, he said to me, "You may call your next witness."

I had no choice but to proceed. "The defense calls Iris Caro."

Iris had dressed for acquittal in a pristine white wrap dress. Jenny had probably prompted that choice. A chunky diamond caught the light as she raised her hand to take the oath. Unlike her husband, Iris trembled as she swore to tell the truth.

I gave her a moment to compose herself before we began.

"Please state your name."

"Iris Satterfield Caro."

Her lips twitched when she spoke. I had Benjamin Gates to thank for her performance anxiety, since she had been calm when we ran through the testimony at my office. Relatively calm, anyway.

"And where do you live?"

Iris answered, and two women on the jury exchanged a glance. The address on Beach Boulevard was well known, a stretch of property occupied by a lavish historic home facing the Mississippi Sound. No commercial or residential structures spoiled the Caros' broad view of the coast.

I skipped the preliminaries. Iris was too shaky for comfort, and I needed to get her off the stand as soon as she provided the gist of her testimony. "Directing your attention to the evening of June thirteenth, can you please tell us where you were on that date?"

"I was at home, alone at home. Daniel was working that evening." When she realized her mistake, she grew agitated. "I'm sorry— Daniel *said* he was working. That's what he told me. He called and said he'd be late. But it's just what he told me. I'm sorry."

"Thank you, Iris." Thinking that she needed me closer, I approached the witness stand, hoping it would settle her down.

She said it again: "I'm sorry."

"No need to apologize, Iris. Do you need a moment before we continue?"

She started blinking rapidly. Her eyes were wet. A box of tissues sat on the judge's bench, and Walker apparently saw signs of an imminent breakdown because he pushed the box toward her.

"I'm all right." She looked away and pressed her lips together. She was wearing lipstick, but it was a muted shade, not too bright. After a second, she faced me and gave me a quick nod.

I said, "Iris, directing your attention to the night in question, tell the jury what happened that evening."

"I'd made a cold supper for us because it was so hot that day.

Chicken salad and sliced tomatoes. Around seven, I decided to go ahead and eat alone. I made a plate for Daniel and put it in the fridge."

I'd told her to include that detail. A covered plate in the refrigerator demonstrated positive aspects of a solid marriage. The jury would like it. "And then what happened?"

"Since I was alone, I ate in front of the TV. I had the television on."

"What program were you watching, if you recall?"

"It was on Netflix. They were streaming a TV series I liked, *Downton Abbey*. I've already seen every episode, but I was watching the one where Mary has her baby and Michael dies."

"And what happened after that, do you recall?"

"While I was watching *Downton Abbey,* I heard Daniel's car in the garage. He came into the house through the kitchen."

"What did you do, if anything?"

"I went into the kitchen, told him I had saved a plate for him, that I had chicken salad in the fridge."

"And what did he say?"

"He didn't want it. He said he wasn't hungry, that he had already eaten."

"What else do you recall?"

"We went into the living room. I remember that I muted the TV, because Daniel didn't watch *Downton*. He's not a fan." She shrugged, stretching her mouth into a resigned smile.

In my office, I'd told her the jury didn't need to hear that. The stress of the witness stand had probably made her forget.

Without prompting, she continued. "I remember that I looked through a magazine while he sat in a chair with his iPad. We went to bed at the regular time, around ten thirty. We go to sleep early because Daniel has morning rounds at the hospital before he goes to the office."

"Iris, do you recall the time that your husband got home that night?"

She answered immediately, her confidence returning. "I do. It was eight thirty. When I heard his car, I checked the clock in the living room before I went to the kitchen. I remember the time. I'm sure of it."

"Please describe your husband's appearance when you saw him that night."

"He wore a sport jacket and a tie, the same clothes he'd had on when he left for work that morning."

"Did you notice anything unusual about his appearance or his clothing that night?"

"No. No, he looked the same as he always does."

"Thank you, Iris." I gave her a warm smile before adding, "No further questions."

Gordon-James rose from the prosecution table. He took his time—buttoning his jacket, checking his notes—before he looked at Caro's wife. He leaned against the lectern and studied her for a moment.

"Do you love your husband, Mrs. Caro?" he asked.

A bewildered expression crossed her face.

The question worried me. I hadn't expected it, hadn't prepared her for it. My thoughts began to spin. *There is no good answer here. If she says she loves her husband, then Gordon-James will argue that that would motivate her to lie on his behalf. And if, for some reason, she says that she doesn't love him, then Caro is irredeemable. The jury won't have any reason to save him.*

Iris's voice was uncertain when she finally responded. "Yes, I do."

"Even though he was unfaithful?" Gordon-James sounded skeptical. "He lied to you, carried on an affair with a patient of his, a girl twenty years younger than you! That didn't bother you at all?"

She cleared her throat. "Of course it bothered me. But I love my husband. I still do."

"How much?"

The question stumped her. She sat in the chair, speechless.

I was edgy and decided to object just to give her a moment to recover. I was rising out of my chair when Gordon-James left the lectern and approached her. "We heard the evidence of your devotion," he said. "It was touching, sincere. You were waiting patiently for him at home. You made him dinner, saved him a plate. You muted your favorite program because your husband didn't enjoy it. That would be an act of sacrifice in any relationship, I'd say."

It was time to cut him off. "Objection! The DA is making speeches again, harassing the witness."

The judge nodded. It didn't surprise me that he'd protect Iris Caro from the DA. In a stern voice, he said, "Ask a question, Mr. Gordon-James."

Gordon-James frowned. "Mrs. Caro, when your husband called you on the night in question and told you he was working late, that was a lie, wasn't it?"

"Yes."

"Did you know it was a lie when he said it that night?"

"No. No, not then. I believed him. He worked late sometimes. OBs have irregular hours."

"And how long have you known the defendant?"

"Since college. We met at Ole Miss more than twenty years ago."

"That's a long time. You probably know him better than anyone, isn't that right?"

She looked at the defense table as if seeking direction on how to answer. Finally, she lifted her shoulders and said, "I guess so."

"You know your husband better than anyone, and you can't tell when he's being truthful and when he's lying?"

Oh, shit, I thought. *Here it comes.*

"Then how can the people in this courtroom possibly believe anything he says?"

I was on my feet before he finished, shouting out an objection—argumentative, badgering the witness. Walker sustained it. But the jury was thinking it over. I saw it in their faces as they stared at the defense table, assessing Caro.

Most of the people in that box had already condemned him. They'd made up their minds.

CHAPTER 30

"LADIES AND GENTLEMEN of the jury, you have a weighty job before you."

Gordon-James stood at the lectern facing the jury. It had been a couple of years since I'd heard him make a closing argument. As I recalled, he relied on a script. But on this day, he didn't have a sheaf of papers. His hand held only the clicker for his PowerPoint slideshow.

"Your job is to find the defendant guilty of two counts of murder in the first degree. The jury instructions contain all the law that applies to this case. What does the law tell you to do?"

He clicked the PowerPoint, and a jury instruction appeared on the screen. It contained the elements of count one, the murder of Aurora Gates.

"This tells you what you must find in order to return a verdict of guilty. Has the State met its burden? Let's review the evidence."

Gordon-James was composed as he walked them through the State's case starting with the fisherman who'd discovered the victim's body. With a flick of his hand, the text messages between Aurora Gates and Daniel Caro appeared. He moved next to the waitress and parking valet, bypassing the in-court identification provided by the Uber driver I'd smacked down on cross-examination.

Then he summarized the testimony of his expert witnesses, clicking images on his PowerPoint, flashing exhibits across the screen.

Too many exhibits, in my opinion. It kept the jury's focus on the courtroom wall rather than on the DA's argument. The jurors looked from the screen to the lectern and back as they tried to follow along.

You're losing them, Gordon-James. They're not hearing you. But that was okay. Better for our side.

He set the clicker down and grasped the top of the wooden lectern with both hands. "Ladies and gentlemen, back on the first day of this trial, I promised you in my opening statement that the State would show comprehensive evidence that would prove the defendant's guilt to you, and I have kept my promise."

At that point in his argument, the DA turned his head and met my eye. I knew what to expect. He was coming for me.

"Counsel for the defendant made an opening statement, too, on that first day. But he didn't make any promises. Because Mr. Penney knew he couldn't follow through on them. What did the defense counsel choose to say in his opening statement? What was his tactic? He attacked the nature of the evidence that the prosecution is bringing before you. Mr. Penney derided our evidence before it was even produced. He spoke of circumstantial evidence as if it constituted some kind of inferior proof. He said *circumstantial* like it was a dirty word, didn't he?"

Several of the jurors looked over at me. I kept my posture relaxed to give the impression that I had nothing to apologize for.

Gordon-James smacked the surface of the lectern with the palm of his hand. "But I'll tell you this, ladies and gentlemen. Circumstantial evidence is the best kind of evidence. Because it can't lie to you. It is what it is.

"Scientific tests. DNA results. Experts' descriptions of gunshots. Photos of abrasions, bruises, genital injury. How can they lie? They are what they are. They can't intentionally deceive you." His voice grew strident: "Now compare the State's case with the defendant's case. What did Mr. Penney present to you? He gave you the testimony of the man charged with two counts of murder who will lose his life or liberty if he's convicted. And he tossed in some character evidence, the personal opinions of the defendant's employees and friends, testimony that had no bearing whatsoever on the facts of these murders. And Mr. Penney wrapped up his case with the testimony of the defendant's wife, a woman who, after years and years of marriage, can't tell whether her husband is lying to her or not."

I had to control my urge to slide down in the seat. Admittedly, the DA's attack on Iris Caro was a pretty good shot.

He went on, even louder: "Think about the credibility of the evidence and the witnesses. Circumstantial evidence doesn't lie. But people can lie. They can and they do. The instructions of law—and you won't just hear them aloud, you'll take them with you to the jury room—state that it's your job to determine the credibility of the evidence and the witnesses and decide whom you believe. If you don't find the defendant Daniel Caro credible, you don't have to believe a word he says. Think about that, ladies and gentlemen. Is he credible? 'I'm working late tonight, honey!' His wife *should not* have believed him. And neither should you."

Another effective shot. It would have been a good place for the DA to wrap it up.

But Gordon-James wasn't finished. He launched into a tirade on the burden of proof, sounding positively resentful of the reasonable-doubt standard. He attempted to define *reasonable doubt* in a myriad of ways that incorrectly diminished the standard, and I objected and shut him down. Four times, in fact.

Every time the judge ruled in my favor, Gordon-James became more vehement. He started going off on tangents, using up time on matters that didn't advance his argument.

As I listened, I thought: *He should've used a script.*

The jurors looked weary. Maybe he noticed it, because he changed direction. With a forbidding expression, he pointed at the door behind the jury box. "You'll be retiring to that jury room shortly. While you're in there deliberating, I want you to use your heads. Think! Think about Aurora Gates and the violence she suffered. As you recall the evidence, I want you to put yourself in Aurora Gates's shoes when you decide—"

As soon as he said *shoes,* I was out of my chair. "Objection, Your Honor! Improper argument!"

Judge Walker was nodding in agreement with me, but I kept on. "What the DA is arguing is personalization. The DA knows that's improper. It's an attack on the impartiality of the jury's judgment!"

"Mr. Penney is correct. Objection sustained."

Keeping his eyes trained on the jury box, Gordon-James didn't acknowledge the ruling. With a weary shake of his head, he said, "There's been so much talk in here. Talk in the courtroom, arguments by attorneys, talk, talk, talk. None of that will be remembered. What I say, what opposing counsel says, even what the judge says—all of it will be forgotten."

I edged forward in my seat, waiting for the opportunity to cut him off. I knew that argument. The DA was borrowing it from the famous closing in the Mississippi Burning case.

"The talk will be forgotten. But what you *do,* what this jury does today, will long be remembered. It will be remembered by Aurora Gates's family as long as they live. It will be remembered by her friends and by the community at large. You have a job to do."

He clenched his hand into a fist and pounded the surface of the lectern. "You must find Daniel Caro guilty so that you can avenge Aurora's brutal death."

That was my cue. "Objection!"

He ignored me, raising his voice to a shout and banging the lectern with increased force. "Her murder and the murder of her blameless unborn child must be avenged—"

At that point, I had to yell to be heard over him. "Your Honor, the prosecution is trying to inflame the passions of the jurors!"

"Avenge her unborn child, who was murdered in the womb by its own father!"

Judge Walker picked up the gavel and beat it on the wooden block. "Mr. Gordon-James, you are out of order."

Finally, the DA stopped speaking. As Judge Walker instructed the jury to disregard his statements, Gordon-James raised his eyes to the ceiling. The lights reflected off the sheen of perspiration covering his face. His breath was coming fast; I could see his chest rise and fall.

He turned his head, coughed into his fist, and cleared his throat before he resumed. "What you do will be remembered. You have sworn to do justice in this case. *Justice,* ladies and gentlemen— that's your job. Sometimes, justice isn't about mercy. This is one of those times. Daniel Caro does not deserve your mercy. In fact, I wish you could show him the same treatment he gave Aurora Gates when he strangled and raped—"

"Objection!"

"Sustained."

The prosecutor paused again, breathing hard. Sweat trickled from his hairline and ran down his cheek. As he struggled for composure, I glanced at the jurors. At least half of them appeared distinctly uncomfortable, averting their gaze from the DA. One guy in the second row looked over at our counsel table and caught my eye. The woman next to him scooted her seat back, away from the DA. I resolved to zoom in on those jurors first when my turn came.

Gordon-James's voice was hoarse. "You mustn't forget what this case is all about." With a shaking hand, the DA held up his

PowerPoint clicker. The new image that appeared on-screen was the autopsy photo of the victim, her body bloated and her face eaten away.

"What if she were your daughter?" His voice broke. "What if she were your niece?"

Another improper argument. It was like he'd forgotten all the rules. Gordon-James was way too close to the case, too personally involved. I stood up to make another objection but hesitated when Gordon-James turned away, presenting his back to the jury. His face contorted with grief, and he began to sob. It looked like he couldn't go on.

So that was it. My old man always said a case could be won with the right closing argument, and sometimes that was true.

As the DA walked away from the jury, I thought, *Maybe a case can be lost in closing too.*

CHAPTER 31

WHEN JUDGE WALKER called me up for my turn, I bypassed the lectern. Unlike the DA, I didn't need to stand behind it or pound it with my fist. Not my style.

I walked straight up to the jury. I held a single note card on which I'd jotted eight or nine key phrases. I was going to talk to the jurors. Not preach, not orate. Just talk.

"Ladies and gentlemen of the jury, I want to thank you for the time and attention you've devoted to this trial. It's no secret that serving as a juror isn't easy. It's hard work, isn't it? Maybe that's why people want to kick their dog when they see that notice for jury duty in the mailbox."

That got a smile out of a couple of them. My guy in the second row nodded in agreement.

"Jury duty is a real imposition, a sacrifice. But it's also the most important job in our judicial system. You, the people in this box, are the ones who keep the scales of justice in balance."

I paused for just a second to adjust the knot of my necktie. It wasn't the lucky tie from Carrie Ann that I usually wore for opening and closing. That morning, I'd opted for a newer tie, one with a regimental stripe in red and blue. I hoped it would give off a patriotic vibe when I urged the jury to return a verdict of not guilty.

127

"Ladies and gentlemen, while I listened to the DA's closing remarks, it occurred to me that maybe *he's* forgotten what this trial is about."

I paused, waiting for Gordon-James to stand and object. I had my comeback ready. But the DA remained in his chair.

I moved down the jury box and fixed my eyes on the gray-haired woman I'd originally pegged as a defense ally. "It's not your job to find Daniel Caro guilty of having an extramarital affair."

She held my gaze, blinking once. I moved on to the woman sitting on her right, who regarded me with a frank expression of dislike.

"That's not why we're here. My client is not on trial for going out to dinner with Aurora Gates. He's not on trial for sending and receiving racy text messages."

When the angry juror rolled her eyes, I stepped to the middle of the box and focused on a juror I thought might be easier to persuade. "He's not on trial for having sex with Aurora Gates over a period of months; he's not on trial for getting her pregnant. He's not charged with having a sexual encounter with her days before her death, which he admitted to you."

My next target: the people in the second row who'd recoiled from Gordon-James's argument. "He's not here today for lying to his wife or for failing to enjoy his wife's television programs." I lowered my voice and said, "If it were a crime to fight over TV choices with your spouse, ladies and gentlemen, we'd all be in jail."

That line got a smirk out of three men in the box. *Bingo.*

"When you think about this case, recall that this is what the State has proven with its evidence—that's it, ladies and gentlemen. The DA proved my client cheated on his wife with Aurora Gates. No doubt about it. And he got Ms. Gates pregnant.

"What you have to find to return a guilty verdict, though, is that the DA proved to you beyond a reasonable doubt that this man,

Daniel Caro—this doctor who faithfully serves our community—assaulted and raped Aurora Gates, shot her in the chest, and threw her body into the water near Popp's Ferry Bridge. You have to find that Daniel Caro committed *those* acts.

"Not that *somebody* did it. We all know somebody did it."

With a sweep of my arm, I pointed at the defense table. "But, ladies and gentlemen, there is not a shred of direct evidence showing that Dr. Daniel Caro did it."

My voice was matter-of-fact when I said, "There's no witness to it. There's no physical evidence tying him to the scene or to the murder. No forensic evidence. And no confession or admission by my client.

"The DA said in his argument that he loves circumstantial evidence! He's crazy about it; it's his favorite kind of evidence." I leaned in like I was sharing a confidence. "You think maybe he's saying that to you because circumstantial evidence is all he's got?"

I stepped to the side and focused on the far seats in the jury box. "And, ladies and gentlemen, if circumstantial evidence can lead you to make more than one reasonable conclusion, then you must listen to that voice in your head when it frames a doubt.

"Because the State carries a heavy burden of proof in criminal cases. Don't let the DA try to diminish or minimize it. He must prove the State's case beyond a reasonable doubt. Let's talk about that."

I took a moment to make sure that all the jurors were tuned in, especially those who remained unconvinced.

"In Mississippi, our jury instructions don't define *reasonable doubt* because our courts believe the words speak for themselves. Y'all know what *reasonable* means. Is it reasonable to think that my client, whose life has been devoted to preserving women's health and safety, would strangle and rape a woman, shoot her in cold blood, then dump her in a lake? And then arrive home at eight thirty in the evening, jacket and tie on, looking as fresh as he had when he'd left the house that morning? Ladies and gentlemen, that's not reasonable.

"Is it reasonable that your neighbors in Biloxi and Gulfport would come to court and swear that Daniel Caro is a law-abiding, peaceable, nonviolent man if he was really a cold-blooded killer? Is it reasonable that he could fool them all? Is it reasonable to think that his wife, under penalty of perjury, would tell you anything about that night that wasn't true?"

It was time to up my energy a notch. I focused again on the woman who was my primary skeptic in the jury box.

"You know the defendant is presumed innocent until found guilty beyond a reasonable doubt. That's the law. And you know that he has the right to remain silent. The defendant doesn't have to testify, doesn't have to put on evidence, doesn't have to say anything. The jury is instructed on credibility by the judge. And the instructions say that only you get to determine the credibility of the witnesses. Credibility is up to you, because you are the ones who see the defendant on the witness stand with your own eyes, hear his testimony with your own ears."

I moved to a more receptive juror.

"You saw and heard my client, Dr. Caro. You heard the witnesses testify to his unimpeachable character. You heard our expert scientist explain that his DNA could have been in Ms. Gates's cervix for as long as two weeks. You heard his wife tell you exactly where he was at eight thirty p.m. on June thirteenth and just what kind of shape he was in.

"The witnesses are credible. You should believe them! And here's a crucial point. The evidence from the defense witnesses does not conflict with the forensic evidence presented by the prosecution, because the forensic evidence doesn't tie my client to the crime. By the way, you can disregard the Uber driver. She backed away from her testimony right before your eyes when she said she'd identified the defendant because the DA told her to."

I expected an indignant denial from the prosecution table. All I got was silence.

"I know that the DA wants someone to pay for this crime. Aurora Gates is dead; her life and her unborn child's life were extinguished. Her family grieves for her. And they want someone to pay, they want someone to suffer.

"But that's not the purpose of this trial. Finding a scapegoat is not the goal of our criminal justice system."

The words were coming to me. I slipped the unneeded note card into my pocket.

"The DA knows he has no direct evidence, but somebody has to pay. Daniel Caro is a seducer, adulterer, heartbreaker. So, according to the DA, Daniel Caro must pay.

"Ladies and gentlemen of the jury, that is not the law. Remember that burden of proof? *Reasonable doubt* doesn't mean 'maybe.'"

I paused and thoughtfully gazed off to the side. "'Maybe it could be him.' 'It's possible, I guess, that it could be him.' 'I suppose, if it's somebody, it might have been him.'" My eyes returned to the jurors. "Is that enough to return a guilty verdict? No! That is not enough to convict, not in this country.

"Do a gut check, please. Is there a doubt? In this case, yes. If you're being honest, you have a doubt. A reasonable doubt."

Without getting loud, I jacked up my intensity. "Knowing that there is clearly reasonable doubt, if you convict my client of murder, will you be able to sleep in the weeks and months to come? Imagine lying in your bed late at night when all is quiet and there are no distractions. If you have wrongfully condemned my client with a guilty verdict, ladies and gentlemen, how will you sleep at night?"

At that, the middle-aged woman met my eye. She was with me; I could feel it. I walked back to where I could view her without obstruction.

"We've all done things we're ashamed of. All of us. My client has too. But that doesn't mean that he should pay for crimes he did *not* commit."

At that, my target juror turned her head to steal a nervous glance at the woman seated next to her — my biggest challenge in the box. I knew I hadn't swayed her. That woman was one of the four Black people in the box of thirteen. She had fixed me with a glare throughout my entire pitch.

I thought of that juror as I wrapped up my argument. Thought of her as I watched Gordon-James flounder through his brief rebuttal and heard the judge read pages of jury instructions aloud.

Right before Judge Walker sent them off to the jury room, he said, "Ms. Tyler, you are juror number thirteen."

The woman who'd glowered throughout my argument looked befuddled. "I don't understand, Your Honor."

Walker said, "You're excused at this time. I'd like to thank you for your service on the jury. We won't need you to stay."

She was the alternate. I had one thought: *For God's sake, don't let anyone on this jury keel over from a heart attack.*

The woman didn't move. I could see the challenge in her expression as the judge's words sank in. She didn't want to be excused. She was ready to go into the jury room with the others and cast her vote.

But she had no choice. Pressing her lips together tightly, she stood and stepped out of the jury box. As I watched her walk away from the twelve other jurors, I breathed a lot easier.

CHAPTER 32

THE JURY had been deliberating all day.

Around four thirty in the afternoon, the jury had sent a message to the judge saying they were deadlocked and couldn't reach a unanimous decision. Judge Walker pulled them into court, sat them down in the jury box, and gave them the dynamite charge.

To give them a push, he read the jury an instruction that said they needed to agree, that it was their duty to return a verdict in the case. There's more to the instruction, but that's the gist. Then he sent them back to the jury room to continue their deliberations.

I sat alone at the counsel table, keeping vigil. Daniel and Iris Caro were in the courthouse lobby with family and friends, trying to steer clear of the supporters of Aurora Gates. Gordon-James retired to the DA's private office down the hall.

I checked the time on my cell phone—it was past six thirty. They'd be giving the jury something to eat pretty soon. I wondered if I could dash down the street to buy a cup of coffee.

While I debated, Mason walked into the courtroom and slid into the chair beside mine. "What do you think? They gonna hang up?"

"Hell, I don't know. Seven hours is a long time."

He tipped the chair back on two legs. "After seven hours, those jurors are bound to be screaming at each other. The jury room isn't soundproof. Why don't you ask Charlene if she's heard any of the deliberations? She's got a soft spot for you, Stafford Lee."

I looked over my shoulder to be sure we were still alone. Mason had known I'd try to wheedle information from the bailiff. "I asked. She had nothing to pass along."

He narrowed his eyes. "Don't bullshit me, Stafford Lee. I know she told you something."

Reluctantly, I nodded. He leaned in for the scoop. In a low voice, I said, "They don't like lawyers."

"Ouch." Mason glanced over at the empty prosecution table. "Well, the DA's a lawyer too. Did Gordon-James really lose his shit in closing arguments?"

Before I could answer, the door to chambers opened. Judge Walker emerged, shoving his arm into the sleeve of his black robe. "We've got a verdict!"

"I'll get my client, Your Honor."

I didn't have to look far. As he'd been throughout the deliberation, Caro was sitting with a sparse group of supporters on the far side of the lobby. I ran down the stairs so that I could walk by his side as he made his way back to court to hear the verdict.

Word of the imminent decision was circulating. Though the courthouse offices had closed at five o'clock, a fair number of spectators remained to hear the outcome. As Caro and I proceeded to the counsel table, the room filled up.

After my client was seated, I turned to offer my support to his wife. Still in the front row, Iris was dressed for the verdict in a black linen suit. Maybe black was an intentional choice, and she was prepared for the worst. When I extended my hand, she clung to it, looking petrified.

Seated next to her was her father-in-law. He looked like he wanted to punch someone—possibly me. "Penney, what's it gonna be?"

I managed, with effort, to answer him in a civil tone. "We'll know in a moment. We're putting Iris in your care, Mr. Caro. In the event of an adverse outcome, you'll need to escort her out of the courthouse."

That shut the old man up. There was a risk of trouble whichever way the verdict went. It wasn't hard to determine the spectators' sympathies. Beside Hiram Caro sat Joey Roman, looking ready for a fight. Two rows back were a handful of my client's friends and a couple of his employees from the clinic. The press stood at the rear of the courtroom, poised for a speedy exit to report the verdict.

The crowded rows on the other side of the aisle were filled with Aurora Gates's family and supporters, uniformed and plainclothes cops, and the staff of the DA's office. I saw the jury alternate seated a couple of rows behind Aurora Gates's stepmother. The alternate had lingered at the courthouse for seven hours to hear the verdict. I hadn't misread her opinion of my client.

It was time to bring the jury into court.

But the prosecution table was empty. We couldn't proceed.

At the bench, Judge Walker looked down at me and said, "Where's Mr. Gordon-James?"

How should I know? I swallowed back the terse response as the DA hurried into the courtroom, followed by the victim's father and the preacher who had been present throughout the trial.

As soon as Gordon-James took his seat, Charlene ushered the jury of twelve into the box.

Judge Walker turned to them. "Have you reached a verdict?"

"We have, Your Honor."

The woman acting as foreperson held the sheets of paper so tightly that the knuckles of her hands were white. She wasn't one of the allies I'd pinned my hopes on.

Judge Walker reached out for the pages. The bailiff took them from the foreperson and handed them up to the bench, and the judge adjusted his eyeglasses before shuffling through the sheets.

He cleared his throat. "The defendant will please stand for the reading of the verdict."

Our chairs slid across the floor as we rose together. I felt Caro's legs shaking.

Here it comes.

Judge Walker studied the top page, prolonging the wait.

If Caro is convicted, what does Joey Roman have planned for me? Will there be more than one assailant? Will it happen tonight or am I doomed to live in a state of dread for days or weeks?

The judge read, "'As to count one, we, the jury, find the defendant not guilty.'"

The phrase soared inside my head. *Not guilty.* But the reading wasn't over. We hadn't heard the outcome on count two, charging Caro with the murder of the unborn child. It would be illogical for the jury to convict on count two after they'd acquitted him of Aurora Gates's murder—but you never know what a jury might decide. We waited in silence.

"'As to count two, we, the jury, find the defendant not guilty.'"

The courtroom remained hushed, as if the onlookers were stunned. Beside me, Caro's trembling became more pronounced. By contrast, I felt my muscles relax. Joey Roman wouldn't be imposing a personal penalty on me after all.

Beyond the unquestionable relief, my reaction wasn't the usual victory rush. Instead of feeling jubilant, I felt like I had done something wrong but managed to get away with it.

Immediately behind me, a whoop of triumph broke the silence. Technically, Hiram Caro's victory cry was premature. The jury instructions had also included lesser offenses: second-degree murder, manslaughter. But as the judge read on, the refrain continued: *Not guilty.*

Finally, the judge set the written verdicts on the bench. Addressing the jury, he said, "Is this your verdict?"

The foreperson replied, "It is, Your Honor."

And then the courtroom erupted.

CHAPTER 33

I HAD never witnessed anything like it.

Sure, I'd seen courtrooms descend into chaos before. But that was on television, in national news coverage of trials in faraway cities. Nothing like this had ever happened in Biloxi, not in my recollection.

The repetitions of *Not guilty* agitated the left side of the courtroom, the pro-prosecution side—a dozen benches filled with people who were outraged by the jury's decision. The murder victim's father was the first one on his feet. Benjamin Gates countered Hiram Caro's victory cry with a shout of his own: "It's not right!"

The Gates family took up the chant, adding their voices to the chorus, and the room echoed with *It's not right! It's not right!* No one tore down the aisle and rushed to the bench, but the courtroom rang with the crowd's discontent and dismay.

As the bedlam continued, I searched the back rows, grateful for the heavy law enforcement presence in the courtroom. But the cops made no effort to subdue the uproar. From where I sat, they appeared to support it. The cops and the DA's staff didn't join the chant, but they were clearly disgruntled. They exchanged unhappy comments, looking daggers at the jury.

Judge Walker wasn't having it. He hit the gavel block hard. "Order! Order in the court!"

His words would have silenced the courtroom on any other occasion, but today they had little impact. Walker turned to the jury box, where some of the jurors were looking frightened.

"Ladies and gentlemen, you are dismissed." He had to raise his voice to be heard over the crowd. "Thank you for your service to the community. Charlene, escort them out."

Charlene hustled the jurors out of the courtroom, and after the doors had shut behind them, Walker slapped his hands flat on the bench and leaned forward.

"This is a court of law, y'all understand that? I'm not putting up with this behavior!" He focused his glare on the rows where the protesters sat, defiant.

One man shouted back, "I'm not putting up with this verdict!"

"I will not tolerate rowdy outbursts or disorderly conduct!" the judge roared directly into the microphone on the bench. It let out an earsplitting whine. "Not in my court, no, sir!"

At that, the noise diminished, but it didn't completely subside. Walker was so infuriated that the lenses of his eyeglasses fogged up. He called out to the DA. "Mr. Gordon-James, I expect the parties and witnesses on both sides will comport themselves in a manner that respects the court. I will tolerate no disruption. If this continues, I'll find unruly individuals in contempt and instruct the sheriff's office to take them to jail."

The threat should have had a sobering effect, but the hissing voices didn't hush until Gordon-James turned in his seat to face the courtroom gallery. He didn't speak, just cast a somber gaze on the crowd.

Gradually, silence fell over the courtroom. After a moment, Judge Walker left the bench and retired to chambers. He slammed the door shut behind him, and the sound was jarring, a cymbal-clash finale to the trial.

People began to exit, but the vibe in the room remained dangerously tense and the noise built again as disgruntled voices resumed their protest. Cautiously, Iris Caro, followed by Hiram and his second wife, Sally (Daniel's mother, Hiram's first wife, had died of emphysema several years prior), approached the defense table. Daniel Caro was near collapse, grasping the back of his chair for support. His father's hug was probably the only thing that kept him on his feet. As the Caros embraced my client, Joey Roman stood back, keeping an eye on the courtroom.

In ordinary circumstances, I'd receive some kudos, handshakes, and slaps on the back. But not that day, not from that crowd. While I wore a phony victory grin, I kept track of the parting insults aimed at the defense table.

Mason and Jenny were in the courtroom. I was glad they'd come to hear the verdict and I tried to catch Jenny's eye. I wanted to thank her for the valuable assistance she had provided during trial preparation. This was her victory too.

I knew Jenny pretty well. She saw me, waved, and slipped out the door with the rest of the Aurora Gates pro-prosecution crowd.

She clearly wasn't happy with the verdict.

A young man shouldered his way through the crowd and up to the counsel table and got right up in my face. "How does it feel, huh? Does it feel good to set a killer free?"

His chest bumped against mine. I stepped back because I didn't intend to duke it out with this dude in a courtroom — no way.

He advanced again, ready to swing at me, and I wondered whether I'd have to let him knock me down.

Then a woman behind him intervened, clutching his arm. "Phil," she said, "back off."

My savior was my former client Arnette, the one who'd given me the cold shoulder outside the courthouse on the first day of the Caro trial.

She tugged on her companion's arm, and he turned away, saying, "Man, you've caused a lot of pain. Hope you find out just what that feels like."

I was glad to see his back. But Arnette had a final word for me.

She said, "I used to think you were a good man. You sure had me fooled."

I could've argued with her, told her that I had performed my professional duty. But the shot connected. I felt a pang in my chest, followed by a surge of self-doubt. Maybe I'd been posing as a good guy when I actually was a villain. Could be I'd even fooled myself.

The Caros finally decided it was safe to leave. Once they were gone, Mason walked up and clapped me on the shoulder. "You did it again, Stafford Lee. Your perfect trial record remains intact! Time to celebrate. Come on, let's go."

I wasn't in a partying mood, but I was so grateful for Mason's support that I didn't argue. My sole thought as I walked alongside him down the aisle and out the door was that in all my years of practice, I had never been so glad to get out of a courtroom.

CHAPTER 34

MASON AND I stood at the eighty-foot ice bar that stretched down the center of Hiram Caro's newest casino. Our drinks sat on the frozen surface of the bar.

The casino had been Mason's choice, not mine. I'd wanted to go someplace less hectic, like Mary Mahoney's, because I still wasn't tossing confetti in the air over that win. I felt more like licking my wounds, having a thoughtful conversation with Mason about the burden of serving as defense counsel and the dilemma we sometimes faced. The system required lawyers to mount a vigorous defense, regardless of the charges or the strength of the State's evidence. But what about the personal costs? I needed space for reflection.

But Mason insisted on a party, and he was the man behind the wheel. We'd left my car at the office. There was no way I'd be driving with even a drop of alcohol in my system tonight. News of the verdict had spread, and I didn't want to give the Biloxi cops a chance to even the score.

Mason was determined to convince me of the wisdom of his choice. Lifting his martini glass from the icy surface of the bar, he said, "This is exactly what you need tonight, Stafford Lee. You've been sitting in a courtroom listening to people talk about death for

142

a week. We're going to hear some music, see some good-looking cocktail waitresses." Nodding to the right, he said, "Check that one out."

A young blond woman strutted by; she was wearing a red bustier top over a skimpy slit skirt. She gave me a friendly smile as she passed.

As I lifted my beer to take a swallow, Mason looked over my shoulder and said in a low voice, "Old man Caro at nine o'clock."

Hiram Caro seized my arm and swung me around. Instinctively, I tried to back away, but he pulled me into a bear hug. I stood there, stunned, with the unpredictable old dude's face pressed into my jacket. Even after he broke the embrace, his hands gripped my shoulders. Warily, I watched his eyes. I was surprised I didn't have a knife between my shoulder blades.

But the man wore a grin big enough to display all his capped teeth. "Stafford Lee, I didn't have the chance to properly convey my appreciation at the courthouse earlier. You did a hell of a good job for my son. Hell of a good job."

Joey Roman stood to the side at a respectful distance. His presence reminded me that on several occasions in the past week, Hiram Caro had forcefully opined that my performance was subpar. But Hiram had apparently forgotten about that. He said, "Stafford Lee, you're the guest of the casino tonight. Dinner is on the house whenever you're ready. Anything you want, it's yours! Hey, boys, how about some free play?"

Mason perked up. "That sounds great, Mr. Caro. Doesn't it, Stafford Lee?"

It didn't sound so great to me. "Thanks, but that's not necessary," I said.

"I insist." Caro turned to Roman. "Joey, contact the players' club. I want Stafford Lee and his friend set up with chips and slot play. I think a thousand dollars each could get them started."

That was a shocker. Next thing I knew, we had shiny players' cards loaded with credit and house chips weighing down our pockets. Mason charged through the crowd, heading for the tables. As I followed, he looked over his shoulder. "We're going to play Texas Hold'em. I feel lucky!"

Mason's feelings were right—he was lucky. We joined a Texas Hold'em table, and Mason was dealt trips on his very first hand. Two rounds later, he got a full house. As soon as the dealer turned over the winning card, Mason pumped his fist in the air. "Damn— look at that! I got a boat!"

The shouting at our table got so loud, it attracted the attention of the blond cocktail waitress who'd caught Mason's eye earlier. Mason was a good tipper—when he was winning. I switched to Jack Daniel's Black Label, because why not? It was Hiram Caro's liquor.

It was a good thing I was playing on the house because the dealer tossed me one losing hand after another while I swilled that good Tennessee whiskey to dull the pain. When the dealer shuffled a new deck of cards, the blond waitress set a fresh whiskey beside me, a drink I hadn't ordered.

She gave me a grin. "Mr. Caro said you had a big day today. We're supposed to make sure you have a fun night."

"Great." I looked at my hole cards. Finally, a pair of aces. I placed my bet.

The waitress lingered, standing by my shoulder. "I saw that case on the news. You must be a real good lawyer. You're, like, pretty famous around here."

Famous for letting murderers walk?

She remained in the spot beside my chair, clutching her tray. "You're totally a VIP at the casino tonight. Anything you want, just let me know."

Something in me snapped. I glanced at her and said, "Go away."

She recoiled. Wearing a baffled look, she said, "What? Huh?"

I didn't bother to lower my voice. "Leave me alone. I'm not interested." And then I tossed a five-dollar chip on her tray.

Her face hardened as she picked up the chip. "You're rude. You're mean, and I will go away. You can get your own drinks from the bar." She threw the chip back at me. It bounced off the table and fell to the floor.

She left, and I saw Mason staring at me. He looked perturbed. "Damn, Stafford Lee. That *was* rude. What the hell's the matter with you?"

I didn't know how to answer, but I didn't want to spend my night at a casino celebrating with a stranger—even a pretty one. I had a wife at home; despite our current rift, that hadn't changed. Thinking about Carrie Ann sparked a longing to talk to her. I wanted to hear her voice.

Studying my lowball glass, I calculated. Carrie Ann had never been receptive to a drunk-dial, and I'd been consuming Jack Daniel's steadily for an hour or more. Still, I didn't think I was too far gone to make the call.

The dealer beat my hand again. Wearing an unapologetic expression, she swept my wager off the felt tabletop.

Mason was organizing his impressive pile of poker chips by color. When I pushed my chair away from the table, he looked up in alarm. "Where are you going? I'm on a hot streak here."

"I'll check on you later. I'm taking a break." I didn't tell him why. He could assume it was due to my run of bad luck.

The casino was loud, with bells ringing from scores of slot machines. At the far end of the casino, I found a relatively quiet spot—the nonsmoking section of a high-limits room. The space was nearly empty.

I sat in the farthest corner of the room, pulled out my phone, and dialed Carrie Ann. When it went to voice mail, I hung up. I slipped the phone into my pocket and sat there for a minute, thinking. I decided that I shouldn't give up. Maybe she was in the kitchen or the bathroom or maybe she'd left her phone in her purse. I'd give it another try.

When she didn't pick up the second time, I left a message: "Hey, Carrie Ann, sorry to miss you. The trial's over. Jury came back with a defendant's verdict. So it's a win!" An old lady using a walker approached and sat at a slot machine next to me. I turned my back to her and lowered my voice. "And I was just thinking about the first jury trial I won after we got married. You remember that one? We'd just bought the house and put every dime we had into rehabbing it. We were so broke, I couldn't afford to take you out to celebrate. We split a six-pack of beer at home and ordered a pizza from Domino's."

The recollection made my eyes misty. Too much whiskey, I thought, rubbing them.

"God, I miss that. I miss you, babe. If I could, I'd turn back the clock. Isn't there some way to do that? Can't we just talk about it?"

I couldn't go on indefinitely. I used my most convincing tone. "I'd really like to come over tonight. Would that be okay? It feels like the moment is right for us to talk this out. Call me back, let me know if tonight's a good time. You just say the word, and I'll walk up to your door with a Domino's box in my hands." I spoke with a teasing note. She used to like that. "Hey, you want wings? You got wings. Sky's the limit tonight, baby. We're living high."

The voice-mail beep sounded; my time was up. I stared at the phone, wondering whether I had made my case. Maybe I'd used up all my persuasive magic in closing arguments.

I hoped there was enough left to convince her to return my call.

CHAPTER 35

JENNY WAS a light sleeper. It was a requirement in her profession.

So when the cell phone on her bedside table rang at 3:43 a.m., she jerked awake. Wondering which hysterical client had interrupted her sleep with a crisis, she pushed her hair out of her eyes and read the name on the phone screen. But it wasn't any client, past or present. The caller ID read **Hank Sweeney**, a detective with Biloxi PD.

She was so surprised to see that name that she fumbled as she tapped the screen and almost disconnected the call. She caught it right before it went to voice mail. "Hello?"

He said, "This is Sweeney."

"Hank?"

"Hey, Jenny."

"What's up?" Her voice sounded foggy. She took a sip from a water glass on the nightstand.

Hank said, "Sorry to wake you."

His voice was solemn. Jenny tensed up, her head clearing rapidly. Bad news was coming; that was certain. She clicked on the lamp and squeezed her eyes shut at the burst of light.

He said, "I'm at a crime scene. I need information and it can't wait."

Jenny experienced a sinking feeling of dread. "What's going on, Hank?" She braced herself and waited.

Hank exhaled. "Stafford Lee Penney has been murdered."

Jenny heard people shouting in the background. "What? What did you say?" She sat straight up in bed, thinking that she must have misunderstood him. She tucked her hair behind her ear and said, louder, "Hank, did you say something happened to Stafford Lee?"

This time, his words were distinct, the message unmistakable. "Stafford Lee is dead. Obviously, it's foul play, no question about that. His wife, Carrie Ann, is also deceased."

Jenny's mind went blank with shock. She struggled to follow the thread of his words as the detective continued.

"They were both shot at close range. There's a third body in the room too. We need to reach next of kin before we make any public announcement. That's why I called you, Jenny. I was wondering—"

She didn't learn what he wanted from her, because a voice in the background interrupted him. Hank turned away from the phone and shouted something she couldn't make out.

She was frantic for information. "Hank! What's going on?"

"Sorry, Jenny. I'll get back to you." Hank ended the call.

Stunned, Jenny stared at the phone, but the screen had gone dark.

CHAPTER 36

CLUTCHING HER cell phone to her chest, Jenny stumbled out of her bedroom and ran down the narrow hall. She paused outside the spare bedroom to tug down the hem of the old T-shirt she used for sleepwear. Without knocking first, Jenny threw the door open with such force that the knob slammed against the wall, probably denting the drywall.

The curtains weren't completely drawn. A thin glimmer of light came through from the streetlamp outside. When Jenny's eyes adjusted, she could make out a figure on the bed. Her heart pounding, she prayed that her eyes weren't playing tricks on her in the semidarkness.

Her loud entrance had roused him. Jenny watched as he rolled over and sat up. His close-cropped hair stood straight up on his head. He ran a hand over his face and blew out a breath that had a faint odor of whiskey. In a groggy voice, he said, "Jenny? Are you okay?"

A wave of relief nearly knocked her flat, because dead men couldn't talk. She sagged against the wall, gasping. After a moment, she pushed away from the wall and padded over to the bed. While she tried to summon the right words, she caught him glancing down at her legs. Self-conscious, she tugged at the hem of her

T-shirt again. But in the present circumstances, the decency — or lack thereof — of her pj's was an insignificant matter.

Jenny sat on a corner of the bed, faced him, and took a breath to steady herself. "Something has happened," she said. She was amazed by the sound of her own voice. It was calm. It didn't break.

"Something has happened, Stafford Lee," she repeated. "At your house."

CHAPTER 37

I SAT in Jenny's car, gripping the dash. I punched the molded plastic with my fist. "Can't you go any faster? Jesus, Jenny."

Her face was taut. "We'll be there in a minute, Stafford Lee." She had to speak over the dinging noise inside the car. In a terse voice, she added, "Would you please kindly fasten your seat belt? The alarm is driving me nuts."

We reached the block where I live and Jenny stopped the car. I flung the door open and bailed out of the vehicle. Police cruisers lined both sides of the street, their red and blue flashing lights illuminating the canopy of tree branches overhead.

My neighbors stood outside their homes wearing T-shirts, sweats, and jersey shorts. I ran past a man who lived three houses down from mine. "Stafford Lee!" he called. "What the hell is going on at your house?"

My property was circled by yellow crime scene tape. I stepped over it, tore across the lawn, and ran up the porch steps. A uniformed officer, some kid I'd never seen before, stood guard. He had a handgun and a Taser on his police duty belt. He said, "Sorry, you can't come in here."

But I had the motivational advantage. Fueled by adrenaline, I shoved the tall kid into a wicker rocking chair and pulled the screen door open. He tried to tackle me, but I knocked him off the porch and into our azalea bushes. He got to his feet, shouting in protest.

Inside the house, I charged past a couple of uniformed cops milling around the living room and another one leaning against the mantel of my fireplace.

When I reached the bedroom doorway, my knees almost buckled. At the first glimpse of Carrie Ann's body in our bed, I bowed my head and bent over. The moment had a weird sense of unreality; I felt like I was stuck in a nightmare.

In the bedroom were plainclothes cops, including a detective I recognized—Hank Sweeney, a good guy. He extended a hand and helped me straighten up.

"Sorry for your loss, Stafford Lee."

The detective's words penetrated my trancelike state. I looked again at Carrie Ann, processing the sight. She lay on the far side of the bed, where she always slept, with a gaping wound in the center of her chest. Her body was completely nude, but her face wore an expression of surprise. Her eyes were open, her lips slightly parted.

I felt a pain in the center of my chest, like a fist squeezing my heart. *She's really gone,* I thought. *I can't stand it. This is gonna kill me.*

Detective Sweeney said, "We're working on the identity of the second victim. Sorry about the mix-up. We just assumed it was you because—you know."

Sweeney pointed at the body lying next to Carrie Ann. My sole focus had been my wife, but at the detective's urging, I looked at the other body. It rested on my side of the mattress; the gory head lay on my pillow. He was a muscular guy, bigger than me, heavier too. Each arm bore a colorful tattoo of a sports team logo, the Mississippi Braves on the left, Ole Miss Rebels on the right.

Like Carrie Ann, the man was naked.

"Any idea who he might be?" Sweeney asked.

I had no words, no clue; I just shook my head. The guy's face was blown away—how could I recognize him?

"So he's nobody you know? Can you make a guess based on the tats?"

I shook my head again.

He said, "You see a killing like this one—" He stopped and sighed. "So much brutality in this crime scene. Makes you wonder. You know what I'm saying?"

I didn't know what he was saying; I couldn't follow the thread. I grabbed the doorframe to stay standing amid the agony of my loss. Who would want to kill Carrie Ann?

Sweeney said, "I'm thinking there must have been passion involved. Heat of passion."

His words barely penetrated my mind. When I didn't respond, he said in a flat voice, "So you can't give us any insight at all about who that second victim is."

"No," I said. Speaking required a huge effort. My gut twisted as I studied the gory remains of his head on my pillow. Looked like the result of a shotgun fired at close range. I didn't offer the opinion aloud.

The young cop I had left shouting in the bushes outside marched up to the doorway. "Detective Sweeney, this man assaulted me and forced his way in."

Sweeney sent a dismissive glance his way. "Get back out front, Officer."

"Are we gonna make an arrest—"

Sweeney cut him off. "Go!"

After the young guy disappeared, Sweeney sidled up to me and said in an undertone, "The third body, the one on the floor. We didn't have any trouble identifying him. Did he give any indication that he was planning something like this?"

Before the detective mentioned it, I hadn't even been aware of the third corpse, splayed on the floor by Carrie Ann's side of the bed. I stepped farther into the room, passing an officer taking photographs, to get a better look.

The third dead body was fully clothed in the suit he had worn to court yesterday. A semiautomatic pistol rested on the rug close to his right hand.

CHAPTER 38

I STEPPED over Benjamin Gates's feet and stood beside Carrie Ann, seized by a protective impulse to pull the bedsheet over her naked body. When I reached out for the cotton sheet, Sweeney stepped up and grasped my elbow.

"Stafford Lee, you can't be in here right now."

A surge of anger blurred my vision. "It's my wife. My house."

His voice was stern when he said, "It's a crime scene. Can't let you contaminate it—you know that. We need to collect evidence. Come on out."

Firmly holding my elbow, he steered me out of the room. I paused in the doorway and turned to take a final look at Carrie Ann's face. I wished they'd let me close her eyes to erase the dazed expression she wore.

But I permitted the detective to escort me away; my feet moved automatically as he led me down the hall, through the kitchen, and out the back door.

Our patio furniture sat in the yard, and Sweeney ushered me to a lounge chair, the one Carrie Ann used to sunbathe in the summertime. I closed my eyes, trying to envision her soaking up the sun.

He took the seat next to mine and said, "Can we get you something? You thirsty, want a glass of water?"

I shook my head. I didn't need anything that he could provide. The image of her face and those staring, unseeing eyes had been burned into my brain.

"I know you've had a shock. But I need you to help us out. One of the officers has a boy at Biloxi High, and he was thinking that it's the coach in there with your wife."

I wasn't following him. I just repeated some of his words. "The coach."

"That's right, the football coach from the high school."

His statement finally penetrated the fog. I sat up straight in the chair. "The football coach?"

"That's what we're checking out now." He pulled out a pack of cigarettes, shook one out, and lit it. "Finding out that your wife's fooling around can break people. I've seen it happen."

Even in my befuddled state, I understood what he meant, and my guard went up. I'd practiced criminal law for years; I knew the statistics. Most murders aren't random acts of violence committed by strangers. Eighty percent of the time, victims are killed by some-one they know. And when a woman is murdered, the likeliest per-petrator is her husband or boyfriend—an argument gets heated, and a firearm comes out. According to the surveys, the deadly arguments often involve accusations of infidelity.

The detective looked away so I couldn't read his expression in the near darkness, but his meaning was clear. Shaking his head, he said, "Hell, nobody knows how they'd respond under that kind of stress until it happens. I've seen men react by doing things totally out of character."

So, I thought. *That's where we're going.* Sweeney was dangling a hook.

Because I was a suspect.

But if this was an interrogation by the Biloxi PD, why hadn't the detective recited the *Miranda* warning? He wasn't permitted to assume that I knew, as I reeled from bereavement and loss, about my right to remain silent. Maybe he was clever enough to hope that I'd say something incriminating and he could claim I'd volunteered the statement out of the blue while we were having a cordial conversation.

It caused me to reconsider my opinion of Sweeney. Maybe the detective wasn't such a good guy after all.

I had opened my mouth to ask him what the hell he was up to when I heard footsteps pounding up the driveway. The gate jerked open and my old man raced into the backyard. I hadn't seen him move that fast in years.

He shouted at me, "Shut up, shut up, shut up! Damn it, boy, you're a lawyer! Shut your damned mouth!"

PART II

EIGHTEEN MONTHS LATER

CHAPTER 39

"THE DEFENSE calls Della Jess Calhoun to the witness stand."

I turned to my client in circuit court and gave a nod, her signal to rise. As I watched her step away from the counsel table and trudge over to the bench, I thought, *Jesus, I should've made her wear jailhouse scrubs to trial.*

She raised her hand to take the oath, and I contemplated her courtroom attire: a worn navy tank top and baggy pink sweatpants. She made a poor appearance for a woman whose liberty was at stake. She was on trial for two counts of aggravated assault and one charge of resisting arrest. As I listened to her swear to tell the truth, a Johnny Cash song ran through my head, the one with the line about finding his "cleanest dirty shirt."

I should've asked her to describe the clothing she'd be wearing when we'd consulted at the jail the prior evening. Back in the day, I would have nailed down those details before trial. But I had wanted to get out of there and head home, where I could do my trial prep and enjoy a shot of bourbon.

I gave her a moment to settle into her seat before I approached. "Please state your name."

"Della Jess Calhoun."

"And what is your age?"

"Forty-seven."

A woman in the front row of the jury box made a choking sound. I couldn't fault her for it. In my first interview with Della at the jail—after the public defender had conflicted out and I was appointed as defense counsel—she'd told me how old she was, and I could've sworn she was lying. With her leathery skin, missing teeth, and thin hair, she looked to be in her sixties. A lifetime of poverty and years of homelessness had taken a harsh physical toll.

"Della, please tell the jury where you were on the evening of April seventh of last year."

"I was just outside the city limits of Biloxi, not too far off Brodie Road."

"And what were you doing?"

"I was sleeping. In my tent."

"So you were camping out there?"

"Yeah. I set up my tent that day under some trees."

"Della, what's your permanent address?"

She grinned, revealing her missing front teeth. "I move around." She turned to address the jurors sitting in the box. "I don't bother nobody."

"Where had you resided prior to pitching the tent off Brodie Road?"

"I'd stayed for about a week or so behind a warehouse in Biloxi. It's deserted—nobody's using it for nothing. I was doing just fine until the cops came. They told me to move along, said I was trespassing. They said I needed to get out of town, that Biloxi wouldn't put up with trespassing or obstructing."

Prior to 2018, it was illegal to be homeless in Mississippi. People could be put in jail essentially for being poor, because our state code made it a crime to be a "tramp" or a "vagrant." In 2018, the state did away with those criminal statutes, so instead of the unsheltered being arrested for vagrancy, they were jailed for trespassing, obstruction, or disorderly conduct.

Della said, "So I got out of town. Packed up my gear and my stuff. And my cat."

I knew she wanted to say more about the cat. She had talked about him at length during our meetings, extolling his virtues. I needed to cut that off. "What happened that night when you were sleeping in the tent?"

"Some boys come up, three of them. Teenagers, not little kids. They tried to knock down my tent, kicked at it, laughing the whole time. Like they thought it was funny."

The three boys she referred to were named as victims in the criminal case. All of them were students at an exclusive private school outside of Biloxi; two of them were sixteen and one was seventeen. They'd already testified in the State's case. They cleaned up good, as the saying goes—they took the stand wearing preppy clothes, their hair freshly cut. One wore his letterman jacket and testified that he'd been benched on the basketball team due to the injury my client inflicted that night.

"And what happened next?"

A flush crept up the sun-weathered skin of her neck as she recounted the events. "One of them boys, the tall one with that team jacket, he tried to grab the sleeping bag, but he run into Boots. Boots was my cat, a big old tom. He was a wanderer, like me. We were family."

She wiped her eye as she continued. "Boots scratched him up good. The boy, he was cussing. I saw him grab Boots by the tail and pull him out of the tent."

She paused, breathing hard. I prompted her: "And then?"

"And then they tore the tent clean down, so I run out. Them boys started throwing my things around, my property. And that one boy had my cat. He was rassling with Boots."

It was important for me to convey sympathy, but I had to fake it because I felt entirely disconnected from her account on the stand. With a manufactured note of concern in my voice, I said, "What did you do, Della?"

"I was shouting to let Boots go and trying to grab my things from them. That's when the skinny boy with the black hair knocked me down, and the fat one started kicking me."

"What did you do then?"

"I tried to fight back, but the fat kid done knocked the wind out of me. But I had to get up because I heard Boots yowling. He was crying something fierce. I seen that the tallest boy, the one in the jacket, took Boots by the tail and started swinging him."

At that, her voice broke. Della's lips trembled and she squeezed her eyes shut.

I gave her a moment to recover before I said, "So what did you do?"

She let out a shuddering sigh and said, "I crawled to my sleeping bag and got that length of lead pipe I keep under it."

"Why do you keep the pipe?"

"For protection. I'm a woman alone. Just me and my cat."

"When you got the pipe, what did you do next?"

"First thing, I went for that boy that was swinging and tormenting Boots. And I knocked him upside the head."

She certainly had. I'd seen the photographs. Della was skinny, but she was no weakling. The boy had suffered a concussion. And the deep scratches that the cat clawed into his arm later became infected. When the boy pulled up his sleeve to show the scars to the jury, my client had to cover her mouth so they couldn't see her grinning with satisfaction. Had I forgotten to counsel her regarding proper courtroom behavior? My brain wasn't so sharp these days.

"What happened next?"

"The skinny boy, he jumped me, got me down on the ground

again, so I socked him in the knee with the pipe. To get him to leave me alone, right? And he went down, and when the fat kid saw it, he had the sense to back off. That's when I seen the cop drive up in his patrol car."

"What did the officer do?"

She sat up straight, radiating righteous indignation. "He took one look around and said I was under arrest. Me! Not them boys! I told him that them boys jumped me and tore through my things. He didn't listen to me. He picked up my piece of pipe. Called for backup and for an ambulance."

"Was the ambulance for you?"

"Nah, it was for the boys who was crying. Carrying on like that after they picked the fight, three on one!"

"Della, when the officer placed you under arrest, did you resist or fight him in any way?"

"No, nothing like that. I got up off the ground and I did try to tell him that I was the victim here. I was minding my own business when the three of them attacked me out of the blue."

"Did the officer listen to you?"

"Nope. He threw me down on the gravel. It scraped the hide clean off my face. Messed my knee up too."

I handed my photographs to the court reporter. I should've had my exhibits marked ahead of time, but I'd been running late that morning. My alarm didn't go off because my cell phone was dead. Guess I'd dozed off before I had a chance to plug it into the charger.

After the court reporter marked the exhibits, I handed Della her standard two-part booking mug shot. In the front view, Della was a picture of misery, her eyes swollen from crying. The side view clearly showed her facial trauma—the skin from her cheekbone to her chin had been scraped raw.

I had no medical records because the county jail hadn't provided medical attention. All I had were the pictures I'd taken with my phone of her black-and-blue knee and the other injuries she'd sustained from her bruising battle with the teenagers.

"Della, are the photographs marked defendant's exhibits one through six fair and accurate representations of the injuries you suffered on the night of April seventh?"

"Yeah. That's what they looked like."

With the exhibits in hand, I turned to the judge. It wasn't Judge Walker. A younger judge, newly elected, had been assigned to preside over the trial.

"Your Honor, the defense offers exhibits one through six into evidence."

The prosecutor didn't object. The photos were admitted.

"No further questions," I said. And I sat down, relieved to be off my feet. I was low on stamina. Exceptionally low.

CHAPTER 40

JUDGE ECKHARDT nodded at the assistant DA. "Ms. Piper, you may cross-examine."

Mollie Piper, a young prosecutor I'd handily defeated at trial three times in prior years, stood and approached the stand. Wearing a stern expression on her fresh, youthful face, she said to my client, "So you admit that you threatened all three of those boys with a lead pipe and struck two of them with the weapon."

The pitch of Della's voice rose: "I had to do it. I loved that cat. He was my family."

The law permitted her to use reasonable force to protect herself. The law was much less interested in the protection of her cat.

We'd gone around on the issue the night before during trial prep at the jail. I'd made it clear as the blue sky: We were trying to justify her actions on the basis of self-defense, so she had to shut up about the cat and talk about the attack on her person. When she argued with me, I lost it. Apparently, shouting her down hadn't convinced her.

She glared at the prosecutor. "Me and that cat took care of each other. We'd stuck together for two years or more. I wish I knew if he was okay. Don't expect I'll ever see him again."

As Della wiped her eyes with the back of her hand, I stole a glance into the jury box. A lot of women like cats, so maybe there were some cat lovers among the group of twelve. If so, they gave no sign.

Piper walked to the counsel table and picked up her exhibit. She carried it to a spot between the witness stand and the jury box so that it could be seen by all.

"Ms. Calhoun, I show you what's been marked for identification as State's exhibit nineteen. Do you recognize it?"

Della ran her hand across her mouth. "Yeah. Think so."

"It's the lead pipe you used to attack those boys on April seventh, isn't it?"

"Could be."

Piper faced the jury and rolled her eyes. I just sat there and watched, trying hard to stay engaged and alert. Della wasn't scoring any points by being stubborn. The police officer had already testi- fied that he'd taken possession of the pipe at the scene. Chain of custody had been established in the State's case.

Piper hefted the pipe and swung it in an arc. I thought about objecting, but I couldn't summon the energy.

"Isn't it true that you kept exhibit number nineteen as a weapon because you believed it could inflict serious bodily harm?"

"I had to use it! They were knocking the shit out of me and tak- ing everything I owned in the world!"

I wanted to sink down in my chair as Judge Eckhardt banged his gavel. Pointing it at my client, he said, "There's no cursing permit- ted in my courtroom."

She wore a hangdog look. "All right."

The assistant DA carried the length of pipe back to the counsel table, set it down with a thud, and aimed a knowing glance at the jury box. Then she returned to the lectern and asked her next ques- tion. "Ms. Calhoun, have you been convicted of any crimes for which you were represented by counsel?" She crossed her arms and leaned on the lectern, indicating that she expected Della's response to go on for some time.

She was right. It did: Public intoxication. DUI. Multiple convictions for trespassing. Misdemeanor larceny. Simple assault, aggravated assault.

Unsurprisingly, the prior convictions had a clear impact on the jury. But the only way I could have prevented the jury from learning about my client's priors was to keep her off the witness stand, and I couldn't do that. Della's only shot at winning was a claim of self-defense, and she was the only person who could offer testimony to support it.

With prompting from Piper, Della recounted her criminal history, which covered many years and had occurred in multiple jurisdictions. The assistant DA wrapped up her cross and sat.

I asked only one question on redirect. "Della, did you believe you were in danger of serious bodily harm from the young men who attacked you?"

"Yes! I thought those fu—"

I took an involuntary step forward. She caught herself just in time. "I thought those no-goods was gonna kill me."

She started to cry. I checked out the jury, hoping to detect a glimmer of sympathy in someone's countenance. Didn't see any. Della cried louder, but those jurors just didn't care.

As her lawyer, I'm ashamed to admit that my fighting spirit had been dampened, and I didn't care too much either.

CHAPTER 41

THEY LOCKED Della in the holding cell outside the courtroom while the jury decided her fate. Before an hour had passed, the jurors sent word that they had reached a verdict.

My client sat on a flat metal bench in the cell, resting her head against the cinder-block wall. Some inmate had laboriously scraped off the bench's gray paint and etched into the metal an angry message: *Fuck the police*.

I was pretty sure that Della hadn't had sufficient time to scratch the words onto the bench. The jury had been out for only fifty-two minutes.

"We've got a verdict, Della," I said.

She nodded, looking as hopeful as I felt weary. When the jurors assembled in the box, I didn't try to read them. Didn't even look at their faces.

Judge Eckhardt held the verdicts in his hand. "'As to count one,'" he read, "'we, the jury, find Della Jess Calhoun guilty.'"

Della swung toward me with a look of dismay. "No! Didn't they listen to what happened out there?"

I shushed her, and she clenched her jaw shut, waiting for the rest. As I stood and waited for the hammer to fall on count two, I tried to be philosophical. Biloxi was like most communities — ordinary

170

citizens tended to approach the homeless in their midst with the popular sentiment "Not in my backyard."

Not my fault. That's what I told myself.

The judge read the jury's third and final verdict: "'Guilty.'" Della came unglued.

She pounded on the counsel table with her shackled fists. "This is bullshit! It ain't fair—didn't you hear me up there? Them boys attacked me first!"

I leaned close and tried to reason with her. "You're not helping your cause, Della. We'll save our arguments for a motion for a new trial. And don't forget, you have the right to appeal."

"I'm appealing now!"

When she stopped yelling to suck in a breath, I heard muffled laughter behind me.

Sitting with their parents in court for the reading of the verdict were the three young men called by the State as victim witnesses. Two of the teens were tall. The benched athlete wore his high-school letterman jacket. The third boy, a short, stocky kid, had the grace to quail under my eye, but his friends continued to snicker.

The judge said to the jurors, "Ladies and gentlemen, is this your verdict?"

The jurors stated that it was. When Eckhardt asked me whether we wanted the jury to be polled, I said, "No, Your Honor," because there was no point in the exercise.

Della yelled, "I want a new lawyer! You hear me, Judge? I don't want him."

The judge's grim expression made it clear that he had no patience for Della's theatrics. I tried again, moving close to her and saying in a whisper, "We can talk about all of this later—"

"I'm not talking to you no more. If I'd had a good lawyer, I'd be getting out. You don't even look like a lawyer. You didn't even shave today! And your breath stinks!"

She was right.

That morning my hands had been too shaky for me to risk shaving. I feared I'd butcher myself with bloody nicks. My suit, the one I'd worn in the Caro trial, was wrinkled. It hadn't been dry-cleaned in over a year. I had gargled with mouthwash after I brushed my teeth, but apparently it didn't kill the residual alcohol smell from last night's bender.

The judge slammed the gavel. "I'm removing you from the courtroom, Ms. Calhoun. Bailiff!" After he threw her out, he dismissed the jury and left the bench.

The courtroom emptied until only I was left to hear the State's witnesses and their parents exchanging triumphant congratulations. At one time, hearing the other side celebrate would have been a novel experience for me. These days, it was my new normal.

Mollie Piper edged up to the defense table and extended her hand. "Good job, Stafford Lee."

It's a long-standing ritual in Biloxi courtrooms for the victor to offer praise and a handshake to the loser. I was supposed to accept the gesture with good grace. But I wasn't up to it. Everyone knew I'd been off my game since Carrie Ann died.

Piper dropped her hand when I made no move to take it. As she hurried away, I wondered whether she was one of the people in Biloxi who still viewed me as a suspect in my wife's death, despite Jenny providing my unshakable alibi.

I wasn't the target of a murder investigation. But my wife's death had changed me. My reputation was in the toilet. I had to chase clients down, scrape together any business I could get.

The court administrators had appointed me to represent Della Calhoun out of pity for my floundering career, not because they wanted Della to receive a vigorous legal defense.

In Mississippi, people believe that tramps and vagrants deserve whatever they get.

CHAPTER 42

JENNY HADN'T been inside Stafford Lee's house on St. Charles Street in ages—at least ten months, maybe longer. Stafford Lee probably didn't even remember that she had a key to the front door.

His recall was spotty these days.

The courthouse rumor mill was churning over his yearlong decline. Jenny needed to find out if the talk was accurate. She stood on the front porch, put the key in the lock, and turned it.

The living room was dark, the shades and curtains drawn across the picture window. When she flipped on the overhead light, she saw his current sleeping quarters. A sweat-stained pillow and a crumpled sheet were strewn across the couch. She shook out the sheet, then switched her focus to the documents and legal pads scattered across the coffee table. A half-empty bottle of bourbon sat next to a dirty glass.

Tears pricked her eyes. Was he drinking all night? She couldn't believe Stafford Lee had sunk so low.

Jenny resisted the impulse to pour the bourbon down the kitchen drain; instead, she went down the hall—glancing briefly into a bathroom littered with dirty towels that had soured with mildew—to the main bedroom.

The door was shut.

Jenny turned the knob, went in, and took in the grisly view of the murder scene.

Though more than a year had passed, all the marks of the crimes remained, with the exception of the corpses and the bed linens and coverings taken as evidence. The bare mattress was stained with the blood of the murder victims. The forensic officers had taken samples, but fragments of bone and dried particles of human flesh dotted the headboard and the wall behind it. Pellet marks from the shotgun blast were also embedded in the wood and the plaster wall. It was a good thing she had a strong stomach.

She spoke out loud to steady herself: "Don't think about Carrie Ann. Just pretend it's somebody else's house."

She had to act like it was standard business. Do a dispassionate perusal. That was the only way Jenny could bear to remain on the premises. So she pulled a tape measure from her pocket. Setting her jaw, she commenced taking measurements, dictating notes into her phone, and snapping pictures.

She had read the police reports Stafford Lee had shared with her. As she examined the bloody carpet where Benjamin Gates's body had been found, she thought about Detective Sweeney's conclusions. The police ultimately attributed the shooting deaths of Carrie Ann and Coach Davies to Gates. They found the shotgun propped against a chest of drawers just a few feet inside the doorway. The blast almost blew the coach's head off, which was why the police had initially misidentified him as Stafford Lee. It was an understandable error. It was Stafford Lee's home, and everyone knew Gates was furious with him after the verdict in the Caro trial.

Benjamin Gates's suicide had occurred on the far side of the room. The reports said Gates had apparently stuck a semiautomatic pistol in his mouth and pulled the trigger; the bullet had exited from the back of his head and lodged in a plaster wall. The handgun was found on the floor near his body.

Jenny squatted beside the bed and aimed her cell phone at the carpet, focusing on a bloodstain left behind by Gates's self-inflicted gunshot. Shaking her head, Jenny pondered the purpose of bringing two weapons into the house. Why use a shotgun to commit the murder when he had a handgun? And why did he opt to walk over to Carrie Ann's side of the bed to pull out the revolver and eat the gun? There was no way to know Gates's intention. The Gates family insisted that they had had no knowledge of his plot.

She strode to the doorway and turned to take a last look at the hideous scene. There was no rational reason for preserving the site of the bloodbath. The investigation was complete. For a price, Stafford Lee could have hired a commercial cleaner to scrub the place down. She closed the door and shivered as she walked swiftly down the hall.

Yet she didn't regret the unauthorized tour of the house. The ghoulish crime scene confirmed her friend's troubled mental state.

Her friend's mind was in a bad place.

CHAPTER 43

I SAT on a stool at the end of the bar at the Salty Dog and drained the last swallow of bourbon from my glass. To get the bartender's attention, I raised the glass up high.

He ignored me, stepping over to another patron. I shook the glass, and the ice cubes rattled inside it. "Another Jim Beam on the rocks, Porter."

He set a fresh drink in front of me. "You're starting early today, Stafford Lee."

"You got that right. I earned it, man."

I was still dressed in the wrinkled suit I'd worn to court, though I had stripped off the necktie before I came into the bar. That court-room defeat in the Della Calhoun case stung, and the first four cocktails hadn't eased the pain.

My conscience pricked me; I wondered if my client was waiting for me to appear at the jail and discuss her post-conviction motions. I'd promised her that I'd come by. Taking a healthy swallow of bourbon, I pushed the thought aside. After the attack Della had launched on me in open court, I had no appetite for the woman's company. When I'd left the courthouse that afternoon, I'd just wanted to sit and drink in peace.

After that hellish shitshow of a trial, I felt like I deserved it.

Mason finally showed up. I refrained from checking the time when he slid onto the stool beside me. He gave me a slap on the back that felt a little too hearty. "How you holding up, Stafford Lee?"

I lifted my glass. "Where have you been, Mason? I've been waiting on you."

He gave me the side-eye. "Doesn't look like you waited. Looks like you started without me."

"You can catch up. Porter!" I pounded the bar with my fist. "We need some service over here!"

The barman walked over to us. "What can I get for you, Mason?"

"I'd like a cold beer. Get me a Modelo."

After Porter set the beer bottle down, Mason turned to me. "Sorry to hear about the verdict. I thought you had a good shot. The homeless gal looked pretty pitiful in those pictures you took of the injuries."

"Yeah, well, nobody cared."

"When the public defender in Gulfport had a conflict of interest, I told the judge that if anyone can win it, it's Stafford Lee Penney. That's a direct quote."

"Thanks." I was starting to resent Mason's repeated reminders of the assistance he'd given me. If he expected my undying gratitude, he was bound for disappointment. My voice cool, I said, "The pay is shit. Maybe you weren't aware."

He avoided my eye. Lifting his shoulder in a shrug, he said, "I thought you might want the business."

I felt my neck heat up like the summer sun was shining on it. I wrapped my hands around my glass. "Damn, that was an ignorant jury. The all-time worst. They couldn't comprehend a legal argument."

"Right."

"And the judge wasn't much better. He's too young for the job—I said so when he was elected. Jesus, Mason, Eckhardt doesn't know how to run a trial."

Mason twisted around on the stool to see if anyone was within earshot.

His caution irritated me. "Don't act like you don't get what I'm talking about. He never practiced criminal law!"

"That's true, he had a civil practice. But he's no stranger to jury trials, Stafford Lee."

I didn't want to hear my friend defend the judge, so I changed the subject. "Sometimes you get saddled with a loser. Good Lord, Mason, you should've seen my client in court today. She looked like a damn clown. And the way she acted? She's a nut, almost got cited for contempt."

"Yeah, you told me over the phone."

I knocked back the bourbon. "The contempt finding wouldn't have made much difference for her. She's not walking free anytime soon." My glass was empty again. I leaned over the bar and called, "Porter! Need another round over here."

Mason took a sip of beer. Looked like he was rationing it, he was drinking so slow. He said, "At least that woman's got a roof over her head. Three hots and a cot, right?"

What Mason said made sense. But in our brief acquaintance, Della had made it clear that she valued her independence and longed for freedom. She'd kept badgering me to find out what the police had done with her tent and her collection of personal belongings and whether her property would be returned to her after she was acquitted.

Well. She didn't need to be concerned about that anymore.

Porter finally appeared with my fresh drink. His face wore a humorless expression. "You're not driving tonight, right, Stafford Lee?"

Affronted, I straightened my back. "What's that supposed to mean?"

"C'mon, don't play dumb—you know the law. We got a dram-shop statute in Mississippi. I don't want to get sued if you leave here and have a wreck."

Mason said, "He's not driving, Porter. Guaranteed."

"Okay, then. I'm counting on you, Mason," he said, and he walked off.

I caught Mason glancing down at my glass of bourbon. The guy was definitely not as fun as he used to be.

As if he could read my mind, he said, "You want to check out the menu, Stafford Lee? Let's order some food. I could go for that fried oyster basket. They got good shrimp po'boys too. You're a fan of their po'boys, right?"

"No, thanks." I slugged back another swallow of Jim Beam. Mason was frowning at me. He looked like he wanted an explanation, so I gave him one.

"I'm not blowing a fifty-dollar drunk on a five-dollar sandwich."

CHAPTER 44

I WAS enjoying a deep, boozy, dreamless sleep. It was interrupted by a literal kick in the ass.

I opened my eyes and found my head resting on my suit jacket, wadded up for a pillow. I could hear the surf pounding on the beach; I smelled salt in the air. I reached out to prop myself up, and my hand pressed into the sand.

With some difficulty, I managed to roll over onto my back. A light shone in my face, blinding me. I lifted my arm to shield my eyes. "What the hell?"

From the darkness behind the beam of light, someone said, "You need to move along."

"Who says? God?"

A second person spoke: "Get up."

That wasn't happening, not yet. I struggled into a sitting position, pulled my knees up, and rested my head on them. My brain was still blurry with all that Jim Beam. I sat like that for an extended moment, hearing the waves crash. When I lifted my head, the flashlight was lowered, and I could make out the figures of two men. Both wore the uniform of the Biloxi police department. I looked down and saw matching pairs of boots on their feet.

I didn't want to be on the receiving end of another kick from one of those boots.

The taller cop said, "Time to get up and go. You'd best keep walking."

Clumsily but successfully, I pushed myself to my feet. Sand fell from my clothing. I tried to wipe it from my face, but the grit got into my eyes.

"You got any identification on you?"

I cleared my throat, coughed up a wad of phlegm, and spit it onto the sand before turning to the cops. "Sure I do." Digging in my back pocket, I asked, "What's the problem, Officers?"

The shorter guy sounded like the younger of the two. "Problem is, you can't pass out on the beach like that."

As I checked all the pockets of my pants, I said, "Now, gentlemen, I'm familiar with the municipal law in Biloxi. I know my rights."

"You don't have the right to crash here." The young cop was getting mad. "Where's the ID?"

I bent over to pick up my jacket, hoping I'd find the wallet inside. My head swam, and I almost toppled sideways. But I recovered my balance, shook the sand off my jacket, and checked the pockets.

No wallet, no keys.

My recall of the night was spotty. Surely I'd remember if someone had robbed me, but someone could have relieved me of the wallet as I lay in the sand, insensible. I groped through my pockets a second time, panic spiking in my muddy brain. A man without his wallet is in a vulnerable position.

"This stretch of beach is public property," I said as I struggled to get my arm into the sleeve of my coat.

The young guy said, "Yeah? And there's no camping on the beach."

I got the jacket on and fastened the middle button as I often did when arguing in court. "I wasn't camping, Officer. Do you see a tent? Any camping gear? There's no campfire. I was simply resting."

The older cop grabbed my upper arm. The abrupt movement surprised me; I'd been focused on the other guy. My reaction was pure reflex—I jerked my arm from his grasp and shoved him away.

Bad move on my part. The young guy pulled a baton from his duty belt, and his arm flew back as he prepared to swing at me. I aimed a punch at his face, and my fist hit his jaw before the baton could connect. He grunted as he went down in the sand.

I watched him fall, shocked that my reflexes had been quick enough for me to outmaneuver him. While I had my eyes on the young guy, the big cop swung his eight-inch aluminum multi-purpose flashlight and landed a brutal hit on the back of my skull.

Now I was on my knees in the sand. As I clutched my head, howling in pain, he struck me again and again, raining blows on my shoulders, back, and arms. The beating stripped away any shred of dignity I'd had left. I cried out, pleading, "Stop! I'm not resisting! For God's sake, I'm not resisting!"

He landed another blow on my hands where they covered the back of my head. I heard him shout at his partner, "Get over here and cuff him, goddamn it!"

My hands were snatched away from my head. I didn't fight him as he jerked my arms behind my back. Once he'd fastened the handcuffs, the cop pushed me into a prone position on the sand and pressed his knee into my back.

The pressure on my torso cut off my wind. I lifted my head and tried to tell him he needed to back off. My words came out in a whisper, the sound lost under the shouting of the cops and the pounding of the surf.

That's the last thing I remember before everything went dark and I passed out.

CHAPTER 45

LATER, I learned that the cops had mistaken me for a vagrant. If I hadn't been so buzzed, I would've realized it immediately.

I was lucky to be alive.

Long hours passed as I sat on a hard bench in the holding cell of the local jail, clutching a bloody towel to the back of my head. A collection of men who'd also been arrested overnight sat talking on benches nearby. I certainly didn't want to compare notes, share details, and recount my experience of being passed-out drunk on the beach before the police inflicted a beating. My disgrace rendered me silent. They mostly left me alone.

I was sitting on the bench in my filthy clothes, reeking of sweat and blood and stale booze, when I heard the footsteps clicking down the tile floor of the hall.

A short guy wearing a black Stetson and a pair of shiny alligator boots appeared outside the cell. Searching the faces of the men behind bars, he called out, "Stafford Lee Penney?"

"Hey, Gene," I said, rising from the bench with effort. As I limped over to the cell door, I added, "Damned glad to see you."

I knew Gene Taylor. He was a local bail bondsman whose smiling face appeared on benches outside court facilities and jails in Harrison County. He didn't recognize me right off. I saw a look of surprise as he took in my filthy appearance; he sniffed, and his nose wrinkled.

He said, "Jenny called and said to get right over here. She didn't tell me you got the shit beat out of you."

Jenny hadn't known. When I was given the opportunity to make one phone call after they booked me, I'd called Jenny. She didn't pick up, so I'd left a short message.

While I sat and waited in the cell, I'd wondered whether I had a prayer of being released anytime soon. It was possible that Jenny had purposely ignored the call. She didn't approve of my new relaxed and laid-back lifestyle. She'd made that clear just a few days ago.

I followed the bondsman to the rear exit of the jail. It was difficult to keep up with his brisk pace; my body was weak, sore, and weary. When we got outside, I was surprised to see that the sun was up. I'd lost track of time inside the jail.

Jenny was waiting in the parking lot, standing by the passenger door of Mason's white Lexus. Mason sat behind the wheel.

I turned to Taylor. "Gene, what do I owe you?"

"Jenny and Mason worked it out. She got me out of bed this morning. You owe her one, Stafford Lee." He pulled a pen from his pocket and clicked the button. "Just need you to sign."

I lifted my right hand, the one with the injured middle finger from the cop's flashlight. The pain and swelling made it impossible to hold a pen. I took the pen with my left hand. "This signature won't be pretty," I said. I pressed the pen to the paper on the clipboard the bondsman held. My hand trembled so violently that the signature was illegible.

Taylor didn't comment. He handed me a copy of the paperwork and said, "Don't you go missing any court dates, Stafford Lee. I know where to find you."

I shuffled over to the car. Jenny looked me up and down. "What on earth? God, Stafford Lee — you're hurt. What happened to you?"

I didn't have the energy to tell the story. "Just get me out of here."

She inspected the back of my head. "Good Lord. Stafford Lee, you need stitches."

"I need a drink," I said. It was supposed to be funny, but Jenny didn't laugh.

She opened the back door, and I crawled onto the seat. When I sank against the upholstery, Mason reached back and dangled a set of keys—my keys.

"Thanks. Hey, do you have any idea what might have happened to my wallet?"

He held it up. "You left your wallet on the bar when you stormed off last night after Porter cut you off and I relieved you of your keys."

I'd inadvertently confessed to a total blackout. I'd have preferred to keep that information close to the chest.

Jenny joined Mason in the front seat and slammed the passenger door shut. She said, "Mason, we have to stop at the ER."

When Mason drove out of the jail parking lot, I ducked down in the back seat. Jenny turned around. Staring at me with a bemused expression, she said, "What are you doing? Are you going to pass out?"

It wasn't outside the realm of possibility. But I said, "Mason is going to drive by the courthouse. I don't want anyone to see me like this."

"Really? You think you can hide?" She turned back around, making an unflattering snort.

That snort destroyed whatever had been left of my self-esteem. Affronted, I said, "What's up with that reaction? Mason knows what I'm talking about. Don't you, Mason? I have to protect my professional reputation."

I couldn't see Mason's face, but his tone was grim when he said, "Jenny's right, Stafford Lee. By ten o'clock this morning, everyone in town is gonna know exactly how you messed up. You can't keep something like that under wraps. Not in Biloxi."

CHAPTER 46

I SHOULD have felt better when we left the ER. The doc had put five stitches in my head and splinted my broken middle finger. An X-ray showed that my ribs weren't fractured; I was just bruised. When I complained of pain, the physician gave me a dubious look and recommended ibuprofen.

But back in the rear seat of Mason's car, I felt worse than I had in the holding cell at the jail. I was sobering up, and everything hurt like hell. All I wanted to do was return to my own house, curl up on my living-room sofa, and sleep.

But before I went to sleep, maybe I'd have a nip of bourbon. Just a small one, for medicinal purposes. It wasn't like I was legitimately jonesing. I'd suffered through a traumatic experience. I needed a dose of liquid comfort to soothe my jangled nerves.

Problem was, I couldn't remember whether I had any bourbon at home. There'd been a bottle on the coffee table, but I might have polished it off the night before trial.

"Mason, make a stop at Big Pop Liquor on the way to my house, okay? I need to pick something up."

Mason and Jenny exchanged a look like a couple of old gossips. I suspected they'd been talking about my liquor consumption behind my back. The thought made me paranoid. "Fine," I said, biting off the word. "Just get me home."

I leaned my head against the leather upholstery and closed my eyes. I'd almost started to doze when I felt the car pick up speed. Confused, I sat up and looked through the window. We weren't headed for my neighborhood. Mason was getting on the highway.

"What the hell are you doing? You taking the exit to Hattiesburg? I'm not going to Hattiesburg."

"No problem. That's not our destination," Jenny said. She was studying the navigation screen on the dash. After several minutes of strained silence, she said, "Hey, Mason, we can take the next exit."

Mason veered off the highway and onto a roundabout. The movement of the car sent bile surging from my stomach into my throat. I lowered the window and stuck my head out just in time to heave. Vomit spewed along the pavement and sprayed the side of the Lexus's shiny exterior. The first round of barfing didn't relieve the nausea, and the involuntary spasms hit my ribs with excruciating agony. As the car turned, I grasped the window frame and rode with my head hanging out, like a dog. The queasiness built to a gag in my throat, and I puked again as Mason's car bumped along on the rutted road.

He finally came to a stop at the side of a remote country lane. We were way out in the boonies, far from Harrison County. I saw no signs of civilization, not even in the distance.

I pulled my head back in, reasonably certain that I wasn't going to retch again in the next few minutes. "Where are we? What are you doing?"

With the car idling, Mason shifted in the seat and met my eye. "Jenny and I think you need to go to rehab."

My muscles tensed. By some miracle, the nausea suddenly evaporated. "The hell you say."

"It's true. We're serious. Right, Jenny?"

She turned to face me. "I care too much about you to keep my mouth shut any longer. You're hurting yourself, and I can't stand to watch it go on. You're ruining your health, throwing away your life. You need help."

"Because I'm partying a little harder lately? Come on!"

"This isn't a party, Stafford Lee. What happened on the beach last night — that's scary. Blacking out, fighting the police, ending up in jail?"

"It was a fluke, a crazy misunderstanding."

"Bullshit," Mason said.

Jenny echoed him. "Yeah, bullshit. It's not a onetime thing. You've cut yourself off from your friends. And you're isolating yourself, getting drunk all alone at your house. *All the time.*"

"You're the talk of the town. Getting so damned drunk you can't try a case," Mason added. "Jesus, Stafford Lee, I can't believe you'd let drinking turn you into a shitty lawyer. Where's your pride? That's not like you. It's way out of character."

"Totally out of character." Jenny reached over the seat and stroked my arm. I moved it away. I didn't want to be patted like a six-year-old.

Jenny wasn't backing down. "Stafford Lee, you know we're right. If Carrie Ann were alive, she'd tell you the same thing. There's no quick fix for this, but it's not too late to turn it around. I want my friend back. You can recover from alcohol addiction at any stage. Will you agree to treatment?"

I wasn't agreeing to anything. "I can't believe you would spring this on me now, out in the middle of nowhere. I need to go home. I'm suffering from a serious injury."

Mason turned back around in his seat, but I could see his eyes in the rearview mirror. "You are suffering from a hangover. You just puked all over my car."

"Send me a bill for the car wash." I jerked the door open with my injured hand and cursed with pain as I bailed out of the vehicle.

Jenny rolled down the passenger window. "Where do you think you're going?"

I shouted over my shoulder as I stumbled down the narrow road, "I'm going back to the interstate. Hitching a ride back to town."

Behind me, a car door slammed, and I heard footsteps pounding on the dirt road. Jenny caught up to me and grabbed my arm right where it had been bruised by the cop's flashlight.

"Shit!" I yelled, jerking my arm free.

Sounding contrite, Jenny said, "Sorry! I didn't mean to hurt you. But you have to get back in the car."

No goddamn way, I thought. "I'm not enjoying the ride. Or the conversation."

"Get. Back. In the car. I mean it." Her face wore a savage look.

"You think you can take me down, Jenny?" Judging from her expression, she intended to try. The idea made me laugh despite my foul mood. "Even in my weakened state, there's no way you can win a wrestling match with me."

She grasped my wrist. "I'm not letting go. I won't stand by and watch you kill yourself." Her face crumpled and she let out a sob. The reaction shocked me. Jenny never cried.

Mason laid on the horn. I could see him through the windshield; he was watching us. "What's going on out there?" he shouted.

"Jenny's flipping out on me," I called back. "Tell her I'm okay."

He just shook his head.

Jenny tugged on my arm, but gently this time. "You can't hitch back to town. No one is going to pick you up and give you a ride, Stafford Lee. You look like an escaped felon. A serial killer." Then in a cajoling voice, she said, "Come on back to the car. Just give us a chance to make our case."

She had a valid point about my hitchhiking chances. I let her lead me back to the car. This time, she slid into the back seat beside me.

"You really need to go for treatment," she said. "You're in a crisis. The situation is urgent—"

I interrupted. "Is this an intervention?" When she said it was, I looked at Mason. He nodded and started driving again. I said, "Huh. Well, that's a first for me."

"Mason and I found a good residential facility in Louisiana, and we talked to the administrator and one of the therapists. Can I share what they told us?"

"Sure. Fire away."

She grabbed her purse, pulled out two sheets of paper, and started to read aloud. It appeared that she'd prepared a pitch in anticipation of our road trip. I slumped down in the seat and sat, not interrupting but also not paying much heed. While Jenny preached the benefits of rehab and Mason drove us toward Louisiana, I tried to think of other things.

CHAPTER 47

SEVENTY-TWO MILES after the state sign welcomed us to Louisiana—and warned us to keep it beautiful—Mason made a turn into the Hope Springs Recovery Center.

We drove down a path lined with oaks draped in Spanish moss that led to a huge white house at the top of a sloping green lawn. Two groundskeepers were hard at work; one was operating a riding mower, the other toiled in a flower bed.

Mason braked in front of the house, and Jenny faced me with an expectant expression.

"It's Tara!" I said.

She frowned. "Don't be a smart-ass."

"It was a compliment. I thought you were taking me someplace with a more institutional vibe. You know, like in *One Flew Over the Cuckoo's Nest,* the facility where Jack Nicholson landed for his lobotomy. This is much nicer."

"Hell yeah, it's nice. Mason and I have dedicated a lot of time to finding the best treatment center in the South. This was a historic property before it was converted into a rehab facility with the feel of a B and B. It's on the National Register of Historic Places."

Mason added, "You can work out while you're here. They've got a great gym. I checked it out. And there's a pool out back."

Deadpan, I said, "Oh my God. I'm on vacation."

Jenny gave me a pleading look. "Stop it, Stafford Lee. Of course it's not gonna be a vacation. But it's beautiful here, right? We wanted to find a place where you could be comfortable while you worked on your problem."

Problem? Was that the diagnosis? Her cautious description of my plight was comical. "Right. It looks exceedingly comfortable. But y'all might as well turn this car around. Ain't no way I can afford this place. I can tell by the landscaping alone."

In a suspiciously casual tone, Mason said, "That's not going to be an issue. Your old man is picking up the tab."

"Oh, shit." I bailed out of the car once again and got ready to haul ass back to Mississippi on foot.

Jenny slid out of the seat after me. "Stafford Lee, just go inside and check it out."

Mason shouted through the open window, "Jenny! You gotta give him an ultimatum!"

"Don't yell at me," she snapped. She turned to me and said, "Stafford Lee, I don't want to make threats—that's not how I want this to go. Won't you come inside just because I'm asking? Talk to the administrator. Please? Will you do that for me?" She grasped my hand, the one without a splint, and tugged on it. "Please," she said again.

Standing on the gravel drive, I looked into her pleading face. I was too tired to fight with her any longer. I figured it wouldn't kill me to go inside. Maybe I'd take a toilet break while we were in there. It's not like I was committing to anything.

I followed Jenny through the front door. She walked up to the receptionist and said we had an appointment with Amy. When the receptionist picked up the phone, Jenny turned and whispered, "Amy's the administrator."

"Got it," I said with a smirk. "Nurse Ratched."

Jenny looked away, shaking her head. Mason joined us, and I followed the two of them into the business office, gearing up for a showdown. I had battled plenty of pompous medical professionals over the course of my career. The admin of an addiction prison couldn't intimidate me. I already had a clear and unflattering mental picture of Administrator Ratched.

Except that she was younger than I'd anticipated, about Jenny's age. Tall and slim as a racehorse. And uncommonly pretty.

As I sat across from her desk in the pristine office, I was painfully aware that I was scruffy and dirty and that the administrator could smell my foul breath and body odor. It put me at a disadvantage, but she radiated compassion. She leaned toward me; she didn't scoot back her chair. While I sat there staring at her like an idiot, she said something I didn't catch. We sat in silence while she fixed me with an expectant look. "Stafford Lee? What do you think?"

"Yeah, can you repeat that?"

She gave me a warm smile. "Sure thing. I just observed that you're fortunate. You have very devoted friends."

I took a moment to digest that statement. "Really?" I looked over at Mason and Jenny, seated to my right. "My friends tell me I have a problem. Apparently, they think I'm a lost cause."

Her smile dimmed. In an earnest voice, she said, "That's not what I heard from them. Stafford Lee, you're not a lost cause. But you have to take steps to reverse course."

I glanced over at Mason and Jenny again. Neither one spoke, but Mason wore a familiar dogged look. He wasn't going to back down.

Jenny's hands were clutched together in her lap. As our eyes met, her nose reddened. She mouthed the word this time: *Please.*

I had to clear my throat before I replied to the administrator. "Beg to differ. I *am* a lost cause, but with very good friends."

They had backed me into a corner, all of them. I was out of arguments. So I waved the white flag.

CHAPTER 48

IN THAT moment of weakness in the administrator's office, I signed on for a voluntary stay of sixty days.

Sixty. Days.

The first week was a blur because I was struggling with the physical symptoms of coming off a yearlong bender. The agony kicked in during my first twenty-four hours. My muscles twitched and jerked; my head was pounding, and weird spots floated before my eyes. The nights were even worse. Without my nightcap, I battled the curse of insomnia. I lay awake in bed, my heart palpitating, suffering through crippling bouts of anxiety. When I caught snatches of sleep, nightmares haunted me.

Mealtime was another form of torture. My stomach was sour, my appetite nonexistent. And because I'd developed pronounced tremors in both hands, holding a fork or spoon was difficult. Though no one in the dining hall commented when my food slipped off my fork and onto the plate or, worse, the table, the shakes made me self-conscious and disinclined to eat in public.

Coping with alcohol withdrawal, the staff told me when I complained, was the first stage of treatment. They advised me to go for walks. Get sunshine, drink water. And, of course, participate in therapy.

By day seven, I'd had it with Hope Springs Recovery Center. At two o'clock in the afternoon on that seventh day, I was seated in one of a dozen chairs placed in a circle inside the sunroom for group therapy. So much soul-searching, talk therapy, blame. It tested my patience way beyond reasonable limits. I didn't even try to play along.

At that moment, Tristan Broussard, my rehab roommate, was sitting directly across from me, talking. Tristan liked to share. I hadn't been forced to room with another guy since my freshman year at Ole Miss. Tristan was third-generation leisure class from New Orleans, and we had nothing in common. Well, nothing but alcohol.

"So I think I was condemned to an alcohol-use disorder at birth. You know? If you're born and raised in New Orleans, there's this culture of excess, a celebration of alcohol. It's inescapable."

A middle-aged woman from Arkansas said, "Because of Bourbon Street?"

Tristan looked down his nose at her. He considered himself Garden District royalty, a class apart from the rest of us. "Not just Bourbon Street. It's everywhere. At my favorite place for brunch, the menu says: 'Breakfast without wine is like a day without sunshine.' That's the town mindset, and I learned it from the cradle. It was preordained that I'd end up right here."

The therapist was a long-haired guy named Marcus who sported round wire-rimmed glasses like John Lennon wore in the 1960s. He gave my roommate a nod of approval. "Tristan, we're glad you're here. Who else feels motivated to share?"

An anorexic woman in her twenties raised her hand. She looked too young to be in rehab, but she claimed to be a bona fide alcoholic. She liked to discuss her personal history at length. To the group, she said, "Marcus said we should think about the triggers in our past experiences that lead to unhealthy behavior patterns. You know, my parents didn't have boundaries."

Oh, we knew. She never stopped complaining about her parents. Her father was an accountant in Baton Rouge; Mom was an English professor at LSU.

"Their language is what I've been focusing on. I think my dad's use of coarse language traumatized me, and that made me want to hurt him and hurt myself. So I started drinking back in ninth grade, and it snowballed really fast."

The therapist said, "Are you comfortable expanding on that? Did your father curse you, abuse you verbally? Because that's definitely a causal factor in addictive behavior."

"No. He didn't curse me, but he turned ordinary words into sexual words. You know deli stuff like salami and smoked turkey? He didn't call it *cold cuts* or *sandwich meat*. My dad called it *horse cock*. He'd be in the kitchen and say, 'Lena, you want a horse-cock sandwich?'"

As she related her tale of woe, I thought, *How about walking into your house and seeing your dead wife in bed, her eyes wide open, her chest blown apart by a shotgun?* That's *traumatic*. But I kept my reflections to myself.

Her voice rose as she reached the climax of her story. "And so when I was in third grade, my teacher said, 'What's in your lunch box?' And I told her it was a horse-cock sandwich."

At the punch line, I made a sound, a cross between a snicker and a scoff. She heard it and turned to me, her eyes accusing.

"You think it's funny? I was nine years old. I didn't even know what it meant."

Actually, it sounded like the kind of joke my old man would've played. But all I said was "I get that it wasn't comical at the time. But it's the type of story that's funny in retrospect, don't you think?"

I turned to the rest of the group and appealed to them. "Am I right?"

Most of the faces in the circle glared at me.

Lena crossed her arms over her chest and lifted her chin. In an injured voice, she said, "I don't feel like sharing anymore."

Marcus gave me a no-nonsense look through his round lenses. I suspected he wore the glasses as a fashion accessory. He struck me as that kind of guy. "Stafford, maybe you'd like to contribute?"

"No. I'm good."

"Really? Still, even after a week? You haven't made any constructive contributions since you joined us. We'd be interested to hear anything you'd like to share."

"I'm not so keen on chewing up my folks for their parenting skills. The way I see it, they did the best they could. And my mom passed away when I was young. I don't like to trash her or talk smack about her."

Marcus didn't want to let me off the hook. "We'll respect your boundaries. Do you want to talk about how you came to be here at Hope Springs?"

I thought about that for a second before I answered. "Nope."

Marcus made a clicking noise with his tongue. "You won't benefit from therapy if you don't take an active part."

"You think people really benefit from therapy?" I asked.

I experienced a buzz of satisfaction when his mouth dropped open. I said, "I'm serious. I've done some reading on it. There are knowledgeable experts who think psychotherapy is futile. It's a shadowy, vague attempt to solve people's problems, and its efficacy has never been proven."

"I disagree," Marcus said. He sounded snippy.

"Yeah, I thought you might. But can we agree that there's this billion-dollar industry that has no guaranteed results? Or even a way to measure success? Does that strike you as pretty absurd?"

The therapist scraped his chair back across the wooden floor. "Why are you doing this?"

He was seriously pissed, and the other faces in the circle mirrored his resentment. The only sympathy coming my way was from a longtime drinker who'd fallen off the wagon for the umpteenth time and landed back in rehab a couple of weeks ago. He claimed he'd recently seen the light—that he'd been born again. With a crooked smile, he told me, "I'm praying for you, Stafford Lee. Alcoholism is an equal-opportunity destroyer. Aren't you sick and tired of being sick and tired?"

I recognized the lingo. He was spouting AA slogans. I tossed one back. "It works if you work it—isn't that what they tell you? But it hasn't worked for you."

The guy's smile dimmed, and Marcus jumped out of his chair. "Okay, Stafford, that's it. I'm not going to let you taunt people who are seriously trying to work through addiction. You're interfering with the recovery of other people in this program."

"What do you want from me?" I said. "You want me to go? Fine. I'll leave y'all to it." Picking that fight in group therapy had agitated me, made me jumpy. I launched out of my chair, tipping it over. I left it lying there.

Just outside the sunroom, I saw Amy. She strolled toward me in slim white pants and a loose silk blouse, looking like she belonged on a fashion runway. She caught me staring. That was humiliating. I certainly didn't want her to think I was attracted to her, even if it was true.

So I gave her a mocking grin and said, "Good afternoon, Nurse Ratched."

She looked into the sunroom, where the circle had one empty, overturned chair. "Aren't you supposed to be in Group right now, Stafford Lee?"

"I was invited to take a recess."

She narrowed her eyes—a Nurse Ratched trick, though it didn't diminish Amy's appeal. "Our program can't help you if you continue to fight it at every turn."

"Can't help me what?"

She looked at me with disbelief. "Help you overcome your addiction. Why do you think you're here?"

"I'm here because my friends coerced me into it. They caught me in a moment of weakness, and you snagged my signature."

Softly, so we wouldn't be overheard, she said, "Have you forgotten about your condition a week ago? The shape you were in when you arrived? Because I haven't."

The reminder was unsettling. But a man's got his pride. "Frankly, I don't think I'm a candidate for rehab. I've been here for a week, but I haven't seen spiders crawling out of the walls. No hallucinations, no delirium tremens. I had a few drinks too many the night before I landed here. That's all."

"Frankly," she began—was she mocking me?—"I think you're smart enough to know you have a problem. It's called alcohol-use disorder. You're resisting the diagnosis because you don't want to deal with it."

"Everybody around here—"

She interrupted me. "Everyone around here is trying to help you. You are the only person standing in the way of your recovery."

She brushed past me without waiting for me to respond. I almost followed her, wanting to prolong the encounter.

But instead, I paced the hall, mulling over the punches she'd landed. I was familiar with the term *alcohol-use disorder*. AUD was a sanitized, modern synonym for *alcoholism*. I knew the signs of AUD listed in the *DSM-5*. Rehab was littered with pamphlets outlining them. There were eleven symptoms. I had nine.

I stopped in the hallway and stood there, working up my nerve. And then I walked back into the sunroom. Picked up the chair I'd knocked over earlier. Sat down on it.

Conversation had halted. Eleven faces were turned to me, exhibiting a variety of reactions to my presence.

I cleared my throat before I spoke so the words would come out clearly.

"I'm Stafford Lee, and I'm an alcoholic."

CHAPTER 49

THEY DIDN'T keep me in rehab for the whole sixty days. I returned home after five weeks, feeling better, stronger, saner. When I landed back in Biloxi, I even got a part-time job. The perfect job. A job having nothing to do with the law.

When I got to work at nine o'clock on Saturday morning, the beach was deserted. Only a couple of seagulls greeted me as I unlocked the units where the rental chairs and umbrellas were stored overnight.

Before long, the resort guests would be stirring, emerging from hotel rooms and strolling down to the water's edge. I started with the umbrellas, pacing off equal distances between them and planting the poles deep in the sand.

It was a young man's job; during high season, you'd see athletic college kids doing the setup, not middle-aged guys like me. But I was in better shape these days. The resort paid my hourly wage by direct deposit, hitting my account with much needed income twice a month.

I unfolded the first pair of wood-framed beach chairs and brushed the prior day's sand from the green fabric seats. A jogger passed me, running on the packed sand. I ignored him, but he stopped several yards away from me and turned to stare.

"Stafford Lee?"

The jogger was Glenn Fielding, a Biloxi trial lawyer about my age. Over the years, he'd been a frequent opponent of mine in court. For a long time, I bested him in our hard-fought legal battles. But not recently.

"What you up to these days, Stafford Lee?"

I wasn't fooled into thinking his interest was friendly. Obviously, Glenn knew what I was up to. He wore a T-shirt and running shorts only on his days off. My work uniform of swimming trunks and flip-flops signaled that I had a teenager's job, sticking umbrellas in the sand for minimum wage.

I clenched my jaw. I felt that old chip on my shoulder, heavy as a cannonball. Defensive comebacks ricocheted inside my head. I knew I could take that snarky guy down in a war of words, make him wish he hadn't messed with me.

And then I recalled the techniques I had learned in Louisiana. With a conscious effort, I relaxed my muscles and gained control of my flaring temper. I tossed that injured pride out with the garbage.

And I didn't try to dodge the truth. "I'm on the job, working as a lifeguard. First order of business, gotta set up the beach umbrellas and chairs."

"What possessed you to take up this occupation? What, are you working on your suntan?" He chuckled at his own joke.

I smiled broadly and glanced up at the yellow ball of the sun. "I'm getting my vitamin D, for certain. It's one of the perks of the job."

He squinted, searching my face like he was trying to read me. "So you've given up the practice of law? Just like that, after all these years? I remember when the *Bar Association Journal* called you the number one lawyer for southern Mississippi. Guess we won't go toe-to-toe in court anymore."

"Sure we will. I'm in the office three days a week, Monday

through Wednesday. I'll see you in court, guaranteed. Looking forward to it."

That was not a fabrication. I was looking forward to taking him down again. But I kept it civil. "Like I said, Monday through Wednesday, my office door is open. You drop in sometime, I'll put the coffeepot on for you."

The guy backed away, preparing to continue his morning jog. "Maybe I'll see you at the White House Hotel for happy hour."

I kept a smile on my face. "Not likely."

After Glenn Fielding jogged away, I finished setting up the chairs. I felt pretty good about the encounter. I hadn't lied, hadn't lost my cool. Hadn't let him ruin my morning.

After I checked the National Weather Service website, I raised a green flag over the beach. The water was calm, ideal swimming conditions.

Before I climbed up the white lifeguard perch, I lifted my sunglasses and swiped zinc oxide down the bridge of my nose. Once I settled onto my chair overlooking the beach, I saw a group of unsupervised kids—maybe nine or ten years old—run up to the water's edge.

I scooted forward on my seat, keeping an eye on them.

When they ran into the water, I tweeted my whistle and called, "Y'all be careful! Don't go in too deep!"

One of the boys turned around and flipped me the bird.

It felt kind of like being in court again.

CHAPTER 50

JENNY INTENTIONALLY arrived at the restaurant five minutes
early; it was important to let people know she respected their time.
But when she walked into Neelah's Soul Kitchen in Gulfport, the
man she was scheduled to meet was already there, seated at a table
near the back.

Pastor Gates would have been hard to miss—a man of his stat-
ure stood out even when he wasn't wearing the black garb and
clerical collar of his professional calling. Approaching the table, she
saw that he was bent over a paperback book. When Jenny pulled
out the chair across from his, he looked up.

"Good afternoon, Jenny." He marked his page and set the book
aside.

"Hello, Pastor. Thanks for meeting me today."

A waitress appeared at his elbow. "Hi, Pastor. Remember me?"

His face lit up. "Imani! Pleasure to see you. How's your mama?"

"She's good, got out of the hospital. She sure appreciated you
coming to pray with her when she was sick. Mama's saying that she
wants to get back to church now that she's feeling better."

"I'm delighted to hear that. You tell her I look forward to seeing
her. To seeing both of you," he added.

The girl gave a quick nod and pulled a small spiral notepad from the pocket of her jeans. "Today's lunch special is smothered pork chops with two sides and a corn muffin."

"I'll have the special. With the yams and black-eyed peas. And a cup of black coffee."

Without bothering to study the menu, Jenny seconded the preacher's choice. "And a glass of ice water, please."

When the waitress walked away, Gates said in a somber voice, "Her mama has had a bad time of it. Cancer. But she puts her faith in the Lord." He glanced over at the waitress and then turned back to Jenny. "We all need to remember to do that."

Jenny placed both hands flat on the table. "Pastor, I'd like to offer my condolences for the death of your cousin Benjamin. More than a year has passed, but I know that time doesn't erase the loss."

"Well. The Apostle Paul tells us that the Lord won't give us more than we can bear." He looked away. When his eyes met Jenny's again, they were troubled. He took a deep breath and continued. "My family has struggled with a weighty load of grief. You're aware of that; everyone around here knows it. We still hadn't recovered from Aurora's murder when Benjamin died. And the scandal around his death—people calling my cousin a killer, saying he'd committed murder and then died by his own hand." Gates shook his head and said with a mournful expression, "I have to wonder if the Lord is testing us."

Jenny had no response, so she kept her mouth shut.

The waitress returned with their beverages and steaming plates of food. Gates smiled and thanked her, bowed his head, and murmured grace. He picked up his knife and fork, then stopped, put down the cutlery, and pushed the plate away. "Benjamin and I grew up in Gulfport together, did you know that?"

Jenny shook her head.

"We lived just three doors apart on the same street. We were close, more like brothers than cousins. I tell you, it's hard to lose him under these circumstances. Almost unbearable." He massaged his temples with his fingers as if his head ached.

Jenny recalled the preacher's presence at the trial. She'd seen him sitting beside Benjamin Gates during the testimony and standing with him in the courthouse lobby. The preacher had been the center of Gates's support network.

She took a bite of the black-eyed peas, silently debating how far she could push her line of inquiry. It was a delicate undertaking. "I don't know whether you've seen the police reports, but they claim that your cousin Benjamin had openly said he wanted vengeance against Stafford Lee Penney. You knew your cousin better than anyone. Does that sound accurate to you?"

"No. No, it doesn't."

She took a breath and tried to finesse the follow-up. "The detective named you as his source of information, Pastor Gates. He said that when they questioned you, you confirmed that you'd heard your cousin say he wanted revenge, that he was angry about what had happened during the Caro trial and about the verdict. The police concluded that those statements provided the motive for the murder/suicide inside the Penney home."

The pastor fixed her with a look of resentment. "Yes, the police questioned me. And I talked to them, answered their questions. But the police in Biloxi weren't listening to my story. They heard what they wanted to hear. They'd already made up their minds about what Benjamin had done and why he'd done it."

She said, her voice soft, encouraging, "I'd like you to tell me what you think happened. From your point of view."

"What do you care?"

She'd expected the blunt question and was prepared for it. "I want to uncover the truth."

Gates pulled his plate toward him, picked up the fork, and

stabbed it into a chunk of candied yam. He chewed slowly as he studied her across the table.

After he swallowed, he said, "It's true that Benjamin despised that doctor. Who can blame him? Caro was a married man who was trifling with Ben's young daughter. My cousin resented the lawyer too. He's your friend, isn't he? Penney?"

Jenny nodded. She couldn't deny it. "Stafford Lee is my friend. We're close."

His brow furrowed and he gave a disapproving sniff. "Sounds like your friend's in trouble. They say Stafford Lee Penney has become a common drunk." He leaned across the table and said in his rumbling bass voice, "'Woe to those who rise early in the morning that they may pursue strong drink, who stay up late in the evening that wine may inflame them.'" He gave her a stern look. "Isaiah, chapter five, verse eleven."

Jenny met his gaze and said, "I agree with you, Pastor. 'Wine is a mocker, strong drink a brawler, and whoever is intoxicated by it is not wise.' Proverbs twenty, verse one." The pastor didn't conceal his surprise. Jenny shrugged. "I was raised Baptist. The verses have a way of sticking in your head. I'm sure you know that."

For the first time since she joined him, he smiled at her. "Yes, ma'am. I surely do."

"But Stafford Lee—he's working on it. I have faith in him; I think he'll turn it around. But about the police report—is it true what the detective said? He wrote that your cousin wanted to see Stafford Lee dead."

"They twisted it, twisted my words. I couldn't deny that Benjamin had made certain statements, that he'd been known to say he wanted Caro and Penney to suffer the same grief he'd borne. It's a natural reaction. I'd counseled him to turn the burden over to the Lord."

She sat back in her chair, studying him closely. "If you were counseling your cousin, why did you feel compelled to share the information with the police? You could've claimed privileged communications. You're clergy."

"He didn't confine those statements to private counseling sessions. He broadcast his feelings liberally, and I was witness to it. But I wanted the police to understand his thinking—that's why I cooperated. Did he want revenge? Yes, but he never would've used violence. The only steps Benjamin took were legal measures."

"What legal measures are you talking about?"

"You recall how distressed and agitated he became during the trial?"

Jenny nodded. She didn't need the pastor to elaborate. They both remembered Benjamin Gates's breakdown in the courtroom.

"While the case was in trial, we prepared letters to send to the State Bar Association and the medical board. Complaints against your friend Penney and Dr. Caro. Before the trial ended, Ben consulted with a lawyer in Gulfport about bringing a slander case."

"Defamation?" Jenny knew that case wouldn't fly, but she wanted to keep Gates talking.

"He couldn't stand the things they said about his daughter at trial, all the insults to Aurora's character. He wanted to sue Penney and Caro for soiling her reputation, hurting her good name. But the lawyers said he couldn't."

Jenny nodded in sympathy. Clients had often come to her with similar issues. "But Aurora was deceased—" she began.

He finished the sentence. "And the dead can't sue for libel or slander. Benjamin was unhappy about that."

"Was he angry?"

Gates met her eye. He knew a trick question when he heard one. "Not that kind of anger."

Choosing her words carefully, Jenny said, "So, in your opinion, could his frustration with the lack of legal options push him to take matters into his own hands? Is that a possibility?"

"Never. Murder wasn't in his nature. Benjamin wasn't a violent man."

Jenny grimaced. "Then what about that scene in court? Your cousin took a swing at Stafford Lee in the courtroom. Stafford Lee tried the rest of the case with a black eye."

Gates brushed her statement off with a wave. "It was a lucky punch, that's all. Benjamin was never a fighter. Even when we were kids, he wasn't any good with his fists. Maybe because he was left-handed."

Jenny picked up her phone and tapped a quick memo to herself. "I wasn't aware of that. I didn't see anything in the reports about Benjamin being left-handed."

"Well, it's true. Here's an irony: In Hebrew, the name Benjamin means 'son of the right hand.' But my cousin favored the left, always."

She set her phone down. Pastor Gates cut into the chop and took his first bite of pork. Ruefully, he said, "I believe we've let our food get cold."

"That's okay." Jenny knew she couldn't clean her heaping plate. Talking about murder had dampened her appetite. "Anything else you can share with me?"

He thought for a moment before he answered. "I truly believe that Aurora greeted Benjamin when he passed through the gate. They're together in heaven; I take comfort in that. But we're still on earth. And a lot of strife and trouble and woe remains in this place. I think we need to be on guard. All of us."

He set down the serrated knife. "There's a killer among us. Because my cousin didn't murder those two people they found in Stafford Lee Penney's house. And I don't believe Benjamin killed himself."

He picked up the knife again. "So—you tell me. Who did it?"

CHAPTER 51

LATER THAT week, Jenny walked onto the patio behind Surfer Matt's Shack on Biloxi Beach near the boardwalk. She spotted Stafford Lee sitting at one of the waterfront tables.

She checked her watch. Stafford Lee was on his lunch break and didn't have much time. When she slid into the chair across from his, she saw that he had already ordered his lunch. On the rough wooden tabletop painted neon purple sat a paper-lined plastic basket and two tall plastic cups.

Stafford Lee handed her a straw. "Is ice water okay? We need to stay hydrated. It's hot as hell out here."

"Water's fine." She peeled the paper wrapper off the straw. "Sorry I kept you waiting."

He waved the apology off. "I beat you by a couple of minutes, so I went ahead and ordered. Want to share?"

He nudged the basket across the table toward her. Nestled inside was a huge fried-shrimp po'boy, cut in half, flanked by a generous helping of fried pickles.

Jenny fanned herself. "God, yes. Looks divine. Okay if I salt the pickles?" She picked up the saltcellar and gave it a liberal shake. Watching Stafford Lee dig into his half of the sandwich, she marveled at the change he'd undergone. "So, what's up? Anything new with you?"

"You won't believe this." The sun glinted off his sunglasses as he grinned at her.

"What?"

"I have a bench trial this week."

Jenny almost choked on her pickle, but she recovered swiftly. "Stafford Lee, how fantastic that you're back in the saddle!"

He nudged his shades down on his nose and peered at her over the rims. "Want to know a secret? I'm nervous. It's my first time trying a case since rehab. I'm feeling a little performance anxiety."

"You are not!"

He glanced around, leaned across the table, and said in a low voice, "I am. Like a kid right out of law school jotting objections on a note card. What if I'm out of practice? What if I forgot how to do it?"

Stafford Lee pulled a woeful face, and Jenny laughed out loud. "Stafford Lee, you are the king. You've been the local trial giant for over a decade."

He gave her a grudging smile.

"As soon as you walk into court, it'll all come back to you. Don't forget, I was your right arm back when you were brand-new to trial practice. Even in the beginning, you had star quality."

His forehead furrowed. "That was ages ago. How much did I pay you back then?"

"Not near what I was worth." Scrutinizing him across the table, she added, "These days you're looking like a sun god. I feel sorry for the lawyer on the other side. Next to you, he or she will look like a pasty-faced dweeb."

"Damn, Jenny. You'd best stop right there. If I start taking you seriously, I'm bound to get a big head." He wiped his hands and changed the subject. "Tell me what you've been up to. I haven't talked to you all week."

The question provided the opening she'd hoped for. "I've been doing some digging, talking to people. Stafford Lee, I'm not satisfied with Detective Sweeney's investigation. I've formed some of my own theories on the murder case." When he didn't respond, she added, for clarity, "Carrie Ann's murder."

He remained silent. With the sun reflecting off his sunglasses, she couldn't read his eyes. "Want to hear what I've come up with?" she asked.

"Not really. Nope." Stafford Lee toyed with the plastic basket. His face wore an expression of distaste, like he'd bitten into a bad shrimp. The mood at the table had altered in a matter of seconds.

Jenny could see that Stafford Lee wasn't ready to revisit the carnage he'd witnessed. But more than a year had passed. It needed to be addressed. "Stafford Lee, I don't want to upset you—"

He cut her off. "Then why do you keep bringing it up?" He rose abruptly and grabbed the check. "I've got to go back to work. I only get forty-five minutes."

She said, trying to keep her voice bright, "Hey, let me chip in for lunch."

He turned to go. Over his shoulder, he said, "I'll take care of it."

As he walked off, she called, "Thanks for lunch! Good to see you!"

He didn't look back.

CHAPTER 52

I HAD to admit that Jenny was right about one thing: As soon as I walked into the courtroom, everything came back to me. It felt good.

I couldn't say, though, that it was just like it used to be. I'd broken some of my trial traditions. I didn't walk to the courthouse toting my big briefcase. Didn't wear the old conservative suit and tie either. Instead, I wore a rumpled—but clean—tan and white seersucker suit and flip-flops. It was an unconventional ensemble, but comfortable? Hell yeah.

Also, I wasn't trying the types of cases I'd handled prior to the Caro verdict. I didn't have the luxury of cherry-picking cases. I had to take any client I could get. And I could no longer demand a retainer up front. If I didn't win, I wouldn't make a dime for my time and effort.

On this particular day, I'd set a civil case for money damages—a tort action for battery, alleging offensive physical contact inflicted by a supervisor on an employee.

My client, Alicia Holmes, a checker at the Dixie Belle grocery store, had been the target of unwelcome sexual overtures from the store manager. Over a period of months, he'd groped her and propositioned her, and when she resisted, he'd threatened consequences related to her employment.

After Alicia confided the harassment to her older sister, Rue, a second-year law student in Gulfport, she stepped in on her little sister's behalf. I wasn't the first attorney Rue called, but I was the one who agreed to take it on.

So we had a solid case of quid pro quo sexual harassment against the employer. And under federal law, we were in a position to sue the corporation. I'd explained to Alicia that we wanted to hold Dixie Belle responsible because the business controlled the workplace. And—not an insignificant consideration—the business had money, the deep pockets to pay the judgment.

We had proceeded against Dixie Belle Inc., alleging employment discrimination and sexual harassment in violation of Title VII. The employer was hanging tough, though. To date, the corporation had refused to make a settlement offer. In our last conversation, I'd accused the corporate attorney of being unreasonable on account of my client's race. She was Black; the store manager was white. It's an old story in Mississippi.

Since they wouldn't take us seriously, I sued the supervisor in state court for battery. The dude didn't have any money, but bringing the battery case against the manager was a strategic move to force the corporation's hand.

So we proceeded to trial. I was trying the lawsuit before Judge Eckhardt, who'd presided over the disastrous case of my homeless client in *State v. Della Calhoun*. I was determined to make a more solid appearance this time around.

The civil battery action was simple and straightforward. It was a bench trial, meaning there was no jury; the judge would decide the case. My client testified first. Under questioning on direct, she described her boss's unwelcome attentions, the improper sexual suggestions, the offensive physical contact he'd inflicted. It was crucial for her to recount in detail the times he'd grabbed her private parts, and though I'd worked with her beforehand, on several

214

occasions during direct, Alicia faltered out of embarrassment, and we had to backtrack. But she had the truth on her side, and it showed.

During the cross-exam, I kept a close eye on opposing counsel, ready to jump out of my chair. Though he went after her, the attorney didn't break her or make her back down from her testimony.

The next witness I called was a checker who worked with Alicia and had witnessed two of the incidents. She was a disappointment; she gave a much less convincing account on the stand than she'd provided in my office. I wondered whether someone had gotten to her before trial. Maybe she was afraid of losing her job at Dixie Belle.

But I knew we'd make a comeback. I was prepared to stake my reputation on the performance potential of my final witness: my client's sister, Rue. When she settled into the witness chair, her demeanor was cool and unruffled.

"Ms. Holmes, are you acquainted with Eddie Hough, your sister Alicia's supervisor at Dixie Belle?"

"Yes, I am."

"Directing your attention to February eleventh of this year, did you have occasion to speak with the defendant on that date?"

"I sure did."

"At approximately what time?"

"I'll tell you exactly what time it was: three forty-three p.m. I know because I wrote it down. I was taking notes on the conversation."

"Tell the court what occurred."

The young woman turned to the judge as if she were an expert witness with years of practice.

She said, "So I was at Alicia's apartment on February eleventh when the store manager called her on her cell. We were sitting on the couch, and she held up the phone; I saw his name on the screen—Eddie Hough. She didn't want to talk to him, but I told her to answer and put it on speaker, so she did."

"Then what happened?"

"As soon as she picked up, he started coming on to her. I heard every word. He said he wanted to see her that night, that they could have a lot of fun. He said she'd been acting like a tease at work, coming in shaking her tits and ass and then pushing him away. That's a quote, you understand. I wrote it down. 'You come in shaking your tits and ass at work, then push me away.' That's exactly what he said."

While Rue testified, my mood lifted. The woman knew how to command a courtroom. I gave her a nod of encouragement. "What else did he say on the call?"

"He said he wanted her to start being friendly to him. And if she kept snubbing him, he could make it tough on her. He could cut her hours back or put her on the late-night shift. He knew she didn't like working late. Alicia's got a baby in day care."

I cut a casual glance at the judge. He looked noncommittal. I wasn't worried. Rue hadn't fired off all her ammunition yet. "And then what happened?"

"Then he started talking real dirty about what he wanted her to do. Specific sex acts. In explicit language."

"Begging your pardon, Ms. Holmes, but you need to tell the court exactly what he said."

She took a deep breath. "He said, 'If you want to stay on my good side, all you got to do is suck my dick once in a while. Or bend over for a quick fuck in the storeroom.'" She faced the judge again. "That's a quote."

She shifted in the chair, looked out at the courtroom, and pinned her gaze on Eddie Hough at his counsel table. I let the defendant squirm for a moment under her righteous glare before I said, "And then what occurred?"

Rue straightened up in her seat. With dignity, she said, "And then I couldn't stay quiet anymore. I told Eddie Hough that I'd heard the whole thing, every word he'd said. And I said if he got within spitting distance of my sister, I'd lay him flat."

The judge smirked. A good sign? I wasn't sure. "What happened the next day?"

"I drove Alicia to her shift at Dixie Belle. I wanted Hough to see me so he'd know I had my eyes open, you understand? As soon as we walked through the door, he came out from behind the service desk and told her to turn around. That she didn't work there anymore."

"What else did he say?"

The defense attorney rose. "Objection! Unless there's an allegation of physical contact on that date, this is irrelevant to the issue of whether the tort of battery occurred."

The judge shrugged. "I'll allow it. Objection overruled."

The defense objection had merit. I hoped the ruling meant that the judge was caught up in Rue's account and wanted to hear how the story ended. I smiled at her. "You may answer, Ms. Holmes."

She faced the judge again. "I said, 'If you fire her, she's got a right to know why.' And the guy said: 'For insubordination.' Then he told us to get out."

With that, I ended direct examination. I had to stifle a laugh when the defense lawyer announced he had no questions for Rue on cross. He wasn't stupid enough to tangle with Rue Holmes.

After we rested, the defense had their turn. The judge admitted evidence over my objection, employment records that showed that my client had never made any written complaint against the supervisor. But I noticed that when the defense attorney passed the paper exhibit up to the bench, the judge set it aside without examining it.

Things were looking good for the plaintiff's case.

The defense rested without calling Eddie Hough to the witness stand. I guessed that it was a corporate decision. Dixie Belle was afraid the store supervisor would say something under oath that might tie the employer's hands in the Title VII sexual harassment case.

We had them dead to rights. There was no way we could lose.

Judge Eckhardt prepared to give us his decision. I picked up a pen and held it poised over my legal pad, prepared to write down the amount of money damages we'd get when Eckhardt announced the judgment in our favor. I'd taken this case on a contingent-fee basis. Even with a win, I'd have to collect the judgment from the losing party.

The judge fixed his eyes on the defense table. "In the matter of Alicia Holmes versus Eddie Hough, the court finds in favor of the defendant," he said.

I wanted to cry out, *Defendant's verdict? No goddamn way. You've got to be kidding!*

Eddie Hough laughed out loud, slapped his attorney on the back, and called out his thanks to the judge as if he were in a barroom rather than a court of law.

Judge Eckhardt ignored him. He rose from the bench, but before he retired into chambers, he turned his focus onto me. "Stafford Lee Penney! The next time you appear in my court, you better be wearing shoes and socks on your feet. You hear me?"

I heard. I wanted to tell him that my footwear choice wasn't as foolish or misguided as his decision in this case, but my getting jailed for contempt of court wouldn't help my client. Wouldn't do me any good either. My throat was tight with anger, but I got the words out: "Yes, Your Honor."

"I'm serious, Counselor. If you don't, there's gonna be hell to pay."

I watched him exit into chambers. As the door swung shut behind him, Alicia Holmes said, "So that's it. We lost."

Her sister walked up to the counsel table. I watched the women exchange a knowing look. Rue turned to me. "You did a good job for Alicia. You took her case on, fought for her."

Wearing an expression of resignation, Alicia nodded in agreement. They were letting me off the hook, but it was too easy. I blamed myself.

"I should've anticipated Judge Eckhardt's pro-defense stance and taken a change of judge. He's got a grudge against me for a prior appearance at trial. Long story—it has nothing to do with you."

Rue gave me a disbelieving look. "Get real, Stafford Lee. His decision had everything to do with us. That judge picked a side. Obviously, he wasn't inclined to support the Black girl checking groceries at Dixie Belle." She turned to her sister. "It's not over, Alicia." Rue looked back at me for confirmation.

"Absolutely. We'll continue to push the Title Seven case against Dixie Belle. And we can appeal the court's decision in the battery case."

"Excellent," Rue said. "How soon can we file that appeal?"

I felt a surge of righteous energy for the first time in months. "As soon as I knock it out on my computer. Which I intend to do right after I get back to my office. If Alicia approves."

My client rewarded me with a genuine smile. "My sister was right about you. Let's do it."

CHAPTER 53

FRIDAY MORNING, the week after the Alicia Holmes battery lawsuit, I made another appearance in court. Following Judge Eckhardt's order, I wore both shoes and socks. I dug a pair of lace-up oxfords out of the back of my closet and left the flip-flops at home.

On that day, Judge Jane Ross presided. Mason told me the new judge, recently sworn in, was capable but also as tough as elephant hide. It was another bench trial. She would decide the case; there was no jury.

In this landlord/tenant case, I represented an elderly tenant who'd been evicted. I called my client, Cora Franklin, to the witness stand. After she was sworn in, she huddled in the chair, clutching a plastic packet of tissues.

I smiled, trying to buoy her confidence. "Mrs. Franklin, how long had you rented the property on Norton Road in Biloxi, Mississippi?"

"Seventeen years. We rented it from the owner when my husband, Dexter, worked in the canning factory." Her voice faltered when she added, "Dexter passed away four years ago, right before Easter."

"During the years of your tenancy, did you make it a practice to pay your rent on time, ma'am?"

My client nodded emphatically. "Yes, sir. My husband always paid it right at the first of the month. After he died, that's what I did too. Even when the new landlord took over last year and wasn't keeping the property up like he should have."

I cut a glance at the landlord, who was sitting with his attorney at the counsel table. He looked bored. "Mrs. Franklin, what did they fail to do with the upkeep of your house?"

"The plumbing in that old house has always been tricky, but my husband could keep it running. Dexter was handy, you know. When it broke down this year, I called the landlord, but I got no answer at the rental office, so I left messages."

"What did you tell the landlord in your messages?"

"I said that a pipe had busted. It flooded the whole basement with over a foot of water. That's when the faucets just quit on me, and after that, I didn't have running water anymore. And then the toilets quit working, wouldn't flush."

To drive home the point, I said, "Mrs. Franklin, are you telling the court that you had no running water in your home and that the toilets did not operate?"

"That's what I'm saying. I had to leave the house and go stay with my daughter. She drove me over to the landlord's office seven times, but no one there would talk to me."

"What did you do about the rent? Did you pay it after the pipe burst even though you had no running water and the toilets no longer worked?"

"I did that first month. But after weeks went by, I told them I wouldn't pay rent until they got the water working again."

I heard an audible snort from my opponent's table. I understood the message. Her failure to pay the rent was problematic, the thorny part of our case. From a tenant's perspective, Mississippi has the most oppressive landlord/tenant law in the country. Mrs. Franklin was obligated to pay that rent, regardless of the circumstances.

But there was more to my client's story. "When you withheld payment from the landlord on the first of the month, what occurred?"

She took a shuddering breath. "My daughter drove me to my doctor's appointment on the afternoon of the third, and when I got home, the landlord was changing the locks."

"What did you do?"

"I begged the man to let me in. I was out of my mind, crying and all. I told them, 'My heart medicine is in there, and the doctor says I have to take it twice a day. Pictures of my grandchildren and my dead husband. All my clothes and dishes and furniture, and my grandmother's cedar chest with the quilt she made for me and gave me on my wedding day.' When I tried to get through the door, a man shoved me away, and I fell."

"What happened to your belongings? Your personal property?"

"Landlord said they'd haul it off, sell what they could, and keep the money." Her voice broke at that point. "He laughed when he said it. Told me my pictures and 'that ratty old quilt' would end up in the landfill."

Cora was crying in earnest. She fumbled with the packet of tissues, pulled one out, and wiped her eyes with it.

When she regained a measure of control, I asked her to identify a series of enlarged photos depicting the overflowing toilets and the flooded basement. Prior to the lockout, her daughter had had the foresight to take pictures of the property conditions and get videos showing every dry faucet in the house. In the event that the landlord tried to claim under oath that the property was in tolerable condition, the pictures would support my client's case more eloquently than a slew of experts could.

The landlord's attorney, a smug bully who specialized in this kind of practice, launched a predictable attack in cross, accusing Cora Franklin of being a lazy, negligent tenant. By the time he concluded his attack, she'd used up almost all the tissues in the crumpled plastic packet.

Judge Ross declared a recess while she considered her decision.

Mrs. Franklin turned to me, wet eyes blinking behind the lenses of her glasses, and excused herself to go to the restroom.

Opposing counsel, Tony Phelps, sidled up to my table. "You had that old Black gal prepped to go, Stafford Lee. Boo-hoo! I haven't seen waterworks like that in a dog's age."

I met his eye. "In your line of work, Tony, I'd expect you bear witness to a lot of heartache."

The slumlord, his client, was listening. Over the past few years, Chad Owens had snapped up a lot of rental properties and he'd become notorious for neglecting them and abusing the system. "Hey, Penney," Owens said. "I know my rights. I can evict any tenant who doesn't pay rent. I'm not running a charity."

His attorney said, "Settle down, Chad." He turned back to me and chuckled. "Damn, Stafford Lee, you must be hard up, wasting your time on a losing proposition like this case."

It never occurred to Tony that I'd been so moved by my client's predicament that I'd decided trying to help her was worth a shot.

"You know the law, don't you? Landlords in Mississippi have the power to do self-help evictions."

He could be right. In Biloxi, the courts were historically pro-landlord. But Cora Franklin's situation was in line with recent case law that frowned on landlord seizure of tenant property in self-help evictions. A federal judge had declared it unconstitutional.

And I might have had a stroke of luck by landing in Judge Ross's court. The new judge with her stern demeanor didn't strike me as a member of the good ol' boys' club. During cross-examination, when the landlord's attorney wrung tears from my elderly client, I'd detected a glimmer of reaction in the judge's eyes.

Judge Ross returned to the bench, and I held my breath, hoping for a miracle.

She scratched an entry on the docket sheet. "The court finds in favor of Cora Franklin and against Laclede Property Management, LLC. And I'd like to tell you why, sir."

The judge looked down upon the landlord from the bench, and her expression was scary. "What you have done to Mrs. Franklin can only be regarded as an act of intentional cruelty, compounding your negligent and illegal management of the property."

The slumlord stammered, "Y-Your Honor—I have the right—"

"Hush your mouth, I'm talking. The evidence clearly shows that you violated your duty under state law to provide a dwelling that is habitable, and in this court's opinion, your failure to comply with your legal obligation was the impetus to everything that came after. In other words, sir, this is your own damn fault."

The landlord jumped up. "Your Honor, I have the right—"

"Sit down and listen," she ordered. She went on to award my client all the relief we'd requested, and then she kicked that landlord's ass all over the courtroom, telling him that if he didn't make things right with my client in short order, he would have to deal with her wrath.

I walked out of court that Friday afternoon feeling like I was ten feet tall. I would have liked to bask in the glow, relish the victory, but I didn't have the luxury. I had to go home and change into my lifeguard uniform; I was on call that day.

When I unlocked the front door, I was still riding that victory high. I felt so good, it took me a moment to realize that someone was in my house.

CHAPTER 54

I FROZE in the open doorway when I heard footsteps tramping across the bare hardwood floor of the main bedroom. (When I'd gotten out of rehab, I'd finally hired a team to clear out the signs of the carnage from my wife's murder, including the bloodstained rug.)

It would have been sensible for me to turn tail and run. Confronting an unknown intruder in a house notorious for murder was crazy. But the situation pushed a button in my brain, setting off a crazy response from me: This was my home. I was under my own goddamn roof. Nobody got to run me off.

So I crept into the house and headed to a guest room I'd been using. I still couldn't sleep in the bedroom I had shared with Carrie Ann. Too much tragedy in there, too many ghosts.

Propped in the corner of the guest room near the head of the bed was a bat, my old wooden Louisville Slugger. I gripped it with both hands and moved as noiselessly as I could down the hall. From the main bedroom, I heard the rustle of fabric. The idea of someone rummaging through Carrie Ann's closet made me see red.

I stepped into the room and raised the bat. I saw someone crouched down on the far side of the bed. I caught a glimpse of blue jeans. "Freeze!" I shouted.

With a shriek, the intruder jumped to her feet and wheeled around.

It was Jenny.

We stared at each other, both of us breathing hard. One of her hands clutched the loose fabric of her T-shirt. The other gripped an industrial tape measure. With her shoulders shaking, she said, "Jeez, Stafford Lee! You just scared ten years off my life!" She dropped onto the bed, gasping for breath.

"What the hell are you doing here?" I lowered the bat but kept gripping it hard. In my panic and fury, I was tempted to swing at something — the wall, the door, a window. I wanted to hear something shatter.

"Stafford Lee, I can explain," she said.

"Explain why it's all right for you to break into my home?"

"It wasn't technically a break-in," she said. "I have a key, you know."

"Damn it, I know you have a key — I gave it to you." My voice was too loud even to my own ears. I leaned against the doorframe, trying to get my emotions under control. "And my trusting you with a spare key doesn't give you the right to come and go at will. This space," I said, indicating the bedroom with a wave of the baseball bat, "this is forbidden territory for everyone."

She hopped off the bed. "Please, Stafford Lee, listen to me for a minute. Will you give me that, just one minute?"

I wanted her gone — out of the room and out of my house. But the look of entreaty she gave was hard to refuse. I rubbed my hand over my face and squeezed my eyes shut to block out the sight of the bed. "Make it brief. One minute, then you're out of here."

She started talking fast. "Stafford Lee, I'm still looking into Carrie Ann's murder. I know you don't want to be reminded, but honestly, Stafford Lee, it doesn't add up."

I studied the floor, searching for patience. How many times would I have to tell Jenny to drop the subject of Carrie Ann?

Relentlessly, she went on. "The police concluded that Gates intended to kill you as payback, to settle a grudge against you. They assumed that you were the target. According to the reports, he brought in two different weapons. He had a double-barreled shotgun that he used to commit the double murder, and then he switched to a handgun to commit suicide. Why? Doesn't that seem off to you?"

I didn't care why she thought it was off. Didn't want to hear it. But she was on a roll. "And the blood spatters. I think Detective Sweeney is overlooking something. It feels to me like the cops are mistaken about the killer's position, the spot where he stood when he shot Carrie Ann and the coach."

I couldn't bear to hear much more. She edged nearer. "But the biggest inconsistency: The police report says Benjamin Gates committed suicide by taking a gun in his right hand, sticking it in his mouth, and pulling the trigger. Just like this. And he fell to the floor and dropped the gun."

She made me watch her act it out. And then she dropped her hand and said, "I don't buy it. That's not how it happened."

Jenny put her hand on my arm; her eyes searched my face.

"I'm right-handed, Stafford Lee. Benjamin Gates was left-handed."

CHAPTER 55

I COULDN'T remain in that room any longer.

I shook off Jenny's hand, backed away, and bolted from the bedroom. She followed close behind me, making apologies. "Stafford Lee! I'm so, so sorry! Let's talk this through. Please?"

I went into the kitchen, walked over to the sink, and grasped the stainless-steel rim, wanting to hang on to something solid as I tried to regain control of myself.

"Stafford Lee? You going to be okay?"

I looked over at her. Jenny stood in the doorway, still clutching the tape measure. Sounding remorseful, she said, "God, I'm totally busted. I thought you'd be tied up in court today. It never occurred to me that you'd find me in that room."

"And that made it all right to sneak into my house? Because you thought I wouldn't be here?"

She grimaced. "I really needed to get back into that room and assess the crime scene in light of the new information I'd learned about Gates. You know the police aren't looking. They decided it was a murder/suicide, and that's as far as they'll go."

With a soft groan, she said, "Can you forgive me? I was wrong to invade your privacy."

I took some deep breaths. Getting out of that bedroom had

228

restored a measure of my sanity. I pushed away from the sink, moved over to the fridge, pulled the door open, and said, "I need a drink."

Jenny froze. "Shit," she whispered.

I took out a bottle of ice-cold Coca-Cola and held it up where Jenny could see it. "You want one?"

She gave a quick nod. As I rummaged through a kitchen drawer for a bottle opener, I remembered that I was on call for lifeguard duty. "I need to call my side hustle, see if I have to be at the beach."

I checked my phone and found a text notifying me that I wasn't needed for the afternoon shift. I tossed the phone onto the kitchen counter, popped the caps off the Cokes, and said, "Looks like I have a rare afternoon off."

We sat at the kitchen table and drank our Cokes straight from the bottle. After a bit, I settled down. I don't know whether it was due to the free afternoon or some magic in Coca-Cola's secret formula, but I started feeling human again.

I wanted to tell Jenny about my courtroom victory. It had been a while since I'd scored a win. I tipped back in the chair. "Did we ever talk about my landlord/tenant case? I represented a sweet little old lady against Laclede Property Management."

She took a sip from the cold bottle. "That's Chad Owens, right, the slumlord? Can't stand that guy."

"Yeah, the case went to trial today. We were David and Goliath."

Her face was eager. "Tell me! Were you victorious? Did David slay Goliath?"

When I gave her a wide grin, she reached out and clicked her bottle against mine. "Here's to seeing justice done! You're back, Stafford Lee! About damn time somebody reined Owens in. I'm so proud of you."

We raised our bottles to each other and swigged. Jenny set hers down and asked, in a tentative voice, "You still mad at me?"

"I'm over it. But I would appreciate advance notice next time you plan to burglarize my house."

"Yeah, I get that. Can I ask you about something else?"

"Sure," I said, but my guard went back up.

"We've never really talked about how the whole rehab thing went down. Mason and I dragged you off without any warning and against your will. Our intentions were good—you know that?"

"I do know that."

"And it all turned out for the best, right? But I can see how you might feel some resentment toward me. A little anger, deep down, for forcing the issue. I've wondered about that."

I shook my head, wishing I had cleared the air before she had to bring it up. "I'm grateful to you, Jenny. Not a bit resentful. You and Mason did me a tremendous service, getting me into rehab. Y'all saved me."

With a wave of her hand, she said, "Oh, hon. You saved yourself."

"You want to hear a confession?"

Her face tensed. "I knew it."

"Knew what?"

She looked down, lifted the glass bottle, and wiped a ring of condensation from the wooden tabletop. "You and that administrator. Amy. I knew she'd caught your eye. Did something happen between you in rehab?"

Damn, I hadn't seen that coming. Her statement shook a laugh out of me. The idea that I could've charmed Amy in my weeks in rehab was downright funny. "God, no. You're way off. I'm telling you this in the strictest confidence—it's about Caro."

She set an elbow on the table and put her chin in her hand. "Daniel Caro, right, your former client? Not Hiram, his father?"

"Yeah, Daniel. I've been thinking, Jenny, about all those suspicions that you harbored during trial. Maybe you were right. Maybe Caro is actually a predator."

I don't know exactly what response I'd anticipated from Jenny. But I had shocked her into silence.

I went on, trying to explain my turnaround. "I started chewing on it back in Louisiana, at Hope Springs. I had a whole lot of time to put the pieces together, think through things I'd been suppressing. For a year, I'd blotted out a lot of cognitive activity with alcohol. Maybe that's where the term *blotto* comes from."

Her face was thoughtful; I could see the wheels turning in her head. Quietly, she asked, "So what are you going to do?"

"I'm going to do some looking, just on my own. I've got an intern who's giving me a hand at the office."

"Intern? You're kidding! That's a hoot, Stafford Lee. Didn't you tell me that student interns weren't worth the trouble it took to explain what you wanted them to do? I'm pretty sure you said that."

Tapping the Coke bottle with my finger, I shook my head. "This woman is the exception. She's a natural advocate, has the magic. You want to meet her? She'll be in the office with me tomorrow, even though it's Saturday, if you feel like dropping by."

"Absolutely." Jenny drained the last of the Coke from her bottle and pushed the kitchen chair back. "Do I know her? What's her name?"

"Rue. Rue Holmes."

I followed Jenny to the front door. Just before she left, she turned, gave me a hug, and went up on tiptoe to kiss my cheek.

After I shut the door behind her, I wondered what to do next. It was Friday, and I certainly had no plans. Maybe I should have asked her to stay. Hang around for dinner. See what happened.

And then I decided that I must be crazy. Soft in the head. What woman wanted to jump into a relationship with a penniless lawyer fresh out of rehab who lived in a house haunted by his murdered wife?

CHAPTER 56

IN MY conference room the next day, I stood over the Mr. Coffee, waiting for the pot to fill. When it was halfway done, I lost patience with it and poured coffee into two chipped mugs, each bearing the logo of the Mississippi Bar Association.

"Rue!" I called. "Do you take anything in it?"

I couldn't make out her response, so I carried the mugs into the reception area and was pleased to see that Jenny had arrived. I handed a coffee to Rue and said, "Well, this is a real pleasure. Ladies, come on into my office and I'll introduce you."

Leading the way, Rue said, "We introduced ourselves already, while you were making coffee. Your coffeemaker is ancient. When your friend Mason came by the other day, he warned me not to operate it because of the risk of electrocution." Rue sat in one of the chairs across from my desk, lifted her mug, and said to Jenny, "You want some?"

"I've been cutting down on coffee lately. Makes me too wired." Jenny took the matching leather club chair next to Rue's and said, "So tell me, Rue. How do you like law school?" Clearly, the women had had a chance to become acquainted while I waited on the coffeemaker.

Rue grimaced. "First year was tough, I'm not gonna lie. The curriculum's hard, and the instructors are old-school. You have to prove yourself. I worried every day that the sky was gonna fall and I'd get thrown out. Now that I'm in my second year, it feels easier, like I finally belong there."

I gave her an empathetic nod. "It was like that for me up at Ole Miss. The faculty still used the Socratic method of teaching. First year was as much about survival as about torts and contracts."

"So are you doing an internship for law-school credit?" Jenny asked. "Is it part of your coursework?"

Rue shot me a grin. "No. I was a witness in my sister's case, saw what Stafford Lee did in court. I was impressed. I'm doing it for the experience." In an ironic tone, she added, "I'm certainly not here for the money. He doesn't have much of that."

"Wish I could afford to pay you what you're worth," I said.

My inability to pay was not a fiction. When Rue approached me about an internship, I'd been up front with her. I told her the unvarnished truth about my financial situation, my lost professional year, the stint in rehab. She surprised me by taking it in stride. She even volunteered to intern for free, but I couldn't permit that. So we struck a bargain: she needed a place to live, and I had a three-bedroom house not far from her law school. That was how I'd come to have a boarder in my home and an intern in my office.

Jenny said, "Rue, do you know anything about Daniel Caro?"

Rue set her coffee mug on the desk. "More than you'd think. I clean his house."

Jenny shook her head. "You're kidding me."

"No joke. I work part-time for Happy Maids, and Iris Caro books two of us every Wednesday. It's a big old place, one of those historic homes. Three stories of hardwood floors, and she wants them cleaned the old-fashioned way, so we have to wax them and buff them. Lord!"

Jenny looked over at me, then back at Rue. "Wow, Rue. You're in law school—that's a full-time job. *And* you have a part-time gig. And on top of that, you intern for Stafford Lee? When do you sleep?"

Rue just shrugged, but Jenny didn't let up. "I'm seriously impressed. What's your secret?"

Rue lifted the chipped mug. "Coffee. You should try it." She took another swallow.

I knew Rue's secret. Rue Holmes possessed incredible drive. Compared to her, I looked like a slacker.

It was time to pull Jenny into our current project. "Jenny, Rue and I have been analyzing the facts of those two cases we talked about last year, the murders of two of Daniel Caro's patients, Aurora Gates and Desiree Whitman. You recall the circumstances around the death of the second woman, don't you? Mason said you and he had a meeting with her husband. He was a deckhand on a shrimp boat."

Jenny gave Rue an inquiring look. "So you're familiar with those cases, Rue?"

"Oh, yeah. People in my community haven't forgotten Desiree and Aurora," Rue said. "Stafford Lee gave me reports. I took that information and made a chart."

Rue leaned over my desk, located a folder, pulled a document from it, and handed it to Jenny. "See how it lines up? Check out the personal characteristics of the victims. You can see that I share those characteristics too, right? So does my sister, Alicia. The chart also sets forth the details of the attacks. I know I'm not a forensic expert, but on the face of it, it looks like the same guy did both crimes." She shivered, although the office wasn't that cool. "It creeps me out to know I'm scrubbing down that dude's shower stall every week. Does that seem bizarre to y'all?"

I expected Jenny to devour the information contained in Rue's chart. After all, Jenny had been the first one to connect the deaths of Desiree Whitman and Aurora Gates. But she didn't even glance at the page; she just rested it on her knee.

Jenny said, "Here's something else that's bizarre. There is a third murder."

"What?" I was so shocked, I almost sputtered. I couldn't even frame a follow-up question.

She looked over and focused on me, her face tense, waiting to see how I'd react. "It's a cold case. I stumbled onto it almost by accident."

"Another patient of Caro's? In Biloxi or Gulfport? How did I miss that?" I could barely believe it. It was true that over the past year and a half, I'd been consumed with my personal loss and the subsequent fallout. But I'd still had access to the local press.

"Not a Caro patient. This particular murder happened about a decade ago. And it wasn't in Mississippi."

I didn't see the connection. Apparently, neither did Rue. She said, "So what's that got to do with Caro?"

At that point, Jenny looked down at Rue's chart. A moment later, she passed the paper back to her. "It's the MO that's distinctive. Every characteristic and element you've identified about the two women in Harrison County also appear in the unsolved case. Including the strangulation evidence. That's a signature. I think all three cases need to be evaluated together."

Rue picked up the chart she had meticulously created and tore the page in half. "Looks like we need to start over. What do you say, Stafford Lee? Are you in? Because I know I am."

"Sure," I said.

Rue's face was stony. "Whether it's Caro or somebody else, he's killing Black women, and law enforcement isn't catching it."

"I can't believe they've overlooked this pattern," Jenny said.

Rue's eyebrows rose. "Really? Doesn't surprise me at all."

CHAPTER 57

JENNY GLASER pulled into the nearly empty lot behind Boulevard Baptist Church in downtown Biloxi. A black Honda SUV was parked close to the back door.

The unlocked church building had the same deserted feeling as the lot; her footsteps echoed on the tile floor. She walked down the hall to an office where a man leaned against a tidy metal desk. Pastor Gates met her eyes with a smile.

"Good afternoon, Jenny. Thanks for coming by." He waved his arm at a doorway to a second, smaller office. "Come on in and have a seat."

Jenny settled into a chair that faced a desk; she observed that Pastor Gates locked the office door after shutting it. As he crossed the room, she said, "Wow. You weren't kidding when you said this would be a private meeting."

He looked somber as he sank into a worn leather chair. "I told the church secretary to take an extra hour for lunch today. I don't want anyone walking in on our conversation because I need your expert opinion as a private detective."

Jenny edged forward in her seat. "You've certainly got my attention, Pastor Gates."

An aged air-conditioning unit rattled the window at Gates's back, but when the preacher spoke, his voice drowned out the background noise. "I received some information in this week's mail. Sent to me here at the church office."

The statement sparked Jenny's curiosity. "Was it a letter?"

He regarded her speculatively, as if he was still trying to determine whether she was trustworthy. When the silence stretched out, she pressed him. "What did it contain?"

The preacher opened a desk drawer and pulled out a manila envelope. "There wasn't any letter, just pictures. Copies of pictures, that is."

"Who sent them?"

"I don't know." He handed her the envelope.

Someone had written *Personal and confidential* on it, and it had a Biloxi postmark. There was no return address. She gave the pastor an inquiring look. "May I open it?"

He nodded, and she slid the contents of the envelope onto the desk. The time-and-date-stamped photos were black-and-white stills that appeared to have been taken from a home-security camera. With a jolt, Jenny recognized the date: the day of the jury verdict in the Daniel Caro trial.

That night, Detective Sweeney had woken her with the news that Stafford Lee and Carrie Ann were dead.

He'd been only half right.

She bent over the first photo, which showed a residential street and part of a house. She pointed at the house and asked Gates, "You're aware that's Stafford Lee Penney's home?"

Soberly, he nodded. "You see that car? Parked on the same side of the street as your friend's house, closer to the camera?"

There were several vehicles in the shot. "Which one?"

"The SUV. You can't tell from the picture, but it's a gray 2014 Toyota. My cousin Benjamin's car."

She squinted at the fuzzy image. The home-security camera that had taken it was not sophisticated. "Are you sure, Pastor? How can you tell?"

"Because he's sitting inside it." Gates reached across the desk and pointed at a blurry figure in the driver's seat who arguably resembled Benjamin Gates.

"Okay, I see what you're looking at," Jenny said. "This places your cousin near Stafford Lee's house at an exact time and date. But why the secrecy, the anonymous delivery? This isn't explosive information. Pastor, you know your cousin was at Stafford Lee's house that night. He was found dead on the floor of the bedroom in the early hours of the next morning." She placed the print back on the desk. "This doesn't tell us anything new."

"Look closer." Gates gave her a heavy magnifying glass with a brass handle. "Look inside the car."

Feeling like a twenty-first-century Sherlock Holmes, Jenny bent over the picture and inspected it through the magnifying glass. "It's hard to make out any detail. What am I looking for?"

"I'd have thought your young eyes would be sharper than mine. Let's get more light in here." Gates snapped on a desk lamp and aimed it toward the photo. When the bright light fell on the page, the shadowy outline of another figure appeared in the car, a barely discernible profile of someone sitting in the passenger seat.

Jenny looked up. When she met Gates's eyes, he said, "Well, Jenny? What do you think?"

She said, "There are two people in the car."

Pastor Gates leaned back in his leather chair. His face was dour when he said, "That's what I think. Benjamin wasn't alone that night."

CHAPTER 58

ON A gray September afternoon, I sat in my lifeguard chair on the beach listening to the pounding waves and the cries of seagulls. Despite strong ocean currents, I'd had an easy shift so far. With school back in session, no kids were playing on my stretch of sand. Cloudy skies overhead had discouraged sun worshippers, and swimming wasn't allowed since I'd raised the red warning flag indicating dangerous surf conditions. A lone middle-aged woman wearing a white cover-up over her swimsuit picked her way along the water's edge.

The deserted beach signaled the end of high season. They would be laying off most of the lifeguards soon. I was ready to hang up my sunglasses and lifeguard whistle. My law practice had picked up in recent weeks, and it was becoming a challenge to set court appearances around my lifeguard schedule. It was time for me to focus on people's problems, to work on resolving their disputes.

But I would miss my time in the high beachside perch. There was something therapeutic about listening to the waves lapping the shore.

My reverie was interrupted by a voice. "Hey! Stafford Lee!"

My new intern ran across the sand and stopped directly in front of me. Looking up, she crossed her arms over her chest. "Why aren't you answering your cell phone?"

Wondering what I'd missed, I unearthed the phone from my backpack. "It's turned off. Rue, I don't sit up here and take calls. I'm on the job, protecting the people in the water."

She turned around and gazed at the deserted beach. When she looked back at me, she said in a wry voice, "Tough job, very important. Stafford Lee, there's not a soul out today."

I couldn't argue with that.

"Come down and talk to me. I don't want to shout over those screeching birds."

While I climbed down, Rue sat cross-legged on the sand and fanned herself with a file folder. As soon as I joined her, she said, "You never told me you turn off your phone when you come out here. When Jenny said she couldn't reach you, I was afraid you'd drowned or something."

I kept my eyes trained on the beach. "What was Jenny calling about?"

"She came across some evidence she wanted to show you. When she couldn't get you on the phone, she came by the house. She was lucky to catch me. I'd gotten back from class right before she rang the doorbell."

I was glad to hear that Jenny was using the doorbell rather than her house key. "What evidence?"

"Some photographs. I promised I'd run you down. Which I did." She handed the file folder to me and added, "You're welcome."

I opened the folder and found six photocopies of pictures depicting a familiar setting. I quickly shuffled through them. They had been taken near my house. There was a date in the corner. A date burned into my brain.

I shook off my emotions and went through the images again, studying each one.

Rue said, "Jenny wants you to pay attention to that close-up of the car."

I already was. Couldn't take my eyes off of it. The picture showed two people in the front seat of an SUV. I recognized the man on the driver's side. It was Benjamin Gates. Probably casing my house before he broke in.

I looked up and gazed out at the beach. Still deserted. "Where did she get these? They need to go to the Biloxi PD."

"Yeah, that's the weird thing. Jenny got the pictures from Pastor Gates, Benjamin Gates's cousin. Someone, he doesn't know who, mailed them to his church. He called Jenny, and she ran them straight over to the police department and showed them to the detective in charge. Sweeney, I think?"

"Right." I examined the pages again. You could see part of my house in one image. "So these are copies?"

"Yeah. She gave the original envelope of pictures to the detective, but she said he wasn't very psyched about it."

"Huh?" I looked up. "Why not?"

"He said it didn't provide any new information. He told her he'd add the pictures to his file. But it's a closed case, he said."

I fixed my eyes on the horizon as I considered Detective Sweeney's reaction to this evidence. A seagull flew overhead, screaming.

The middle-aged beach walker stretched out on one of the chairs and shrugged off her cover-up.

Rue said, "What do you think of the latest response from the Biloxi PD?"

"Dunno." Hearing that the Biloxi PD wasn't interested in new evidence hit me like a punch in the gut. The file folder I held started shaking in my hands.

I needed to subdue my resentment and get my shit together so I could unravel the meaning behind the evidence. I cleared my throat and said, "I'm pretty sure I can tell the source of these images. Looks like they came from Roland Shank's security camera."

"That's good." She waited. "You gonna call your neighbor?"

"I am. Just give me a minute."

"Okay." We sat on the sand in silence until Rue asked, "This neighbor a friend of yours?"

I looked down at my shaking hands. "Not particularly." But I pasted a tight smile on my face, grabbed my phone, searched through my contacts, and hit Shank's number. As I waited for him to pick up, Rue whispered, "Speaker!"

I hit the Speaker button right before he answered. "Stafford Lee? What's up?"

"Roland, I've called to ask a favor. I came across some photos that were taken on the night my wife was killed. The stills sure look like they're from a security system at your house."

The line went quiet for a moment. Then: "Yeah?"

"Yeah. I'd like to see the tape—if you still have it."

"Well, no. I don't have it, not anymore." He sounded genuinely confused.

I could feel my muscles tense up. "You sure?"

"We replaced that old system last year. Thought we needed more security, you know, after your wife was..."

He let the sentence trail off, unfinished. I quit trying to sound friendly. "I see."

Ironically, my house was still equipped with the same security system that had been there when we'd bought it years ago. No camera, just alarms on the doors. I was careful to set them before I went to sleep at night. But now that Rue and I both came and went, we didn't bother to set them in the daytime.

My neighbor spoke again, sounding defensive but not insincere: "But, Stafford Lee, the Biloxi police talked to everybody in the neighborhood. They came to our house the next day. I wasn't there, but my wife was. She showed them the tape, said they could have it."

I said, "Someone with the Biloxi PD took it?"

"That's what my wife said. Like I told you, I wasn't home."

There was no reason for Shank or his wife to lie. From what he'd said, Sweeney had had the tape for over a year. Rue and I exchanged a look of disbelief.

Roland said, "Sorry I can't help you."

After I ended the call, I sat there trying to process the information. If the police had the tape, they must have noticed that two people were in Gates's car that night. Why did they close the case? Why weren't they looking for a witness or a coconspirator? If Jenny was right about Benjamin Gates, did that mean that another person had committed the murders in my house?

The questions went off in my brain like gunshots while I stared out at the water. I watched as the lone woman left her chair and waded into the surf, ignoring the red warning flag that meant no swimming.

Rue broke the silence. "So if the tape from your neighbor's security system was in a closed police file, how did copies of those pictures make it to Benjamin Gates's cousin?"

I didn't respond; I was watching as the swimmer went farther from shore and encountered the current. Rue nudged me with her elbow. "Why have they closed your wife's file if the cops have a tape showing another person at the scene of the crime?"

I couldn't answer that. It didn't make any sense at all. But my student intern had a better grasp of the issues than the detective in charge of my wife's murder investigation.

That was a sobering thought.

The middle-aged swimmer was shoulder-deep in the ocean before she began to struggle. Though she wasn't far from the shore, she floundered as she fought the current.

I stood, grabbed the rescue buoy, ran across the sand, and dived into the surf.

Her face was twisted with panic as she tried to fight the rip current pulling her deeper into the waters of the Gulf. By the time I reached her, she was terrified, shrieking for help.

"I've got you!" I shouted. "Stay calm." I tried to hand over the rescue buoy, but instead of taking it, she grabbed my neck and clutched so tightly that she almost took me under.

Once I got her clinging to the buoy rather than my neck, we swam together, parallel to the beach. When the pull of the current eased, the waves began to push us toward the shore.

Back on the beach, she collapsed onto the sand and burst into tears, still clutching my hand. I knelt beside her while she recovered.

And people think that being a lifeguard is easy.

CHAPTER 59

A WEEK later, I sat at my desk, my fingers moving across the keyboard as I drafted pleadings for a new personal-injury case referred to me by Mason.

My office was quiet that day. Rue was in Gulfport attending her commercial law class. Jenny hadn't checked in with me that morning, but I hoped she'd stop by later. Mason was planning to come by after a docket call in Eckhardt's court. After Eckhardt's unconscionable ruling in Alicia Holmes's case, I'd filed motions for a change of judge in all my cases in his division.

My current client had sustained injuries in an auto accident. I was composing the final paragraph of the plaintiff's petition when a call came in on my office line, a landline phone sitting on the credenza behind my desk. The screen read **Caller Unknown**.

Too many scammers and unwelcome solicitations out there. If Unknown wanted to talk to me, he'd have to leave a message.

I was back on the computer when the office phone hummed to signal a new message. I wrapped up the plaintiff's petition for damages, saved it, hit Print. While the printer churned out the pages, I played the message on speaker. A male voice came on the line. It sounded robotic, as if it had been filtered through a voice-changer app: "Hey. This is for Stafford Lee Penney."

The voice paused. I waited for the caller to identify himself. But he didn't give a name.

The message continued. "It's not smart, digging into the stuff that went down at your house. You're lucky to be alive — you realize that, right?"

I pulled the chair up to the credenza and stared at the phone as the message played on.

"Just walk away, Counselor. You walked away once; shouldn't be hard to do it again."

I waited, listening, my complete attention focused on the phone. There was a long moment of silence and then a beep. The call had ended.

I was still trying to get my head around that message when I heard the front door open. Rue's voice rang out in the reception area: "Stafford Lee! It's me!"

"Back here," I called. She appeared in my doorway with her keys in hand, smiling. But when she saw my face, the smile vanished.

"What happened?" she asked. "Bad news?"

I shrugged, unwilling to describe what I felt. "I just got a message that I need to listen to again."

She hesitated. "You want me to leave?"

"No, stay. I'd like you to hear this."

Rue walked up beside me, and we both stood near the phone on the credenza as I replayed the message.

At the first words, Rue gave me a startled look and whispered, "There's an app for that."

Despite the robot trick, I'd hoped I might recognize the guy's voice when I heard it a second time. But I didn't.

When the caller said I was lucky to be alive, I heard Rue gasp. "What are you going to do?" she asked, clutching my arm.

"I'm not sure." It was true. I didn't know how seriously I should take it.

"It's a threat, Stafford Lee. You have to do something."

Privately, I agreed with her, but sounding chill, I said, "It's not an overt threat. There's no mention of violence or references to harm." But when I took a step back and considered it dispassionately, I realized that maybe Rue was right. I unplugged the phone, intending to take it over to the Biloxi PD and share it with Sweeney.

But what was Sweeney supposed to do about it? The caller's identity was a mystery, and his statements didn't rise to the level of a crime. Sweeney might think I was asking for consolation or emotional support. The last thing I needed was sympathy from the detective.

But the call had shaken me. From Rue's troubled expression, I could tell that she was worried too.

I wanted to calm her down, so I said, "Rue, I do understand if you have second thoughts about staying at my place. My security system is over fifteen years old. You might not feel safe there. I get that — it's a legitimate reaction."

Maybe she was already weighing the risks. She took her time before she answered. "I think I'll stick around. We're talking about my compensation — free housing. But I'm sleeping with one eye open."

CHAPTER 60

JENNY GLASER stayed up late, binge-watching a new series. When she started to nod off, she hit Pause on the television remote and fell asleep immediately.

When she awoke and saw pitch-black through the bedroom window, she checked the time on the nightstand. The digital clock read 2:34 a.m.

Huh. That's funny, she thought. *Two-three-four.* She lay in bed wondering what had awakened her. It wasn't a phone call or a bad dream. In fact, she had no recollection of dreaming at all. She didn't have to use the bathroom. Wasn't thirsty.

Then she heard the soft rattle that her back screen door made when it closed. It was followed by the thud of the wooden door and the click of the latch bolt against the lip of the brass strike plate.

She lay there, frozen. *I locked it, didn't I? Before I went to bed? I never forget to lock up.*

Of course she'd locked up. The noise the intruder made must have woken her.

The sound of footsteps in the house broke her paralysis. Jenny rolled out of bed, got down on her knees, and thrust her arm between the mattress and box spring. She kept a handgun for her protection, a Glock 19. And she knew how to use it.

But the firearm was shoved in too deep. She wasted costly seconds groping for it and only managed to graze the metal of the barrel with her fingers as the footsteps pounded into her bedroom. She barely caught a glimpse of the man who came through the door. He grabbed her around the waist and pulled her roughly to her feet and away from the bed. A second guy closed in on her. He was big, brawny, wearing jeans and a black hoodie. The hood was pulled over his head, and a cloth gaiter covered the bottom half of his face. He advanced on Jenny, muttering words that didn't register. She hiked her right leg up high, then shot it out, aiming directly for his crotch.

The kick connected, and he shrieked as he went down. The guy holding her loosened his grip on her left arm and shouted, "Shit! Fucking bitch!"

She wrenched her left arm free, pivoted her hips toward him, lifted an elbow, and, with all the force she could muster, struck him in the chin.

The blow must've surprised him; he let go. Jenny ran from the room, jumping over the intruder who lay curled up on the floor. She tore down the hall and headed to the front door, which was the nearest exit.

She'd just thrown the dead bolt when the guy she'd shaken off caught up to her. Her elbow strike hadn't incapacitated him. He grabbed her arm and jerked her around. His face was masked with a gaiter. He was huge, more than a head taller than Jenny. When he punched her the first time, she stayed on her feet, though she heard a bone in her nose crack. The second blow knocked her to the floor.

He cursed and gave her a vicious kick in her ribs. As she writhed on the rug, she saw the other man stumble into the room to join them. He was breathing hard.

The man who stood over her said to him, "You want a turn? Payback for kicking you in the nuts?"

The other man shook his head. The bigger one bent down, grabbed her arm, and jerked her up off the floor with such force that he dislocated her shoulder.

While he beat her, Jenny heard herself scream over and over until she passed out.

When she came to, she was sitting in the back seat of a car. The movement of the vehicle as it bumped over the road brought fresh agony to her dislocated shoulder, her ribs, and her head. She had to lock her jaw to keep from crying out.

The man riding beside her said, "Hey, she's awake. Should I knock her out again?"

The driver glanced at them in the rearview mirror, then shook his head.

She whimpered when the car slowed to a stop. The man riding in the back seat with her—the one who'd beaten and kicked her in her living room—opened the car door and dragged her out. After she made a pitiful attempt to resist, he carried her down a driveway and up the front steps of a house.

It was a house Jenny knew.

When she realized she'd been delivered to Stafford Lee's front porch, she was afraid to believe it. She thought she might be out of her head, hallucinating from trauma.

He dumped her on the doormat. When her injured shoulder hit the hard surface, she cried out.

The man pushed the doorbell more than once; she heard it ringing in the house. Right before he ran down the steps to the waiting car, he snarled, "Tell your buddy we said hello."

CHAPTER 61

IN THE middle of the night, my doorbell rang.

"The hell?" I sat up in bed, groggy. I hadn't imagined it; the bell rang again and then a third time. I'd just gotten out of bed when I heard a knock at my bedroom door.

Rue was out in the hall. "Did you hear that?" she said.

I pulled on jeans and a T-shirt. "Yeah. I'm up. I'll go check."

I grabbed the bat. I was thinking about the caller who'd left a message on my office line, wondering if he was trying to throw another scare in me. I gripped the wooden handle, determined to let him know exactly how I felt about the early-morning wake-up call. In my present mood, I was inclined to knock someone's head in.

Rue followed me as I stormed down the hall. When we reached the living room, I stopped abruptly. "You stay back, Rue. This has nothing to do with you."

She held up her cell phone. "Want me to call the cops?"

"No. This could be someone's stupid idea of a joke. You know my crazy friends."

Through the picture window over the couch, I saw a car back out of my driveway and speed away with its headlights off. I ran up to the window, trying to get a look at the license plate.

The car didn't have any plates.

Rue was at my shoulder, peering through the glass. "I guess that was your late-night door ringer. Looks like he moved on. We can go back to bed."

I pushed the buttons on the keypad by the door to disarm the alarm system. "You go on. I'd better take a look around, see if he did any damage."

I don't know what I expected to find. Something vandalized, maybe. When I pulled the door open, I almost stepped on her.

It was a woman. Laid out at my front door. Someone had beaten her badly. Her face was covered in blood; her hair was matted with it. I knelt beside her on the front porch, trying to figure out who she was and what she was doing on my doorstep.

Rue stood in the doorway, her hand over her mouth.

I said, "Rue, turn on the porch light!"

When the light came on, I couldn't believe it. Not Jenny.

Under the bright light, Jenny squeezed her eyes shut. She winced when I stroked the hair away from her face. Blood came from both her nostrils; it was smeared across her face, had spilled down her neck. Her clothes were stained with it. Her nose was broken, that was certain, but it didn't seem like that could be the source of so much blood. And then I found the head injury. I ripped off my T-shirt and pressed it firmly against the wound.

She was barely conscious, but I needed information. I grasped her arm. When I shook it, her eyes opened wide and she let out a ragged scream.

Rue was shouting into her phone. "A woman's been attacked, she's bleeding! We need an ambulance!"

Jenny's lips moved. I bent my head close to hear her.

"My shoulder."

My hand moved to her shoulder. This time, I barely grazed it with my fingers. I could tell what the problem was. Someone had wrenched her arm so violently that he'd dislocated her shoulder. Rage made my head pound, but I held my anger back. Jenny needed my help, not my fury.

Rue's voice was loud in the doorway. "I don't know who attacked her! Somebody dumped the woman on the front porch!"

Jenny was making unintelligible sounds, trying to communicate something. Her face became frantic, and she turned her head back and forth.

I wanted to hold her, give her comfort, but I was afraid to do anything that would cause her more pain. If I made any move that hurt her, it would gut me. So I just clasped her hand, not too tightly, and said, trying to sound reassuring, "We've got an ambulance coming, Jenny. We're gonna get you to the hospital. You're gonna be fine."

Her head stopped moving, and she made eye contact with me. I wasn't certain if she could understand what I was saying, but I had to know. "Who did this to you?"

She shook her head once but didn't respond otherwise. I shouldn't have pressed her, but I needed to, because I wanted to find him.

Then take the baseball bat and beat the shit out of him.

"Tell me," I whispered. As I waited for a name, one thought ran through my head: *Anyone who'd do this to Jenny ought to be dead.*

She finally said, in a broken voice, "I don't know."

After that, she began crying in great, gasping sobs. Kneeling beside her, I felt so helpless, I wanted to howl myself. There was nothing I could do to relieve her suffering.

I shouted into the house, "Rue! Where are the EMTs?"

"They're coming!" she called back.

With an effort, I lowered my voice and said, "Hear that, Jenny? They're on their way." I tried to sound calm, upbeat. Like I wasn't about to fly apart.

Jenny blinked as she looked up at me. "How long?" she whispered.

At that point, I'd gladly have let someone dislocate my own shoulder in exchange for the sound of a siren nearing the house. But the night was almost silent. I could just make out the distant rumble of traffic from the highway.

So I lied. I smoothed her hair away from her face and said, "I hear the ambulance. Not much longer now. Everything's gonna be all right, Jenny, I promise. You'll be fine."

CHAPTER 62

WHEN I walked into my house just before noon, I was beat. I'd pulled an all-nighter at the hospital, pacing the waiting room while I waited for news about Jenny.

Rue called from the kitchen, "Stafford Lee! You want coffee? There's half a pot left."

It sounded good. I trudged in and pulled a mug out of the cabinet. Rue sat at the kitchen table wearing her white housekeeping uniform. Her hands were wrapped around her own coffee cup. Looking worried, she asked, "So she's going to be all right?"

I dropped into the chair beside her and nodded. "They got her shoulder back in its socket, and they don't think she'll need surgery on it. Sewed up her head."

Her eyes widened. "Wow."

"They did a CT scan to make sure she didn't have any bleeding or bruising in her brain, but I don't know what the results were."

"So they're keeping her in the hospital?"

"They'll keep her overnight. I'll go back this afternoon. Visiting hours start at three o'clock."

Rue went to the coffeemaker to refill her mug. Leaning against the counter, she said, "I've been thinking."

I rubbed my eyes; they burned from sleeplessness. "Yeah? What about?"

"It wasn't Dr. Caro who broke into her house."

I slid down in my chair so I could rest my feet in the opposite seat. "I agree. He didn't."

"Right? She'd know him, even in the dark, because she put in a lot of hours on the trial prep, was at meetings with him at your office. Was Jenny able to tell you who did that to her?"

The question sent a stabbing pain through my head. "The police took her statement. There were two men, wearing cloth gaiters over their faces. One of them had a hood over his head. She didn't recognize them, didn't know the voice of the man who did all the talking. But if one of them had been Caro, Jenny would certainly have known."

Rue took a sip from her mug. "We've been working on this project with the cold cases. Talking to people, including the police. You know how news travels in this town." She paused. When I didn't respond, she continued. "Out of nowhere, you got that crazy message at your office telling you not to dig into stuff, to walk away. And then they went after Jenny, and when they were done, those men brought her to your house. So we've got to figure the attack on Jenny must have something to do with you."

When she spoke those words, I gripped the handle of the mug so tightly that it broke off. As I dropped the shard of pottery on the kitchen table, Rue said, "Stafford Lee? Are you okay?"

I couldn't meet her eyes; I was too busy wrestling with the guilt that had worn me down over the past nine hours. "The attack had to be related to me. The cops asked me about it at the hospital."

"What did they say?"

"The last thing the thug said to Jenny after he dumped her on my porch, she told the cops, was something like 'Tell your buddy we said hello.'"

Rue turned away from me, so I couldn't read her reaction. Briskly, she washed her mug with a soapy rag and set it upside down in the dish drainer. She stayed silent as she dried her hands with a kitchen towel. We needed to address the elephant in the room, the clear possibility that associating with me was hazardous to people's health. I said, "Rue, did you ever hear that Caro's father has Mob connections? That he was part of the Dixie Mafia?"

She finally turned my way and gave me a weary look. "On my side of Biloxi, everybody knows what Hiram Caro's capable of. And he has an army of thugs who follow his orders."

"You need to consider that. For your own safety." I'd thought about that all night after I'd heard about the message they'd delivered to Jenny. It made sense that the old man was behind it. He had access to the manpower, the kind of criminals who dealt in brutal intimidation tactics.

"I'll be keeping that in mind, I promise you that," she said.

Rue was smart. She understood the danger inherent in working with me, living in my house. She might start packing up her stuff. Anyone else would have. I should've insisted on it.

But she just said, "I need to head out now. If I'm late, she docks my pay."

The words set off an alarm in my head. "Where are you going? Who are you supposed to work for today?"

She grabbed her bag. "There's no point in fussing about it."

I followed her out of the kitchen. "Rue! You can't go to Caro's house, not today."

She slung the bag over her shoulder and strode to the front door. "Get real. It's my job, Stafford Lee."

"Call in sick." When she kept on walking, I pulled my phone from my pocket. "Hey, I'll do it for you. I'll call the agency, tell them you're running a fever, and you can't come to work, you don't want anyone to catch it."

She pulled the front door open. "I never get sick."

"Rue, please, just listen to me. You can't risk further association with the Caros. You're a target, you understand? You fit the profile."

She sighed and turned around, her car keys held firmly in her hand. "Forget it. Just stop."

"You saw what they did to Jenny. You're not immune, Rue. People know you're working in my office, living in my house. There's already courthouse gossip. People are speculating that we're romantically involved. If the women associated with me are being attacked, it's probably best if you distance yourself from me, at least for a while."

Her face was stony. "I don't think you understand my situation — probably because you can't relate to it. I have to go clean that house. If I don't work, I can't pay my tuition, make my car payments. And don't even think about backing out on our internship-for-rent deal."

Without looking back, she ran down the front steps and out to her car. I wanted to follow, but despite all my years in the courtroom, I couldn't find a way to rebut the argument she'd made. Because she was right — I'd never walked in her shoes.

So I watched her drive off. And then I shut the front door and wandered over to the couch.

I figured I'd sleep, but I couldn't drift off. Every time I closed my eyes, I thought of Hiram Caro.

CHAPTER 63

I DIDN'T even change clothes before I headed out.

When I parked at the front door of Hiram Caro's casino, I was wearing the same blood-spattered jeans I'd worn overnight at the hospital. The young valet gave me a leery glance. I held up a hand because I wasn't inclined to argue with him. "I'm leaving the car right here. This won't take long."

I drew startled stares from onlookers as I jogged down the brightly flowered carpet, passing the casino entrance and the hotel check-in. I didn't stop until I reached the business offices. And when I pushed the door open and the receptionist stammered out a greeting, I didn't pause to inquire if Hiram was in or if he was available. She left her desk and followed me down the hallway.

"Mr. Penney? Can I assist you?"

She couldn't.

I didn't knock on the door of Caro's office; I just turned the knob and shoved open the door.

The office offered a floor-to-ceiling view of the hotel pool and, beyond that, the Gulf Coast. But Caro's seat didn't take advantage of the view; his desk faced a wall of screens displaying live footage of the activity on the casino floor.

The old man sat all alone in there at his massive wooden desk.

That surprised me. I was prepared to find him flanked by security goons and bodyguards. I couldn't recall the last time I'd seen him without Joey Roman at his elbow.

"Who let you in here?" he asked.

He didn't appear to be flustered by my unannounced appearance, not that I could see. His hand was steady as he tapped his cigarette ash into an ashtray, a large brass replica of a roulette wheel. FABULOUS LAS VEGAS was embossed around the metal rim.

I said, "Nobody let me in."

I took a seat in front of the desk as his receptionist poked her head into the office. "Mr. Caro, I'm so sorry!"

"Shut the door," he said without glancing in her direction.

She closed it with a quiet click, and I said, "Last night, my investigator's home was broken into. Two men attacked her."

His face didn't betray any reaction. "That's too bad."

"You're right, it is. That's some cowardly bullshit, striking out at me by beating up a woman who works for me." It was an intentional choice, characterizing my relationship with Jenny as strictly business. Revealing the depth of our friendship would make her more vulnerable, and she was already in jeopardy.

Caro said, "I can't disagree with that."

Grasping the arms of the chair, I leaned toward the old man. "Don't try to play me, Caro. I know you unleashed your hired thugs on Jenny Glaser last night."

"You're crazy. This is the first I've heard about it." He stubbed his cigarette out in the center of the roulette wheel.

"I think you're lying."

His face broke into a grin. "That's funny, Penney."

"What the hell's funny about it?"

"That you came over here because you actually believe I give a shit about what you think. Want to hear the goddamn truth?"

I wanted to take the metal ashtray and use it to smash his face, crush his nose, pay him back for what his thugs had done to Jenny. But I remained in the chair.

He went on. "I'm not interested in you or your friends. And I don't care what you think I've done to your friends." Caro's eyes strayed to the closed-circuit television screens filming the casino floor. Then he returned his attention to me and placed his hand on the receiver of the telephone that sat on his desk.

"The only reason you're still sitting in that chair is that I respect what you did for my son. If I wanted you gone, all I'd have to do is pick up this phone. But you know that."

It was true. I was keenly aware that with one word from Caro, I would be planted at the bottom of a dumpster filled with oyster shells.

"But my son might not like that. He's high-minded. Daniel wouldn't be comfortable with his defense attorney getting rough treatment at a Caro casino. Daniel's delicate about things like that. He's always been sensitive. That's what makes him such a good doctor."

He spoke the word *doctor* with obvious relish. He picked up a pack of cigarettes and shook one out. He lit it, exhaled the smoke, and said, "My son is still trying to get past the turmoil and scandal that the Gates girl created in his life. Here's what I recommend. I suggest that you and your investigator leave my son alone. He was found not guilty. There's no reason for Daniel to continue to be tormented by that trial."

I was about to ask him what he meant—it sounded like he was aware that I was looking into the events surrounding the trial—but at that point, he picked up the phone and said, "Opal, send security in." After he hung up, he said, "You ought to quit thinking about Daniel altogether, start straightening up your own mess. Look at you. Law practice shot to hell, you're a middle-aged man with a part-time job on the beach. Everyone knows you're a drunk."

There was no point in arguing with him. No opportunity either. The door opened, and two men in matching black security uniforms appeared. As they escorted me out of the office, Caro took one last shot.

"If you're sober, you can give me a call next spring. We hire lifeguards to sit by the casino pool from May to September."

CHAPTER 64

IF HIRAM CARO thought his abuse would discourage me, he was wrong.

I was determined to keep digging until I found the person responsible for the attack on Jenny. But at that moment, I had to head home. I needed a shower and a change of clothes. I could grab an hour of sleep, and when I woke up, I hoped I would be sharp again. Then I'd go back to the hospital, talk to Jenny, piece the puzzle together.

I got into my Prius, still parked at the front door of the casino, and drove off through town. My empty stomach growled. I considered pulling into a drive-through to get a burger.

As I scanned the fast-food options, I passed Daniel Caro's ob-gyn clinic.

"Son of a bitch," I said aloud.

On impulse, I made a U-turn and drove into the clinic parking lot. Scaring pregnant women wasn't my style, but I was itching to bust through the doors and confront Caro in his office. Then I saw that his personal parking spot—marked DANIEL CARO, MD—was empty.

The digital clock on the dash read 1:30 p.m. Caro was probably eating lunch somewhere. I was still debating what to do when he pulled his Bentley into his designated parking space.

I was out of my car in a flash, and I trotted up to the Bentley just as he exited. I heard the beep as he locked it with the fob, saw his taillights blink. When he saw me approaching, he recoiled and grabbed the handle of the car door as if he was going to get back in and drive away. Then he changed his mind, apparently, and took off at a run to the clinic entrance.

But I beat him there. Leaning against the glass, I said, "Hey, Daniel. We need to talk."

His face was flushed. "If you need to speak with me, call my office for an appointment."

"I want to talk right now."

"That won't be possible. I have to get inside; I have patients waiting."

He grabbed for the door handle, but I blocked him. "What I have to say won't take long. Jenny Glaser was attacked last night. Two men broke into her home."

His eyes blinked behind his glasses. "Jenny who?"

The anger surged in my chest, making me blurt out words without weighing them first. "You despicable shit—you know exactly who Jenny is. She was the investigator who helped keep your worthless ass out of prison." I grabbed the lapels of his coat and jerked him toward me. "It was you, wasn't it?"

"Me? Break into someone's home like a common burglar?" He let out a high-pitched laugh; it sounded almost like a giggle. "Are you insane?"

"You engineered it. Didn't you?"

"Oh, please." He rolled his eyes like a teenage punk. The eyeroll pushed me over the edge. I thought of Jenny beaten and bloody on my doorstep.

I grabbed his throat and squeezed. "Don't bullshit me. I know what you're capable of doing. I'm your lawyer, remember?" He struggled, but I tightened my grip. "There's evidence. You know that?"

"I was acquitted!" When he croaked out the words, spit sprayed in my face.

I wiped my chin on my sleeve. "I'm not talking about Aurora Gates. You've got double-jeopardy protection on her. I'm talking about other women. What about your patient Desiree Whitman? Let's talk about her."

His mouth dropped open. Then he broke free from my hold and pounded the window beside the door with his fist. "Brenda!" he cried. "Let me in!"

I gave him a shove, and he stumbled. I said, "Jesus. That's typical, screaming for your office help to come to your rescue. Telling some woman to save your ass."

I stepped out of his way. He grabbed the door handle, staggered inside, closed the door, and turned the lock. Once he was safe, he shouted at me: "You're crazy. All that drinking affected your brain."

I could see a cluster of women sitting in the waiting room. They were staring at me through the glass, looking frightened. I was forcibly reminded of my appearance, my bloody clothes and uncombed hair.

Those women had it backward. They had nothing to fear from me. Their physician, though? He was a suspicious character. They needed to watch out for him.

CHAPTER 65

A COUPLE of days later, I sat at my desk scouring the internet for unsolved murder cases around the Gulf Coast. If another patient of Daniel Caro had suffered a mysterious death, I was determined to find her. I would be on it like a bloodhound.

Mason came into the office and pulled up a seat. "How's she getting along?" he asked.

I looked up from the monitor. "They discharged her. She's recovering at home."

He looked relieved. "Hey, does she need any help? Running errands or something?"

"I did a Target run for her yesterday, but you never know. Why don't you give her a call? I know she'd be glad to hear from you."

He shifted in the chair like he couldn't get comfortable. "It's hard to know what to say in a situation like this. I wish there were somebody I could sue on her behalf. Or even take outside for a rumble, although fistfights aren't my strong suit."

I got a call on my cell phone. I checked the screen: **Harrison County Jail**. Without hesitation, I picked it up. I was back in the law business. "This is Stafford Lee Penney."

"Stafford Lee? It's Rue. I'm in trouble."

It didn't sound like Rue. The voice on the line was high-pitched and shaky. "Rue, tell me what's going on."

"I'm in custody. The Biloxi police picked me up at your house. I wanted to call or leave you a note, but they wouldn't let me."

I couldn't believe what I was hearing. "The police came out and arrested you? Did they have a warrant?"

"Yeah, they did. I demanded to see it. It said I was under arrest for larceny."

"What?" It had to be a mistake. Maybe a store employee had made a false accusation.

Her voice dropped to a frightened whisper. "Grand larceny."

That stunned me. It meant that this was no trifling matter, no misunderstanding at the grocery store's checkout counter. In Mississippi, grand larceny is taking personal property valued at five hundred dollars or more. It's a felony, punishable by imprisonment for up to ten years or a fine of up to ten thousand dollars. Or both.

Mason waved his hand to get my attention. "What? What's going on?"

I set the phone on the desk and put it on speaker. "Rue, Mason is here. We are both on the line now. Is that okay?"

"Yes," she said.

"What are you accused of taking?"

"A necklace. A diamond pendant necklace," she said, her voice breaking. "I don't even know what she's talking about. I didn't go through her jewelry. I've never touched it."

"Where's the accusation coming from? Whose jewelry?"

"Iris Caro's."

I met Mason's eye across the desk. It was starting to make sense in a perverse, underhanded way. It was opportune timing for the accusation, less than forty-eight hours after my confrontation with Daniel Caro at his office. Or maybe the move had been triggered by my conversation at the casino with the old man.

Rue said, "Stafford Lee? They're asking if I qualify for a public defender. What do I say?"

That was easy to resolve. "Tell them no, Rue. In fact, you tell them hell no. You have counsel."

I heard an audible sigh of relief on her end of the phone. She said, "They told me they're bringing me before the judge this afternoon for a first appearance on the felony charge."

"I'll be there," I said.

Mason leaned over and spoke into the phone. "Me too, Rue."

"Hear that, Rue? You'll have two lawyers defending you. Don't worry, we've got this. Okay?"

When she didn't answer, I repeated, "Okay, Rue?"

"Okay. I know we'll get this straightened out. See you this afternoon."

I was glad to hear her sound confident again, even if it was just for show.

After I hung up, Mason swore a blue streak and said, "Why's Caro throwing your intern in jail? Hell, that man had a narrow escape from incarceration last year. Why is he so eager to see someone else locked up?"

It was on me; I was sure of that. "I've made the Caro family unhappy. The timing of the attack on Jenny, and now this accusation against Rue—it's payback or a warning."

Mason pulled out his phone and called the clerk's office. He said, "Hey, Reagan. I've got a client in jail, a woman named Rue Holmes. They're bringing her over for a first appearance today. What time do I need to be there?"

He listened, nodding. "Thanks. See you then." He hung up and said, "They're bringing her in for arraignment in an hour. I'll meet you over there."

After Mason left, I checked a coat tree that stood in the corner, where I kept a couple of emergency wardrobe items: a tie and a navy sport coat. I hadn't dressed for court that morning. I'd come to the office in jeans and an old button-down oxford that was frayed at the collar.

I pulled the tie off the coat tree, slid it under my collar, and tied a double Windsor knot. Then I slipped on the jacket and stepped into the office restroom to inspect myself in the mirror.

It had been a long time since I'd worn these items. The red tie had a visible grease spot, and scrubbing at it with a paper towel didn't make it disappear. And the jacket, which had hung on the rack for over a year, looked like it was long overdue for a trip to the dry cleaner. While unsuccessfully trying to tug the jacket sleeves straight, I noticed that the cuffs of my shirt were frayed too.

I frowned at my reflection. Rue deserved better.

CHAPTER 66

WE HAD a stroke of good luck.

The clerk informed me that Rue's case had landed in Judge Ross's court. Ross was the judge who had handed me a victory in my recent landlord/tenant lawsuit. If I could have, I would've brought every client I had in front of her.

Mason was already in the courtroom, talking to Charlene, the bailiff. When I walked in, they turned to stare. I headed down the aisle, and Charlene gave an ear-piercing wolf whistle.

She called, "Just look at you, Stafford Lee! You getting your picture made today?"

Charlene's reaction was over the top, but I had cleaned up. I'd decided against appearing in court wearing a soiled tie and wrinkled jacket and headed home for a wardrobe change.

Mason squinted as I joined him at the counsel table. "The spit shine on those shoes is so bright, you're blinding me."

"Shut up."

Charlene sidled over and gave me an admiring glance. "New suit?"

"Nope. Just haven't worn it in a while." I'd found the three-piece suit hanging in a bag at the back of my closet. The charcoal wool wasn't ideal for the heat of September, but it was clean and pressed and had a sharp crease down each pants leg.

Mason nudged me. "Looks like you've taken Judge Eckhardt's advice. I heard him bitching about your casual courtroom attire."

The door to chambers opened. Judge Ross leaned out and said to Charlene, "Are we ready to handle the afternoon arraignments?"

"I'll bring them in, Judge."

Charlene hustled out the side door that led to the holding cell. A minute later, the bailiff reappeared leading a short line of inmates.

Rue was among them, dressed in orange jailhouse scrubs. After the defendants were seated, I stepped over to speak to her. "Rue, how are you holding up?"

She raised her chin with a shadow of her usual confidence. "About like you'd expect."

The bailiff called out, "All rise!" and I returned to the counsel table. When Judge Ross took her seat at the bench, she looked down to where I sat with Mason.

"Gentlemen, on whose behalf are you appearing this afternoon?"

I said, "Your Honor, Mason Burnett and I are appearing on behalf of Rue Holmes. She's here on a first appearance."

The judge sorted through her files, pulled one out, and opened it. "Grand larceny?"

"Yes, Your Honor."

"Bailiff, escort Ms. Holmes to the counsel table."

Rue's hands were cuffed. When she joined us at the table, I whispered to the bailiff, "Lose the cuffs, Charlene." She hesitated. In a low voice, I said, "They're unnecessary. I swear."

With a worried wrinkle over the bridge of her nose, Charlene took a key from her belt and unlocked the restraints. Rue sat down between Mason and me, rubbing her wrists.

Judge Ross said, "Let the record show that defendant Rue Holmes appears in person and with counsel, Stafford Lee Penney and Mason Burnett. Ms. Holmes, you're charged with one count of grand larceny. Shall I read the charge aloud to you?"

Rue spoke up in a firm voice. "I'm innocent, Your Honor."

I placed my hand on her shoulder. "Judge, defendant waives formal reading of the complaint and enters a plea of not guilty."

Judge Ross nodded. "I'm setting the case for preliminary hearing on October ninth, two weeks from today."

"Yes, Your Honor."

She glanced down at the file. "The district attorney's office has recommended that bail be set at ten thousand dollars."

Rue gasped and looked at me with alarm. "I can't raise that, I don't have it," she whispered.

Mason stood and said, "We request that Ms. Holmes be released on her own recognizance, Your Honor."

The judge folded her hands on the bench. "Tell me why you believe that would be appropriate in this instance."

I stepped away from the counsel table and approached the bench. "Rue Holmes is a lifelong resident of Biloxi, a model citizen with a spotless record. She's an honors graduate of Mississippi State University, currently enrolled in law school in Gulfport. She maintains employment in Biloxi, resides in Biloxi, and works as an intern in my law office. She's no flight risk, Your Honor. And she certainly poses no danger to this community."

The judge listened closely, nodding as I spoke. "Ms. Holmes, I'm releasing you on your own recognizance. You understand that with an ROR, you're obligated to show up for your scheduled court appearances, and you're assuring the court that you will not engage in any illegal activity."

Rue expelled a deep breath and said, "Yes, Your Honor. I understand."

Judge Ross picked up her pen and made notations on the file. I said to Rue, "They'll process some paperwork, but it won't take long. I'll wait for you at the jail."

In a fierce whisper, she said, "Stafford Lee, it's a false accusation. I didn't do it."

"You think I don't know that?"

CHAPTER 67

ON MONDAY afternoon, Jenny was holding down the fort at Stafford Lee's office.

He'd headed off to Gulfport with Rue. News of her felony charge had quickly spread on campus, so Stafford Lee arranged an afternoon meeting with the dean of her law school, hoping to allay the dean's fears and convince him that the charge was bogus, the underlying allegation unfounded.

Jenny sat in a chair in the reception area, balancing an open file on her knee. Stafford Lee had used his powers of persuasion to convince the DA's office to provide early disclosure of the evidence against Rue. Jenny bent her head over the police reports, carefully reviewing them.

At several points, Jenny snorted with disgust. The investigation was flimsy. The cop's report was filled with conjecture. No convincing evidence connected Rue to the disappearance of the pendant. It was the very weakest kind of circumstantial case.

Jenny flipped through the pages looking for Iris Caro's witness statement. While she hunted, the file almost slipped off her lap. Her injured arm was in a sling. The doctors said she'd have to wear it for at least two more weeks, to keep her shoulder in place and prevent further injury. Jenny hadn't realized how difficult it was to get things done one-handed. Even the simplest tasks posed a challenge.

She found Iris's statement at the very end of the report. Mrs. Caro had pointed the finger of accusation directly at Rue: "I keep my jewelry inside a velvet box in my dressing room, just off the main bedroom. Rue Holmes cleans the second floor of the house; she's the only person with access to those rooms."

Jenny muttered, "What about your lousy husband? He goes up there, doesn't he? Maybe he gave your diamond to a new girlfriend."

In the statement, Iris Caro recounted a conversation she'd allegedly had with Rue on an occasion when Iris was wearing the necklace. "The maid kept going on about it. She wanted to know whether it was real, commented on how big the stone was, asked how much something like that cost. I distinctly remember the conversation because it made me uncomfortable."

Jenny knew that Rue had no recollection of the conversation. Rue had said she rarely had occasion to talk to Mrs. Caro, because Iris didn't hang around the house when they cleaned. She'd go out — shopping, lunch, errands. Rue speculated that someone else had complimented the necklace, maybe another employee from the housekeeping agency. Her coworkers included several young women of color, and Rue suspected that whoever it was, Iris confused that woman with Rue. "Mrs. Caro's the kind of person who can't tell us apart," Rue had said.

Jenny was reading through the statement a second time when the front door opened and two uniformed officers walked in.

Jenny knew one of the cops, Terry Horton. She'd done some work for Horton's ex-wife in their divorce, found out about his extramarital activities.

Officer Horton remembered Jenny too, she could tell. His eyes flickered down to her sling and back up to her face.

It took some getting used to, being seen in public with her face in this condition. Her nose was swollen, and she had two black eyes. Other bruises on her face were starting to change color.

Jenny didn't intend to discuss her injuries with Horton. "Officers, what can I do for you?"

"We're not here to see you."

She almost laughed. Officer Horton was downright rude. But that was no surprise, given what she'd learned about him during the divorce. "Stafford Lee's not here right now. Do you want me to give him a message?"

"We're looking for Rue Holmes. Is she on the premises?" Horton demanded. He put his hand on his duty belt like he intended to use one of the items it carried.

Jenny's gut prickled a warning. "What do you want with her?"

"We have some questions."

Her indignation mounted as he strode through the office looking around as if he thought Rue might be hiding under a piece of furniture. When he opened the door to Stafford Lee's private office and peered inside, she said, letting the sarcasm drip, "Is Iris Caro missing more of her precious jewelry? Maybe a diamond tiara this time?"

Officer Horton came to a dead stop, then turned slowly to face Jenny. "You think that's funny? You're speaking ill of the dead. Iris Caro has been murdered in her home."

CHAPTER 68

AS I drove through Gulfport on Monday, I thought about the rocky weekend my friends and I had had.

After Rue's arraignment before Judge Ross, Mason had volunteered to contact Iris and try to reason with her. He drove to the Caros' house on Saturday. Unfortunately, Daniel Caro met him at the door and shut the conversation down.

On Sunday, Rue tried and failed to get in touch with her boss at the housekeeping agency. Rue was right to be concerned that she'd be terminated. In Mississippi, an employment-at-will state, an employer can fire a worker for any reason or for no reason as long as it doesn't violate an employment discrimination statute.

By Monday morning, Rue was determined to find a way to save her job and her academic standing. She was going to go to the agency and talk to the manager, then meet me at the dean's office.

I had some court settings that day, but I made it to the dean's office just before four o'clock. On the surface, it was a reasonably successful meeting. Rue vowed that she was innocent, speaking with the utmost sincerity. She didn't hedge, never faltered, and maintained eye contact with the dean throughout the conference. And I made my case on her behalf. After assuring the dean that the accusation was false, I promised that we'd get it sorted out. I wasn't bullshitting him. There was no way the larceny charge would stick because Rue hadn't done anything wrong.

The dean, a lanky silver-haired academic, nodded politely as he listened to what we had to say. He'd graduated from law school with honors, and under his diploma, on the credenza, was a bronze statue of Lady Justice holding the scales, a representation of the impartiality of the court's decisions.

But on two separate occasions, I saw his eyes dart to a computer screen angled just out of my view. Were we boring him? Or was he receiving third-party communications about Rue's criminal case? When I shifted in my chair to get a look at the monitor, he hit a key and the screen went dark.

After that meeting in Gulfport, I headed for my next destination: the Harrison County DA's office, First Judicial Circuit. Henry Gordon-James kept his main office in Gulfport, and it was time to talk with the man face to face.

When I stopped at a red light on Twenty-Third Avenue, I pulled out my cell phone and turned it back on. Rue had begged me to turn off the phone before we entered the dean's office. She said that the law faculty was strict about cell phone use, especially during lectures.

I'd missed three calls and two messages from Jenny in the past hour. I called as the traffic light turned green.

"Thank God," she said. No greeting, no hello. She sounded rattled.

"Jenny, what's up?"

"Did you get my messages? I've been trying to reach you."

"Sorry, I had to turn off the phone in the dean's office. You'd think we were meeting with a Supreme Court justice. Is everything okay? You sound upset."

"The police were here, Stafford Lee. At your office."

"The hell? What did they want?"

"They're looking for Rue."

If they wanted to speak to her, they had to go through Mason or me, her legal representation. The Biloxi PD knew the rules. I was working up a good case of righteous indignation when Jenny said, "The police said Rue is a suspect in the death of Iris Caro."

As I absorbed that statement, I damn near ran a red light. I hit the brakes just in time, barely missing another car in the intersection. As the driver swerved away from my Prius, he laid on the horn and shouted at me.

Jenny said, "Stafford Lee? What's that noise? Did you hear me?"

"Say it again." I gripped the steering wheel.

She enunciated each word: "Iris Caro is dead. And they want to talk to Rue."

I needed to get off the road. A Taco Bell sat at the corner of the intersection; I pulled into the parking lot. I was shaken by the news of Iris's death. We'd gone to school together. When we were younger, I knew her pretty well. Fighting off shock, I took a breath and said, "That's crazy, absolutely nuts. How can they possibly believe that Rue had anything to do with it?"

Jenny said, dropping her voice as if she didn't want to be overheard, "When I couldn't reach you, I called a friend of mine at the Biloxi PD. She works in the Criminal Investigations Division. The CSU."

"The crime scene unit? What did you find out?"

"She gave me some information, strictly on the down-low. Cause of death is suffocation, they think. But there's blood all over the scene. Iris also had a head injury. Looks like there was a struggle."

"Has anyone talked to Iris's husband? He should be the top suspect."

"Daniel has an alibi, ironclad. He was in surgery in the morning, labor and delivery in the afternoon. They're not looking at Daniel, Stafford Lee. There's forensic evidence. She claims they found physical evidence that points to Rue."

"I don't believe this."

"Stafford Lee, I'm just telling you what my friend said."

Curtly, I asked, "What evidence?"

"Fingerprints. Rue was fingerprinted when they booked her for larceny. The prints at the murder scene in the Caro house and in the room where Iris's body was found—they're a match."

I breathed easier. "They found her prints in the Caros' home? Jesus, Jenny, that doesn't mean anything. Rue works there, she cleans the place. Her prints are all over that house."

"They've taken hair samples too."

"So? Same thing. She's in the house every damned week. People shed hair—cops know that. This is insanity, I don't understand—"

Jenny broke into my tirade. "They think they have footprints too. Tracking across the floor. Tracking Iris's blood across the floor."

CHAPTER 69

I PEELED out of the Taco Bell lot and headed back to the law school, buzzing through narrow back roads to avoid the Gulfport traffic; my tires squealed with every sharp corner I took.

Two calls I made to Rue went straight to voice mail. She'd explained that the law students were scared to let a phone go off during lecture, so I hoped she was in class.

Every spot in the school parking lot was taken except one. A sign declared the prime spot was reserved for Dean Forrest Albert, JD. I didn't hesitate, just wheeled the Prius in. *Tow me,* I thought. I slammed the car door shut and broke into a run. Half a block from the lecture hall, I heard the wail of a siren.

A blue-and-white Biloxi PD patrol car sped by me, its light bar flashing, and pulled up in front of the school. When the uniformed officers emerged from their vehicle, I tore across the neatly mowed grass and chased them into the law school building.

Inside, I saw the cops board the elevator, so I took the stairs two at a time and arrived on the third floor just as the elevator doors opened and the police stepped out. Breathing hard, I followed them into a classroom at the end of the corridor.

It was a big, auditorium-style lecture hall with a pitched floor and tiered seating. Students sat quietly with their laptops or notepads resting in front of them on curved desktops. A large screen displayed a PowerPoint slide that read *Sixth Amendment Protections*. Next to it, a professor scrawled on a whiteboard with a blue marker.

The policemen marched swiftly down the aisle. The lead officer approached the instructor and said something to her. Her mouth dropped open, and the marker she held made a zigzag line across the board. The room began to buzz as the policemen scanned the students' faces. I stood at the back of the room, hunting for Rue.

The instructor stammered, "Wh-what's going on, Officers?"

The lead cop said, "We have an arrest warrant for Rue Holmes. We're here to take her into custody. Is she present?"

That's when I spotted Rue, seated in the middle of the second row. As the students turned wide eyes on her, Rue clutched her neck.

The professor pointed her finger at Rue and asked in a squeaky voice, "What's the problem, Officer?"

Jesus. It was shocking to know that the woman quaking at the front of the room actually had a law degree. I bet she'd never seen the inside of a courtroom.

Making damn sure I sounded more authoritative than the professor, I said, "Officer, I'm Rue Holmes's attorney. There's no need to execute this warrant. I can guarantee Ms. Holmes's appearance."

I strode down to the second row as the other cop entered from the opposite aisle. He reached Rue's side before I did and held out an arm to ward me off. He must have recognized me, because he said, "You stay back, Stafford Lee."

I kept coming. "She's my client. I'm entitled to see the warrant. Who issued it? Which judge? I want to see the probable-cause statement."

The officer ignored me. He looked down at Rue. "Rue Holmes, you're under arrest."

And then some asshole law student decided to play enforcer. He jumped out of his chair and blocked my path. "Back off, dude!" the kid shouted. "You're obstructing a lawful arrest."

The cop grabbed Rue by the arm and pulled her from her seat. She didn't fight him. I saw Rue place her hands behind her back. The cop snapped on the cuffs and began to recite the *Miranda* warning. "Rue Holmes, you have the right to remain silent."

I shoved the interfering student out of my way, but it was too late to stop the arrest. The cop continued, "Anything you say can and will be used against you in a court of law. You have the right to an attorney. If you can't afford an attorney, one will be provided for you."

"She has an attorney. I'm standing right here." The cop ignored me.

She didn't protest or hang back as the officer pulled her past her classmates. Both cops walked her up the tiered steps.

I followed them out of the classroom. Once we were in the hall, I shouted my own warning. "You know your rights, Rue! Don't answer any questions. Remember that they'll use anything you say against you!"

She turned and looked as if she had something to tell me. But the officers tugged at her arms, which made her stumble on the tile floor. When I ran up to assist her, one cop wheeled around and said, "You want to be arrested too? We got another pair of cuffs, Stafford Lee."

I took a step back and said, my voice bouncing off the marble walls of the hall, "Rue, I'm going straight over to the jail! Don't let them talk to you without counsel present. You insist on it. I'm your lawyer, Rue!"

As they took her into the stairwell, Rue finally turned and met my eye. Her jaw was clenched tight; I could see a muscle twitch. When they escorted her down the steps, she walked with dignity, holding her head high.

CHAPTER 70

THE POLICE took Rue to Biloxi.

I kept my promise. I drove directly to the jail and informed them that I was counsel for Rue Holmes. They confirmed that they had her in custody, but they wouldn't let me see her.

That set me off. I went to the Criminal Investigations Division of the PD and kicked up a fuss, demanded to talk to Detective Sweeney. When he wouldn't see me, I tried to shoulder my way inside the unit. They locked the doors to keep me out.

So I returned to the front desk of the jail. I was told that Rue was still being processed. Come back in a couple of hours, the officer advised.

I got back in my car, intending to drive to my office and wait it out there. Iris Caro was dead and Rue was in custody on suspicion of homicide—the local news outlets would pick up the story any minute. Rue's sister, Alicia, was a client of mine, and Rue's mother was caring for an aunt who had suffered a stroke in Picayune, a town on the same news circuit as Biloxi and Gulfport; I didn't want Rue's family to hear about her arrest from the radio or television. I called Alicia, but she didn't pick up, and I sure as hell couldn't deliver this shocking bombshell about Rue in a voice-mail message.

I needed to reach her mother. I didn't have her number, but Rue would have it somewhere in her room at my house, so that's where I headed next.

I pulled into the drive and sprinted inside. I stopped short in front of Rue's bedroom. It didn't seem right to intrude on her private space, but under the circumstances, I was certain she wouldn't mind.

The bedroom was tidy—no surprise there. Looking around, I wondered whether it was a challenge for Rue to tolerate my half-hearted attempts at housekeeping in the rest of the house.

Her schoolbooks and papers were stacked neatly on the bedside table, but her laptop was missing. She'd probably had it with her in class. I made a mental note to contact the law school and pick it up for her later.

When I didn't find the information in her papers, I approached the dresser, but I was reluctant to go through the drawers. I saw a collection of sticky notes on her mirror, and I scanned the hand-written reminders and to-do lists until I spotted a yellow note with her mother's name, an address in Picayune, and a phone number with a Mississippi area code.

As I was entering the information into my phone, the doorbell rang. Immediately after that, someone pounded on the front door. I decided that whoever it was could wait.

And that's when I heard something slam against the wood, followed by a crash. Sounded like my front door had literally been kicked in.

That got me moving. "What the hell?" I shouted, bolting out of the guest room.

It took me only a few seconds to grab my baseball bat and get to the living room, but three officers were already there, prowling across the floor. A fourth cop was trying to fasten a document to my shattered door with a thick strip of tape.

When I bounded into the living room holding the bat, one of the cops pulled his service handgun and pointed it at me. I dropped my bat and froze, my hands in the air. The guy at the door called to his fellow officer, "Put the gun away, you don't need it. It's Stafford Lee Penney."

The cop returned the gun to his holster; I lowered my hands, walked over to my front door, and tore off the paper the cop had stuck to it. Belatedly, the cop said, "We've got a warrant, Stafford Lee."

I looked at the document. Unbelievable. They did, in fact, have a warrant, a warrant to search my house.

The door was hanging off the hinges. Pointing at it, I demanded, "What possessed you to come busting in here like that?"

The cop who'd taped up the warrant appeared to be the officer in charge, and I knew him. I had cross-examined Sergeant Gorski on the witness stand on many occasions.

He said unapologetically, "Come on, Penney—we knocked first. No one responded. We're empowered by law to enter the premises to execute a warrant, you know that."

The other officers stood by, poised to take me down if I made trouble. Gorski cleared his throat and said, "Stafford Lee Penney, are you the person in control of these premises?"

"Cut the bullshit, Sergeant. You know it's my goddamn house!" I was too angry to be intimidated. My hands were shaking, but I wasn't afraid; I was furious. Still, though I was almost blinded by rage, I didn't lose sight of how unwise it would be to tell them to get the hell out.

So instead I said, "This is an illegal entry."

Gorski scoffed and turned away. "Read it, Penney. It's signed by a judge. Authorizes a search of these premises for evidence related to the murder of Iris Caro."

While the cops trooped down the hall, I tried to make sense of the document. The words swam across the page; the only thing I could comprehend was the signature. The judge who'd signed the warrant was Eckhardt. He'd authorized the search of the residence of Rue Holmes at my address in Biloxi.

The officers were stomping through every corner of my home. I ran into the hall and shouted, "Tell me what you're looking for!"

I saw one of the cops open the door of the bedroom I'd shared with Carrie Ann, and my outrage exploded, making my vision gray out at the edges. I yelled, "Don't! Do *not* enter that room. You have no right." I ran down the hall, shoving past one of the other officers who stood by, eyeing me with suspicion.

I stopped in the open doorway of the main bedroom, still unwilling to enter that space. The officer had thrown open a closet door and was aiming a flashlight beam inside. At the sight, I felt my throat tighten. "Get out of this room," I choked out. "No one stays in here. Not since my wife—" I couldn't say her name aloud, not in his presence. "Whatever you're looking for, it's not in here, I swear to God."

The young cop ignored me, so I went off in search of Gorski, hoping to convince him to back off. He probably had the power to limit the scope of their intrusion. Maybe if I used the right words, I could persuade him of the futility of his pursuit.

I found Gorski in Rue's bedroom, pawing through the contents of her dresser drawers. I said, trying to sound reasonable, "I've read through your warrant, Gorski. I guarantee that it's illegal and over-broad, and the language is too general. Come on, Gorski! You know the Fourth Amendment. It prohibits the kind of search you are doing right now."

When he paid me no heed, I stepped up to the dresser. "Your search won't stand up in court, I swear it. Why don't you tell me what you're hunting for? Maybe I'll know where it is. I'm not consenting to anything, I'm just trying to figure out what it is that you want."

"Get out of here, Penney." He gave me a look of warning. "I won't tell you again."

I backed out of the room and walked down the hall. When I passed the bathroom, I saw they'd already been inside, had thrown towels out of the cabinet and onto the floor. The next room I passed was the bedroom I currently used. An officer was on his hands and knees in my closet, digging through shoeboxes. My clothes and underwear were strewn across the floor. He'd dumped the contents of the hamper onto the rug.

Standing in the doorway, I said, "This is a violation of my constitutional rights."

My voice startled the guy, and his hand went to the gun in his holster. He turned to me, and I didn't like the expression on his face. I stepped out of the doorway because I didn't want to become a search-warrant fatality. But I kept talking. "Have you ever been subpoenaed to testify at a hearing on a motion to suppress? Because you'll be on that witness stand for certain if you dare to take one single item out of my house. I'll serve you personally, cross-examine you myself. I'll take the hide off you, man."

He just snorted, bent back into my closet, and continued to dig.

Gorski came up behind me. "Penney, I'm giving you one last chance. If you keep on hindering and obstructing, I'm gonna kick your ass and haul you in. That's a promise."

I almost gave him a shove—I was *this close* to doing it. But he had a Taser on his belt, and a nightstick, and a gun. I'd lost one physical battle with the Biloxi PD in the past calendar year. I wasn't eager for a rematch.

So I went back to the living room and collapsed on the sofa. Then I picked up my phone and called Rue's mother. She was devastated by the news, but I had to keep the conversation brief. With the noise and commotion the police were making, it was impossible for me to sound reassuring. After I ended the call, two officers descended on the living room. One cop flipped up the lid of Carrie Ann's piano bench and flung sheet music onto the floor. This time, I kept my mouth shut and just watched the carnage unfold.

CHAPTER 71

I WAS stretched out on the hard leather couch in the reception area of my office. My clothes were rumpled; I'd slept in the shirt and pants that I'd worn to meet the law school's dean the day before. My suit coat was rolled up on the armrest, a makeshift pillow, but it hadn't provided much of a cushion. Also, the couch was short. My bare feet hung over the side.

Someone rattled the knob on the office door. I remained in my spot on the couch. I was in no mood to greet the public, not after the past twenty-four hours.

But when I heard the lock turn, I rolled over and raised myself up on my elbows. Only two people had keys to my office: Jenny and Rue. I knew that Rue wasn't on the other side of that door. She was locked up tight at the city jail. So I wasn't surprised when Jenny walked in. She carried her purse and a McDonald's bag in one hand. As she shut the door, she said, "What on earth, Stafford Lee? Have you been here all night?"

"Yes, ma'am, I have." I sat up with a groan and set my bare feet on the floor.

"Why did you sleep in your office?"

"Actually, I didn't sleep much in here. This couch isn't particularly comfortable." My neck was stiff. I rolled my head and listened to the cracking noises that the movement made. "But the cops tore my house apart with their bogus search, and I just couldn't stand to be there."

I grabbed a sheaf of papers sitting on the end table and held it out to her. "This is the inventory from the search. It's crazy, what all they took. You want to see it? I swear, you're not going to believe it."

Jenny reached out for the inventory with her good arm, the one that hadn't been dislocated. But she took the pages and set them back on the table without bothering to read them. I noticed that something was different about her that morning. "Hey, Jenny, where's your sling? Aren't you supposed to be wearing it?"

"I'm not fooling with it anymore. It slows me down."

That bothered me. "What did the doctor say? Hey, you're not driving, are you? The doctor gave you specific instructions about that. I was there."

She shrugged one shoulder—the undamaged one. "Don't worry about it. Look, I brought you some breakfast." She handed me the paper bag. An Egg McMuffin was inside. I unwrapped the sandwich and viewed it without enthusiasm. I wasn't hungry.

But Jenny was watching me like a hawk, so I took a couple of bites so I wouldn't look ungrateful.

She said, "There's a hash brown in there, did you see? You like those, right? You gonna eat it?" She was talking about a fast-food breakfast, but her voice had a definite edge. It made me take a closer look at her. Under the bruises on her face, Jenny was pale and seemed tense. She had something on her mind other than McDonald's. I wadded up the bag and tossed it at the trash can. My aim was off—it hit the floor.

I was inclined to let it sit there, but Jenny picked it up and dropped it into the can. Then she dragged a chair up to my make-shift bed, sat beside me, and took my hand.

She said slowly, as if she'd carefully thought out the words in advance, "I got a call this morning from my friend who works in the crime scene unit."

"Did you tell her they're wasting their time? Dragging Rue out of class in handcuffs and kicking in the door of my house—I'd appreciate it if you'd inform her that the Biloxi cops have lost their freaking minds. They've gone batshit-crazy on this case."

She pressed her lips together. I knew Jenny; she was flipping out about something and struggling to hide it. "She said they found something. There's evidence that was taken from your house. And they think that forensics can tie it to evidence from the Iris Caro murder scene."

I jerked my hand away from her icy grip. "Bullshit. Impossible. Don't even try to go there, Jenny. I don't want to hear it. There's no way that Rue is capable of murder."

Jenny rubbed her eyes as if they were full of grit. Her lips trembled. "It's not just that." She took a breath. "Stafford Lee," she began. Her voice was soft, almost inaudible. I braced myself. I knew how Jenny acted when she was breaking bad news. Really bad news.

"She says they've got something on you, Stafford Lee. They think you were in on it with her."

I felt like I blacked out for a moment, like my brain lost the capacity to function. "What the hell are you trying to say? What do they think I was in on?"

She whispered the words. I guess she thought they were too horrible to speak in a normal tone.

"That you were in on killing Iris Caro."

PART III

OCTOBER

CHAPTER 72

TWO DAYS had passed since Jenny informed me that the Biloxi PD was eyeing me as a possible suspect. But I couldn't get anyone to confirm it because no one in law enforcement would talk to me.

I'd tried to reach out to Henry Gordon-James, had called him repeatedly over the past forty-eight hours to ask what the hell was going on. He wouldn't take my calls. I left urgent messages. He didn't acknowledge them.

Meanwhile, Rue was still locked up tight. She was being held at the county jail in Gulfport. The police considered her to be a primary suspect in the murder of Iris Caro. They said as much in a statement to the press. The police chief said in an interview that the community wasn't in danger, that they knew who the perpetrator was. When pressed for details, he would say only that they were on the case.

Whether the community was reassured by his statements, I couldn't say. But I sure as hell wasn't. Because I knew for certain that Rue Holmes hadn't killed Iris Caro. The killer was still at large, and the police weren't looking.

The previous day, Rue had made an initial appearance before a judge in Biloxi. I stood beside her as he informed her of the murder charge. They gave us a copy of the charging affidavit. Her bail was set at seven hundred fifty thousand dollars. That's a fortune in Mississippi—well, it's a fortune anywhere. She'd never be able to come up with that much money. They wanted to make sure she stayed put.

In the courtroom, I kicked up a fuss, stormed the bench, argued the lack of probable cause, protested the bond amount as unreasonable. Rue hadn't been indicted by a grand jury yet, and there was no telling when an indictment might be handed down. The judge informed her that she had a right to a preliminary hearing to determine whether there was probable cause that Rue had committed the crime. But she had to formally ask the court for a prelim if she wished to receive a hearing.

And now I was sitting in my office, fine-tuning the written request. The rule stated that the hearing had to be held within fourteen days, but I knew how the game was played. After the hearing date was set, the district attorney would try to postpone it, claiming they needed to wait for evidence or results from the crime lab. The delay could stretch out for months while Rue remained locked in a cell.

I'd already called the DA on the issue, trying to get a firm date for the preliminary hearing. But no one would talk to me about that either. Not Gordon-James, not any of his assistants. The silence was deafening.

My fingers flying on the keyboard, I pumped more fire into the request to the court. I needed to submit it that day, because as soon as it hit the court file, the clock would start ticking. And I intended to hold everyone's feet to the fire on Rue's behalf.

The phone rang. The caller ID showed that it wasn't coming from the courthouse or the Harrison County DA's office, so I let it ring. I had a deadline to meet.

When I heard the front door of my office open, I wished I'd thought to lock it. I decided to go tell whoever was out there to come back later.

The door slammed shut. "Stafford Lee Penney!"

I knew that voice. With a jitter of trepidation, I pushed away from the desk, stepped out of my office, and went into the reception area. Sergeant Gorski and one of his fellow officers stood just inside the door.

He said, "We have a warrant for your arrest." He held it in his hand.

It felt like my heart stopped.

Maybe I shouldn't have been surprised. Jenny had warned me that it was going down. But hearing the words spoken and seeing the uniformed officers waiting to take me into custody — the reality sent me into shock.

My body went cold when they cuffed me. Despite the disconnect in my brain, I heard myself speak to Gorski. They read me my rights, but the words I knew by heart didn't even register. Inside my head, a voice kept insisting: *This isn't possible. It can't be happening. I haven't done anything wrong.*

I haven't done anything.

My brain continued the litany of disbelief as they pulled me out to the squad car. One of them put a hand on my head and pushed me into the back seat. While I sat in the patrol car, staring at the officers through the battered prisoner partition barrier, the numbness faded and was replaced by a very different sensation.

It was fear.

I'd been arrested for murder. *Murder.*

This was really happening, and I was scared. Scared shitless, like they say.

They were going to lock me up. I might never walk free again.

CHAPTER 73

I'D BEEN arrested before, less than a year ago.

This was different.

Back then, they'd dragged me in for passing out on the beach. After my drunken scuffle with the cops, when I was banged up and miserable, they'd tossed me into the drunk tank with the other lowlifes, and I'd waited to be released.

This time, I wasn't going anywhere.

At the jail, they fingerprinted me, took a mug shot. After I was processed, I figured they'd take me to a jail cell. They took me to an interrogation room instead.

I sat alone in the room for a time. On my feet, I wore white crew socks and orange Crocs. The jailer had issued them to me along with my jailhouse scrubs, and I'd stared at the shoes I'd never worn before until he said, "We started using these to cut down on escapes."

"What?"

"So you can't get away. They're hard as hell to run in. You're not going to make a break for it if you're wearing Crocs."

They kept me cooling my heels in the interrogation room for about an hour, I think, but I had no way of knowing for sure. They'd taken my phone, my wristwatch. My clothes were stored in the inmate property room. The orange jail scrubs I wore were a poor fit. My feet and ankles stuck out from pants made for a man much smaller than I was.

Figuring someone was watching me through the camera mounted on the wall, I tried to sit still and not let them see me sweat.

But I *was* sweating, big-time.

Finally, the door opened. I was surprised to see Detective Sweeney enter, carrying two foam cups. I had naively assumed he would avoid a confrontation with me. We had a history from Carrie Ann's death.

Sweeney was accompanied by another plainclothes officer, a detective named McGuire. McGuire held a folder in his hands. They sat, and Sweeney nudged one of the cups across the table. "I thought you might want some coffee," he said.

Ah, he's the good cop.

McGuire passed the folder to Sweeney. The detective opened it and pulled a pen from his inside jacket pocket. "I've got a *Miranda* waiver here."

I took a sip of coffee. It was weak and tepid. It made sense that they wouldn't trust a suspected murderer with a cup of piping-hot brew.

"You want me to read it aloud?" he asked. "I know you know what it says."

When I didn't answer, Sweeney cleared his throat and began. "This is a *Miranda* warning and waiver. I'm filling in the date and place. And the time is"—he checked his watch—"one thirteen p.m. Your rights. 'Number one. You have the right to remain silent. Number two. Anything you say can and will be used against you in a court of law. Number three. You have the right to talk to a lawyer—'."

I broke in. "I'm not going to sign it, Sweeney." No sense in wasting everyone's time. Even though, admittedly, I had a lot of time to spare.

He continued reading as if I hadn't spoken. "'And have him present with you while you are being questioned.'"

I didn't interrupt again. When he finished reading me my rights, he said, "The waiver of rights states this: 'I have read this statement of my rights and I understand what my rights are. I am willing to make a statement and answer questions. I do not want a lawyer at this time. I understand and know what I am doing. No promises or threats have been made to me, and no pressure or coercion of any kind has been used against me.'"

He pushed the paper across the table and tapped it with his pen. "Signature line is right here. Detective McGuire and I will sign as witnesses after you execute it."

He set the pen down on the form. I didn't touch it. Crossed my arms over my chest.

Sweeney left the form where it lay. "We know you're well aware of your constitutional rights. Shoot, Stafford Lee, you're the expert on criminal procedure in this room." He turned to his partner. "Right, McGuire?"

"Sure." McGuire looked eager, like he was hungry to bite off a piece of me. "We just figured you'd want to give us your version of the facts."

Hastily, Sweeney added, "We want to offer you that opportunity, Stafford Lee. Like I always say, there're two sides to every story."

I'd never heard him say that. It was bait, just bullshit. Sweeney wasn't a guy who examined an issue from all perspectives. It was a trap. But though they had waylaid me, I hadn't completely lost my wits. I kept my mouth shut.

After a moment of uncomfortable silence, McGuire said, "We heard about your recent falling-out with the Caro family."

I almost twitched and raised an eyebrow. Stopped myself in time.

Sweeney said, "There were some angry confrontations. That's what we heard."

His partner tipped back in his chair. "At the casino, with Hiram. And later on at Dr. Caro's clinic. You were on a tear that day, weren't you? Sounds like you lost it, were out of control."

I didn't respond.

"The old man can be hard to get along with, can't he?" Sweeney's voice rang with false sympathy. "Stafford Lee, you and me, we're Old Biloxi. We know Hiram's background. He was your father's client, wasn't he? That time they tried to take Hiram down with the rest of the Dixie Mafia?"

McGuire was impatient. He wanted to bring it back to me. "There were witnesses that day you went to see Hiram. His secretary in the casino business office and two security guards. And there was a whole mess of women inside Daniel Caro's clinic. They all say you were out of your head, making threats. Acting violent."

My breath came faster. Had I laid hands on Daniel Caro that day? Maybe I had. To an outsider, a spectator, it would have looked bad.

Sweeney made a mournful face, the corners of his mouth turned down, feigning regret. "Stafford Lee. We know about your history with Iris."

I stopped breathing then. *What?*

He went on. "You were romantically involved with her in the past, weren't you? When you were younger. People don't forget something like that, Stafford Lee. Not in Biloxi."

I almost lost my resolve to stay silent because I desperately wanted to deny it. Iris and I hadn't had a deep romantic connection in the past. We'd gone on a couple of casual dates back in undergrad, and that was the extent of it. And it was more than two decades ago. I didn't even remember if I'd kissed her.

They stared at me, waiting for me to crack.

Finally, McGuire took a new tack. "Tell us about those flip-flops."

I didn't have a clue what he was talking about.

"You wore them to court, right? Everyone at the courthouse

knows the judge chewed you out about wearing flip-flops. Were they the same ones you wore to your job at the beach?"

Asking about my flip-flops? *Really?*

"When did you wear them last? Can you recall? If you could share that information with us, it would be helpful. I mean, it could help *you* out."

He dangled that, trying to goad me into speaking. I knew better.

When I didn't respond, McGuire slammed his fist on the table, knocking over my coffee. The movement took me by surprise; I almost jumped out of my chair.

As the puddle of cold coffee spread across the table, he stood and shouted, "Goddamn it, you candy-ass lawyer! Since when have you got nothing to say? You think you're being smart?"

Sweeney picked up the *Miranda* waiver to keep it dry. In a humorless voice, he said, "McGuire, sit down."

They kept me in the interrogation room for a long time, going off on tangents and then returning to the same questions.

I was rattled, but I hadn't lost my mind. Not yet. I knew to hang tough. I kept my mouth shut.

CHAPTER 74

WHEN THEY escorted me out of the interrogation room, I expected to be transported to the county jail in Gulfport. It was a big jailhouse; Rue was currently one of around eight hundred inmates there.

But they took me deep inside the Biloxi jail to the medium-security detention area. In my defense experience, I'd seen it used as a temporary holding place for people who'd been arrested and were waiting to be brought before a judge. I'd interviewed clients there, so I knew that in this part of the jail system, prisoners were kept in single cells.

Funny thing was, though, I had a cellmate.

He lay stretched out on the only cot, grinning at me. He said, "Looks like they're double-booked at the city jail."

I stood in the center of the tiny cell, which was furnished with the cot and a toilet bowl and nothing else. Having represented criminal inmates for fifteen years, I wasn't surprised by the primitive accommodations; I just didn't know where I was supposed to sit my ass down.

My cellmate sat up in bed, scooted around, and dropped his bare feet onto the floor. He patted the end of the mattress he had just vacated. "Join me?"

That wasn't happening. I checked out the toilet—metal; no seat or lid—and swiftly glanced away. I backed up, slid down the wall of painted concrete blocks, and squatted on my haunches. The cell floor made for a dirty seat, but it was a better option than the toilet.

I wondered how long I would remain in the city lockup. Maybe, I reasoned, they were taking me before a judge. With luck, I'd have a chance to bond out. I didn't have much cash in the bank or any liquid assets, but I had some equity in the house. It might be enough, depending. And in the worst-case scenario, I could appeal to my father.

And then I recalled that Rue's bond amount had been set at seven hundred fifty thousand dollars. Could I afford a bail bondsman's percentage fee on a figure like that? Maybe I was being overly optimistic.

My cellmate said in a cordial tone, "I'm Lou. You might as well get comfortable. You're not going anywhere for a while."

I wondered how he knew that, but I wasn't disposed to ask him. Suddenly, I realized that I was weary, bone-tired. It felt like the adrenaline that had fueled me until now suddenly ran dry. I slid all the way down to the floor and rested my head against the wall.

God, I wanted a drink. The thirst for alcohol came out of nowhere and hit me hard. I was in no danger of falling off the wagon, though, not on these premises. I tried to ignore the craving. I said, "I'm Stafford Lee."

Lou regarded me with undisguised curiosity. "What are you in here for? Some kind of white-collar crime? You look like a better class of felon than the rest of us."

Did I? I felt lower than a snake's belly.

I turned my attention to Lou. We were dressed identically, living proof that scrubs were not one-size-fits-all. Lou was probably half a foot shorter than me, so the length of his pants wasn't a problem, but he was about seventy pounds heavier, and his soft gut hung over the elastic waistband.

Lou laughed and said, "I bet you were caught for some kind of scam—maybe a Ponzi thing. You look like you could sweet-talk old ladies into signing over their life savings."

He clearly thought that he was paying me a high compliment. I just shook my head.

Suddenly, his face lit up. "Holy shit! You're that lawyer, aren't you?"

I groaned. It had been too much to hope for, that the orange scrubs and clogs would provide anonymity.

Lou was excited by his realization. "Don't tell me your last name, I'll think of it. You won a big trial a while back. Penney! You're Stafford Lee Penney."

Reluctantly, I nodded. I could hardly deny it. My presence in the jailhouse would be common knowledge in Harrison County soon, if it wasn't already.

"I'm in here on a parole violation," he volunteered. "I pissed hot on my drug test. Hey, you'd know if there was some way to beat a bad urine test, wouldn't you?"

I didn't ask the nature of the charge he'd done time on prior to parole. His hands, the palms and fingers, were cracked, marked with dark lines, like a car mechanic's. If I'd had to guess, I'd have figured him for property crimes. Maybe a fence, dealing in resale of stolen goods, like scrap metal or copper or even catalytic converters—the metals they contained made them big items on the black market. He looked like a guy who ran a chop shop, dismantling stolen cars and selling the parts. Maybe he was a small player in a broader enterprise of organized crime.

He pressed me. "Is it worth it, fighting the urinalysis? If I want to go that route, I'll have to hire a lawyer. Will I be throwing my money away?"

I wasn't in the mood to hand out free legal advice. "I couldn't say."

He slumped down on the bed, looking disappointed. After a moment of silence, he abruptly broke wind with a long, wet release of gas.

He struggled to his feet. "You wouldn't believe what they feed you—it's about done me in. How many times can a man eat sauerkraut?" He jerked his pants down and sat on the toilet. "They really ought to give us more privacy in here."

Fervently, I agreed.

After he flushed and returned to the bed, he snapped his fingers and pointed at me. "So you were Caro's lawyer. That guy, the son of the casino owner."

"Yeah."

"You got him off, right? How much he pay you for that? What's it cost, getting a guy off?"

"The fee is confidential. But, Lou, the client pays for representation, legal services. The outcome isn't guaranteed. It's in the jury's hands."

He didn't look convinced. "I caught some of that trial on TV when I was doing time. I remember when they showed that doctor's wife on the news. She's good-looking in a tight-ass way. But hell, I'd nail that."

I didn't upbraid him for the disrespect. He probably didn't know that Iris Caro was dead. How could he? He'd been closed off in this cell.

"I hope you hit the Caros up for a big payday. They can afford it. You ever go to the old man's casino, ever play there?"

I'd been to the casino the week before. The detectives had drilled me on it for over an hour. But I didn't mention it.

Lou wasn't put off by my uncommunicative attitude. He kept talking. "Caro's slots don't pay out, especially for max bet. And I'm in a position to know. From time to time, I've used the slots to avoid RICO problems. My partners deposit my payment in a slot machine, then I sit down and play for a while before I cash it out. Caro's machines never pay! How do you think he controls that? Like, they got some button or something they push to make the machines so tight? Seems like you'd have to win once in a while unless he's rigging it."

He rambled on, talking about the table games, card games he'd played and money he'd lost. The words swirled overhead like a swarm of birds flying in circles. My mind drifted.

"You ever feel like doing that?" he said.

The question broke into my reverie. "Doing what?"

"You know, I just told you how my buddy thought the dealer was cheating, and he punched his face in. But what good does it do to hit the dealer? We ought to be kicking Hiram Caro's ass, right? He's the one who's cheating us." Lou leaned back on the cot in a relaxed posture. But his eyes were sharp and piercing as he regarded me. They reminded me of a possum's eyes, dark and beady. "You ever feel like doing that?" he asked again. "Getting back at Caro for something?"

I clenched my jaw. I finally understood. Maybe the trauma or the shock had kept me from catching on sooner. They were setting me up for a jailhouse confession. They'd struck a bargain with my shithouse buddy. Lou was on a mission to trick me into making incriminating statements.

CHAPTER 75

THEY KEPT me in the Biloxi jail overnight. At some point, they dragged in a second cot. It was a tight squeeze. I stretched out, lying flat on my back, to avoid bumping into my cellmate, Lou.

The next day, the jailer took me out and led me through a maze of corridors. I asked what was going on, but he didn't respond. When we reached a holding cell, he pulled open the door and announced, "You got visitors."

In the room, Mason and Jenny sat at a folding table.

Jenny pushed back her metal chair and stood, looking like she might burst into tears. She leaned toward me as if to give me a hug. Glad as I was to see her, I just couldn't accept it. My self-control was hanging by a thread, and I couldn't let it break. I dropped into an empty chair and focused on Mason.

The question I needed to ask him stuck in my throat for a second, and not because I was afraid of being overheard. The holding cell was reserved for criminal defendants to meet with counsel. There were no cameras mounted on the wall, no ears listening at the crack of the door. I didn't have to be on my guard, not in there.

"How bad is it?" I asked.

Mason and Jenny exchanged a look. She ducked her head, bent

over her phone, and swiped at the screen. Mason picked up a pen and tapped it on his legal pad in a rapid beat.

I knew Mason. The news was bad enough to make him nervous. But he wouldn't conceal the information. Mason wouldn't bullshit me.

"It's bad," he said. "We're trying to read tea leaves here because no one is saying exactly what it is that they've got. But they've set your bail at the same amount as Rue's, and they're proceeding against you and Rue as codefendants."

Jenny said in a hushed voice, "Coconspirators."

My leg started jiggling. I forced myself to still the movement. Once I composed myself, I said, "Mason, I need a favor."

He waved off my request. "You don't even need to ask. I'll enter my appearance immediately. Consider yourself represented, Stafford Lee. I'm here for you."

Jenny added, "I'll help on the investigation side. Anything I can do. You know that. Anything at all."

I shook my head. It wasn't that I didn't appreciate the support— I did. I was sincerely thankful. But the help they offered was not the help I sought. "I'm going pro se. I intend to represent myself."

They were both facing me, so I couldn't miss their reactions to my announcement. Their expressions cycled from disbelief to dismay to disapproval.

Mason spoke first. "What the absolute—" He glanced at Jenny, then looked back at me. "You trying to be funny? Making a joke?"

Jenny pinned me with her stare. "No. You can't."

I opened my mouth and began to explain, but Mason stood, cutting me off. His voice boomed as he said, "You're crazy. You know what they say, Stafford Lee?"

"He knows," Jenny said.

I sighed, dreading the argument. I knew the old expression.

Mason said, "Come on, Stafford Lee. Tell me. What do they say about a lawyer who represents himself?"

We stared each other down. Did he really want me to answer? What the hell; I wasn't afraid to say it. "He's a fool."

"No, that's not it. Get it right, friend. 'A lawyer who represents himself has a fool for a client.' That's you, Stafford Lee."

"We're not going to debate this," I said. I was trying to sound reasonable. Pleasant, even. Like I said, I appreciated what they were trying to do.

But they wouldn't drop it. Jenny said, "That applies even to you, Stafford Lee. In case you weren't aware."

"I'm aware."

She tapped her phone. "Mason was serious when he said it's bad. This is the coverage in today's paper. You need to see it."

She set the phone in front of me. I didn't pick it up. To Mason, I said, "So, about that favor. I want you to take Rue's case, Mason. She can't afford to hire a lawyer."

Mason was conflicted, I could tell. "They'll appoint counsel. She'll get a public defender."

"The public defenders are overworked, Mason. Their caseload is too heavy, and a lot of them are young, inexperienced. She won't get the representation she needs. It's got to be you."

He didn't look happy, but he didn't flat-out refuse either. I was confident Mason would do the right thing.

Jenny had the stubborn look she got when she had no intention of backing down. She shoved the phone right in front of me so I couldn't ignore it. "You gonna read it or do I have to read it to you?"

I looked down. Below the headline, the story had photos of each of the three principal parties: a portrait of Iris Caro, taken from coverage of some society event; my regular headshot, a fairly recent professional photo the newspaper kept on file; and Rue's picture, which was taken from her mug shot. The contrast between the jailhouse picture and the posed photographs was profound.

I shoved the phone away.

Jenny said, "Okay, you don't have to read it; I'll give you the gist. There's a probable-cause statement. The cop swears that the charges against the two of you are supported by forensic evidence tying you to the murder scene—"

Mason interjected, "Doesn't say why or how."

"Right," Jenny said. "And the sworn statement says they found online correspondence on your laptop, Stafford Lee, showing threats against Iris."

"E-mails," Mason said.

I could barely keep up. "What? No. Not possible. Who were the e-mails from?" I was genuinely baffled.

"From you. There are veiled threats that if she rejected you, you'd harm yourself and her. Implying murder/suicide. They're filing a motion to get access to your cell phone."

Though I knew I'd entered nothing incriminating on my phone, the statement made me wince. The phone was in the property room, out of my control. The idea of Sweeney and McGuire reading through my communications was offensive—and nerve-racking.

I shook my head helplessly. Mason cleared his throat and said, looking embarrassed, "Someone's pitched a theory to the press that you're obsessed with Iris. They don't name the source. A long-ago love affair, this individual is claiming, that reignited when you represented her husband in the Aurora Gates murder."

"We know, Stafford Lee, it's absolutely nuts," Jenny hastened to add.

But Mason looked determined to say his piece, to convey every twist of the damning news article. "Someone called the police, told the cops that during the trial, you tried to coerce Iris into having sex with you."

"What? No!"

He ignored me. "And she spurned your attentions."

"Insane!" I said, my voice rising. "This doesn't even make sense."

Jenny said, "And the theory is that Rue assisted you in the killing. She was motivated by revenge because Iris had turned her in to the police for larceny but also because she's in love with you."

That did it; I exploded. I jumped out of the chair, picked it up, and flung it against the wall. "It's all lies! It's crazy!" I swung back to my friends. "Who would believe any of that?"

As my voice bounced off the cinder-block walls of the holding cell, it struck me that Jenny and Mason looked scared. That made me wonder: Were they frightened for me? Or frightened of me?

CHAPTER 76

WHEN I returned to my cell, I lay on my cot with my back to Lou. The guy wouldn't leave me alone. I felt like I was on the witness stand being cross-examined.

"Hey, Stafford Lee! You were gone for quite a spell. Where'd they take you, what did they do with you?"

I closed my eyes and snored softly.

"Stafford Lee? You awake?"

When I didn't respond, I felt him nudge my hip with his bare foot. I tensed with the urge to jump up and throttle him. As I was searching for a way to silence my companion without incurring additional criminal charges, I heard footsteps on the concrete floor outside the cell.

The jailer appeared, unlocked the cell door, and swung it open. "Penney, come with me."

Lou whined, "When's it my turn? I'd like a chance to get out of this box, stretch my legs."

I slid my feet into the Crocs, stood, and turned around so the jailer could cuff my hands behind me. "Where am I going?"

He didn't answer until we'd exited the cell and he'd turned the key, locking Lou inside. "You're getting bonded out."

Lou heard him. "You're shitting me! Penney's getting out?" he

313

shouted. "Where'd he come up with three-quarters of a mil? I can't believe it!"

Frankly, neither could I. I was dumbfounded as the jailer escorted me down the long, dingy hallways of the facility. I tried to figure out which of my friends had made the sacrifice on my behalf. A bondsman's percentage fee on seven hundred fifty thousand dollars was a crippling amount of money. Had Jenny and Mason joined together to raise the sum? I couldn't let them do it. It was asking too much.

Even my father would struggle to come up with that amount. And he and I were on the outs. He'd made it clear that he was unhappy with what he considered my bohemian lifestyle. He'd complained about the casual courtroom attire, and he really lost it when I brought an unmarried Black woman into my house as a boarder. Lately, we'd avoided each other even more than usual.

I suspected the jailer might have overheard some details of my release, but I held off asking. The guy wasn't likely to part with any information. His face was closed, and he hurried through the jail at a pace too fast for someone who was slogging down the concrete floors in soft plastic shoes with his hands cuffed behind his back to keep up.

We emerged in a lobby, a space at the back of the jail used for bondsman visits. The release personnel sat behind a glass window, and I saw a uniformed woman talking to a bondsman through an intercom. As the jailer released me from my cuffs, I spied Gene Taylor, the bondsman who'd secured my release after my prior arrest. He was leaning against the far wall, dressed in his signature Stetson hat and cowboy boots, his head bent over a clipboard. He looked up, saw me, and came over, grinning. "Stafford Lee, I'm getting you out of here."

The words sounded like a symphony, soaring and powerful. I experienced elation, a relief so pure that it bordered on ecstasy.

Without question, I wanted to accept the offer of liberty, run through the door, and breathe the outside air.

He led me into a cubicle to execute the required paperwork. As I sat on a hard bench while he scanned through the pages on the clipboard, I was literally shaking with the desire to get out. But still, I needed to know the circumstances of my release.

"Did they lower my bond?" That was the only conclusion I could reach. Maybe the judge had decided to knock it down, due to my status as a longtime Biloxi resident. If it was reduced to a quarter of a million or less, Mason could have managed that.

The bondsman gave me a wry look. "Nope, bond set at seven hundred and fifty K. You're my big score for the month, Stafford Lee. Tonight, I'm taking my girlfriend to dinner to celebrate. Gonna buy her some fancy lingerie." Obviously happy about the situation, he winked and handed me the pen. I wrote my name with a scrawl that didn't resemble my actual signature.

He picked up the clipboard and stood. "Let's get you processed out. I reckon you'll be glad to get back into your own clothes. Tell you what, I'm tired of looking at your hairy legs. Couldn't they get you some longer pants?"

"Hey, Gene," I said. I needed him to tell me the name of my benefactor while we were here in the cubicle, where no one else could hear. "Who paid your fee?"

"My fee?" He gave me a curious look. "You don't know?"

"I figure it was Mason Burnett." When the bondsman didn't say anything, I added, "Or Jenny Glaser. Is that right? Did Jenny contact you?"

He snorted like he knew a joke I wasn't in on. The sound was unsettling.

For my final guess, I croaked out, "My father?"

"No, sir! A client of yours paid it."

I was stumped. I'd had many clients over the years, and sure, I'd worked hard to foster positive professional relationships with them. But I couldn't think of any man or woman I'd represented who would bail me out of jail.

"Can't guess?" he said.

I shook my head. The bondsman shuffled through his paperwork until he came to the sheet setting out the indemnitor's information. He set the clipboard back on the table and placed his finger right under the name. I looked down. Thought at first my eyes were deceiving me. But there it was, in black ink. A signature I'd seen before.

Daniel Caro, MD.

CHAPTER 77

TWO DAYS later, I walked out onto the oak-shaded courtyard of Mary Mahoney's Old French House restaurant. Daniel Caro was already there. I couldn't see his eyes behind the dark sunglasses, but I suspected that he'd chosen the meeting spot for its relative privacy. The glass-topped tables on the brick-paved courtyard were spaced farther apart than those inside the eighteenth-century house where Mary Mahoney's had done business for fifty years.

I sat down on a metal patio chair and jumped right in. "What's going on here, Caro?"

His face remained expressionless. "Excuse me?"

Perspiration started beading on my forehead despite the shade. "Is this some game you're playing? Posting my bond and bailing me out?"

He adjusted his sunglasses. "Your reaction surprises me. I assumed you'd want to be released. I must confess, I thought you'd be more appreciative. If you're not responsible for my wife's death—"

I broke in, my words tumbling out in a rush. "No—God, no! It wasn't me, I'm innocent. You know that I would never harm Iris."

The slight nod he gave me didn't provide sufficient reassurance. I wanted—no, needed—a definitive sign that he believed me. To set the facts straight, I said, "The police theory made it into the

317

press. They concocted a love triangle, said that I seduced your wife and killed her in a crime of passion and that I'd also romanced my intern and used her to aid and abet me in my crime. Daniel, it's absurd, absolutely crazy. I swear on my life, I never harmed Iris. I never had any designs on your wife. Iris and I, we were never—"

He raised a hand to silence me. "Enough."

Enough? I shut up, but I wondered what it meant. Had I convinced him? Or did he think I was lying? Maybe I needed to backtrack. "I apologize—I haven't offered my condolences. Please know how sorry I am about the death of your wife. It's a terrible loss, a senseless tragedy. Iris was a wonderful person—" I would have said more; I was prepared to mention some of her virtues. But Caro cut me off.

"You're right about that. She was wonderful. I was very fortunate to have Iris as my spouse for all those years. I knew her well. And she was never interested in you, Stafford Lee."

That shut me up. I sat back and listened.

He said, "I'm aware y'all knew each other when you were young. Had a date, maybe. And I also know it didn't go anywhere. Iris told me she never found you particularly attractive or likable, not even when you were in college."

The nature of the conversation was so bizarre, I had an inappropriate urge to laugh. To suppress it, I covered my mouth with my hand and coughed.

A waiter appeared with glasses of ice water. "What can I bring you gentlemen this evening?"

"Just water," I said.

Caro said, "I'll have a Grey Goose martini, up. Dry."

After the waiter walked away, Caro took off his sunglasses. He had dark circles under his eyes. His face bore marks of strain. "About Iris. Our marriage wasn't perfect, of course. We went through some stormy times; you know that." He glanced away from me and paused for a moment. "I put her through a lot with the Aurora Gates affair and the murder trial."

I didn't argue.

He went on. "And Iris had her own faults. At times, she engaged in flirtations, played the coquette, acted out her glory days as a college belle. But she never betrayed me, never broke her vows. Iris wasn't unfaithful."

I said, "I'm sure you're right."

Memories of my own wife, Carrie Ann, came flooding in. Even after all this time, I still found it hard to believe she'd brought a lover into our bed. I'd never suspected that she was unfaithful. But who knows? It was possible that Caro knew his wife better than I'd known mine.

He met my eyes. "Do you want to hear my opinion? About my wife's death?"

"Yes." It was the absolute truth. I scooted forward until I was literally on the edge of my seat. I'd never been more eager to hear what Caro had to say, not even when he was paying me by the hour.

"I know you didn't kill her. And that employee of yours, the law student—" He stopped, looked up at the branches above us. "Holmes? Is that her name?"

"Yes. Rue Holmes."

He sighed, shaking his head. "She didn't do it either."

CHAPTER 78

RELIEF SWEPT over me when I heard Caro's statement. I eased back in the chair, picked up the water glass, and drank, mentally composing an expression of gratitude for his refusal to buy into the dark theories surrounding Rue and me.

The waiter appeared just as I was about to speak. He set a martini glass in front of Caro and asked, "Do you gentlemen need dinner menus?"

"No," I said. I had no intention of lingering.

But Caro overruled me. "Leave the menus. We'll order in a bit." When the waiter left, Caro lifted his martini glass and studied it before taking a sip.

I wanted to say my piece and make a quick departure. "Thanks so much, Daniel. I'm in your debt for arranging my release. It was incredibly generous, and I intend to repay you. I'm also grateful to hear that you understand that I'm not responsible for your tragedy. I can vouch for Ms. Holmes as well." I stood and extended my hand.

He didn't take it. He gave me a cool look and said, "I'd appreciate it if you'd give me a few more minutes of your time. Since, as you just said, you're feeling beholden to me. You may recall that the last time we spoke, you were less than civil."

That was an understatement. The last time I'd seen him, I'd had my hands around his throat. When he put it that way, it gave me no choice. I dropped back into the seat.

Caro picked up the olive skewer and used it to stir his drink. He leaned in close and said, "I'm aware that the Biloxi police are capable of chasing the wrong theory in a murder case." Then he paused to eat one of the olives.

To fill the silence, I said, "That's true. As a criminal defense attorney, I've seen it happen."

"Well, I've observed it from personal experience," Caro said. "The prosecution and the police nearly destroyed me when they accused me of killing Aurora."

I couldn't figure the guy out. His wife had been murdered, but he sat at Mary Mahoney's calmly sipping a martini. He exhibited no pain, no anguish. He waited for me to respond. I gave a stiff nod, which seemed to satisfy him.

"I was a scapegoat," he went on. "They had to pin the crime on someone, and I was the most convenient person. Her pregnancy, I suppose, made for a tidy theory. Something easy for them to comprehend."

The courtyard was filling up with dinner customers. I said softly, "But they were unsuccessful. You were acquitted—the jury found you not guilty."

"Exactly—*not guilty*. Those words don't go far enough. That verdict isn't exoneration. My reputation, every aspect of my life, is still sullied by that trial. I continue to live under a cloud."

I was certain that the couple seated at the nearest table was eavesdropping. It was a relief when the waiter returned and asked, "Would you like to hear this evening's specials?"

Caro held up a hand like he was making a royal gesture. "Not necessary. I'll have the flounder imperial. And I'll start with a cup of gumbo, of course."

The waiter turned his attention to me. *Oh, what the hell,* I

321

thought. If I had to remain here, I might as well sit back and enjoy it. There's no better food this side of New Orleans. "Shrimp and crab au gratin, please. And the gumbo."

When the waiter walked off, Caro continued. "So, as I was saying, I live under a cloud of suspicion. If you want confirmation, just look around."

I did. When I focused on the table to my right, I caught a woman sneaking a glance at us. I stared her down. She looked away, flustered, and whispered something to her companion.

Caro sipped the martini. "You can see what I encounter, what I have to contend with. That's why I bailed you out of jail. I want to hire you."

That knocked me flat. "Excuse me?"

"Stafford Lee! Did you think I made your bond as a selfless act of mercy? Or because I felt sorry for you?" The corners of his eyes wrinkled with wry amusement. "I want to hire you to prove me innocent in the death of Aurora Gates."

I'd grown increasingly leery of him as the meeting went on and now I regretted agreeing to it. It would have been far more prudent to write my thanks on business stationery and put it in the mail.

Caro said, "Having a jury proclaim that you have not been proven guilty beyond a reasonable doubt—which was the outcome of my trial—isn't the same thing as being proven innocent. I'm sure you understand the difference. In a primitive, nonintellectual fashion, laymen realize it too. That's why many people in the community still regard me as a killer. Before this, I never followed social media, never paid any attention to it. But I can hardly ignore it now. The things they say. Terribly distressing."

He turned away, shaking his head. Studying his profile, I was amazed to see that he was entirely serious. Caro's wife had just been murdered, but his chief concern was his public reputation.

Caro sighed. "Thank God my patient suffered complications

with her delivery on the day of Iris's death. If I hadn't had an alibi, they'd probably blame me for Iris as well as Aurora."

I needed to put distance between us because I was seized by an impulse to get up and knock him out of his chair. How could Caro obsess about his public image when he should be mourning his wife? I knew what grief felt like, what it looked like. Caro didn't exhibit the signs. I didn't expect him to follow my miserable example and become the town drunk, but he sure didn't seem too torn up about Iris. He didn't appear to be thinking about her at all.

The gumbo arrived. I had a moment to compose myself while Caro tasted it, then nodded his approval.

While he ate, I clutched a soupspoon as an internal debate ran through my head. I didn't believe in Caro's innocence. I still harbored suspicions about his role in the death of Aurora Gates. And since the trial, Jenny had planted new seeds of doubt from her digging expedition into the death of his other patient.

A search for the truth could turn up startling results—not necessarily the outcome Caro sought.

Caro finished his gumbo and gave me an inquiring look. "Well, what's your answer? I have no problem meeting your hourly rate. I know you can get results."

He was right about that. I could do the job. A lawyer is a hired gun. I'd devoted my career to it. But we needed to negotiate. If Caro wanted me to go to the mat for him, he would have to provide me with a compelling reason to cooperate. "I'll work for you, Caro. On one condition."

I could see the satisfaction in his eyes. He thought he'd already won. "Good! That's good, I'm glad to hear it." He paused, then added, as if it were an afterthought, "What condition?"

"You're going to bond out Rue Holmes."

CHAPTER 79

MY LAW office was officially closed. The front of the building was locked up tight, shades drawn, lights out.

The back conference room had been transformed. Jenny, Rue, and I had plastered the walls with charts, photos, reports, and news articles. Every scrap of information we could uncover on the string of local murders—Iris Caro, Aurora Gates, Desiree Whitman, Benjamin Gates, Coach Davies, and Carrie Ann—was on display.

It was a gut-wrenching immersion, I can't deny that. I spent my days surrounded by images of the violent execution of my wife, the nearly headless body of her lover, and the corpse of Aurora Gates after the fish had eaten her face away.

Under normal circumstances, no one would have been able to work in that room, engulfed by the hideous sights mounted on the walls. But these weren't normal circumstances. My life was at stake. Rue's too.

Rue sat silently at one end of the conference table, seemingly oblivious to the grisly images. I sat at the opposite end, scribbling the particulars on a notepad. There was no absolute pattern. The causes of death weren't identical. The race and gender of the victims varied. If there was a common thread, I couldn't see it yet.

Jenny stood near the wall that was devoted to the Iris Caro homicide. Fewer exhibits were tacked up there. We didn't have all the information yet. I had made a written request for discovery, and Mason had filed one on Rue's behalf. But Gordon-James was in no hurry to turn over his file. We were still in the dark on the particulars of the police investigation.

"Stafford Lee?" Jenny said, looking up at the enlarged news clipping with Iris Caro's portrait. "This is incomplete."

"Hell, Jenny, you think I don't know that? The DA will hold out as long as the rule permits." I sounded impatient, and I knew I needed to rein it in. But I was so wired, it didn't take much to make me snap.

"I'm thinking about what we've put up here. The probable-cause statement says Iris's death was the result of suffocation, not trauma to her head. So why haven't we added the out-of-state victim? I want to devote some space to that cold case."

"Why?" I asked.

"There was evidence of strangulation in that one."

"Strangulation and suffocation are different," I said.

"But they're also alike, don't you think? It's an intimate crime, requires close contact. Both involve depriving the victims of air, making them unable to breathe. We definitely shouldn't close our minds to the possibility that the homicides are all related."

Jenny raised a valid point. I went back to my legal pad, made a new note: *Strangulation versus suffocation?*

Jenny backed away from the wall and looked around. "When I scope it all out, it's so blatantly obvious. Daniel Caro is still the likely suspect. Not you, not Rue."

I glanced at Rue to assess her reaction. She had no response. Rue's listlessness worried me. It was completely out of character. I said, "Caro has convinced the police that his alibi is solid."

Jenny shook her head, bemused. "So why would Daniel Caro be motivated to bond y'all out? I know what he told you, Stafford Lee, but still, it doesn't add up."

For the first time in a while, Rue spoke. "He wants to throw Stafford Lee off the scent. It's a trick, a ruse."

Jenny asked, "What do you think of his alibi, Rue? He had a patient in labor and had to perform an emergency C-section."

Rue said, "Doctors come and go, right? He doesn't have to punch a time clock. Besides, he could've killed her before he left for work. The coroner's time of death is just an estimate."

She lapsed back into silence. I was considering her words when I heard the rattle of the lock to the front door. Had to be Mason Burnett. I'd recently entrusted him with a set of keys.

"Stafford Lee?" he called.

"Back here," I replied.

He walked in, pulled out a chair, and tossed his briefcase onto the conference table. He looked grim.

Jenny said, "Glad you're here, Mason. I want you to weigh in on something."

Mason just slouched over the conference table.

Jenny continued anyway. "I was telling Stafford Lee and Rue that we need to open this up wide, all the way. I want the statement you took from Germain Whitman, the shrimp-boat worker whose wife was murdered; we need every detail on that case. And we should add the other cold case with the same MO. You remember the one I'm talking about?"

Mason sat up and shrugged. He opened his briefcase and pulled out two file folders.

"Come on, Mason," Jenny said. "It's a good theory, right? Tell me what you think."

He groaned, a sound that came from deep in his throat. "I think we need to narrow our focus, not broaden it. You can start by tearing all that shit off the wall."

Affronted, Jenny said, "I don't get it. Why are you acting like this?"

"We need to concentrate on keeping their butts out of prison. That's the goal."

"I respectfully disagree." Her words were tart. It was clear that Mason had raised her ire. "The murder walls are important. They show the whole picture. We can't isolate the Iris Caro death, can't separate it from the others. They could all be related."

Mason grabbed the files he'd just pulled from his briefcase and shoved them across the table, one toward me, the other to Rue. "I just got discovery from the DA's office."

"How did you get it?" I asked.

"Called in a favor. This is the whole prosecution file, everything they've got—reports, statements, exhibits, photos. I received it as counsel for Rue Holmes, but I made a copy for you, Stafford Lee." He slumped down in his chair.

I picked up the file. We'd been anxiously awaiting the information, but I couldn't bring myself to open it up. The prospect terrified me. Gripping the file, my hands betraying me with tremors, I asked Mason, "How bad does it look?"

I caught Mason's eye. When he glanced away, I figured I could predict what he was about to tell me.

Mason said, "I think you need to ask yourself why someone is trying to frame you for killing Daniel Caro's wife. They have forensics that tie both you and Rue to Iris's bedroom. And they've got Iris Caro's blood on items seized from the search of your house."

He slid even lower in his seat. "If I didn't know you better, I'd think you did it."

PART IV

MAY

CHAPTER 80

I SAT alone at the counsel table, waiting for my trial to begin.

It was a speedy trial setting. Only thirty-one weeks had passed since my arrest for the murder of Iris Caro. I could've bought some more time, demanded a continuance. But it was important to have my case heard before Rue went to trial. This way, Mason would have the benefit of seeing the State's evidence, hearing the testimony, and watching the way the DA laid out his case.

I shifted around in my chair to check out the spectators, wondering whether my friends were present. I saw Mason sitting at the end of the bench in the very last row. He sat alone too.

He acknowledged me with a somber nod, and I continued searching, scanning every face in the courtroom. I would have sworn Jenny would be there for the first day of trial. Would have staked my life on it.

I pulled out my phone to check where she was on the tracking app. Jenny had talked Rue and me into signing up to share our whereabouts after some creepy calls came into the office. Mason wasn't interested, said he thought location-sharing apps themselves were creepy.

A blinking dot showed Jenny on a highway, heading out of town.

An excruciating stab of disappointment made me slump down in the chair. Maybe she was working, but it would've been nice to see her there. Our relationship had undergone some changes in the past thirty-one weeks. Significant changes.

But hell, even my own father hadn't bothered to show up and offer support. He said he had a conflict, a court setting in another county. Bullshit. I suspected he was conflicted, all right—because he was ashamed. Maybe he'd finally written me off.

The jury had been selected. Fourteen men and women were squeezed inside the jury box in the courtroom in Biloxi. Judge Holly Ostrov-Ronai was presiding over my trial, and she had insisted on seating two alternates in addition to the jury of twelve. She didn't want to take any chances, she'd said. Didn't want to throw out the case in the event someone caught the flu.

That wasn't the way we usually did it here. In Biloxi, one alternate was considered sufficient insurance. But this judge didn't hail from Harrison County. All the judges in our district had speedily disqualified themselves. While the case bounced around the judiciary looking for a place to land, another half a dozen judges had to recuse. Some of them were friends of mine or knew my father. One judge from Hattiesburg had a long-standing feud with my old man; I was relieved to see him drop out. Ultimately, they had to bring Judge Ostrov-Ronai in from Jackson.

Ostrov-Ronai wasn't a Mississippi native—she was actually from New York City, had been born in Bayside, Queens. She'd taken Jackson by storm when she opened her plaintiffs' personal-injury firm. Her practice was so successful that the local lawyers were relieved when she took the bench as a circuit judge. I'd heard about her phenomenal trial practice, but she'd never spent much time in the southern part of the state and had no connection to me.

The jury had also been imported from the state capital. The fourteen jurors had been transported from Jackson to Biloxi by bus and were lodged in a Best Western near the courthouse. Free breakfast, flat-screen TV, nice pool.

They wouldn't be using the pool, though. A sequestered jury stays locked up tight.

Judge Ostrov-Ronai emerged from chambers. After she instructed the jury, she looked at the DA and said, "You may begin opening statements."

That took me back to the start of the Caro trial, when I was still on top of the world. Toting my briefcase to the courthouse, ready to wow the jury with the opening statement I'd rehearsed at the office in front of my two best friends.

As I watched Gordon-James pull a script from his files, I had the distinct feeling that the best opening statement in the world couldn't help me today. I debated reserving my own opening for the start of the defense case. Maybe I'd get more mileage from it then, after the jury got to know me.

But my opponent was ready. He surged up out of his chair as if he couldn't wait to begin. "If it please the court," he said, his voice soaring out over the room.

As he approached the jury box, he looked like a warrior launching a crusade. His expression was predatory, and though he didn't gaze directly at me, I knew I was the prey.

It hit me then—the *hunted* sensation I was experiencing was how criminal defendants felt when they were on trial. My former point of view, that of defense counsel, wasn't remotely similar. This time, I was the accused. It was terrifying.

The prosecutor wanted to nail me on the murder charge. That desire was etched in his face. I could hear it in the intensity in his voice as he began to speak. "Ladies and gentlemen of the jury, I appreciate the sacrifice y'all are making, coming all this way to hear this case. Permit me to introduce myself. I'm the district attorney of Harrison County, Henry Gordon-James."

Unlike the local judges, Gordon-James hadn't opted to recuse himself. He could have claimed a conflict. We'd known each other for years. But my old nemesis had willingly stepped up to orchestrate my destruction.

CHAPTER 81

AS JENNY GLASER drove down a farm road on the Mississippi Delta with her car radio on for company, she wrestled with the regret that had plagued her since she'd left town that morning.

I ought to be in Biloxi.

Jenny had intended to go to court and take her place among the spectators. Though it would be a painful exercise, she wanted to be present as a show of support. Stafford Lee didn't have many friends who were still willing to stand behind him and be there on his behalf.

But a call had come the night before, a possible break. She couldn't pass it up. She'd been tracking this man for months, trying to pin him down. It was important to seize the opportunity.

She was doing it for Stafford Lee, and the clock was ticking. He'd taken the May trial setting even though she begged him to ask for more time. She needed to find evidence compelling enough to convince a jury—or the DA—that they had the wrong guy.

About fifty yards up the road, she spotted a sign that read PETTUS PECAN GROVES. As she turned into the drive, the local radio station started playing an oldie. The familiar melody of "Stand by Me" drifted through the speakers of Jenny's car, but Ben E. King's plaintive baritone sounded like a rebuke. She hastily grappled with the knob to turn off the radio, but she upped the volume by mistake.

The music blared as she pulled up a gravel drive to an old two-story farmhouse with a wraparound porch. Two big dogs appeared out of nowhere and ran toward her car, barking like crazy.

A sandy-haired man in denim overalls opened a screen door, stepped onto the porch, and shouted at the dogs. When they retreated, Jenny got out of her car. "Jenny Glaser, that you?" the man called.

Jenny waved, flashed a big smile. "Detective Pettus, I sure appreciate you agreeing to talk to me today."

They shook hands on the porch. He said, "Call me Bill, okay? I haven't been a detective for quite a while." He gestured toward a pair of wicker rockers. "We can sit out here, if that suits you. No flies yet, a little too early for them. Can I get you some tea? It's no bother, we keep a pitcher in the refrigerator."

"No, but thanks so much," Jenny said. After all the trouble she'd had setting up this meeting, she didn't want to let him out of her sight. They sat down in the wicker chairs. "You said you're leaving for a trip soon? I was lucky to catch you before you left town," Jenny said.

"We've got a new grandson in Little Rock. We're eager to get to Arkansas and meet the little guy. He's our first."

"That's just wonderful. Congratulations." Jenny gazed out at the trees. "This is a beautiful orchard, Bill. I can see why you left police work to move out here. I love Biloxi; I've lived there all my life. But this spot is special."

"It's my family's place. My dad harvested pecans from the old natural groves on the river. But I've added to it since he passed on, put in some seeded orchards. We're doing right well, got a good crop of the Kiowa nuts and the Elliot pecans."

The farm was tidy, well maintained. The barn behind the house was new, had probably replaced an old structure on the same spot. The former detective had worked hard to preserve the family farm.

Keeping her voice casual, she asked, "You ever miss it? The police work?"

He looked thoughtful. "I did at first. The circumstances of my departure weren't ideal. I got mad and quit. Don't know whether you heard that."

She had, but she didn't comment, just waited for him to say more.

"I'd just come into the detective job, rose through the ranks in Gulfport. So I was a real fire-eater, wanted to see every case solved, tied up tight. I couldn't take it when they let the case of that woman who washed up on the shore go cold."

This was Jenny's cue. "You're talking about Desiree Whitman. Right? Her body washed up on the beach in Gulfport." When he nodded, she said, "I started looking at Desiree's case when Daniel Caro was on trial for the murder of Aurora Gates." She pulled out her phone and set it on the small wooden table between their chairs. "I'd like to know more about the Desiree Whitman investigation. That's what I came to talk to you about."

He frowned down at the phone. Crossing his arms over his chest, he said, "This is off the record, ma'am."

She was disappointed, but she didn't want to push her luck. Jenny turned off the phone, holding it so he could clearly see her do it, and tucked it away in her bag. "Tell me about the case," she said. "The cause of death, the condition of the body—what do you recall?"

"She'd been shot through the forehead at close range. There was evidence of strangulation prior to the shooting, bruising on the neck. And she had been sexually assaulted."

"Was there evidence that was improperly handled? I've talked to the victim's husband, Germain. He said he was told something about the rape kit not being stored correctly so the samples weren't preserved."

"Bullshit," Pettus said. He had been rocking in his wicker chair, but the movement ceased abruptly. Jenny studied his expression, sensing that he was ready to unburden himself, confide a secret he had kept for too long.

He said, "I was a newcomer in the detective division, not a member of the inner circle. But we had some evidence; I was building a case. Hell, the woman's body told a story. We were comparing it to some other assaults and violent crimes in the region. We hadn't narrowed it down to one suspect, but we were getting there. I could feel it. You know what I'm talking about? When you can feel a case getting ready to crack wide open?"

He paused. Jenny held her breath, scared he would lapse into silence.

Pettus started rocking the chair again. It creaked under his weight. "I had some theories. But I'm not sharing them with you, not after all this time. I don't want to run my mouth and get slapped with a lawsuit. I'm not letting some jerk sue me for slander and end up with a piece of this farm."

She was disappointed. Her mind whirled as she tried to figure out the best way to keep him talking. "Bill, I'd love to tour your property. Will you walk me through the pecan groves?"

"Nope." His answer was abrupt, and his manner had become taciturn. "This isn't a tourist destination, ma'am. I'm a working farmer now, and I've got things to attend to before I can head to Little Rock." The chair stopped rocking and he rose with a grunt. "I'd best not say any more or I'll get myself in trouble. I'll walk you to the car, Ms. Glaser. The dogs might come running from the barn. They're friendly, basically, but they get pretty excited with strangers. Little old gal like you might get knocked down."

Jenny was grateful for the escort. She suspected that either one of the dogs could knock her flat. As they walked across the yard, she admired the dogs, hoping to get on Pettus's good side. "Those are two fine-looking dogs. And they're just doing their job, right? Letting you know when somebody comes onto the property?"

"That's right."

She lingered by the car door, trying to prolong the conversation. "Is there another time we can get together? I'm glad to do whatever fits your schedule. I could take you to lunch when you return from Little Rock. Or to dinner."

He laughed out loud. "Oh, my wife would like that, all right. If I was to tell her I was meeting a pretty woman from Biloxi for dinner, you'd be fishing *me* out of the Gulf with a bullet between the eyes. I guarantee you'd find my dead body on the beach with a note saying, 'Served that sumbitch right.'"

Jenny didn't find the joke very funny, but she faked it, gave him a conspiratorial wink. "The offer still stands."

He opened the car door for her. "I like you," he announced. "Gonna let you in on something. But if you ever repeat it, I'll swear you're a liar."

Jenny froze. Her heartbeat accelerated as she waited for him to speak.

"Nobody ever said a word about evidence being mishandled or samples not being preserved or insufficient evidence—not until after somebody put on the squeeze."

She waited for him to continue. After a moment, he did.

"Why he was able to shut a police investigation down, I don't even know. Did he have something on somebody, someone higher up the food chain than me? Probably. Cops are like anybody else. Some of them have their vices; they dabble on the dark side."

Jenny nodded. "So you think it's possible that someone was able to influence the outcome of the murder investigation?"

"At the time, that was the only thing I could figure. And I couldn't live with it, just couldn't abide it. So I quit." He hawked and spit on the ground. "If Hiram Caro is running Gulfport's police department, I ain't working there."

CHAPTER 82

I SHOULD'VE reserved my opening statement.

Clearly, not one of the fourteen men and women on the jury was ready to hear anything I had to say. All refused to make eye contact with me, and their faces expressed a daunting variety of unfriendly emotions, everything from suspicion to resentment to frank dislike.

As I stood there trying to engage them, it occurred to me that maybe Mason and Jenny had been right about the pro se decision. Could be that by not hiring a lawyer to represent me, I'd proved the truth of that old saying. It sure looked like I was a fool.

I hadn't forged any positive connection with the judge from Jackson either. When I finished my opening statement, Judge Ostrov-Ronai turned a solemn face to Gordon-James and said, "Are the parties ready to proceed?"

I didn't respond. She wasn't talking to me.

Gordon-James said, "Yes, Your Honor."

"The State may call its first witness."

Gordon-James rose. "The State calls Sergeant Carl Gorski to the witness stand."

The officer marched into court wearing his full uniform. Gorski hadn't opted for plainclothes, not for this appearance. He wanted that Jackson jury to see the shiny badge pinned to his chest.

After Gorski was sworn in, Gordon-James jumped right in; he barely asked for the witness's name and occupation before he directed his attention to the investigation of Iris Caro's death. The DA picked up his first exhibit.

"Sergeant, I'm handing you what's been marked for identification as State's exhibit number one. Can you tell us what it is?"

"It's a photograph of a footprint found near the body of the deceased, Iris Caro, in the bedroom of her home in Biloxi."

The question shook me. Not because I didn't know what was coming—I was aware of the evidence against me. What startled me was the DA's strategy. I'd expected the case to roll out in the usual manner, with the consecutive order of events—the discovery of the body, the medical determination of the cause of death. He'd forgone a sequential buildup. Gordon-James was aiming directly at me from the first minutes of this trial.

"Describe the footprint, Sergeant."

My head was reeling. Kicking off the case with that footprint drove home a stark reality: I was in the fight of my life. That evidence had been planted in my home. I was falsely accused. And no one was in my corner. Mason's primary duty was to his client Rue, and Jenny hadn't bothered to come to court.

For a moment, I thought I was going to lose it.

Gorski said, "It's a print we found on a wool carpet. The footprint is a reddish color, consistent with the color of blood."

Gordon-James walked over to the counsel table and pulled a plastic bag from a cardboard banker's box. "Sergeant, I hand you State's exhibit number two. Can you identify it?"

As the witness turned the clear plastic bag over and examined it, I experienced a eureka moment—I knew what I had to do. I ditched my carefully devised trial strategy and seized on a new plan. *Screw the rules*. Proper courtroom demeanor, process, practices—forget that shit. Playing by the rules wouldn't save me.

Holding the bag up so the jury could see it, Gorski said, "This bag contains a man's shoe made of plastic. It's what's commonly called a flip-flop."

"What, if anything, do you observe about the exhibit?" asked the DA.

"The sole of the shoe is covered with a substance that appears to be dried blood."

"Do you know where the bloody shoe was found?"

I couldn't wait for the cross; I needed to be heard. I jumped up and shouted, "What he's about to say is nuts, ladies and gentlemen. It's absurd!"

Everything stopped. Jurors gaped at me. The judge lost her power of speech for a moment. She quickly found her voice, but her judicial bearing was rattled. "Sit down!"

I sat. In Jackson, they said Ostrov-Ronai was tough as nails. Looked like it was true.

The judge said, "The witness will answer."

The cop gave the DA an apologetic grimace. "Can you repeat the question?"

I sat there with every muscle tensed, poised to create more chaos. After the court reporter read the question from the record, the cop nodded. "We found the shoe in the search of the defendant's home in Biloxi. It was at the back of his bedroom closet, inside a trash bag—"

That was my cue. I was on my feet again before he finished his sentence. "That's what I'm talking about! Why would I keep a shoe covered with the victim's blood in my bedroom closet? That's crazy!"

"Objection, Your Honor!" Gordon-James said.

I took a step away from the table and appealed to the jurors in the box. "I mean, who would do that? I'd have to be a moron to stash that shoe in my closet. Believe me, I'm not that stupid!"

The judge pounded her gavel. "Mr. Penney, you're out of order!"

That was true, I certainly was. But my outcry had seized the jury's attention. A handful of them were finally looking at me.

The judge was too. She pointed a finger in my direction. "Take your seat at the counsel table, Mr. Penney. You know better than this; you can't claim ignorance of courtroom proceedings. Sit down! I don't want to have to warn you again."

I stepped back to my chair. The judge gave me a threatening glare. I met her eyes and shook my head. Didn't pretend to look repentant. She'd tried a lot of cases in Jackson and knew that jury trials involved theater.

I figured I'd let Judge Ostrov-Ronai wonder what I might do next.

CHAPTER 83

JENNY REACHED the Biloxi city limits around midafternoon. The road trip through the Mississippi Delta had cleared her head, afforded her a chance to think. She'd gone round and round trying to find a way to discredit the evidence that pointed to Stafford Lee as Iris Caro's killer. By the time Jenny headed through the outskirts of downtown Biloxi, she was a woman on a mission, ready to execute her new plan.

She pulled into a parking spot directly in front of a run-down one-story building. She'd passed the structure dozens of times without ever venturing inside. A portable roadside sign topped by a flashing arrow read COMPUTER GEEKS UNLIMITED, BUY, SELL, TRADE.

Jenny walked in. Behind a glass counter was a dusty collection of laptops and towers poised perilously beside ancient Apple computers. A printed sign tacked over a door leading to the back of the store stated the company's policy: PAYMENT DUE IN ADVANCE!

Only one employee could be seen on the premises. Jenny scrutinized the guy behind the counter. He might have been in his late twenties, but it was tough to say. At first glance, he looked younger. He was rail-thin, his face unshaven, with a head of untamed bushy brown hair. He wore a T-shirt emblazoned with the image of some comic-book superhero Jenny had never heard of.

She strolled up to the counter, but the guy didn't look up. He was playing a game on his cell phone. The phone was set to max volume and emitted loud zapping sounds as he furiously tapped the screen with his thumbs.

Jenny waited, gazing at the merchandise on display under the glass countertop—a jumbled assortment of computer chips, hard drives, and power supplies—as if she were considering a purchase.

Finally, the clerk muted the phone and set it down. "You here to pick something up?"

"No. This is the first time I've set foot in this shop. I'm Jenny. Are you the owner?"

Jenny wasn't a gambler, but she would've bet money that he wasn't the owner. He said, "No, he left. Won't be in until tomorrow morning."

He wore his lack of interest like a badge. To put her plan in motion, she needed to engage him. "What did you say your name was?"

He hesitated before answering. "Raymond. You need something fixed?"

"Raymond, you've got an interesting business here. What services do you offer?"

"The usual. You got a broken screen on your iPhone or iPad, I can replace that. Or I can repair your computer or your phone."

He sounded bored. He seemed to assume that she was seeking a simple fix for something.

Jenny shook her head. "I need something a little more, umm..." Her voice trailed off as she sought the correct word. "Sophisticated."

A glimmer of interest showed on his face; his eyebrows rose slightly. "We can reset passwords, that's no challenge. I can clean up your hard drive. Override and delete files. You need to get rid of something?" He cracked a small smile. "I can defrag your porn, get rid of those files for you, if that's your problem. Is that what you came in for?"

345

He regarded her curiously. Jenny suspected he was trying to guess exactly how much porn she had on her device and why she needed it erased. She laughed. "No! That's not why I'm here, I swear."

He shrugged and reached for his phone again. Hastily, Jenny laid on the compliments. "It's amazing, how knowledgeable you are. Tech just isn't my thing. You're so smart, it's really impressive."

He nodded absently as he pulled the game back up on the screen. She was losing him.

Jenny's mother, a genuine Mississippi belle, had attempted to school her in the art of flirtation. Jenny hadn't paid much attention because she didn't want to follow in her mother's footsteps. But she recalled one of her old sayings: "Tell a handsome man he's smart; tell a smart man he's handsome."

"Oh. My. God. I just figured out who you remind me of!"

He blinked at his phone.

She stepped back from the counter. "That guy from the Avengers movie."

His eyes came up and focused on hers. "Which one?"

Hell, she didn't know. "I get the titles mixed up. But you remind me of him so much."

"Thor? Or Iron Man?"

Which answer was the right one? she wondered. She took a stab at it. "Thor."

"Chris Hemsworth?" A blush turned his complexion bright red. "You're kidding."

"I'm not! I know what I'm talking about. I noticed it when I came in here. Something about the way you carry yourself. And your eyes! You have that same look, that appeal." Jenny gave him the megawatt smile she saved for occasions like this. Seemed like her mother's tip was working. She could see him warming up to her.

"The first of his movies was the best. A classic," he said.

"Agree. One hundred percent." She leaned in close. "So I'm going to tell you why I came in here. Because I get the feeling that you can do anything. Like you've got tech superpowers."

He gave her a shy smile. "Yeah, maybe."

She went up on tiptoe and whispered in his ear, "Malware."

He looked intrigued. "What do you want?"

"I want a tutorial. I want you to teach me how to plant malware and spyware on someone's computer."

He glanced around, though no one was there to overhear. He said, his voice low, "You'll need a discrete computer."

"How do I find that?"

"I have one. Built it myself."

Jenny sighed like she was starstruck. "Raymond, you're a dream come true. Will you show me?"

He straightened, tugged at the hem of his superhero T-shirt. "Yeah. I can do that."

CHAPTER 84

A NEW day, Tuesday. A new State's witness testified on the stand, a forensic expert from the crime lab. He was talking about trace evidence collected at the scene of the crime.

Specifically, he was discussing three human hairs found on the pillow and sheets of the bed where Iris Caro's body was discovered.

The witness wasn't a DNA expert. The hair collected at the crime scene didn't have the roots attached to it, and roots of the hair are necessary to extract DNA. He was testifying about old-school hair comparison, the kind you did under a microscope.

Gordon-James said, "Mr. Stein, did you perform a microscopic examination of these hairs?"

Before he could answer, I called out from my counsel table, "Since he's an expert and I'm the one on trial, can he explain what my head was supposedly doing on Iris Caro's pillow? I've never been inside that house!"

Gordon-James turned to the judge. "Your Honor—"

I jumped in again. "Judge, I was at my office that day. Is a State's witness ready and willing to testify to that?"

Judge Ostrov-Ronai was fed up. "One more outburst and I'll instruct the bailiff to escort you to jail. You can participate in the remainder of your trial virtually."

The threat shook me up. If they removed me from the court-room, I wouldn't have a prayer. Besides, I had a decent legal basis on which to attack the hair evidence. "I understand, Your Honor."

The DA repeated his question. Mr. Stein stated that he had performed a microscopic examination of the hair taken from the scene.

"And thereafter, did you conduct a comparison of the human hair from the pillow and sheets of Iris Caro's bedroom to hair samples taken from the defendant, Stafford Lee Penney?"

It was time to get back on my feet. "Objection, Your Honor!"

Judge Ostrov-Ronai looked at me with poorly disguised loathing. I'd been on my feet a lot in the past two days. "Grounds, Mr. Penney?"

"The question is improper because hair microscopy is a faulty science. Scientists have shown that it is completely unreliable!"

Gordon-James looked daggers at me. "Again? Really? Your Honor—"

The judge said, "That will be grounds for argument, Mr. Penney. It goes to the weight of the evidence. Overruled."

Under ordinary circumstances, I would have sat down and shut up. The threat of removal from court was dire. But I had a valid point, and I needed to make it. "No, Your Honor! There's nothing to argue about! Hair microscopy isn't science and therefore doesn't merit an expert opinion. Are you aware that three defendants—*three*, Judge— were recently exonerated in Washington, DC, after the FBI hair-microscopy evidence used at trial was later proved to be wrong?"

Gordon-James pounded his fist on the counsel table. "He's making speeches again, Judge!"

I stepped into the space between my counsel table and the witness stand. "The jurors have the right to hear this information so they can view this witness's testimony in the proper light. I request leave to voir-dire this witness, Your Honor."

The judge squeezed her eyes shut like she was fighting a headache. After a moment, she nodded. "Proceed."

I didn't waste any time, just sailed right in. "Mr. Stein, you testified under oath that you've undergone FBI training for hair analysis and hair microscopy, isn't that true?"

The expert gave a bare nod. "It is."

"But are you aware that the FBI and the U.S. Department of Justice have admitted that for decades, every FBI expert gave flawed testimony about hair comparison in criminal cases? That's true, isn't it? The DOJ and the FBI have gone on record, haven't they?"

"I can't speak for the DOJ or the FBI. I work for the state crime lab."

I laughed at him. "I see. Will you admit that microscopic hair comparison analysis has become extremely controversial in the criminal justice community?"

He was miffed. I was happy to see it; I wanted to shake him up. After a pause, he said, "There is a division of opinion on the issue."

"All right, now we're making progress! So which side do you fall on? Let the jury know where you stand on this. Do you agree with the FBI, who, according to your testimony, trained you in this unscientific and imprecise discipline? Because the FBI is doing an internal review of thousands of hair-microscopy cases in which their lab improperly reported a match. And it's been reported that the FBI, your source for your so-called expertise, overstated hair matches in more than ninety-five percent of those cases. Ninety-five percent, Mr. Stein! What's your score? How many times did you get it wrong?"

There was a moment of silence. The witness looked confused. "What's the question?"

Hell, even I didn't remember. I turned to the judge. "Your Honor, I contest the witness's expertise to give an opinion on this issue."

"Overruled," she said shortly.

It looked like I had lost that round, but I suspected that my objection had done some good because when I sat down, Gordon-James turned his back on the hair-microscopy witness and said, "No further questions."

So the guy never got to state his opinion, which most certainly would have been that the hair from my head was a match to the hair found in Iris Caro's bed. The point I'd made in court about hair analysis was true. The FBI had backed away from it. But privately, I had to wonder: Were there really strands of my hair on the pillow and sheets in the room where Iris died? Who had set me up? Who had come to my house, taken samples of my hair, and planted them in Iris's bed? Daniel Caro? His old man, Hiram? Someone I'd sued or some cop who held a grudge? Could it even be Gordon-James himself?

Why choose me as the fall guy for the crime?

The DA had a new witness on the stand, another expert from the crime lab, the guy who did DNA testing. The DNA evidence wouldn't be so easy to contest. No one at the FBI was hanging their head in shame over DNA evidence. It was still considered solid, incontrovertible.

Gordon-James pulled that plastic bag from the box again. My gut churned when I saw the bloody shoe the police had seized from my bedroom closet. As I watched him and his witness wave the flip-flop around, I wanted to grab it, stuff it back into the DA's exhibit box, get it out of sight. After he'd laid the foundation, Gordon-James came around to the crucial question.

"Did you do a DNA profile on the blood found on the flip-flop, State's exhibit number two?"

"I did."

"How does the DNA profile on State's exhibit two compare to the known sample of blood taken from the body of Iris Caro, which is marked as State's exhibit ten?"

"There are no differences."

Then he elaborated, of course. Explained that it was a match, that it was essentially impossible for the blood to have come from any other individual.

I couldn't make my bloody shoe disappear, even if I grabbed it out of the witness's hand and flushed it down the men's room toilet. Couldn't discredit the expert either. When Gordon-James held the exhibit up for the jury to see, I averted my eyes.

I considered making another spectacle, shouting that the discovery of the shoe was meaningless because only a fool would keep such damning evidence of guilt. But the futility of the argument — and the judge's threat — kept me in my seat. Facts are facts. It was indisputable: Iris's blood was on the sole of my shoe, the one found in a trash bag inside my bedroom closet.

Someone hated me so much that he or she had set out to destroy me. Who was it?

CHAPTER 85

WHEN JENNY finally made it to the courthouse on Tuesday afternoon, the courtroom was empty. Morning proceedings had ended, and they had recessed for lunch.

She checked the tracking app on her phone, but Stafford Lee had apparently turned his off; the screen read **No location found.**

So she hunted down Charlene, the bailiff, who was eating a tuna sandwich in the clerk's office. Charlene always kept track of Stafford Lee's whereabouts when he was trying a case, but now she said, "I don't know where he goes at noon, Jenny. He's not my job. I'm only responsible for criminal defendants who are in the custody of the county jail."

Jenny turned on her heel and started looking for Mason, but she couldn't find him in any of the courtrooms. She went to Stafford Lee's office, but the place was empty and dark. She turned on the light in the conference room and scanned the murder walls. She stopped in front of a collection of autopsy photographs and peeled one away.

Back in her car, she drove to Red's Shooting Range. Red Thompson, the proprietor, sat behind the counter in a webbed folding picnic chair, thumbing through a firearms catalog. He looked up when she walked through the door.

"Well, look who's come to see me! How are you getting along, Miss Jenny?"

She returned his smile. "Doing all right," she said. Red had been a close friend of her late father. Her dad had started bringing her out to Red's range when she was just a kid; he'd taught her to shoot when she was in middle school. She had known Red for so long, she could even remember when his hair was fire-engine red. It had faded over the years to a rosy blond.

"Look at you, girl, just as pretty as a movie star. Surely you're not still single. You ever find a guy, get remarried?"

She dodged the question. "I don't have any time for husband-hunting, Red."

Red shot her a wink. "You'll change your tune when the right guy comes along. So, you out here for some target practice? Don't want you getting rusty."

"No, not today."

"You still carrying your Glock?"

"Yeah."

"You ready for an upgrade? I just got the newest Glock, the Gen Five. They keep getting better. Everyone who's tried it says the accuracy is unbeatable. You could check it out."

"No, thanks, Red, maybe another time. I'm here to ask you about shotgun evidence. You're my number one adviser, lots smarter than those guys at the crime lab."

He snorted. "Them pencil necks? Shoot, not much competition there."

Jenny reached into her bag and pulled out the autopsy photograph she'd removed from Stafford Lee's office. "Okay, Red. I want you to take a look at this photo. It's a close-up of the chest wound, see? She was shot with a shotgun in a murder-suicide."

Red rose from the picnic chair and stood on the opposite side of the counter. He grimaced when he glanced at the image showing the gunshot wound in Carrie Ann Penney's chest. "That poor lady. Who is she? Anyone we know?"

Jenny didn't answer directly. After a moment, she said, "Yeah, I knew her. It's not a new case, but I've been reviewing it, and I have some questions. Judging from the shotgun wound you see on the victim's chest, can you determine the distance between the gun and the victim when the shot was fired?"

"Sure. See there, those little burned pieces, powder and stippling? They can't travel very far. So the barrel of the shotgun had to be pretty dang close, within about two feet of that woman when it was fired."

"Two feet, you think? That's your best guess?"

"Yeah, from this picture. But if you've got the shotgun, you don't have to guess."

"What do you mean?"

"I mean that if they found the gun at the scene and impounded it, you can get a definite answer on distance. A shotgun fires multiple pellets that simultaneously spread out in a wider pattern until they hit the target. So you test-fire it from different distances and angles until you find the range that made the pattern left on this woman's chest. You can figure out distance that way, and it's pretty darn accurate."

Jenny pulled the firearms report from the murder-suicide case out of her bag. She skimmed it and said, "The police took custody of the shotgun found at the scene. But they didn't do any distance testing. The report doesn't specify whether any firearm tests were done."

"Yeah, they don't do distance testing at the sheriff's department or the PD. They'd have to send it off to the State Highway Patrol headquarters and make a special request."

The close-up photo of Carrie Ann's chest lay on the countertop. Jenny examined the stippling, the powder marks, tried to determine the pattern the projectiles had left behind. While she studied it, Red stepped over to a gun rack behind the counter and said, "You want to go out on the range and try it, see what I'm talking about?"

Red unlocked a gun case, pulled a shotgun from the rack, and held it out to Jenny. She didn't take it from him because another gun in the case had caught her eye, a twenty-gauge shotgun that was the most beautiful hunting gun she'd ever seen. The wooden stock was polished walnut with an elaborately engraved side plate; its barrels were buffed to a high sheen.

"Red, where on earth did you get that?" she asked reverently. She pointed up at the shotgun. He acknowledged it with a nod.

"Ain't she a beauty? That's a custom Perazzi, made in Italy. It's not for sale, but you and me, we couldn't afford it if it was. See the gold inlay in the side plate? Genuine gold, no kidding. That shotgun costs more than I make in a year. Heck, maybe two years."

She leaned on the counter, longing to feel its weight and balance. "Can I hold it? Just for a second? I'll be careful, I promise."

He shut the case and turned the lock. "No, Jenny. You can try any gun in this place, but I can't let you lay a hand on that one. It's not mine."

She was disappointed. "I'd be careful, Red. You know that."

He looked adamant. She could tell that no amount of cajoling would change his mind. "You can't even breathe on it, Jenny. That particular gun is part of a personal firearms collection. It's here for yearly cleaning and maintenance, and they're coming by any time to pick it up."

He tucked the key into his pocket. "It's the property of Hiram Caro."

CHAPTER 86

JUDGE OSTROV-RONAI had called for lunch recess to end at exactly one o'clock. I made it back to court with five minutes to spare—and damp cuffs on my suit pants.

I had used the lunch break to drive to the boardwalk, sit in a secluded spot, and watch the water. I wanted to listen to the waves, breathe in the salty air; I'd hoped it would be a balm for my troubled spirit.

And it was. The water called to me. I kicked off my shoes, pulled off my socks, rolled up my pants, walked across the sand to the shoreline, and let the water rush up to cover my feet. It was restorative. But I stepped in too far and caught a wave that splashed almost up to my knees.

In the courtroom now, I inspected my pants, wondering whether the jury would notice the fabric was wet and wonder why. I was trying to dry them off with a handkerchief when Henry Gordon-James appeared at my counsel table.

I was surprised to see him standing so close. He hadn't spoken directly to me since the trial began. I braced myself for a tirade or an angry confrontation. But when he spoke, his voice was soft, deliberately casual.

He said, "I really hate to admit being wrong."

I stared at him, waiting for him to make his point. I knew this wasn't idle conversation.

He continued. "I don't like it, but the way things are shaping up, I might have to do that."

Honestly, the silent treatment was preferable to mind games. "You're speaking in riddles, Henry. If you've got something to say to me, just say it."

He jammed his hands into his pockets. "They're taking a close look at some old murder cases, some unsolved files. Gulfport PD and Biloxi PD are working together, along with the county sheriff's department."

"Great. Congratulations. Best of luck; hope they get to the bottom of whatever it is."

He went on as if I hadn't spoken. "There are some similarities in some of those cases, and they're assessing them and also comparing them to the Iris Caro murder. Looking for a signature."

His words kindled a spark of hope. My friends and I had been going through the same inquiry at my law office. I started to volunteer the information about the murder walls we'd constructed in my conference room, but something about the way his eyes bore down on me made me hesitate.

He said, "When you put it all together, all those pieces, it lends clarity. Shows the common denominator. Some of my best people in law enforcement are saying that you are the common thread. You're the one responsible."

I opened my mouth to protest. He spoke again before I had the chance.

"And you were right under my nose this whole time. I used to think that Daniel Caro was a cold bastard, an unfeeling predator. But you're worse."

During the conversation, the bailiffs had wandered back into court. We had an audience.

Gordon-James said, "You are a monster."

CHAPTER 87

THAT NIGHT, I sat in my conference room with a list of witnesses that the DA had provided. I sifted through the prosecution file, trying to predict who Gordon-James would call the next day.

It was a guessing game that required my complete attention. I suspected that the DA would unleash the damning e-mails I'd supposedly sent to Rue after the murder that contained incriminating statements of criminal responsibility. They had one they'd purportedly found on my computer instructing her to put on her housekeeping uniform and get inside the Caros' house to get the shoe I left behind.

Or they might open with the short series of threatening texts I'd purportedly sent to Iris, evidence of a one-sided romantic obsession. A flurry of texts that supposedly came from me appeared on Iris's phone the day of her death. Texts declaring love, demanding that she leave Daniel. The final text said that I'd commit suicide if she refused but that I'd make sure she died first. Scanning the phony communications, I wondered how I could convince the jury that they were fake. Did I have any hope of persuading them?

Someone knocked on my front door. I didn't look up. The only friends I had in Biloxi had their own keys and could let themselves in. And I didn't intend to grant entry to anyone else. I wasn't inclined to speak to a reporter, and I sure wasn't up for a confrontation with a random angry member of the public who wanted to tell me off. I had received more than my share of abuse that day at the courthouse.

Now someone was pounding on the door, beating on it so violently that the hinges rattled. Still, I was determined to ignore it. But then the shouting started, a voice I knew well. Groaning, I rose and stepped into the reception area.

He was yelling, "Stafford Lee, I know you're in there, damn it!"

I unbolted the lock and pulled the door open. My father stood at the threshold, his face florid from yelling. "Didn't you hear me knock?"

"Yeah, I heard you."

He strode in, heading straight for the conference room. I followed, asking, "What are you doing here?"

"I came over because of all the talk around town." When he reached the doorway of the conference room, he froze. "Jesus Christ!" He swung around to face me, and his complexion was so red, it bordered on purple. "What the hell have you got going on in there? Have you lost your goddamn mind?"

"It's research," I said. The explanation didn't sound convincing. I knew how unsettling the room looked to someone who was not part of the investigative team.

He strolled up to the nearest set of photos and studied them. "Good God, Stafford Lee. Is that your wife?"

I stepped away from the room. "Let's go into my office, okay? I've got stuff organized on the table in here, and I don't want anything disturbed."

He muttered as he left the conference room. When he settled into a chair in my office, I heard him mumble something about me needing a straitjacket.

I sat behind my desk and faced him. His hair was disheveled, his collar unbuttoned, and his necktie hung loose. He scowled at me. "I was at the courthouse today. It's buzzing like a beehive over there. People say that the DA went after you, accused you of being a serial killer."

My stomach knotted. It sickened me to know that the talk was making the rounds at the courthouse. "I guess he did."

"You guess? They said he called you a monster. Is that a quote? He used that exact word?"

"I don't want to talk about it. I need to get back to work, Dad. I'm in trial."

"You are not just *in* trial, son. You are *on* trial. Why the hell are you representing yourself? Of all the crackpot things I ever heard! Why didn't you ask me? I'd have stepped in to take your case. What, you think you can't afford my fee? As if I'd charge my own son."

The mental image of my father seated next to me at the counsel table was frightening. "That never occurred to me. You know what they say, a close family member shouldn't take on representation."

He gave a scornful laugh. "I'd sure as hell have done a better job than you're doing. I know what you're up to in there, Stafford Lee. People can't wait to stop me on the sidewalk and fill me in. You're putting on a carnival sideshow in court. Why would you act like a lunatic who doesn't know the law? You're not a layman; you have the benefit of a legal education."

In a knee-jerk reaction, I started to defend myself. "There's a method to what I'm doing, Dad. I had to get the jury to listen to me."

"Oh, shut up."

I fell silent, quit trying to explain my tactics. Seeking my old man's understanding was a losing proposition.

He said, "I've given the matter some thought. And I figured a way out for you. How you can plant the seed of reasonable doubt you need for acquittal."

In spite of myself, I perked up, ready to hear his advice. Because I needed a miracle, and maybe he had one.

He knew he'd gotten my attention. His eyebrows lifted and his face took on a wily expression. "It's so obvious, I don't know why you didn't think of it yourself. You should have stepped right up in opening statements and laid it out."

"What?" I was eager to hear his strategy.

"It's time to cast suspicion on that cleaning lady, Rue Holmes. She's the one who had the opportunity to commit the crime. She worked in the Caros' house, for crying out loud! And she's no law-abiding citizen. She stole a necklace from Mrs. Caro."

My mouth opened. Nothing came out, I was speechless. Dad didn't notice.

He went on. "And that's not all. That gal is the one who set you up, I'm sure of it. You've got to realize that, son. I know you're soft-hearted when it comes to people like her. You have a blind spot. But think about it. She lives in your house. How hard would it be to get samples of your hair from the shower drain or a brush in the bath-room? And that bloody shoe? Clearly, she took your beach shoes to the scene, stepped in the blood, brought one back to your house, and tossed it in your closet, wrapped up in a trash bag so you wouldn't notice."

He must have read something in my face, because he started to get defensive. "I'm not just shooting in the dark here, Stafford Lee, flailing around to blame anyone but you. I've thought it through, and the facts lead me to one reasonable conclusion. She's responsi-ble. She set you up. Either she committed the murder herself or she knows who did, because she's covering somebody's tracks. And she's covering those tracks with your beach shoes."

I was stupefied. It took me a minute to compose myself suffi-ciently to speak. "You haven't offered up an explanation. You skipped right over the issue of **why**. Why would Rue do it? What possible motive would she have to either kill Iris or frame me?"

"Eh, motive. Well, that's always a mystery, right? That's why they don't include it in the criminal charge. Hell, I'm not a mind reader, and I don't know the girl. You do, though. Could it be jealousy? Resentment? Did you do something that made her mad?"

Adamantly, I shook my head. He was mistaken, way off the mark. It wasn't possible.

My father's voice grew strident as he argued his point. "With women, you never know what sets them off. Women are vengeful creatures. Who knows how their minds work? That's why people used to think they were witches. Women are sneaky, secretive, underhanded."

Jenny appeared in the doorway. I'd been so focused on my father's accusations, I hadn't heard her come in.

Her eyes narrowed as she glared at my father. "What did you just say about women?"

For an old guy, he moved pretty fast; he shot up out of his chair. "I said I'm on my way out." He looked back at me. "Stafford Lee, you think about what I told you!"

CHAPTER 88

JENNY FLOPPED down into the seat my dad had vacated. She propped her feet on the edge of the desk and said, "One of these days, Stafford Lee, I'm afraid I'm going to deliver a slap-down to your dear old dad."

"When it happens, I want to be there to watch. Promise me."

"Okay, I promise. If I know about it beforehand." She gave me a keen glance. "How's it going? How are you doing?"

"Hmm. Not great."

She dropped her feet back to the floor. "Okay, I want to pitch a theory. You up for this?"

Jenny was buzzing with excitement over something, I could tell. And I was certainly in the market for ideas. "I'm listening. Run it by me."

"I think we're looking at the wrong member of the Caro family."

Well, that wasn't what I expected. "What? You've been harping on Daniel since he was on trial for Aurora Gates."

"Yeah, I know. But I'm starting to wonder whether it's Hiram Caro. Some pieces have surfaced that point in his direction. Should we be focusing on the father rather than the son?"

Her switch made my head spin. I couldn't even pretend to be encouraging. "Come on, Jenny. This isn't helpful."

"Think about it. Hiram would have every opportunity to enter the Caros' home. Iris wouldn't raise an alarm if she saw her father-in-law in the house. And that old reprobate could take her down. He's not too old to win a wrestling match with a woman her size. Shoot, what did she weigh? A hundred twenty pounds?"

"Opportunity isn't enough to even raise a suspicion."

"Did you know he has a cache of weapons? A whole collection of them. Handguns, rifles, shotguns. I was talking to Red about it at the shooting range."

"But Iris wasn't shot with a firearm. She died of suffocation after she sustained a blow to her head. The head wound resulted in heavy bleeding, but it wasn't the cause of death, although it may have rendered her unconscious." I was reciting the coroner's report from memory. I'd had a lot of time to study it.

Jenny said, "About the weapons in Hiram's collection. They could connect him to the other murders we've looked at—Aurora Gates, Desiree Whitman. Those were committed with handguns. Maybe if we go back and check ballistics in old cases, the guns in his collection would match up. He also owns a custom shotgun, a very special model. Testing could show if the projectiles from his shotgun make a specific pattern."

Once I realized she was talking about Carrie Ann, my gorge rose. Closing my eyes, I willed myself to calm down.

Whether she was aware of my discomfort, I didn't know. But Jenny kept talking. "And Hiram has ties to organized crime. I mean, your dad was his lawyer when he was part of the Dixie Mafia. You know what that means. He has minions who would plant evidence for him, people who wouldn't hesitate to take a flip-flop from your closet and use it to create evidence against you."

"This is so far-fetched, Jenny."

"More far-fetched than you and Rue and Iris in a love triangle? Here's something I just found out. Hiram Caro had an insider working at Gulfport PD, someone on his payroll. Whoever it was, he or she bungled the Whitman investigation on orders from Hiram Caro."

That gave me a jolt. "Wow. That's something. Who is it? Did you get a statement?"

"I talked to Bill Pettus, a former detective. He's not ready to go on the record yet, but I think I can wear him down."

It was apparent that Jenny had been striving to make a breakthrough. God knows I appreciated her efforts, but she had only gathered fragments, bits and pieces that didn't fit together to create a substantial defense. It meant the world to me that she'd put up such a valiant fight. I reached out, squeezed her hand, and said, choosing my words carefully, "Jenny, speculation won't turn this case around. And casting suspicion in a random fashion isn't going to convince anyone of anything. It's too late to try to raise a non-specific Other Dude Done It defense. The ODDI defense works only when there's a plausible, solid, substantial reason to point the finger at another person."

I turned her hand over, kissed her palm. Then I pushed my chair back and rose. "I've got to go back to the conference room and prep for tomorrow."

"Right now? I've got more to tell you."

"Yeah, right now. Pretty sure I know what is coming up next. Tomorrow morning, I think he'll introduce the e-mails that supposedly came from my computer and the texts they found on Iris's cell phone. I'm trying to figure out a way to combat those. I don't know how I'll convince the jury that I didn't send them."

Jenny broke into a triumphant smile. "That's my best news! I was saving it for last. I found a witness to refute all that."

That stopped me. I dropped back into the chair. "What have you got?"

She pulled a huge wad of handwritten notes from her bag. "I haven't turned this into a formal memo for you yet because I've just spent about thirty-six hours with my new best friend, Raymond Plummer. He's a geek, a tech whiz kid."

I tried to scan the notes, but her writing was illegible. "What will he say?"

"He knows all about malware and spyware. He can explain to the jury how the e-mails were planted on the computer and the texts were sent to her phone. He can even do a demonstration, if the court will permit that. Make it happen right before the jury's eyes."

"Will it sound feasible?"

"Oh, yeah. People know that hacking is a thing, but they don't understand how it works. Malware and spyware can be used to gain information, like passwords, contacts, personal ID details. One tool is the Trojan Horse. It can install backdoors to bypass normal authentication procedures."

"Then what?"

"Then your phone is the hacker's phone, and the hacker has complete access—he can send e-mails, texts, whatever."

I could feel my spirits lift. Was it possible that Jenny had unearthed a bona fide lifesaver? "How will he look on the stand? Will he inspire confidence?"

She wrinkled her nose. "Working on that. I'm hoping we can clean him up for the stand. Maybe a haircut. If he wears a superhero T-shirt to court, would that be a disaster? Because it might happen."

"Superhero? You mean like Spider-Man?"

"No, I'm thinking Thor. In fact, I'd bet on it. And speaking of betting, I think I'll leave you to your trial prep. I've got someplace to go."

I didn't want her to leave, even though I'd informed her just minutes before that I needed to go prep. I considered asking her to stick around for a while, just for the comfort of her company. She was the only thing that made life tolerable, the single bright spot in my miserable existence. "Where are you headed?"

"The casino. I can see that I haven't convinced you that my gut feeling about old Hiram is valid, so I'm going to do some digging."

She grabbed her bag and headed out of the office. I called after her, "Jenny, no! I don't want you going over there."

I heard her laughter. "I didn't ask you!"

She was under the mistaken belief that I was kidding around. I ran into the lobby and caught her before she reached the door. "Do I have to drag you into the conference room and lock you inside? I'm serious. The Caros are trouble, both of them."

I had her arm in a firm grip, but she didn't appear to be remotely moved by my speech. "Stafford Lee, my ex-husband thought he could boss me around. That's why it didn't work out." She jerked her arm from my grasp. "Just because we're sleeping together doesn't mean you can tell me what to do."

She left, slamming the door shut behind her.

CHAPTER 89

JENNY WISHED she hadn't snapped at Stafford Lee. He was under crippling pressure—he was on trial for murder and juggling his own defense. His whole life was spinning out of control, so it made sense that he wanted to exert some power over the investigation.

Problem was, Jenny wasn't the kind of woman who took orders. Not even when she loved the guy.

And she loved Stafford Lee. Not in a love-you-like-a-friend way either. Jenny had fallen hard, head over heels.

She couldn't decide if the timing was disastrous or fortuitous. Maybe both.

She pulled into the parking lot of Hiram Caro's waterfront casino. The lot was packed. She steered her car up and down the lanes, hunting in vain for a vacant spot. The tall pylon sign in front of the casino flashed a huge message on its reader board that explained the parking crush: VIP SLOT TOURNAMENT TONIGHT! $50,000 JACKPOT!

She circled around to a parking area clearly marked CASINO EMPLOYEES ONLY and pulled into a forbidden space. Looking up, she saw surveillance cameras in the lot. She was taking a risk. She assumed the casino's promise to tow unauthorized vehicles wasn't an idle threat. There was a distinct possibility that her car was being watched by Hiram's goon squad—and that was a dangerous prospect.

But this was for Stafford Lee, and time was certainly of the essence. As she jogged to the casino's side entrance, she passed another surveillance camera. Jenny didn't cower. She lifted her chin and stared into it defiantly. *Here I come, Caro.*

Inside the casino, Jenny walked through a maze of dinging slot machines to the hotel lobby. She didn't see a tournament under way, but the casino floor was packed. Every seat at every card table was taken, and the craps tables had attracted rowdy crowds. Someone was winning; she heard shrill cheers.

Somewhere on the property, a country-western band was playing. The powerful bass lines blasted from the subwoofers, shaking the floor. She wanted to cover her ears. Once she reached the hotel lobby, the noise was muted. Jenny walked first to the casino business offices, though it was after hours. She saw that the front windows were dark, and when she tugged on the door, it was locked.

But Jenny wasn't discouraged, not yet. She knew how casinos operated. The gambling action was hottest when the sun went down and the neon lit up the darkness. As a casino owner, Hiram Caro didn't have a nine-to-five existence. She knew he liked to hang around when business was brisk.

Jenny opened the door to the VIP club, certain those offices would be open. High rollers went to the VIP club for comps, personal service, and private check-ins when they arrived from the airport in the casino's private limousine. The stretch limo, emblazoned with a smiling woman behind a roulette wheel, was a common sight around town.

Now she observed a couple arguing with the desk attendant, complaining about accommodations and demanding a suite. Jenny waited behind them, her foot tapping with impatience as they haggled. When the man started to negotiate more free play as a substitute for the suite, she couldn't remain quiet any longer. Stepping around the couple, Jenny said to them, "This will just take a second." She addressed the woman employee in a no-nonsense voice. "I need to speak to Hiram Caro."

The VIP hostess was a trim woman in her forties with big hair and heavy makeup. She eyed Jenny speculatively. "Was Mr. Caro expecting you?"

The female high roller at Jenny's elbow gave her a shove and said, "You've got a lot of nerve. We're checking in here."

Jenny ignored her. Keeping her focus on the hostess, she said, "Where can I find Hiram? It's urgent."

The employee looked uncomfortable. Jenny tried a good-natured appeal; she turned on a winning smile. "I know you want me out of your hair. Just tell me where he is, and I'll go away."

The employee's hand slid under the counter. Jenny caught the movement. *Uh-oh. Panic-button alarm.*

Her suspicions were proved correct when two guys in security uniforms burst into the office. They each grabbed one of Jenny's elbows, pulled her from the VIP desk, and hustled her down a short hall to a private office inside the players' club.

They brought her into the room and shut the door. Jenny was flustered, but she was determined not to show it. She sat in the chair closest to the door, figuring that would be the best position for a getaway. Easing back in the chair, she looked up at the guy standing over her and asked, "Is Hiram going to join us? I need to talk to him."

"He heard you're looking for him."

Jenny turned her attention to some brochures on a small table beside her chair. She picked up an advertising trifold, crossed her legs, and pretended to read it, making an effort to appear completely at ease.

After four or five minutes, the office door opened. She looked up, hoping to see Hiram Caro.

She was disappointed. Hiram didn't walk through the door. Instead, his personal bodyguard stalked in. Joey Roman.

CHAPTER 90

JOEY ROMAN closed the office door and locked it. Then he leaned against the door, folded his arms across his chest, and gazed down at Jenny.

Roman's attire distinguished him from the other security personnel. He was dressed in a slim-fit sport coat over a crisp white shirt paired with indigo jeans. Joey didn't need to wear a security uniform or badge to give off a dangerous vibe. She knew he wanted to intimidate her. Locking her into a room with three men and blocking the door so she couldn't get out—it was an act of aggression. Jenny was determined to send a message right back: *I'm not scared of you.*

She gave Roman a side-eye before returning her attention to the advertising brochure. Reading aloud, she murmured, "'Loosest slots and hottest table games in Biloxi.' Wow. Impressive."

Silence in the room. She counted to ten before she spoke again. "Is Hiram on his way down?"

Roman sounded almost friendly when he said, "Mr. Caro's not available. What do you want? I can pass along the message."

Jenny's impatience gave her voice a sharp edge. "I don't want to go through the messenger boy, Joey."

The two young security guys tensed up and exchanged a look of surprise. Jenny noted their reaction. She figured it meant that Joey Roman was rarely disrespected on casino property. She would have to proceed more cautiously.

She forced a smile. "Joey, you know I'm a private investigator, right? I'm here in a professional capacity. I want to talk to your boss about a case."

His eyes were hooded. "What kind of case?"

"A murder. A case where someone's been falsely accused."

"Why would he care about it?"

Jenny didn't like the atmosphere in the room. It gave her an edgy feeling, like the walls were closing in on her. "He might have some relevant information to share, that's all."

"What's the case?"

It was becoming clear that Hiram Caro would not be walking through that door. Jenny needed to regroup; she could use Joey to accomplish her goal. She said, "The death of his daughter-in-law, Iris Caro."

She watched Roman closely. If Hiram was involved in the woman's death, Roman might know something. He was Hiram Caro's top henchman. But Joey Roman's face betrayed nothing, gave no flicker of reaction. He stepped over to Jenny and plucked the advertising pamphlet from her hand. "This is a casino. If you're not here to enjoy the casino activity, you should run along. I guarantee Mr. Caro won't appreciate your nosy questions about his son's deceased wife."

"Okay. I hear you." At that point, Jenny was itching to get out of the office. She had no desire to prolong her captivity in the VIP club with Joey Roman, but she needed to plant a seed with his boss. If she couldn't corner Hiram, maybe Roman could make a delivery for her.

She decided that it was time to dangle the bait. She pulled a flash drive from her bag and held it up. "Be sure to tell Hiram I'm looking for him. When he sees this, I guarantee he'll want to talk to me. I have evidence that clears Stafford Lee Penney."

Joey snatched the flash drive from her. "Great. I'll give it to him."

"Hey!" Jenny protested. She stood and held out her hand. "That's my property. Give it back to me."

Roman flipped the lock, pulled the door open. To the uniformed guards, he said, "Escort her out of the casino. And make sure she leaves the property."

Jenny had to walk at a brisk pace to keep up with security. As they marched her through the casino and out the exit, she replayed the exchange in her head, battling uncertainty. Had she set the trap effectively? That flash drive needed to be delivered to Hiram Caro, and soon.

Stafford Lee's life depended on it.

CHAPTER 91

IN THE conference room, I sat in a chair facing the wall where Iris Caro's autopsy photo was posted. I was poring over Officer Mueller's report, scribbling notes in the margins. Mueller was the cop who would authenticate the texts and e-mails I had supposedly sent to Iris. The DA needed to convince the jury that I was a jealous lover and those messages were the proof. I framed my attack on the testimony, devising cross-exam questions and anticipating the cop's responses. Someone knocked at the outer office door.

I ignored it.

After a second round of knocking, I heard the rattle of a key in the lock. Some of the tension left my shoulders. Thank God—Jenny must be back from the casino. The door creaked open. I called, "Jenny! I'm back here!"

"Stafford Lee!" It was Mason. "You got a minute?"

"Sure." I marked a stopping point on the police report and pushed it to the side.

Mason stepped into the conference room and took a seat at the table. He glanced around the room and grimaced. "Good God, Stafford Lee. I don't know how you can concentrate in here. Too many horror stories on the walls."

I nodded, looking at the images of Iris, Aurora, Carrie Ann,

Desiree. There were other faces too, victims in cold cases that Jenny had uncovered. "You'd be surprised. It doesn't interfere with my focus too much. Actually, it serves as a reminder. Keeps my feet to the fire."

He shuddered. "Everyone has his own tricks of the trade, I guess." Shooting a glance out the door, he said, "So Jenny's not around right now?"

"No." I cursed under my breath. "She took a wild notion to run over to Hiram Caro's casino tonight. Said she wanted to do some digging. I couldn't talk her out of it. I promise you, I tried."

Mason blew out a breath. "Good, glad it's just us."

"Really? Because I'm tied up in knots knowing she's over there. If she pisses Hiram off, there's no telling what he'll do."

Soberly, Mason nodded. "That's kinda what I wanted to discuss. Do you think Jenny's going off the rails?"

I stiffened. It was one thing for me to grouse about Jenny's pursuit of Hiram, but no one else could criticize her. Not even Mason.

He must have read my reaction. "Stafford Lee, I know she's motivated by loyalty. And she's all about doing whatever she can to attack the State's case. But there're limits, you know? There's a line you can't cross. And Jenny's crossing it."

I tipped my chair back on two legs. With a chill in my voice, I asked, "What line are you talking about?"

"I got this crazy e-mail from her today about cyber-evidence. She said she wanted to keep me informed because it could help Rue. She claims she's found a tech witness who's gonna pull a rabbit out of his hat." He ran a hand over his hair. "Stafford Lee, you sure that's smart?"

I shrugged. "Why wouldn't it be?"

His voice dropped to a whisper: "Buddy. What the tech guy's doing? It's not strictly legal."

Mason was right. But in my current position, that didn't eliminate the tech guy as a resource. "That's my problem, Mason. Don't worry about it."

"Goddamn it, Stafford Lee, it's my problem too. Everything that goes down in your case, I have to live with. Because—as you'll recall—I represent your codefendant."

"I'm aware of that."

"Are you?" He stood and looked down on me with a resentful glare. "Do you recall that I took her case on at your request? As a favor to you?" He looked like he wanted to say more. But the office's front door flew open and banged against the wall, and Jenny called out from the lobby, "I think we've got him!"

CHAPTER 92

GOD, I was glad to have Jenny back in the safety of my office. I ran into the reception area, grabbed her, gave her a hug.

Then I stepped back, held her at arm's length, and studied her face. To my immense relief, she looked like she was fine. Better than fine; she was beaming.

"What happened?" I asked.

"I planted a virus. At least, I think I did."

Mason joined us in the lobby. He gaped at Jenny. "A virus? You mean a computer virus?"

"Yes! Malware."

I let out a whistle. I was seriously impressed. "No kidding?"

"Yeah. Raymond is coming by—the kid from the computer store. No telling what will happen, but we'll see what goes down."

Mason groaned. "Oh, shit. We're all going down. Y'all realize this is illegal, right?"

Jenny gave him an eyeroll. "Mason, please. What are you afraid of? It's not like the Biloxi PD has a cybercrime division."

"Are you familiar with an agency known as the Federal Bureau of Investigation?" he asked. When the tech kid walked into the office a moment later, Mason was clearly uncomfortable. He made a dash for the door. "I'm out of here," he said. "See you at the courthouse, Stafford Lee."

Jenny said, "Stafford Lee, I'd like to introduce my expert consultant, Raymond Plummer."

My spirits fell when I saw him. The kid didn't look like any expert I'd ever seen. His shorts drooped down to reveal his underwear, and he hugged an old laptop to his chest. He said to Jenny, "Where are we setting up?"

Jenny pointed him to the conference room. As Plummer headed off, Jenny pulled me aside. "Stafford Lee, Mason's not all wrong—we're getting into murky waters."

I'd already thought of that. And disregarded it. I didn't have much confidence in the Gen Z dude setting up his equipment in my conference room, but I was desperate for a break. Any kind of break from any source.

"If we run afoul of federal law, the feds will have to stand in line behind Henry Gordon-James to get a piece of me." I nodded toward the conference room. "I say we give the kid a shot."

Jenny joined the tech guy, and I locked the entrance and tugged on the doorknob to double-check. If someone interrupted us, he'd have to kick in the door, so at least we'd have some warning.

I heard Jenny talking excitedly to Raymond Plummer, and I strolled back to join them. My spirits were rising, though there was no cause for celebration, not yet. As far as I could tell, my circumstances hadn't changed. I stepped into the conference room and saw that the tech guy had stationed himself at the far end of the table behind a battered laptop decorated with comic-book-character stickers.

The sight set me back. Was this the man we'd entrusted with a crucial element of the defense? Did my fate rest on his narrow shoulders?

Jenny stood behind his chair, looking at the screen. She saw me, gave me an encouraging smile, and waved me over. "Raymond found public Wi-Fi. Unsecured."

The kid clicked on the laptop for several excruciating minutes. "Cool. Making some progress," he said.

I didn't want to be a sucker and buy into false hope. Maybe that's why I acted like a jerk. "Hey, Raymond. Is that really your hacking equipment? The old laptop?"

To his credit, the kid didn't get huffy. Without looking up, he said, "It's not the hardware that's important, it's the software. And also, you know, the skill set of the person doing it."

Jenny shot me a warning glance. "We know how lucky we are to have your help, Raymond. You're a pro. There's nobody better."

I reserved judgment. There was a long period of silence while the dude played with his laptop with Jenny as an attentive audience.

The stress was giving me jitters. To disguise it, I sat at the table and pretended to work on the cross-exam I'd been composing before Mason arrived. But I was totally faking it. I felt like something was about to explode.

At length, the kid made a snort of satisfaction and gazed up at Jenny. "We're in."

Jenny's hand went to her chest. "You think?" she said.

I pushed my chair back. "Into what?"

Jenny said, "Stafford Lee, I took a flash drive to the casino, one that Raymond gave me. I needed to get that flash drive into Hiram's computer system. I figured I could con the old man into planting it himself if I had the chance to talk to him, but he wouldn't meet with me. So I showed it to Joey Roman, held it out like bait."

The scenario Jenny described was exactly what I'd wanted her to avoid. "Joey Roman? Jenny, you don't want to mess with Joey."

"But it worked! He grabbed it right out of my hand and said *he* was going to give it to Hiram Caro—and it looks like he did! He must've gone straight to Hiram, didn't even wait until tomorrow to pass it on."

A sense of anticipation took hold of me. "So what does the flash drive do?" I asked. I was a lawyer, not a tech guy. I was still trying to figure this out.

Jenny said, "The flash drive Joey snatched from me contained a virus."

Raymond ran his hand over the computer screen. "The virus in the flash drive infects the computer it's inserted into. Then the virus replicates itself and attaches to software and stored files."

"It gives us access. To everything." Jenny was so pumped, she was glowing with triumph.

"You mean we have access to Hiram Caro's computer? Right now?"

"Yeah, we do." She rubbed her arm. "Oh my God, I've got goose bumps. What should we open up? What do you want to dig into?"

The tech guy said, "He's got a shit-ton of pictures. You want to look at his photos, see what he's got stored?"

I wanted to share Jenny's enthusiasm, to believe that this wild attempt could pay off.

Jenny said, "It's a starting place. Come over here, Stafford Lee."

I couldn't imagine Hiram Caro taking a bunch of personal pics, but it was worth a shot. I joined Jenny, put my arm around her. "Yeah, let's take a look at Hiram's pictures."

The photos appeared on the screen, a composite of small images. It wasn't what I expected to see. I glanced at Jenny. She was squinting in concentration, her brows drawn together.

"I don't understand," she said.

Her hopes had been dashed when she viewed the display—so had mine.

The photos weren't pictures of Hiram. They were shots of Joey Roman. Joey, Joey, Joey, one picture after another. Joey at the beach, at the casino, in a boat. And nude pictures he'd taken of his reflection in a mirror or by sticking his phone down his pants.

The tech geek said, "Wow. He stored a lot of dick pics. The dude is reckless with his digital footprint."

No argument there. Jenny turned away from the screen and buried her head in my shoulder. She muttered, "I'm sorry, Stafford Lee."

Hiding the sinking feeling in my gut, I whispered in her ear that I was grateful for everything she'd done. Jenny had no reason to apologize; she'd risked way more than she should've, tangling with Joey Roman.

But Raymond Plummer seemed fascinated with the photo montage. As he scrolled through the images, I saw Joey holding up a redfish he'd caught on his boat; Joey's meal at a restaurant; Joey in Vegas, on Fremont Street. And there were lots of selfies with a variety of women.

"Hold on!" I said to the hacker. I edged up close to the table and tapped the laptop screen with a finger. "Who's that?"

He enlarged the selfie of Joey. It was a clear well-lit shot. Joey stood with a good-looking woman wearing a skimpy cocktail-waitress uniform.

At first, I thought maybe my eyes were playing tricks on me. But no, I wasn't seeing things. I recognized her face.

It was the cold-case victim from Gulfport.

Desiree Whitman.

CHAPTER 93

JENNY CLUTCHED my arm. "Oh my God, oh my God, oh my God."

The hacker didn't look up. "Wow, she's hot. Somebody you know?" he asked.

I couldn't take my eyes off the screen. Automatically, I replied, "Somebody we've heard about. Never met."

Jenny released my arm and bent over the guy to tap the image on the screen. "We need that. Save it on the flash drive for me."

He nodded, hit some keys. "Okay, done. Where do you want to go next?"

I said, "Keep scrolling through photos. Slowly, okay? We want to examine every picture containing a female."

The tension filled the room like a fog, making it difficult to breathe. Time seemed suspended as we surveyed the images, looking for a second hit.

Then I caught it. "That one, we need to see it."

Jenny made a choking sound when he pulled it up on the screen. We exchanged a look. "What do you think?" I asked her.

She stepped over to the murder walls, pulled down a front-page article from the *Sun-Herald*, the daily newspaper based in Biloxi that covered the Mississippi Gulf Coast. She returned to the conference table. Her hand trembled as she held the picture next to the laptop screen.

She whispered, "You think?"

I nodded. "Yeah. Pretty sure."

I was certain, actually. The pictures were a match. Joey Roman had saved a candid shot of a young woman whose death was a cold case, a murder with the same MO as the other victims on the murder walls.

My mind was going haywire, spinning in different directions, as I absorbed what the images meant.

And then I had a hunch. "Can you scroll back to find the photos he saved from three years back? Start with pictures from the month of March of that year."

It didn't take long to spot her. Aurora Gates was there.

Jenny pulled out a chair and sat. "I'm getting light-headed," she said, her voice cracking.

We studied the photo. It was another standard selfie taken by Roman. He was grinning like a chimpanzee and he had his arm around her, his fingers digging into her shoulder.

Aurora's head strained sideways and her eyes looked away from the camera, like she was plotting her escape. Her smile was not convincing. It could easily be interpreted as a wince.

"Look at the background," Jenny said. "They're in Caro's casino."

She was right. The selfie was a close-up, so not much of the setting was depicted. But behind Roman's head, a portion of a sign read CEDAR.

The restaurant promoted as the casino's high-end-dining option was the Red Cedar Steak House.

"Can you check the date on that picture?" I asked the guy.

"Sure," he said. "Here you go."

The cursor pointed out the date.

"Jesus," I whispered.

Jenny jumped out of the chair to check the date against the Aurora Gates coverage on the wall. "Stafford Lee. The date—that's the date of offense on the criminal charge. Daniel Caro was accused of murdering Aurora Gates on the day that selfie was taken."

I didn't need Jenny to confirm it. I'd tried the case, seen the date on the criminal charge accusing Daniel Caro of murder, heard it from witness after witness on the stand.

I said, "Daniel Caro testified that they met for dinner at the casino steak house that night. Then she drove him back to his car. It was the last time he saw her alive."

Jenny returned to the table. She stared at the picture, then at me. "What do we do with this information, Stafford Lee?"

I didn't reply. My focus was on that computer screen, on the image of Aurora wincing as she was held captive by Joey Roman. My eyes scanned the pictures that followed. They had different subjects now, no more Aurora Gates.

"Go farther back. A year before. See what the pictures show."

We scrolled back until we found more Aurora Gates, pictures from the early stage of her relationship with Joey. She was smiling in those. In the beginning, anyway. And then she dropped out of sight.

To the hacker, I said, "Let's look at his videos."

The kid pulled them up. Compared to the photo files, there were relatively few videos. The tech kid played them for me, starting with the oldest. In the first one, Roman had filmed a stripper giving him a lap dance at some seedy club, maybe on Bourbon Street. In the next, Joey had filmed the water from the beach during hurricane season, when the waves were high and the weather was wild.

Plummer paused before pulling up the next one. The thumbnail was almost black; it looked like it might have been downloaded by mistake. "You want to play it?" the guy asked.

I checked the date. When I saw it, I shuddered. June 13, the day Aurora Gates was murdered. "Yeah, definitely."

Jenny broke in, sounding anxious. "Stafford Lee, we've gotta figure out what we're going to do with this."

Plummer's hands hesitated. I nudged his shoulder and said, "Go ahead."

He enlarged the video and played it. It was a short recording, taken in near darkness.

The three of us fell silent as we watched. Once I realized what I was seeing, it was difficult for my head to grasp it.

The video ended.

I said, my voice hushed, like we were attending a funeral, "Play it again."

The second time through, I knew. There was no mistake.

The dim footage of the video showed Aurora Gates, naked. She was bound and battered but still alive as she lay in the hull of a boat that was bobbing in the water.

CHAPTER 94

ON WEDNESDAY morning, I stood outside the courtroom on the second floor of the courthouse in Biloxi. And I waited.

The open design of the 1960s architecture gave me a bird's-eye view of the main entrance to the courthouse as well as the activity in the lobby. Press had been gathering for the past thirty minutes. At first, there were just a few. Then the news vans began to arrive. Reporters and camerapeople streamed from vehicles. By 8:45, they swarmed into the lobby.

No one tried to hunt me down. They were awaiting the arrival of the main attraction, the DA of Harrison County. Henry Gordon-James drove to Biloxi from Gulfport every day and parked in his designated spot in the lot on the east side of the courthouse.

On Wednesday, he was running late. Because he was tardy, he arrived just as the big county van pulled up to the curb. I saw the vehicle through the lobby windows. It was the van that transported the jury to and from the Best Western.

Talk about timing. This was getting better and better.

I gripped the balcony railing and watched the scene unfold. When the DA strode up to the entrance, reporters converged on him, pelting him with questions. Meanwhile, the fourteen jurors from Jackson slowly emerged from the van, struggling for space on the sidewalk as they awaited their escort to the jury room.

While the bailiffs hollered at the press, trying to clear a path for the jurors, the reporters shouted at Gordon-James. The cacophony of voices was music to my ears.

The bailiffs finally managed to hustle the jurors into the courthouse and up the stairs. But Gordon-James was still making his way through the sea of people in the lobby. I heard him say over the bedlam, "What's up? Y'all expecting some fireworks today?"

I had to give him credit. He wore his game face, didn't appear to be shaken, though I knew he must be wondering what the hell was happening. He'd been left out of the loop.

One TV journalist got a microphone right up in the DA's face and shouted, "Henry, what do you think about the new evidence?"

On the balcony, I tensed as I waited to hear his response. A flash of uncertainty crossed his features, but it was gone in a second. "You know the prosecution can't comment. Save it for after the verdict."

Once the DA reached security, he was able to leave the mob behind. He tore up the steps, reached the landing, and walked past me without a glance.

Not a surprise. I hadn't anticipated a greeting from him. The last time we'd spoken, he called me a monster.

I followed him because we had important business to discuss.

When the courtroom door shut behind me, I said, "Hey! Gordon-James! What's all the excitement?"

He didn't respond. I approached the counsel table where he was setting up his laptop. I stood close enough for him to see my phone as I pulled it out. I said, "I wonder if all that hubbub is related to the e-mail attachments I received this morning."

He still wouldn't look at me. In a chilly voice he said, "Step away from my counsel table, defendant."

I hit Play on the video. The image of Aurora Gates appeared. "Have you seen this?"

He wouldn't acknowledge it, wouldn't even look. "Remove your phone from the prosecution's space or I'll notify the bailiff."

So that's how it was going to be.

"The judge is waiting for us," I said as I pocketed the phone. "She wants to see us in chambers."

That got his attention. His head jerked up; his eyes met mine. I could swear I saw the wheels turning in his head as he tried to figure it out.

I headed to chambers. Behind me, Gordon-James demanded, "What's going on? What are you up to?"

I decided it was my turn to be closemouthed, so I didn't answer. But if I'd been inclined to speak, I might have said a single word to the DA before I knocked on the judge's door:

Surprise!

CHAPTER 95

IN CHAMBERS, Judge Ostrov-Ronai looked flustered. Her black robe was unzipped, and her face was flushed. The DA and I had barely stepped into the room before she said, "What the heck is going on out there?"

I settled into my seat and glanced over at Gordon-James, inviting him to weigh in first. His expression was stony. He said nothing.

So I said, "Judge, I'd say there's been a new development."

Ostrov-Ronai straightened her eyeglasses. "Well, I wish someone would enlighten me. The press mobbed me on the way in, and I didn't have any idea what they were ranting about. I'm telling you, they jumped me. Is this how judges get treated down here? There's more decorum in Jackson, thank God."

I was gripping my phone hard enough to crack the screen. I needed to chill out or I'd give myself away. There was too much at stake; I couldn't blow this. In a measured voice, I said, "I think I have the answer. I opened an e-mail this morning. It contained some shocking attachments."

I leaned forward and set the phone on the judge's desk. I flipped through the selfies first, giving her a chance to look them over.

Gordon-James scooted his chair closer to the desk. As the selfies of Joey Roman and the murder victims swept across the screen, Judge Ostrov-Ronai shrugged. "I don't see anything very shocking."

I pulled up the video of Aurora in the boat. Hit the arrow to play it. Joey Roman's voice could be heard, taunting her. The judge grimaced. Gordon-James reared back as if he couldn't bear to look at it. A sheen of perspiration broke out on his forehead. In different circumstances, I'd have been sympathetic. After all, Aurora was his niece.

But I was fighting for freedom. Mine and Rue's. If I faltered, we wouldn't have another chance.

When the judge looked up from my phone, she appeared genuinely baffled. "That's terrible, a horrific thing to see. But the woman in that boat, she's not the victim in this case."

"No, Your Honor," I said.

"These other pictures, they're just regular cell phone shots; they don't show criminal activity of any kind. What's the connection to this case, the one we're trying in court?"

"All of these women were murdered, Judge." I refreshed the screen and flipped through the selfies again for her benefit—and the DA's. "To my knowledge—as I understand it, there was a similar MO in those cases."

Ostrov-Ronai shook her head. "I don't know the background of those cases. Were the perpetrators convicted?"

I looked at Gordon-James. Waited to see how he would respond.

He didn't mince words. "No. Cold cases, mostly."

"That's dreadful. Appalling." Ostrov-Ronai tipped back in her chair, digesting the information. "Are the cases local? Sounds like you'd want to get to the bottom of it, Mr. Gordon-James."

I grabbed the lead-in. "The DA told me yesterday that he's got an investigative team looking into those cold cases right now."

"Is that right?" the judge asked the DA. When he confirmed it with a brief nod, Ostrov-Ronai said, "Mr. Penney, let me see those pictures again."

I opened the phone, thumbed slowly through the images. As Judge Ostrov-Ronai studied them, she said, "And the man? It's the same man in all those pictures, I think. Do you know who he is?"

"Sure, everyone in Biloxi knows him. He serves as personal bodyguard for Hiram Caro, the father-in-law of Iris Caro."

Ostrov-Ronai's brow furrowed. "You said you received these in an e-mail? Who from?"

I lifted my shoulders in a shrug. "It was a phantom e-mail address. Subject line read 'Connect the Dots.' Given all the excitement this morning, I'm betting that the reporters out there got the same e-mail I did."

Gordon-James swung around to face me. "An inflammatory smoking-gun e-mail in the middle of the murder trial? You sent it, Penney. Admit it."

"I did not. I swear."

It was the truth; I hadn't sent it. The tech kid did. And he'd made sure he wasn't on my internet server when it went out.

The DA turned to the judge. "This isn't a problem for us, Judge. It has no bearing on this case. That video..." His voice failed him. After a moment, he rallied. "It isn't related to the trial, has nothing to do with Stafford Lee Penney or the murder of Iris Caro."

I said, "There's a photo, a selfie, of that guy and Iris. Don't know if you caught that."

There was; we'd found one in the photo library, further back. But it was a wider shot, a picture of Joey with the whole Caro family: Hiram, Daniel, Iris.

Gordon-James ignored me. "Judge, you can't take this seriously. An e-mail, really? No one sent it to me—don't you think that's significant? We don't know the source of the information."

"I can send it to you, Henry." I sounded cool, unruffled. Which surprised me, because my stomach was churning. "Shall I forward it to you too, Judge?" Ostrov-Ronai nodded and gave me her e-mail address; I tapped the phone and sent the e-mail to both of them.

Then I slipped the cell phone into my pocket and announced, "I request a mistrial, Your Honor."

Gordon-James roared, "No!"

The judge looked at the DA like she thought he'd lost his mind. "Sit down, sir."

The DA sat on the very edge of his seat. He gripped the arms of the chair. "I beg your pardon, Judge. But the defendant's request is preposterous. There's no basis for a mistrial, certainly not the sudden appearance of a mystery e-mail with no bearing on the case. The anonymity discredits it even if it was related. There's nothing to support its validity."

I had to admire his quick recovery. But this was no time to try to reach a consensus with the opposition. "Judge, the DA's argument is disingenuous. Everyone in this courthouse knows that the trial's been affected. Just take a look at the crowd out there."

We could hear the buzz of voices as we sat in the judge's chambers; people had obviously moved into the courtroom.

There was a soft rap at the door. Charlene, the bailiff, stuck her head in. "Sorry to interrupt, Judge. There's some issue with the jurors. Four of them overheard something on the way into the courthouse this morning about new evidence. One of them has the idea they've found a video."

Ostrov-Ronai closed her eyes. "Oh, my."

"Yeah, she told the whole panel there's video of Mr. Penney killing the murder victim, and she's got everyone else worked up about it. They've got questions."

I almost jumped out of my skin; I hadn't anticipated that. "Good God, Judge! You understand what that means for the defense? How am I supposed to get a fair trial from that jury?"

"Well, this morning just gets worse and worse," Ostrov-Ronai said. "Bailiff, tell the jurors we're delayed. And they're forbidden to discuss the issue."

"Yes, Your Honor." She shut the door behind her.

The judge took off her glasses and rubbed her eyes. "Gentlemen, we have a problem."

That was progress. A problem at trial is good for the defense, bad for the prosecution. And Ostrov-Ronai was calling me a gentleman. I felt a spark of hope—despite the fact that the jury empowered to decide my fate believed there was video proof that I was a killer.

The DA said in a strained voice, "You can instruct the jury to disregard, Judge. Remind them that they've sworn an oath to base their decision on the evidence alone. Poll them if you think it's necessary."

"You think that's the remedy?" The judge swiveled her chair around and stared at a bookcase holding a set of law books—hardcovers that no one used for research anymore now that everything was online. We sat in silence while she thought it over. I had to fight to remain still. I wanted to push, but my instincts said it was best to hold my tongue. Let her reflect while she gazed at the set of books containing decades of case law.

At length, she swung the chair back around to the desk and said, "I'm no believer in beating a dead horse. Once a jury is tainted, that's it. No point in keeping a jury locked up to reach a verdict that can't stand."

I wanted to leap out of that chair, shout, pump my fist in the air. Somehow, I kept my composure. I said, "I'll make my request for mistrial on the record, Your Honor. In open court."

Ostrov-Ronai stood and started to zip up her robe. Gordon-James said in a bleak voice, "I'll vigorously oppose it, Your Honor."

Once her robe was zipped, the judge pulled a lipstick from her leather tote bag. Getting ready for the cameras, I supposed.

"Gentlemen, you'll both get to say your piece. But this jury is going home."

CHAPTER 96

THREE DAYS later, I was cooling my heels in the interrogation room at the Biloxi PD. Detective Sweeney had called first thing Saturday morning to schedule a meeting.

It was unnerving, sitting in the cinder-block room again with the mounted camera aimed down at me. Sweeney hadn't revealed the reason for the interview other than to say he had an inquiry. And the last time I'd been escorted to the stifling space, I'd just been arrested for the murder of Iris Caro. So I was tense.

While I waited, I gave myself a mental pep talk. These circumstances were different. Sweeney had framed the interview as a request. I'd come to the PD in my Prius rather than the back seat of a patrol car. And I was wearing my own clothes. No orange scrubs this time, no Crocs on my feet.

The memory of the Crocs made my feet itch. I was about to kick off a shoe when the door to the interview room opened. Sweeney entered. He was solo. That was a good omen. No good cop/bad cop routine this time.

He carried a brown paper envelope. As he scraped back his chair, he gave me a nod. "Appreciate you coming by today, Stafford Lee."

I perked up. The detective sounded somber but not unfriendly. I hoped he had a bombshell on Joey Roman, one that would set me free for good. But I didn't let down my guard, not yet.

"Detective, just so we're clear. I don't waive my rights to silence or counsel regarding any matters related to the death of Iris Caro."

He rested his hand on top of the paper envelope. It was small and marked EVIDENCE. The bottom of the bag was printed with signature lines to preserve chain of custody. "This isn't about Iris Caro."

He pulled a pen from his pocket. For a moment, he was silent. I was curious, eager to learn where this conversation was headed. I wanted to hear him utter Joey Roman's name.

At length, he said, "We received information this week. I expect you know what it was. The tip enabled us to obtain a search warrant. We executed it yesterday. Searched the home of Joseph Roman."

Bam! I clenched my jaw shut, waiting for the big reveal. The search must have borne fruit or I wouldn't be sitting at the table. I wondered what he'd try to fish from me. I was impatient to hear the outcome of that search, but Sweeney wasn't forthcoming. Trying to sound chill, I said, "Come on, Sweeney. What did y'all find? Hell, you're working on a Saturday. The search must have revealed something significant."

"I can't go into detail, you understand that. But I need to show you an item of property we found in the search."

He clicked his pen, signed and dated the envelope. Then he opened it, pulled out a clear plastic bag, and placed it on the table directly in front of me.

I looked down. The bag held a ring, a gold wedding band. I began to shake. My throat closed up.

Sweeney's voice held a note of sympathy. "If you'd examine it, please. Without opening the bag. See if you can identify it."

I picked up the bag, but my hand trembled so violently that I was in danger of dropping it. I'd recognized the contents at first glance.

There was no mistaking it. The bag held Carrie Ann's wedding ring.

Before our wedding day, I'd had the inside of the band engraved. Through the plastic evidence bag, the letters jumped out at me: *SL & CA forever.*

My eyes burned. I set the bag down, thinking of the hubris of youth. We'd been too young to understand the tenacity that *forever* would require.

Sweeney's voice broke into my misery. "You recognize it, Stafford Lee?"

I nodded. Couldn't speak.

"He kept souvenirs. Stored them in a hollowed-out dictionary, one of those books people use as a safe."

His words conjured up an awful image, a dictionary filled with mementos of violence and death.

Sweeney said, "We've got a warrant out for him, an APB. We haven't picked him up, can't locate him just yet. Caro says he's not showing up at the casino. It might take time. He could be out on a boat in the Gulf."

I struggled for composure. Sweeney returned the ring to the brown evidence envelope. As he sealed it, he said, "But he'll turn up. Don't want you to worry about that. A guy like him, he can't hide forever."

There was that word again. *Forever.*

That's when I started to cry.

CHAPTER 97

JENNY AWOKE with a start and sat straight up in bed.

It was early morning. The sky outside the bedroom window had just begun to brighten to deep blue. Too early to rise. She should lie back down, try to catch another hour's sleep. Her sleeping patterns had been disrupted by the stress of the murder trial. But she was getting better. Much better, actually.

She looked down at Stafford Lee, sleeping beside her. His left arm rested on top of the sheet. Jenny reached for his hand and touched him softly so she wouldn't wake him.

She studied his left hand. When their relationship began, he'd put away the wedding band he'd worn for eight years. Now the matching ring was stored in the evidence room of Biloxi PD.

Revisiting Carrie Ann's death had been hard for him. New facts had come to light; a witness told the detective that Joey Roman had pursued Carrie Ann when she and Stafford Lee were separated. Carrie Ann had rebuffed him—the rejection of his attentions was surfacing as a common theme in all his crimes. The police believed Roman had lured Benjamin Gates to the house to provide a convenient cover-up for the double murder.

Joey was pretty good at covering his tracks, smarter than Jenny had realized. That's how he'd gone so long without being caught.

She thought the discovery would ultimately bring Stafford Lee peace. Jenny knew he'd held himself responsible for her death, believing that he'd triggered the murder by inflaming Benjamin Gates in court. He could put those fears to rest now.

Together, they'd dismantled the murder walls in his conference room. The charts, pictures, and reports were neatly organized in cardboard bankers' boxes stored beside the filing cabinets. Jenny privately wished they could burn them, convert the memories to smoke and ash. But they couldn't dispose of the files, not yet. As the investigation into Joey Roman picked up steam, the DA had agreed to put off Stafford Lee's and Rue's trials indefinitely. What he hadn't yet done was dismiss the charges.

Stafford Lee had asked if Jenny wanted to wait until the prosecution decision was settled before she moved out of her place and into his. He said he didn't want her to bear the burden of his legal woes.

Jenny slid down in the bed and curled up next to Stafford Lee. She knew that some people in Biloxi might think her plan to set up housekeeping with him was too hasty, even ill-advised. But the past months had brought matters into sharp perspective for her. Adversity had a way of making priorities crystal clear.

She needed to seize the day. Be with the man she loved. Nail down every opportunity to be together.

She was already a nightly guest in Stafford Lee's house, sharing the spare bedroom he'd occupied since the murder of Carrie Ann. When Jenny finished moving her stuff in, Rue would move over to Jenny's place. It was more convenient for Rue, closer to the law school's campus. Moreover, Rue commented that the new "love nest" vibe at Stafford Lee's house was a little too intense for comfort. She liked to remind them that she had predicted the romantic outcome before either Stafford Lee or Jenny admitted to it.

A few dim stars were still visible outside the window in the dark-blue predawn sky. Jenny lay on her side as Stafford Lee slept, marveling at the joy that had bloomed during the period of hardship in their lives. She felt deeply, supremely happy. It seemed like nothing could mar that perfect moment.

Her muscles suddenly went taut.

She heard him right before he appeared in the doorway of the bedroom. He wore a Kevlar vest over a white T-shirt. And he carried a shotgun. It was the Perazzi; she could see the shape of the wooden stock and a glint of gold on the side plate.

As Joey raised the shotgun, he said, "Bet you didn't expect to see me again."

In a flash, the Glock was in her hand and aimed at Roman's head.

"Bet you didn't expect this," Jenny said as she emptied the chamber.

CHAPTER 98

THE WAITER set a dish of turtle soup on the white tablecloth directly in front of Jenny. After he served us, I picked up my spoon and waited for her to taste it. I was eager to see her reaction.

When I'd recommended it, she said she'd never tried turtle soup. I insisted that she order it, told her she was in for a treat. The turtle soup at Brennan's is legendary.

But now she just stared down at the dish, toying with her spoon. I went ahead and had a taste of mine. "Oh, wow. Delicious."

She set the spoon back down on the tablecloth. With a rueful sigh, she said, "I'm so sorry, Stafford Lee. I can't eat it."

That was a novel reaction coming from Jenny. She wasn't squeamish about anything. Certainly not food.

"Are you all right?"

"Yes! I'm fine—great, in fact. It's just that I'm feeling a little sorry for the turtle."

This was getting interesting. "I wasn't aware that you had a soft spot for turtles."

She raised her eyebrows. "See? You thought you knew everything about me. Well, I used to play with them in the backyard when I was a kid. I kept one in a shoebox for a while. Even named him."

The confession made me smile. "What did you name him?"

She whispered, "Slowpoke."

When I laughed, it made her blush. She took a sip of water from her glass and looked around. "Stafford Lee, I still can't believe you brought me here. All the time I've spent in New Orleans, I've never had dinner at Brennan's. This is a first. I'm a fish out of water in this place. But I'm loving the experience."

I'd reserved a table for two in the Chanteclair room at Brennan's, looking out on the courtyard. I wasn't a stranger to the restaurant, but the occasion marked a first for the two of us.

Our relationship had commenced during a tempest in our lives. We'd clung to each other as we confronted obstacles, fear, strife. We'd never had the opportunity to get dressed up, go out for a special evening.

I wanted to change that. Jenny needed a break from the storm that still whirled around us. We both did.

She said, "Have you ever seen such a beautiful place? After tonight, my new favorite colors are pink and green. This was a wonderful surprise, Stafford Lee. It's nice to get out somewhere without everybody looking at me."

It was good to have a change of scene, a relief to enjoy some anonymity. My murder charge had generated unrelenting public scrutiny. After Jenny took out Joey Roman, the stir she created in Biloxi was overwhelming. We couldn't go anywhere in Harrison County without attracting notice.

"You turned heads when we walked into Brennan's tonight, Jenny. But it's because you're beautiful."

Jenny always looked great. But that night, wearing a blue silk dress with her hair down around her bare shoulders, she was striking.

She glanced at me. "Want to know a secret?"

I nodded.

"I used to daydream about a night like this. With you, us going out on a real date." She hastened to add, "Not when Carrie Ann was in the picture. That's a line I never crossed, even in my head. But after that, I'd think about it. In the daydream, I knew all the right things to say and do. I was a siren."

I reached across the table and took her hand. "Well, that's all true. You are a siren. Completely irresistible."

She looked away. "I kept a scrapbook."

I scooted my chair closer to the table. "Beg pardon?"

"All your trials. I cut the articles out of the *Sun-Herald*. Kept them in a big binder. I've got over a decade's worth. I told myself I was doing it for professional reasons. But then I'd go over the articles sometimes just to read your quotes. Look at your pictures." She lifted her shoulders. "It was a crush. I was a total fangirl."

I was astonished. "Where have you been keeping that scrapbook? I want to see it."

She laughed and said, "You've never seen it because it's hidden in the bedroom at my place. And I better unearth it before Rue finds it. God, she'll think I'm nuts."

The soup had gone cold. The waiter removed it, replaced it with entrées of blackened redfish and striped bass. As she cut into the bass, Jenny assured me she hadn't kept any fish as pets.

At length, Jenny nudged my knee under the table and said, "You're not playing by the rules."

"What? What do you mean?"

"We were playing Truth or Dare, and you haven't taken your turn."

I sipped my water before I responded. "What if I take the dare?"

"I dare you to tell me the truth." She leaned toward me and whispered, "Tell me something about you I don't know."

I gave the question some thought. "Okay. Here's a true fact. I started to fall for you when I was in rehab."

"No! Really?"

"Yeah, really. I thought about you all the time. But I wouldn't admit what I was feeling, not even to myself. Not for a long while. Through all these dark times, the only light I could see was you." I swallowed hard because I hadn't said it to her yet. "I love you, Jenny."

It took considerable courage to admit it out loud. I studied her across the table, waiting for her reaction.

Her eyes were bright; she dabbed at them with her fingertips. "I have to go to the restroom. I need a Kleenex."

When she stood up, I rose, like my mother had taught me. Jenny came up to me and whispered something. I bent down to listen.

She repeated it. "I need a dollar, Stafford Lee."

That wasn't quite what I'd expected.

As I reached for my wallet, she said, "They've got a ladies' room attendant in there. I think I'm supposed to tip her. I didn't even know that was a real thing, thought it was just in old movies."

She ran off to the restroom and returned a couple of minutes later. She had a glow to her—it sounds corny, but that's the only way to describe it.

When we finished the entrées, Jenny sighed. "I'm stuffed, but it was so good I had to eat every bite."

"How about some dessert? You know they invented bananas Foster here. They'll make it tableside, set it on fire. It's a showstopper."

I could see her think it over. She shook her head.

I said, "Hmm, better reconsider. I think there may be a law against leaving Brennan's without ordering dessert."

She played along. "State statute? Or federal?"

"A city ordinance. I'm fairly sure."

She laughed. Then she said, with a note of regret, "Stafford Lee, we still have to get back. It's a ninety-minute drive to Biloxi."

I smiled. It was a perfect opening to spring the surprise. "About that. We're not going back tonight. I reserved a room for us at the Royal Sonesta."

I'd been pretty sure she'd like the idea. When she lit up like a firefly, she looked so happy I was afraid I'd need a Kleenex.

"You did not!" she said.

"I did. We've got a balcony on Bourbon. It wasn't easy to score a Bourbon Street balcony on short notice. I had to call my dad. He pulled some strings."

She grabbed my hand, squeezed it hard. "That's perfect. I love the Royal Sonesta. They've got a jazz bar with live music."

A jazz bar sounded okay, if that was what she wanted. But I'd been staring at her in that slinky blue dress all through dinner.

She must have read my face. "What are you thinking?"

I cleared my throat, lowered my voice, said, "I got some beads."

She looked perplexed. "Oh? You want to throw them off the balcony? To the people on Bourbon?"

I said, "I wasn't thinking I'd waste them on strangers."

She gave me that look. Picked up her purse. "No dessert tonight. Hurry up and get the check, Stafford Lee."

My arm shot up to signal the waiter.

CHAPTER 99

MASON BURNETT was early for our meeting. He walked into the office shortly before eleven o'clock.

I was standing in the reception area, waiting. "Mason! Come on in and have a seat."

Mason followed me into my private office and dropped into a chair facing my desk. "You're looking good, Stafford Lee. Back to normal. How's Jenny?"

I glanced away. "She's okay."

He made a sympathetic clicking noise with his tongue. "She's holding up? Not carrying a load of trauma over Roman's death?"

"She's working through it. It's a process, gonna take time."

Mason shook his head in wonder. "Drilled him right between the eyes. Where'd she keep that gun of hers?"

"She's been sleeping with it on the bedside table since that break-in last year. If it had been under the mattress, we'd both be dead."

"How'd she pull it off? Was it a lucky shot?"

"Mason, it wasn't luck, it was skill. She's a dead shot. You should know that, after all these years."

"She never bragged about it." He looked pensive. After a moment, he shook it off and grinned at me. "So! What's up, what's the news

407

that you wouldn't tell me over the phone? Got to be something big for you to drag me over here to hear it in person."

"It's big."

"Is it Gordon-James? Has he finally come around? I keep thinking he's gonna call, tell me he's dismissing the charges against you and Rue."

I picked up a pen, twisted it in my hands, put it down. "The murder case hasn't been dismissed."

"Sorry to hear that." I watched him. He did look sorry. "So. What's up?"

"The FBI is investigating."

"Really!" Mason gazed off, digesting the information. "Hadn't heard that."

"The state police called them in after the search of Roman's home. They found evidence of multiple victims over the years, crossing state lines. They're pulling out all the stops, looking at cold cases all across the Gulf."

"Wow. Incredible."

"They called me in for another interview."

"Again? I know you had to go in to ID Carrie Ann's wedding ring." Mason grimaced. "Taking her ring. God, Stafford Lee. That's sick."

"Yeah. Really sick."

Mason's brow wrinkled. "You never mentioned it was missing."

"The coroner said she wasn't wearing a ring. I figured she'd gotten rid of it."

That led to an awkward pause. Mason broke the silence. "Shit, Stafford Lee—that had to be tough. Hard on you, bringing up bad memories. Is Jenny still set on moving in with you? You could put it off, I guess."

My voice was calm, controlled. "No, we're not putting it off."

"Excellent. I'm glad to hear you're moving on, going forward. You've had a rough time."

"True. We have, both of us. A close call."

"But everything's okay?"

"Yeah. We're alive. And I'm free, for now. It's lucky I'm not in prison. Locked up for the rest of my life."

Mason slid down in the seat, shaking his head. "Come on, Stafford Lee — that was never gonna happen. You would've beat that case. The evidence wasn't strong enough to convict you."

"You think?"

"Damn straight! The jury wouldn't have convicted. Not a chance."

My throat was tight. I had to take a couple of deep breaths.

Finally, I said it. "Is that what you told yourself?"

CHAPTER 100

MASON'S HEAD jerked back as if he'd been struck.

"Huh?"

I repeated, "Is that what you told yourself? To justify it in your own mind?"

He tried to look shocked, like he couldn't comprehend what I was saying. "What are you talking about, man?"

I wanted to launch out of the chair and punch the injured expression off Mason's face. "Come on, Mason. My old friend. It's time to shoot straight with me."

He lifted his shoulders, shook his head helplessly. "We're still talking about Joey Roman, right? He's a killer."

"The cops didn't find any kind of souvenir for Iris Caro. Nothing in the hollow book, nothing anywhere in Roman's house, connects him to that murder."

"Then they need to keep looking."

I laughed a little at that. The irony, I guess. "That's right, they do. Because Roman didn't kill Iris. And I know *I* didn't do it. And Rue didn't."

Mason grabbed the arms of his chair and started to rise. I pointed at him. "We're not done here, Mason."

He sat back down, perching on the edge of the chair. "You think

I'll sit here and let you fling crazy accusations at me? I won't stand for that."

"So why didn't you ever tell me about Iris?"

"Tell you what?"

"That she came to see you last year about filing for divorce. In all this time, you never mentioned it."

He glanced at the door and back to me. "I couldn't tell you. Client confidentiality."

"But she wasn't just a client, was she? Jenny's been thinking that you started carrying a torch for Iris. She says you swore her to secrecy when you asked her to tail Daniel Caro and get compromising pictures of him."

"Because it would be easy to do! He was a philanderer. He lied under oath when he said Aurora Gates was his only affair. Iris told me the first time she came to my office. She broke down and cried." He scowled as if the recollection made him angry. "Daniel Caro is a serial womanizer; he's toxic."

"I don't care about Caro's shortcomings as a husband. But I'm pretty goddamn interested in why you set me up."

Mason's knees were shaking. He clutched them to still the movement. "I would never—you can't think I'd really do something like that."

"Yeah, I wouldn't think so. Except Jenny's tech witness found out where those texts and e-mails came from, the ones I supposedly sent to Iris. You did it. You took over my phone, my e-mail. They came from you."

His face was white as parchment. He didn't deny it.

I went on. "We knew my neighbor had video on their security system, checked it out back when this all began. We never thought anything of you coming and going from my house. You had a set of keys. You were a frequent visitor. Always welcome, right?"

He didn't say anything, so I kept talking, determined to force a response. "That made it easy to plant evidence. Because nobody'd think twice about you walking through my front door. Because you were my best friend."

I was starting to lose it. "The kind of friend who set me up to rot in prison for a crime you committed. You don't have a shred of decency left—you actually took on Rue's defense! You were acting as her attorney when she was on trial for a crime you'd committed! What has she ever done to you? I guess Rue's life was just collateral damage, was that it?"

"No!" Mason said.

"No?" I had to restrain myself; I wanted to fly over the desk, take him down. "You made the anonymous tip about the stupid god-damn love triangle! You set us up!"

His face had turned gray. Saliva sprayed as he cried out, "I set it up so you could beat it!"

CHAPTER 101

HE WIPED the spit off his face with the back of his hand. "It was a shit case! Anonymous tip? One bloody shoe? And the hair! I knew Gordon-James couldn't resist presenting the hair evidence; he's been doing that for years. And I knew you'd discredit it. We went to that criminal defense conference together, remember? In Jackson? The federal public defender talked about all those hair cases the FBI had backed away from. Remember?"

I acknowledged the statement with a stiff nod. *Keep talking,* I thought.

"I figured you'd find some way to contest those texts. They didn't sound like you, did they? That was intentional."

I opened my mouth to speak. Changed my mind, shut it.

He was babbling, talking so fast it was hard to keep up. "I wanted to represent you myself—I offered to do it. Hell, I knew where the holes were; I planted them. Could've cruised to an acquittal without any problem. But you didn't want me, you batted my offer away like a pesky damn fly in your face. You could've hired anyone—the best damn lawyer in the country—to handle your defense. Problem is, you still think you're the king, you wouldn't entrust your defense to anyone else. And then"—Mason was gasping for air; he looked like he was going to pass out—"then you decided to throw effective trial practice right out the window. Act like a lunatic in court. You were blowing it! This is all on you, Stafford Lee!"

I couldn't believe what I was hearing. "All on me? You committed the crime."

"But it wasn't a crime!" His voice had risen to a shout; he caught himself. He dropped it to a hoarse whisper. I walked around the desk and stood by his chair.

He said, "It was an accident, honest to God, I swear it. I thought that after she was divorced, we'd be together. I was crazy about her. I'd have done anything for her. You want to know why it was a secret? Because she said it had to be! Said we couldn't tell a soul, nobody, not even you."

His nose was running. He swiped it with his sleeve. "Then she texts me one day and calls it all off. The divorce, the relationship—canceled. All over. No reason."

I leaned back against the desk. "Iris breaks up with you by text, so she ends up dead?"

He shook his head, rubbed his face with his hands. "I went to her house to talk with her. Told her I deserved an explanation. She said her husband was suspicious. Daniel had figured out something was going on. She said she'd taught him a lesson. Can you believe that? She'd let him know how it felt, gave him a taste of his own medicine. And then she told me again it was over."

His shoulders were hunched. He gave me a pleading look.

I said, "So who killed her?"

"Nobody killed her! It was an accident. Didn't I say that already? She told me to get out, but I followed her upstairs. She'd made me nuts. I was out of my mind. I asked her to give our relationship a shot, that was all I wanted. She wouldn't listen. I guess I grabbed her, and it scared her. She pulled away from me, fell, and hit her head on the table by her bed. She was screaming. I just wanted her to quiet down. I took the pillow off her bed."

He broke into a sob. "I never meant to hurt her. I was crazy about her." He drew a ragged breath. "It was an accident, Stafford Lee. Swear to God."

He bowed his head. His shoulders shook as he wept. "When I realized what had happened, I couldn't believe it. She was gone. I flipped out. I panicked. I never should've aimed it at you. I thought I could use Rue as a distraction. Rue was accused of stealing from her; she was already on their radar. But it didn't seem credible enough. And I knew if they came after you, you'd beat it. Shit— you're Teflon, Stafford Lee, nothing sticks to you. You're the luckiest guy alive." He said it like maybe he resented my supposed good fortune.

He rubbed his wet eyes on his sleeve. "But it's all going to work out. We'll wait and see what Gordon-James does next. I think we're all gonna walk away from it, just like I hoped. I found that damned diamond necklace in my front seat at the car wash—how about that? It must have slipped off when Iris and I were messing around. We'll come up with a cover story for Rue, something that sounds reasonable. The DA has got to drop the charges. The whole town will rise up against him if he takes you to trial a second time. You and Jenny are legends now."

He looked at me, his eyes pleading. I had to harden my heart. "I don't want to wait, Mason."

"What's that supposed to mean?"

It was time. No more games.

"I'm wearing a wire."

The door to the conference room creaked open. We heard the tread of footsteps making their way to my office. Detective Sweeney appeared in the doorway.

CHAPTER 102

DETECTIVE SWEENEY stepped into the office, followed by two uniformed officers of the PD. Jenny lingered outside the door with Henry Gordon-James. Her face was red; she'd been crying back there.

Sweeney stepped over to Mason. "Mason Burnett, you are under arrest for the murder of Iris Caro."

Mason didn't respond to the detective. He swung to me, his face contorted with righteous fury. "I can't believe you'd do this! After all I've done for you? When you were a drunk, I pushed your sorry ass into rehab, remember?"

One of the uniformed cops pulled Mason's hands behind his back and cuffed him as Sweeney said, "You have the right to remain silent."

Mason shot me an accusing look. "This what you want, Stafford Lee? You happy now, seeing them drag me away?"

My gut was sour; I felt like I was going to vomit. "Happy? Are you kidding? This is killing me. Tearing me apart."

He snorted. Sweeney ushered Mason into the lobby. A cop pulled open the front door. The other cop grabbed Mason's arm as Sweeney continued to recite the *Miranda* language: "You have the right to an attorney."

Mason was still focused on me. "My heart bleeds for you, Stafford Lee. It must be so goddamn tough to be you. Always landing on top."

Sweeney tugged on his other arm and wrapped up the warning as they escorted Mason through the door and shut it behind them.

Henry Gordon-James stepped up. "I'll issue a press release today after I dismiss the case against you and Ms. Holmes." His voice was neutral, unapologetic. "It will be nonspecific. I'll make a reference to newly discovered evidence."

I nodded but didn't speak. If the DA thought I was going to thank him, he was wrong. He made his exit; I was glad to see him depart.

Jenny ran up to me and buried her head in my chest. I put my arms around her and held her tight. We stood together until I pulled away to study her face. "Are you okay with this?"

She nodded, said, "Yeah, I'm okay." Her voice had a tremor, though.

"No regrets? You don't wish we could go back, do it some other way?"

She shook her head but didn't meet my eye. It made me nervous. Maybe she was having second thoughts.

But then she sighed and said, "There wasn't another way. It had to go down like this." After a moment, she stepped back. "Stafford Lee, you need to call Rue. She went to class today, but she's waiting to hear."

"You're right." I pulled my phone out of my pocket and hit Rue's number. She picked right up.

Her voice was breathless over the phone. "Yeah?"

"Good news, Rue. It's over. The DA is dismissing the case. He'll announce it today."

Apparently, she wasn't alone, because I heard her shout to someone, "Charges are dropped!" A noisy cheer went up. Her fellow students had been rooting for her. She came back to the phone. "Talk to you later. I've got to call my sister and tell her the news."

I ended the call, and the realization started to sink in. It was over. I felt a lightness overtake me, like a leaden weight had dropped away.

I started unbuttoning my shirt. "Jenny, help me out of this wire, okay?"

She stepped up to assist, freed me up in a flash. There are some unique advantages to dating a private investigator. She set the equipment aside and said, "Let's get out of here. We're taking the rest of the day off."

"Really?" I glanced at her. "What are we going to do?"

"We're going to the beach. You know how long it's been since I had a beach day? I want to get out in the sun, play in the water like a kid. I need to wash this whole sad mess off me."

CHAPTER 103

ONCE JENNY had the destination in mind, we wasted no time. After a quick stop at home, we drove up to the boardwalk and parked. I popped the trunk to get out the beach gear. Jenny was impatient. "Hurry up, Stafford Lee. I'm dying to jump in."

We walked together across the beach; the water of the Gulf sparkled under the sun. It was breezy, and the beach flag rippled and flapped in the wind.

"Yellow flag, Jenny. Sure you want to swim? It might be a little rough out there."

She patted my arm, flashed me a smile. "I'm not worried. I'm with a certified lifeguard."

"Did you know that I actually saved a swimmer one time? It was in September."

"Yes, I do know that. Because you told me about it like six or seven times."

"Ouch." I stopped and dropped the gear onto the sand. "I obviously need to come up with a new story. Something that will impress you with my valor."

She laughed. "Shoot, Stafford Lee. You don't need to sell yourself to me. I already know your good qualities."

I nudged her. "And my flaws."

"Those too." She gazed out at the water. Her expression was serene.

The sight of the nearby lifeguard stand brought a glimmer of nostalgia. "You know, being a lifeguard was a lot more fun than practicing law."

"Forget it, Stafford Lee. You're back on the job tomorrow, bright and early. Time to get your law practice in order." She stood on tip-toe, kissed my cheek. "But you did look really hot back when you used to sit up in that chair wearing nothing but swim trunks and shades."

She took off and ran into the surf. I kept an eye on her while I unfolded the beach chairs and set up the umbrella. Jenny dived into a wave and disappeared. When she didn't surface immediately, I started to sprint across the sand.

Before I reached the shore, she popped back up. Standing waist-high in the water, she looked like a sea nymph as she shook out her hair.

She sang, "Come on, Stafford Lee! Get on out here!"

She waved her arm, beckoning me. I followed her into the Gulf, wading over the shifting sand toward my redemption.

ACKNOWLEDGMENTS

Several attorneys provided valuable assistance as we shaped the court cases and legal issues our characters encountered. Special thanks go to James L. Farrior III and Corban Gunn for their aid on trial practice and procedure in Biloxi, Mississippi, and to John Appelquist for his expertise in criminal law and procedure.

ABOUT THE AUTHORS

James Patterson is one of the best-known and biggest-selling writers of all time. Among his creations are some of the world's most popular series, including Alex Cross, the Women's Murder Club, Michael Bennett and the Private novels. He has written many other number one bestsellers including collaborations with President Bill Clinton and Dolly Parton, stand-alone thrillers and non-fiction. James has donated millions in grants to independent bookshops and has been the most borrowed adult author in UK libraries for the past fourteen years in a row. He lives in Florida with his family.

Nancy Allen practised law for fifteen years in her native Ozarks and served as a law instructor at Missouri State University for sixteen years. She is also the author of the Ozarks Mystery series and the Anonymous Justice series.